A city [illegible] rina **Cudmore** lives in Cork, Ireland, with her husband, four [f]ive children and a very daft dog. A psychology [gra]duate, with an MSc in Human Resources, Katrina spent [m]any years working in multinational companies and can't [b]elieve she is now lucky enough to have a job that involves [d]aydreaming about love and handsome men! You can visit [K]atrina at katrinacudmore.com

[M]**ichelle Major** grew up in Ohio but dreamed of living [in] the mountains. Soon after graduating with a degree in [j]ournalism, she pointed her car west and settled in [C]olorado. Her life and house are filled with one great [h]usband, two beautiful kids, a few furry pets and several [w]ell-behaved reptiles. She's grateful to have found her [p]assion writing stories with happy endings. Michelle [l]oves to hear from her readers at michel[lem]ajor.com

Also by Katrina Cudmore

Tempted by the Greek Tycoon
Christmas with the Duke
Resisting the Italian Single Dad
Second Chance with the Best Man

Also by Michelle Major

Falling for the Wrong Brother
Second Chance in Stonecreek
A Stonecreek Christmas Reunion
Anything for His Baby
A Baby and a Betrothal
Always the Best Man
Christmas on Crimson
Mountain Romancing the Wallflower
Sleigh Bells in Crimson
Coming Home to Crimson
Fortune's Fresh Start

Discover more at millsandboon.co.uk

BEST FRIEND TO PRINCESS BRIDE

KATRINA CUDMORE

THE BEST INTENTIONS

MICHELLE MAJOR

MILLS & BOON

All rights reserved including the right of reproduction in whole or in part in any form. This edition is published by arrangement with Harlequin Books S.A. This is a work of fiction. Names, characters, places and incidents are either the product of the author's imagination or are used fictitiously and any resemblance to actual persons, living or dead, business establishments, events or locales is entirely coincidental.

This book is sold subject to the condition that it shall not, by way of trade or otherwise, be lent, resold, hired out or otherwise circulated without the prior consent of the publisher in any form of binding or cover other than that in which it is published and without a similar condition including this condition being imposed on the subsequent purchaser.

® and TM are trademarks owned and used by the trademark owner and/ or its licensee. Trademarks marked with ® are registered with the United Kingdom Patent Office and/or the Office for Harmonisation in the Internal Market and in other countries.

First Published in Great Britain 2020
by Mills & Boon, an imprint of HarperCollinsPublishers,
1 London Bridge Street, London, SE1 9GF

Best Friend to Princess Bride © 2020 Katrina Cudmore
The Best Intentions © 2020 Michelle Major

ISBN: 978-0-263-27872-9

0320

MIX
Paper from
responsible sources
FSC™ C007454

This book is produced from independently certified FSC™ paper to ensure responsible forest management.

For more information visit: www.harpercollins.co.uk/green

Printed and bound in Spain
by CPI, Barcelona

CHAPTER ONE

KARA DUFFY HIT the mud with a yelp. Cold muck and pebbles dashed her face. She sagged into the soft earth, every inch of her body aching.

Sucking footsteps, in a fight with the quagmire, approached behind her.

Could this day get any worse?

Not only was she, the poster girl for the charity's first ever fun mud run, going to be one of the last to cross the finishing line, but now one of her volunteer race marshals was having to come and rescue her. She needed to get up. Now. While she had some dignity left.

She pushed with all her might but her hands disappeared into the sogginess and her knees slipped and slid all over the place.

She gave a grunt and flipped over. Swallowing her pride.

But instead of a race marshal, three men, all in their thirties, all muscled and tanned, wearing top-to-toe tight-fitting black clothes, stood watching her. Two were considering her with professional concern, while the guy in the centre was trying desperately to hold back a laugh.

Prince Edwin of Monrosa and his royal protection officers, Domenico and Lucas.

Oh, what? Clamping her hands to her face, she gave a

moan. Between her fingers she spotted Edwin grin. She giggled, relief surging through her, the weeks of disquiet over his lack of contact vanishing more swiftly than the grey March clouds scuttling across the sky behind him.

Lowering her hands, she grinned back at him, all of her work worries, her crabbiness over being so cold, her frustration at lagging so far behind in the field of competitors, disappearing in the face of his entrancing sorcerer's smile.

Edwin's hand reached down and he hoisted her out of the mud, an embarrassing squelching sound accompanying her escape.

With a barely detectable nod from Edwin, Domenico and Lucas moved away in the direction of the two event marshals who were standing at the stone piers at the top of the field that led out onto the return road to the event's tented village.

'You look exhausted.' Edwin paused, that smile still dancing on his lips. 'I'd offer to carry you but I don't want to be yelled at like the last time I pulled you up from a muddy field.'

Puzzled, she yanked her jacket down from where it had twisted around her waist and then she laughed. Of course! He was talking about the first time they had met. She had been seventeen and playing in a rugby cup game and had just been tackled by a prop forward built like a small garden shed. Winded, she had been trying to gather herself when she had been hoisted off the ground. She had expected a teammate but instead she had turned to find a dark-haired guy towering over her, the concern in his golden eyes stealing away her indignation. From the get-go, Edwin had appointed himself as her protector, her rock of good sense…and after Michael, her brother and

Edwin's best friend, had died, despite her resistance he had become her mentor, her modern-day guardian angel.

Now, aching for a shower and hot chocolate at the finishing line, for once she was seriously tempted to take him up on his offer of assistance but of course didn't do so. 'You need to be careful with your back at your age.'

Edwin folded his arms. 'I'm only three years older than you.'

She gave him a sympathetic smile. 'Every year counts.'

He raised an eyebrow, his thumb flicking across the tip of her nose. She shivered at the fierce concentration in his expression. Then, showing her his thumb, now covered in a smear of dirt, he said with his usual quiet humour, 'I'm guessing you don't need this particular memento of today's run,' pausing, he ran his eyes down the length of her mud-encrusted body, 'especially when you are already heading home with a small garden's worth.'

Kara blinked. And stepped away. His touch always made her feel peculiarly vulnerable. 'I need to get to the finishing line—the fundraising team will be regretting persuading me to front up the campaign.' Rolling her eyes at Edwin's grin, she admitted, 'I can't believe I actually agreed to pose for those photos and marketing video of me dashing across the finishing line—I should have known they'd come back to haunt me.'

Turning away, she tackled the mud bath before her. He came and walked alongside her. 'So what has brought you here today? Isn't there some exotic beach or skiing trip missing you?' she asked.

'I decided to forgo my usual Sunday morning haunts to spend some time with you.' Taking hold of her hand again, to help her out of a deep hole she was failing to free herself from, he pulled her out and said gently, 'I know how much today means to you. I wanted to support you, especially as the race is named in Michael's honour.'

An ache for Michael rose up from the pit of her stomach and spread into her chest cavity like a smothering vapour until it wrapped around her heart, the loneliness of it physically hurting even a decade on. She swallowed down that ache to a place deep, deep inside of herself, balling her fists to create the energy to be upbeat and teasing with him. She lifted her head to meet his gaze. The man with the golden eyes and golden heart. 'I always appreciate your backing.' She gave him a wicked smile. 'As does the rest of my team—Kate and Triona were only lamenting earlier this morning the fact that we haven't seen a lot of you in the office in recent months.'

'Where are your team anyway? Why aren't you with them?' Edwin asked.

'I told them to go ahead, I was only holding them up. They needed to get to the finishing line early to thank everyone taking part in the run before they left. We had hoped for a bigger field today and need to persuade as many runners as possible to come back next year. If we can get the numbers right, this run will be a great way to raise funds and promote the work of the charity.'

Edwin's mouth tightened as once again he had to yank her out of the mud. 'Somebody should have stayed with you.' Nodding towards her trainers—well, what was visible of them beneath the inches of mud—he added, 'And equally someone should have told you to wear something more practical.'

She gazed down at his feet and smirked. 'Like your special forces-issue boots, you mean? And don't go denying that you were trained by the Monrosa army—no one goes away, as you claim you did, on a three-month diplomatic tour and returns with biceps that would rival those of a heavyweight boxer.' As expected, Edwin gave his usual non-committal shrug, so she added, 'There was no need for anyone to stay with me for the race. I was doing fine until I came to the incline.'

He made a disbelieving sound. And her heart missed a beat as his gaze continued to hold hers with an unsettling intensity. Only now that he wasn't looking away did she realise just how rarely he fixed his eyes on her for any prolonged period. Disconcerted, she asked, 'Is something the matter?'

For a moment the faint lines around his eyes tensed, but then he turned and, still holding her hand, led her towards Domenico and Lucas, who were waiting for them alongside the course marshals. 'There's something I want to ask you. I need your help. But we can discuss it later.'

She allowed him to guide her out of the quagmire, wondering if this was the first time in all their years of knowing each other that he was asking for her help.

From the first moment that they had met he had helped her, and had shown no sign of stopping. There must have been a time when he had asked for her help…but for the life of her, she couldn't remember one. Yes, she had given him the support of friendship, shared his passion for old black and white movies and mountain trekking, the writing of Douglas Adams, but Edwin, so self-contained, so self-sufficient, so private, had never directly asked for her help. Even in those dark days and weeks after Michael's death, when grief had been chiselled into his face.

Now, as he led her out of the field, she inhaled a shaky breath, her chest tightening. How would she have coped if Edwin hadn't been there for her after her darling, her beloved, her troubled older brother had died? Her parents had fallen to pieces. They had idolised Michael as much as she had. The first family member to go to university.

And Oxford at that. Their pain after his death had been unbearable to witness. Knowing Michael had taken his own life had been too cruel, too senseless, too wrapped in guilt and what-ifs. Kara had stood by and watched her dad try time and time again to reach her mum, searching for support, but her mum had shut him out, disappearing into a world of her own where there was no time or energy for anyone else. She had watched her dad plead, grow angry and eventually shut down. It had crushed Kara's idea of love and relationships to see all of that pain and helplessness wrought on her dad.

As their marriage fell apart and during their eventual divorce Kara had leant on Edwin, needing his support, his encouragement, his advice, his reproaches when she had self-destructively gone off the rails. She had somehow managed to sleepwalk her way through her A levels in the month after Michael had died and gone on to university. But there had been so many bumps along the road, including dropping out of university for a month, until Edwin had made her see sense.

And when she had finally taken her finger off the self-destruct button five years ago, for the first time accepting just how destructive her relationship with her ex-boyfriend Nick was, she had realised that there was one thing she wanted to achieve in life—to set up a charity focused on the mental health of young adults, particularly targeting the difficult years of transition after leaving school. Five years on, the charity had seven centres throughout the UK, ran transitioning and education programmes in conjunction with several universities and provided a twenty-four-hour helpline. But there was so much more that they needed to do. There were so many more young people and their families they needed to help, but the lack of resources was holding them back. The need to do more consumed her.

At the gateway out onto the road, they paused and Edwin shook hands with the marshals, who did a reasonable attempt at appearing to be nonchalant in meeting him, an actual, real-life prince.

When it was her turn to greet the men she pulled them into a group hug. 'Thanks for volunteering today. We couldn't hold fundraising events like this without the support of our volunteers.'

Both men held themselves as stiff as a board and when she released them they eyed her as though they were worried for her sanity and their own safety.

'Kara's the founder and chairperson of Young Adults Together,' Edwin explained with amusement.

Both men relaxed.

One of them, heavily built with long hair and a skull nose piercing, said in a pronounced Cornish accent, 'This morning I was up before dark to come and do my bit.' Reddening, he cleared his throat, rolled his shoulders, and continued, 'My daughter…went through a bad patch last year.'

Kara swallowed at the confusion and fear in his voice. He cleared his throat noisily. 'Your counsellors gave us a lifeline when we didn't know where to turn.'

Kara pulled him into another hug. This time he wrapped his arms around her.

After she had extracted a pledge from both men that they would continue to volunteer for the charity, she hobbled as quickly as she could alongside Edwin on the internal estate road that led back to the tented village which had been erected adjacent to Fairfield House, thanks to the generosity of Lady Fairfield, who, along with Edwin, was a patron of the charity.

Domenico went ahead of them, while Lucas stayed a distance behind.

After graduating, Edwin had worked in the City of London for four years before returning to Monrosa to act as global ambassador for its financial sector. His job brought him to London on a regular basis but for the past month he had remained in Monrosa and his contact with Kara had mainly consisted of the occasional rushed text. 'I haven't heard from you recently—have you been busy?'

Beside her Edwin came to a stop. Kara's heart did a somersault at how troubled he suddenly seemed.

'You're limping.'

Giddy relief ran through her. For a moment she had thought something was seriously wrong. She reached down and rubbed the back of her thigh. 'I think I pulled something.'

Crouching down beside her, Edwin said, 'Show me where exactly.'

Kara pointed to the mid-centre of her thigh with her index finger. 'There.'

His hand touched her mud-strewn thigh, his warm fingers softly tracing over the skin beneath her running shorts. Every muscle in her body tensed as she resisted the temptation to yelp, giggle, move away.

'You've pulled your hamstring. We need to get you back to the finishing line quickly so that you can ice and elevate it.'

His gaze moved up to gauge her reaction.

'Why are you here, Edwin?'

Instead of answering her question he stood and said, 'I'll carry you to the finishing line.'

Kara laughed but she soon stopped. He was being serious. 'I'm fine. And anyway, I have to make my own way there—my sponsorship depends upon it.'

'How much is your sponsorship worth?'

'Close to two thousand pounds.'

For long seconds he held her gaze and Kara's heart gave a little kick. She should look away, make some quip, but now that he was here she realised just how acutely she had missed him over the past month.

'I'll match your sponsorship.' And then, with one of those utterly charming smiles of his, where she felt as if she was the centre of his world, he added softly, 'Now, please let me carry you. You're injured.'

For a nanosecond she actually contemplated his offer. But then good sense kicked in and she walked away. 'I've only pulled my hamstring. And how would it look to all of the other participants if the event organiser not only finished last but also had to be carried over the finishing line? By you of all people.' A safe distance away from him, she turned back. 'You know the media would have a field day if you're spotted carrying me. When are they ever going to accept that we're only friends?'

Edwin came alongside her. 'My father and mother had an arranged marriage. They started off as friends.'

Why was he telling her this? And she couldn't remember the last time he had spoken about his mother, who had died when he was a teenager.

Before she got the opportunity to ask him what was going on, his arm wrapped around her waist and she almost jumped out of her skin. They weren't the touchy-feely variety of friends.

'Your limp is getting worse. If you refuse this help then I'm going to instruct Lucas to carry you to the finishing line.'

Preferring the unsettling effect of being so close to Edwin over the ignominy of being carried by Lucas, who frankly scared her a little with his silent-killer type intensity, she allowed him to support her, but didn't lean as much into his strength as she really needed to.

'My father still misses my mother. They were a good team. Maybe practical marriages are the answer.'

Okay, this conversation was getting odder and odder. 'Answer to what?'

Nodding in the direction of the tented village, which had just come into view, rather than answer her question Edwin asked, 'How much will the mud run raise for the charity?'

Why hadn't he answered her question? 'Close to twenty thousand pounds, which will secure counselling services in Southampton for the first three months of next year.'

'You know I'm happy to provide more funding.'

This was an ongoing argument between them. 'Yes, and I appreciate your offer. But I don't want you funding the charity…there are so many others you support. I want Young Adults Together to be funded by the local communities—it builds a better understanding and ownership of the issues involved, along with helping to destigmatise mental health issues.'

He gazed at her with a fondness that burnt a hole right through her heart. 'I'm very proud of you, do you know that?'

Kara shrugged, rolled her eyes, trying not to let her delight, but also alarm, show. When he spoke to her like that, it made her feel totally exposed and fearful as to what her life would be like if he wasn't part of it.

Leaving the dual carriageway and following the main artery into Brighton, a sea of red brake lights appearing ahead of him, Edwin slowed and eventually brought his SUV to a stop.

Beside him, Kara sighed heavily. 'There are roadworks ahead. They've been causing traffic chaos for the past week.' Turning to glance at the car directly behind them, she added, 'There really was no need for you to drive me all the way home to Brighton. I feel so guilty Domenico and Lucas are having to drive my car back for me.'

Studying his protection officers in his rear-view mirror, Edwin grinned at their scowls and at how they were taking up every spare inch of space in the front of Kara's tiny car that made him wince each time he saw it, not just because of its canary-yellow bodywork but also because he doubted it would offer her much protection in an accident. She refused to trade it in on environmental grounds. 'I didn't want you driving when you should be resting your leg.'

Kara let out an impatient huff and shifted the icepack he had earlier taken out of the first-aid kit in the boot.

'It's a pulled hamstring and not even a seriously pulled one at that. It's fine,' Kara protested, her nose wrinkling with annoyance, the freckles on her cheeks she usually covered with make-up standing clear and proud.

'I like you without make-up and your hair like that. It reminds me of how you looked when we first met.' He hadn't meant to go out onto the rugby field that day, but seeing her brilliantly dodge endless tackles through intelligent and courageous play the length of the pitch, only to be thwarted at the try line, he had roared in frustration, and then, seeing her inert on the ground, her face buried in the earth, her limbs sprawled, he had raced onto the pitch, the need to get to her, to protect her all-consuming. And to this day that need to protect her was still there. A need that had solidified after Michael's death. Seeing her despair, her loneliness as her family fell apart, he had vowed to protect her, to always support her.

Michael's funeral had been a nightmare. Kara's parents, who were both deeply private individuals, had resented the media attention Edwin's presence had attracted and, already wracked with guilt over whether he could have done more to help his friend, he had listened to Kara say quietly and with a heartbreaking dignity in her eulogy that she had lost her first ever best friend, her inspiration, and he had silently pledged he would always be there for the little sister Michael had adored.

At times, he had struggled. Her pain had mirrored his own grief—not only for the loss of his best friend, but also from losing his mother and the unearthed memories and feelings he wanted to keep buried. But as they had got to know each other over the years their relationship had moved to one of firm friendship, and Kara, with her straight talking and dry sense of humour, gave him balance and perspective and a sense of normality he could so easily lose in a life where people were always way too eager to please him.

Was he about to put their entire relationship in jeopardy? Was he about to compromise the trust between them? Frustration towards his father and fear for the future had him wanting to open the car door and break into a run.

Oblivious to the bombshell he was about to deliver to her, Kara gave him a horrified look, flipped down her sunshade and stared at her reflection in the mirror. 'Are you kidding me? I can't believe I forgot my make-up bag this morning. And as for my hair…' She paused and lifted her long, honey-blonde curls with a grimace. 'Remind me to arrange for there to be a few hair straighteners in the women's changing rooms next year.' She gave a shiver and flipped the sunshade back up. 'I look terrible. I need a serious dose of sunshine—I look like I've spent ten years locked away indoors.'

Admittedly there was the hint of dark circles on the delicate pale skin beneath the sweeping brush of her long eyelashes, but the brilliance of her crystal-blue eyes hid that tiredness from all but the keenest of observers. 'I take it you are still working insane hours.'

Ignoring his comment, she flicked the radio to another station and then another, not settling until she found one playing jazz. She knew he hated jazz.

Ahead there was still no movement in the traffic. Flicking the radio off, he said, 'I saw you hobbling around the refreshment marquee when you were chatting to the runners—my guess is that your leg is a lot more painful than you're letting on.'

She rolled her eyes but then turned in her seat and regarded him with an appreciation that always caught him right in the gut. She followed it with the double whammy of her wide smile that always exploded like a firework in his heart, radiating a lightness inside him that always threatened the protective cloak of royal circumspection he had been taught to adopt from an early age.

'Thanks for coming in to say hello. The runners were thrilled to see you. I think you've guaranteed the success of next year's run. We were inundated with runners asking if they could sign up,' she said.

'I'm sure their interest in participating next year is down to how well the event was organised today and nothing to do with me.'

'Oh, please. You know the huge crowd waiting at the finishing line were there for a reason. And it certainly wasn't to cheer me on. Apparently there was a stampede back to the finishing line once word got around that you were spotted starting the race late—from our female runners in particular.' Nodding in the direction of the car behind them, she added with a grin, 'You and the guys did look rather fetching in your tight running gear.'

When was the traffic going to move again? He had things he needed to say to her. Things that were tying his stomach in knots. He had spent the last couple of weeks with a team of lawyers trying not to be in the position he was now in. What he had to ask of her was huge and unfair. He didn't want to drag her into this mess that wasn't of her making. But there was no one else he could trust. Dryly he responded to her teasing, 'I'm glad we proved to be of some use.' Then, unable to resist teasing her back, he added, 'I reckon it might be safer if you stick to the sidelines next year, though.'

'No way! I mightn't be special-services fit like you but I can hold my own. Trust me, I've learned my lesson and I'll pace myself much better next year.' She gave him a hopeful smile. 'It would be great if you could take part again. I can get Triona to contact your office with the date and hopefully if you are free they'll be able to schedule it into your diary.'

He arched his neck. Being stuck in a traffic jam was not the ideal place for this conversation but he couldn't go on pretending his life hadn't been turned upside down any longer. 'I'm not sure I'll be in a position to take part next year.'

For a moment she frowned but then she visibly paled. Her hand shot out to touch his arm. 'You're not ill, are you? Is that why you haven't been in touch recently?'

Her immediate concern for him only ratcheted up his guilt. He had sworn he would protect Michael's little sister, and here he was, asking her to step into the unrelenting scrutiny of the entire world.

He and Michael, who had both been students at Oxford, had met through the aikido club. As it had turned out, both of them were in Mansfield College studying Politics, Philosophy and Economics, Edwin a year ahead of Michael. On several occasions, Michael had brought him to his family home in London, claiming he needed to be exposed to the reality of how others lived. In London, Michael had taken him to the homeless charity where he had volunteered when in sixth form, and to his local aikido club, where he heard about their programmes to encourage teenagers into sport and away from knife crime. And Kara had tagged along, listening attentively to Michael's opinions, smiling when Edwin and Michael disagreed over some issue. She had visited Michael in Oxford and had gone to parties with them, the only person to ever persuade Michael out onto the dance floor. Kara had idolised Michael and their parents had worshipped him. Edwin used to tease him over it, Michael always shrugging it off until one evening during his second year in Oxford, when they were both at a house party. Michael was drunk and fell and spilt a drink all over someone's laptop. The owner screamed at Michael. Michael just stood there staring at the girl as she ranted at him, not reacting, looking as though nothing was registering with him. And then he disappeared out of the house. Edwin followed him, unsettled by the blankness in Michael's expression.

Edwin finally found him in the gardens of Mansfield. He almost backed away when he realised Michael was crying. Edwin had been brought up to hide his emotions. He didn't know how to cope with someone else's. But he went and sat down next to Michael. And they must have sat in silence for at least twenty minutes before Michael admitted just how much he was struggling to fit in at

Oxford, how apart he felt from student life, his constant anxiety, how he feared disappointing his family, how riddled his mind was with dark, negative thoughts. Edwin listened, tried to help, but he was way out of his depth and ill-equipped to deal with Michael's despair. He encouraged Michael to reach out to the support services in the university and offered to pay if Michael would prefer to go to see someone privately.

And after a lot of resistance, they ended the night hugging, Michael promising to contact the university health services. But in the weeks that followed, Michael shut Edwin down whenever he asked how he was doing. He disappeared off campus or spent days locked away in his room, claiming he was studying and didn't want to be disturbed.

In the run-up to their end-of-year exams, Edwin spoke to the college authorities about his concern over Michael's welfare. Michael learned of his intervention and went ballistic, refusing to speak to him again. Edwin called Michael's parents one night, a call he had agonised over for days, not wanting to betray Michael's privacy or to panic his parents unduly. He spoke to Michael's dad, who responded with disbelieving bewilderment. He told Edwin that, while he appreciated his concern, he was certain he was wrong. For hadn't Michael only told them the previous weekend just how much he was enjoying university life and was looking forward to staying with Edwin in Monrosa over the summer?

Michael failed his second-year exams. The day after he learnt his results he caught a train to the south coast and took an overdose on the beach that night. Early the following morning he was found by a local man.

His parents were away on holiday. Kara was the first to be told.

Kara called Edwin in Monrosa, sobbing and, despite several attempts, unable to tell him what was the matter. It was their neighbour who quietly whispered those words of horror down the phone to him.

Within an hour he was on his way to London. Once there, he held Kara, his heart torn in two by her mute, violent shivering, all the memories of holding his youngest brother, Ivo, the morning of their mother's funeral haunting him, reminding him how Ivo too had shuddered with grief, his fragile bones rattling in his arms.

When his mother had died he had thought that the grief of losing her would simply be about the gut-aching sadness and disbelief—he had never anticipated the ugly swamp of consequences that kept flowing back into his family's lives and swallowing them whole. Their father's angry, authoritarian way of trying to be an effective single parent, Luis's rebellion, which had seen him constantly in trouble with authority, Ivo's avoidance of them all, his own deliberate distance.

Loving someone too much destroyed you.

And in the aftermath of Michael's death, all those emotions had been stirred up again and he had relived the agony of losing someone. Through the shock and grief and guilt he had somehow managed to care for and support Kara, encouraging her to continue with her studies, and to accept her university place, and as time passed they had become close friends, their relationship managing to survive media intrusion and endless arguments when Kara was testing every boundary possible, crying out for attention.

And now he was about to ask her a question that could blow apart the one friendship that kept him sane.

He lowered his window. Drops of drizzle immediately speckled the interior of the car door but he needed some air to clear his brain. On a deep inhale he admitted, 'I might not be able to take part in the race next year because by then I might have succeeded to the throne of Monrosa.'

For long moments Kara stared at him, grappling for words. 'When did this happen?'

'My father has decided to abdicate.'

'And you're next in line.' Looking away, she stared at the still stationary traffic and said distractedly, 'There must have been an accident ahead.' Then, her gaze shifting back to him, she shook her head. 'Wow. I didn't see that coming. But you don't seem very excited. I thought succeeding was what you always wanted.'

In the distance a siren sounded, and it came closer and closer until a police car passed them on the hard shoulder. He winced at the piercing sound. 'Both the royal court and the public will be slow to accept this change in ruler, especially when I push through my reforms to halt the ever-increasing mass tourism to allow for more sustainable development on the island to protect the environment.'

For long seconds Kara studied him, her ability to get to the core of a problem apparent in the reckoning in her eyes. 'You need to sell your vision of the Monrosa you want to rule. Ground that vision in what you already stand for—prosperity for all while protecting both the environment and the vulnerable in society. Look at all the changes you've already made by persuading your father to reform environmental policy. And there are all your ideas on housing and healthcare reform. I know you'll rule with loyalty and compassion while ensuring Monrosa continues to thrive. And the people will come to see and appreciate that too, with time.'

He could not help but laugh at the passion in Kara's

voice. 'Maybe I should employ you as my press officer.' Then, sobering at the thought of the momentous battles he would have in the future, he added, 'Those environmental reforms aren't enough—they are only the start. Changing the mind-sets of the people, especially those heavily invested in the tourism industry, will not be easy. Environmentally responsible tourism and the attraction of other service industries, especially the financial-services sector, has to be the way forward for Monrosa's economy.' He let out a heavy sigh, '*Dio!* We have ruined long stretches of the coastline already with overdevelopment. My father sees no issue with it, but it's unsustainable. I need to succeed to the throne to stop any further development. We need to set in place a twenty-year plan for keeping the economy viable whilst protecting the unique environment of Monrosa.' His mother had been a passionate campaigner for protecting Monrosa's unique microclimates and biodiversity, and Edwin was determined to put the protection of the environment centre stage during his reign.

Kara nodded. 'And you will succeed in putting that plan in place. I know you will.' Then, pausing to bite her lip, she added, 'I'm guessing I'll get to see even less of you once you are crowned. Is that why you haven't been in contact recently?'

'I've spent the past month trying to persuade my father to stay in the role. I'm not convinced he's abdicating for the right reasons.' Seeing Kara's quizzical look, he added, 'He believes it's time for fresh ideas and a new energy in the role.' Then, rubbing his hand over his jaw, Edwin admitted, 'My father also says that he wants to ensure he has grandchildren before he's too old to enjoy them.'

'What has your father abdicating got to do with him becoming a grandfather?'

Edwin inhaled a deep breath. 'My father quietly passed a new piece of legislation last year on succession in Monrosa. From now on, only a married individual can be sovereign.'

Kara tilted her head and gave a small exhale of puzzlement. 'What does that mean?'

Doubt and misgivings and fear stirred like a trinity of foreboding inside him. He wasn't into relationships, never mind marriage—there was too much expectation around the need for love and intimacy. And Edwin's heart was too closed to ever risk loving another person again. Was he really prepared to enter into the minefield of marriage because it was his duty to do so? That question was easily answered. His destiny was to be crowned Sovereign Prince. He owed it to his country, his family, his people. 'I have to marry or my aunt, my father's sister, Princess Maria, will succeed to the throne.'

Kara laid her head against the headrest and let out a heavy, disbelieving breath. 'You're getting married.' She looked away, out to the grey and abandoned-looking industrial estate on the opposite side of the road, her hair obscuring her face.

'That's why I'm here today, to tell you. There's something I need…'

Before he could say anything more Kara twisted back to him, shifting in her seat and giving him a smile that didn't reach her eyes. 'Well, I suppose congratulations are in order. Who's the lucky woman and when is it all going to happen?' Then with a brief laugh she added, 'No wonder you disappeared off the face of the earth for the past month. I thought you were caught up with work and royal duty, not planning the wedding of the year.'

'My father intends on announcing his abdication next

Thursday. The coronation date of the next monarch is already arranged—it will take place on the first of June.'

'So you have to be married by then?' Not waiting for him to respond, Kara said, 'That's just over two months away. So who are you going to marry? Are you already engaged? Is the wedding date set?'

Another police car, siren blaring, passed on their inside. He waited for the sound to fade out before he said, 'Earlier I said I needed your help…'

Kara waited for him to continue. After years of embracing bachelorhood, his brain was still struggling to keep up with the new reality his father had decided to foist on him.

Folding her arms, Kara said, 'Please don't tell me you want me to be your best woman or something like that. I'm sure Luis can manage to behave himself for once and deliver a fitting best man's speech. And if not, I'm sure Ivo could be persuaded. Eventually.'

Did she really think he would become engaged to someone else without forewarning her or at least telling her he was heading in that direction? 'No! Not that. What I want to ask you…' he paused, gave her an uneasy smile that did nothing to diminish her unimpressed scowl '…I want to ask you to marry me. I want you to be my wife.'

CHAPTER TWO

HAD SHE BANGED her head earlier, when she had fallen? She could have sworn Edwin had just asked her to marry him. Was she suffering severe confusion as a result of concussion?

A loud rapping on Edwin's window made them both jump. Domenico was standing there and gesturing ahead, pointing out that the traffic in front had moved on and now Edwin was holding things up.

Nodding, Edwin pulled away.

Kara studied him, and it felt as though she was truly seeing him for the first time in ages. Was this man—this prince, this soon-to-be sovereign—actually asking her to marry him? His concentration was on the road ahead, his mouth pulled into a tight line, a hint of colour in his high cheekbones.

She laughed and said, 'Nice joke, Edwin. Now, why don't you tell me who you're really going to marry?'

He darted a look in her direction, the cleft in his jaw more pronounced than usual. He was seriously hacked off. 'I wouldn't joke about asking you to marry me. Surely you know that?'

Yes, she did. Edwin wasn't cruel. He was honourable and selfless. But right now she was grasping at straws in a bid to try to make sense of this conversation.

'I'm serious, Kara. I'd like you to be my wife.'

'Wow. I never thought I'd be so lucky as to be proposed to somewhere as romantic as a gridlocked dual carriageway on a gloomy Sunday in March.'

'I promise you a nice honeymoon.'

Kara laughed. 'Have you completely lost your mind?'

'Remember the time you rang me in the middle of the night and said that if we both got to thirty and were still single then we should marry?'

Oh, God, she'd hoped he had forgotten about that.

'I was tipsy and emotional at a friend's wedding. I wasn't being serious. I'm not interested in marrying.' In the immediate years after witnessing her parents' marriage implode, she had steered well clear of any relationship that could end so painfully. So she had dated guys who she knew wouldn't hang around, and for a while that had suited her fine. But after graduating, with her family home sold and living alone in Brighton because of work, she had craved stability and closeness. She had thought Nick was the answer to her embarrassing hunger for intimacy and she had embraced their relationship like someone famished. But his early attentiveness had slowly morphed into claustrophobic controlling behaviour and had once and for all firmly convinced her a single life was preferable to the minefield of relationships and the hurt they spawned. Now, folding her arms, she pointed out, 'And anyway, I'm not thirty yet.'

'In six months you are.'

'Thanks for the reminder.' She had a good life, one that was hard fought for after years of uncertainty and grief—supportive friends, a career that gave her meaning, and, most important of all, an uncomplicated personal life that left her free to focus on work, and work alone. Why, then, did hurtling towards thirty leave her with a nagging sense of unease? Was it the frustration of knowing there was an ever-increasing demand for the charity's services both in the United Kingdom and abroad? She desperately wanted to do more. There was so much work to be done in addressing mental-health issues and educating both young people and those who supported them about dealing with matters before they got out of control. Was it this constant feeling of not doing enough that left her unsettled as she faced her thirtieth birthday?

At a pedestrian crossing on a suburban street, Edwin stopped to allow a young man pushing a pram and holding hands with a little girl to cross the road. Kara shared sporadic phone conversations with her parents and usually they were short and revolved around the weather, but a few months ago her mum had surprised her when she asked her what she thought Michael would have been doing by now? Would he have had a career in political activism, as he had dreamed? Would he have been married? Had children? And after the call, she had sat in the silence of her apartment and wondered once again if she could have prevented Michael from dying.

Her gaze shifted to Edwin. He had been her constant, her steadying influence over the past decade. His marriage proposal was not only insane but it was also sending a tidal wave of uncertainty into her life when she had thought she had finally got a handle on it. 'There must be a long line of more suitable women out there—shouldn't you be trying to forge some strategic alliance, or whatever it is you royals do?'

Edwin waited until he had pulled into her street and found a parking space before he answered. 'I need to marry someone I can trust.'

Killing the engine, he unbuckled his seatbelt and turned and regarded her with that regal look of his that spoke of pride and honour. 'And there's no one I trust more in life than you.'

Her heart catching at the sincerity of his voice, she unbuckled her own belt. 'That's not exactly a solid basis for a marriage, though, is it? I'm sure you trust Domenico and Lucas but you're not about to marry one of them.'

Edwin eyed her with a raised eyebrow. 'I can't. They're both married. And there isn't time for them to get divorced. I need to announce my engagement before Thursday; my father is insistent on announcing his abdication then.'

Domenico came alongside the car. Edwin nodded that they were ready to go into Kara's flat. Reaching for the handle of his door, Edwin added, 'I reckon trust is the most important part of any marriage. At least we have that.'

Should she tell him that she didn't want him to come inside? She needed some time and space to make sense of his bombshell proposal. But what was there to think about? There was no way she could marry Edwin.

Inside her basement apartment, she placed her gym bag in the tiny utility room off the kitchen and went and filled her kettle.

Turning to Edwin, she said with a sigh, 'I'm a working-class girl—I have no idea how to be a princess. Even saying the word "princess" feels ridiculous. Me, a princess? No way.'

'The title would be Her Serene Highness, Princess of Monrosa,' Edwin said, removing his black padded jacket and hanging it on her bulging coat rack.

'See—I didn't even know what the correct title would be.'

He shifted the stool he always sat on away from the kitchen counter to allow for the extra-long length of his legs. Sitting, he shrugged. 'You're not expected to know royal protocol. None of that is of importance. What is important is that I have a wife I can trust, a wife who understands that what we'll have is a working marriage. I know how keen you are for the charity to be able to help more people—you could use your status to achieve that.' Rubbing the back of his neck, he said, 'I know what it is I'm asking of you, Kara, and I'm not asking it of you lightly. I have spent the past week agonising over whether to do so, but I think we can make it work. Neither of us is looking for romance…at least that's what you've always claimed.'

His last sentence sounded like a challenge. As though he was testing her constant refrain over the years that marriage was not for her. 'It isn't just a love marriage I'm not interested in, Edwin. It's all types of marriage.' Filling the teapot with boiling water, she added, 'I know this might sound a little rich coming from me, given my outlook on love, but *you* shouldn't discount love—you've never given it a chance. At least I gave it a go. You've always ended relationships way too early.'

Edwin made a grumbling sound and, leaning heavily against the counter, sent a teaspoon clattering across the marble surface. 'I'm happy being single.'

Placing four teacups on the counter, Kara stepped back, folded her arms and raised an eyebrow.

Edwin's gaze narrowed. 'What?'

Kara continued to hold his stare.

'Look, I just like to be careful who I trust. You've done pretty much the same since Nick,' he argued.

'Agreed, but then I'm not the one who now needs to marry. Maybe if you had been more open to those few women you actually dated over the years, willing to trust them, then you wouldn't have to resort to asking your friend to marry you.'

Edwin stood and, pacing the tiny floor space of her

kitchen, raised his hand in exasperation. 'Like how I trusted Salma Rosucci?'

Kara winced. 'I'll admit it was unfortunate that Salma told the paparazzi you were holidaying together in Sardinia.' Biting back a smile, she added, 'On the positive side, the photos they took of you sunbathing cheered up millions of women across Europe.'

Edwin scowled. Then, walking towards her, he placed a hand on the countertop next to her and asked with quiet pride, 'Would marrying me be that bad?'

For a moment something deep inside her wanted to say no, that marrying him would be…would be okay. Better than okay, in fact. She would get to spend her days with him. Would that be such a bad thing? But then logic kicked in. Picking up the teapot, she poured tea into all four cups. 'The media are going to go crazy.'

'Let them. They'll soon come to recognise what an incredible person you are.'

'They'll eat me alive first. I can see the headlines—*"Prince Edwin to Marry Builder's Daughter."* Or how about, *"Why is Kara Duffy Marrying Billionaire Prince Edwin?"* And what will your family say?'

'Luis and Ivo don't care about what I do—they're too busy leading their own lives.'

'And what about your father?'

'He doesn't have the right to an opinion. He may have forced my hand on marriage but he has no say in who I marry.'

Kara buried her head in her hands. 'In other words, he's not going to be happy when he finds out you've chosen me.' At best Kara would have said his father was indifferent to her whenever she visited the palace, and there were certainly times when he seemed to think she was an annoying creature sent to test his patience. 'I know he still blames me for that time I went out racing with you both and cost you the competition because I was so seasick we had to go back to the marina.'

'As I've said before, don't take it personally—my father is cantankerous with everyone. Including his own children.'

'But he rarely speaks to me and the last time I visited the palace he called me Salma...not only does he not know my name but he also mistakes me for one of your ex-girlfriends. Does he know you want to marry me?'

'No.'

A thought snaked its way into her brain. 'Asking me to marry you wouldn't be your way of getting back at your father, would it?'

Unbelievably he grinned at that. 'I hadn't thought of it that way, but it could be an added bonus.'

Shaking her head at the constant tension that existed between Edwin and his father, she pushed a cup along the counter towards him. 'I'd almost be tempted to say yes, just to witness first-hand how you and your father manage the succession; you'll drive each other insane with your alpha-male jostling.'

She carried the other two cups to the front door.

Edwin followed her. 'Alpha-male jostling. Where the hell did you get that idea from?'

She laughed at his indignation. 'It's a constant battle between you two—can't you see that? You and your father are too alike—that's why you clash. You both always want to be in control, the decision maker, the leader.'

He gave her a disbelieving look. 'No, we clash because my father is stubborn and work obsessed.' Indicating the teacups, he added, 'You know, you really don't need to give tea to Domenico and Lucas.'

'So you pointed out the last time you visited, and the

time before that. And several times before that too. I hate the thought of them sitting out there in the cold with nothing to drink.'

Unlatching the door, instead of standing aside to allow her to go outside, Edwin took the cups from her. 'I'll bring them out—you should be resting. And making tea for the protection team will be a definite no when you're a princess.'

'I hate to point out the obvious, but I haven't agreed to be a princess.'

He gave her a grin. 'Not yet. But you will.'

He stepped outside. She called out, 'And you think your father's stubborn,' before going into the sitting room, where she turned on some table lamps against the fading light of the day and then lit the fire before going back into the kitchen to fetch their teacups.

Back in the hallway, she met Edwin on his way back in and she gestured for him to follow her into the sitting room.

She took a seat on the occasional chair beside the fire. Edwin carried a low stool from beneath the window and placed it before her. She lifted her leg onto the stool, wincing at the tightness that gripped her thigh.

Edwin sat on the sofa facing the fire, tucking a leg under himself, an arm running along the back of the navy sofa that was too small for his bulk. The flames from the fire cast shadows on his face. And then his eyes met hers. Silently he waited for her answer.

'I can't marry you, Edwin.'

'Why?'

'Where do I start? My background. What if something goes wrong? I like being your friend. I don't want to lose that.'

He shifted forward in his seat, his eyes holding hers all the time. 'I promise never to hurt you.'

Edwin always kept his word, but what if he couldn't do so in this instance? Sometimes, despite their best intentions, people hurt each other. Not in a deliberate way like Nick, but purely due to human fragility. Look at what had happened between her parents. At first Kara had stood on the sidelines, bewildered and frightened, watching their pain and guilt and dismay over losing Michael destroy their love for one another. They had once loved each other. She was certain of that. But just not enough to counter the tsunami of grief losing Michael had caused. Her dad had looked to her mum for support, but she had pushed him away. Day after day she had watched her mum turn her back on her dad, grow more remote and uninterested in everything, while her dad had become more desperate, constantly trying to get through to her, to make things okay. Eventually, and not surprisingly, her dad had stopped trying, and had become bitter and defensive. It was the speed of it all that still astounded her: within weeks their family life had been stripped away and they were behaving no differently to three strangers living under one roof.

'What are you most scared of?'

She stared into the fire, considering his question, and then studied her ring-free fingers. Nick had given her a ring to mark their anniversary of dating for a year. He used to sulk when she didn't wear it. She hadn't worn a ring for years. The thought of even doing so now made her wince.

She understood why it was so important to Edwin to marry and she hated not being in the position to help him on this one occasion that he had asked for her support, so, despite the tightness in her throat, the wave of vulnerability rolling through her, no matter how sickening it was to have to rake up old memories, the least he deserved was her honesty. 'I'm scared of feeling suffocated, losing myself in a relationship, even in a marriage of convenience.'

'I'm not following.'

She swallowed, the ability to talk suddenly vanishing. 'After Michael…well, you know how crazy my life got for a while…' she tucked her hands under her legs, liking the way her thighs squashed the tingling in her hands at the memory of Nick's ring on her finger '…too much partying and drinking and getting into relationships and friendships that weren't healthy.'

Edwin shrugged. 'You were trying to work things out.'

She exhaled, remembering how much it had cut her to see Edwin's disappointment each time he had learnt of yet another of her long litany of disastrous acts and decisions in the years after Michael's death. Studying him, she bit her lip, wondering if she could dredge up the courage to ask the one question she'd always wanted to ask him, but never had the guts to—why he stuck around. She couldn't bear the thought that it was just because he pitied her. 'You were incredibly patient with me back then.'

Moving even further into his seat, he placed his forearms on his knees, his hands clasped, his gaze holding hers. Her heartbeat rose and rose as the seconds passed. 'You were hurting.'

She blinked. Nodded, her throat knotted with emotion. Was it losing his mother that made him so empathetic to how deeply she had grieved Michael?

'Once I graduated and moved here to Brighton for work, I thought for a while that I had my life under control. Mum and Dad's divorce had gone through and I wasn't having to constantly deal with their arguments. I was enjoying work and I had my own little flat, which I loved. But I knew nobody here in Brighton. And then you moved back to Monrosa.' Picking up her teacup, she held the warm porcelain in her hands. 'With you out of the country I didn't even have someone to give me earache about my lack of judgement.'

Edwin smiled. 'Not earache, guidance.'

With a deep inhale she admitted, 'And then I met Nick. He seemed to be everything I was looking for—really attentive, and he wanted to be with me all the time. Our relationship made me feel safe.'

She shuffled her chair a few inches away from the fire, a burning, embarrassed heat flaming inside her, knowing she needed to continue her explanation as to why relationships terrified her. 'It's hard to explain, but over time I began to realise that he was just too into me. He was constantly texting and calling me. Most evenings he came around here. He'd get angry when I had to work late or if I wanted to go out with work colleagues. He started to call me several times a day. Wanting to know where I was and who I was with. He said he called just to make sure I was okay. And then about a year into our relationship he entered a phase where he'd blow all hot and cold. One day he'd be kind and attentive and the next day he'd totally ignore me. I never knew where I stood with him and it utterly confused me.'

Edwin's nostrils flared.

She could understand his anger.

She rubbed the back of her neck. Would she ever stop feeling embarrassed for being so clueless? Would she ever stop feeling somehow responsible for Nick's behaviour?

'My self-confidence took a dive. I lost all direction and sense of myself. I felt so confused. You probably won't remember this, but you came to visit after you had attended a financial summit in London. You knew something was wrong, so I pretended I was sick and just generally stressed out by work, and you insisted I take some annual leave. You brought me back to Monrosa to stay in your family's villa in the mountains.'

'I remember. You said it was a virus—you never said anything about Nick.'

'I didn't really understand myself what the matter was. I just had this overwhelming sense of panic. So I thought it was something physically wrong with me—some type of stress response to missing my parents and being so busy with work. What I failed to face up to was how destructive my relationship with Nick was.' Kara swallowed at how Edwin's mouth was pulled into a tight line, anger sparking from his eyes.

'Why didn't you tell me?'

Because I didn't want you to know that I had messed up once again. I wanted you to see me as a peer. Not Michael's little sister who kept tripping up in life and needing your help.

'It was during my week in Monrosa that the idea to set up a charity started to form in my mind. I thought about Michael and how he struggled in university. And how I had struggled when I moved to Brighton, away from everything that was familiar to me. I wondered if there could be more support and awareness-building for young adults on managing major transitions and their mental health. I also faced up to the fact my relationship with Nick wasn't healthy, so I broke up with him when I returned to England.'

His eyes narrowing, Edwin asked, 'How did he take that?'

Grimacing, Kara admitted, 'Let's just say it took him a while to accept it.'

Edwin let out an angry breath. 'Did he harass you?'

'I had to block his number.'

Edwin sat forward, rolling his shoulders, his expression perplexed. 'Why didn't you ask for my help?'

'Pride and embarrassment, along with a dash of disbelief.'

Edwin threw his head back and studied the ceiling before returning his gaze to her. 'I wish you had told me.' Then, with integrity burning brightly in his eyes, he said quietly, 'I understand why you'd be cautious about getting into a relationship again and I swear to you I would never hurt you…but I get it, Kara. I'm not going to try to persuade you into something you don't want to do.'

Oh, thank God.

But boy, did she feel guilty.

'Is there anyone else you can ask?'

'There's no one else I can trust.'

She leant back in her chair feeling weak with the simple sincerity of his softly spoken words. 'I know how much this means to you.'

'It's my problem to sort out, not yours.'

'Can you challenge the new law your dad passed?'

'I've spent the past month trying to do just that. He's refusing to budge.' He stood and moved towards the door. 'I need to go back to Monrosa tonight.' Turning, he added, 'Thanks for listening and I hope you can understand why I asked you—people respond to you so positively. Despite what people might like to think, being a royal requires a strong work ethic, empathy and above all the ability to be a strong role model—and you have those qualities in bucket loads.'

Was that how he saw her? Really? Not the chaotic young adult who tested his patience endless times, or the charity CEO with a propensity to over-commit?

'I assume it'll be a temporary arrangement…if you find someone to marry.'

He paused and considered her for a moment. 'I can see no reason why it couldn't be permanent.'

'But what if you meet someone else? Actually fall in love?'

'I have liked being single and not being tied down, but that doesn't mean I won't stay true to my marriage vows. This may be a working marriage but I will respect the marriage even more for that. I will respect that whoever marries me will do so in good faith and deserve my utmost loyalty.'

Thrown, she asked, 'But what of your father's wish for grandchildren? How is that going to happen?'

A hint of a smile lifted on his lips. 'Are you asking me for a sex-education lesson?'

'No!'

'I've told my father he may have forced my hand in marrying but that he has no say in whether or not I have children.'

'How did he react to that?'

'He was surprisingly unperturbed. I can't help but think he didn't want to give away his annoyance that he hadn't included the need for children to be born in the marriage to be part of the succession rules.'

Edwin left the room and, lost for words, Kara studied her hands. They were shaking. How hadn't she noticed that before now? His footsteps echoed on the tiles of the kitchen floor. He came back into the sitting room, shrugging on his jacket. She moved in the chair to stand. He gestured for her not to.

As usual he went to give her a hug goodbye.

But rather than hug her for the normal quick squeeze they usually shared, he laid his hands gently on her shoulders, their warmth seeping into her bones, his cheek brushing against her hair. Pinpricks of awareness bubbled on her skin. An air of sadness, almost vulnerability, surrounded him.

She went stock still. How much must it have taken Edwin to ask her to marry him—this proud, self-sufficient man who never asked for help or support? A whoosh of admiration for him hammered through her. Edwin would have agonised over this and would not be asking her to marry him lightly. He *really* mustn't have another option. She knew what it meant to him to succeed to the throne. All his ambitions for Monrosa. Her head swam with all the reasons why saying no was the only sane thing to do. But how could she turn him down when he had been her lifeline so many times before?

He straightened. Her heart beating like a trapped butterfly, she tried to keep her voice steady. 'I'll give you two years. After that we can divorce. Anything less would seem…unbecoming.'

'Are you saying yes?'

'I think so.'

Edwin pulled her into a hug, his arms holding her tight. Her head swam again. His chest was solid warmth, his scent the usual reminder of the mountain forests of Monrosa.

When he pulled away his gaze held hers. 'I need to leave for my flight. Think about your answer overnight. Call me tomorrow. I don't want you rushing into a decision you may later regret.'

With that he left the room and a few seconds later she heard the front door open and quietly shut. She let out a long exhale and clenched her shaking hands. Her gaze ran around her sitting room. This was her home. Was she really prepared to move away from this life she had built for herself to live in a country where she would know no one other than her pretend husband?

CHAPTER THREE

KARA ATTEMPTED TO join the other early Monday morning joggers as they ran along the promenade, but after a few hobbled steps she gave in to the tightness in her thigh.

It was still dark, a heavy mist dancing around the street lights. She should have stayed in bed. But her jumbled thoughts had needed air.

Last night she had created a pros and cons list for marrying Edwin when she hadn't been able to sleep. On the cons side she had listed in no particular order of importance:

Losing my privacy
Leaving my job and home
Moving to a new country
The media sensation when we marry and divorce
I have no idea what is involved in being a princess and I'll just mess up
My parents' disapproval—they might like Edwin, and in truth not show much interest in my life, but I can't see that stopping them having conniptions to see their only child agreeing to such a public and high-profile pretend marriage
Having to fake being in love in public
The damage it could do to our friendship

On the pros side she had put:

It could be fun??

But she had crossed that out for being too frivolous and then had written in capital letters two single points:

It's my turn to help Edwin
It will give me the platform to raise the international profile of Young Adults Together

On a daily basis, the Young Adults Together internet forums received messages from people from all over the world looking for help and support. And the only way to ensure they reached as many people as possible was for local communities to get involved in the charity's work and fundraising.

It hadn't taken her long to realise that the cons side of the list was heavily weighted towards the impact of accepting Edwin's proposal would personally have on her. While the pros side was about her giving back. It was no contest really.

However, there was an extra con she hadn't even been able to write down last night, hating to think that Edwin was anything like Nick, but what *if* he was manipulating her? Just as Nick had used to do. Was he using her to antagonise his dad or perhaps to divert the media's attention away from his succession to the much juicer speculation as to just why he had chosen her to be his bride? She knew she could trust Edwin—for crying out loud, he had done nothing but support her for the past decade...but that nagging doubt was still there.

Cheers, Nick. You've really managed to make me paranoid about everyone's motives.

Hobbling back to her apartment, she knew she had to make a decision. Edwin deserved a final answer from her.

Opening the front door, she went towards the kitchen, where she had left her phone charging last night. By the hall table she paused at the collage of photos on the wall, realising it had been a long time since she had stopped to look at them.

Her gaze sought out one particular picture amongst the dozen others.

Herself and Edwin and Michael, sitting in the beer garden of a pub in Oxford, wearing layers of clothes against the coldness of the winter's night, Michael sitting in between herself and Edwin, his arms thrown around their shoulders, staring into the camera, his expression earnest. Michael had approached life with an intense but passionate seriousness, as though he owed the world a debt. Had university triggered his depression or was it something he had always struggled with?

She blinked as tears washed over her vision, obscuring the photo of her two best friends.

She had lost one.

She wasn't going to lose the other. And she certainly wasn't going to let Nick's behaviour influence her decision either.

Edwin answered immediately. 'Hi.'

His voice was low and husky. Was he still in bed?

Edwin lying in bed... Did he wear pyjamas? Somehow she couldn't imagine him pulling them on. Wait... What exactly would their living and sleeping arrangements be when they married?

Despite her throat being suddenly tighter than her dad's wallet, she said in a tumble of words, 'My answer is still yes. I'll marry you. I'm assuming I'll need to move to Monrosa...but then what?'

There was a pause on the other end of the line. 'I'm glad.'

Her heart galloped at the reserved relief in his voice. She could hear a rustling sound of paper and then the soft tread of footsteps. She had been wrong. He wasn't in bed. Was he having breakfast, in his office? Then he spoke again. 'After we marry we will use the royal apartments within the palace. The south-wing apartments have been recently renovated and will suit us perfectly. There's an office there with a balcony that overlooks the mountains that will be perfect for you.' He paused. She could hear his footsteps again. And then he sighed. 'We'll need to share a bedroom, and a bed —our staff are usually very loyal but sometimes there can be a rogue insider who informs the media about our personal lives.'

Was he serious? Share a bed!

'How big is the bed we'll be sharing?'

'It's an antique four-poster.'

Any antique beds Kara had ever come across were always on the miniscule size. 'How big?'

Edwin cleared his throat, but not before she heard him chuckle. 'I guess you could say it would be a cosy fit for two.'

She huffed. And was grateful he couldn't see her red cheeks right now. 'Order a new bed and make it a super-super-king-size.'

She ended the call to his laughter.

And then she laughed too.

Had she lost her mind?

Wednesday afternoon and the usually tranquil white drawing room of Monrosa Palace, with its walls draped in white and gold silk brocade, fragile French gilt-bronze furniture sitting on handwoven silk rugs, reverberated with impatient mutterings.

'This atmosphere is more akin to that of a funeral than an engagement announcement,' Edwin muttered to Victor, his personal secretary.

Victor eyed the rest of the room. Alongside Edwin's father, who was getting increasingly agitated at the delay in starting the afternoon's proceedings, the Secretary of State, the First Aide de Camp to His Royal Highness, the Chamberlain and various other advisors close to His Highness had assembled for the engagement announcement. And clearly none were happy with his father's earlier declaration in a private briefing that he was going to abdicate the following day.

'His Highness has ruled Monrosa for thirty-five years. We are a conservative society. In time the people will accept his decision,' Victor replied with his usual understated diplomacy.

Turning his back on the room, Edwin studied the news reporters gathered at the far end of the internal courtyard of the palace. The palace, once a Moorish fortress, had been extended and renovated by practically every generation of the Prado family, which had ruled Monrosa for the past six hundred years. His ancestor, Prince Louis II, had erected a low arched gallery supported by three hundred and sixty-five marble pillars around the internal parameter of the courtyard. His father's contribution had been to commission the restoration of the frescoes painted by Miotto and Formano in the south wing of the palace.

Even from the opposite side of the vast courtyard, originally constructed with another enemy in mind, Edwin could sense the media's anticipation that something of importance was about to happen. His father addressed the press every Thursday afternoon. Only something of major significance would warrant a separate press gathering the day before.

It's about to happen.

He balled his hands and breathed deeply into his diaphragm. He needed to ground himself, banish every reason why he didn't want to do this and focus on the succession. Too much thinking and ruminating got you nowhere.

The mumbling behind him had ceased.

He whipped around.

Standing with his aunt, Princess Maria, at the threshold of the room, her hair straightened into sleek waves, her professionally applied make-up emphasising the blue depths of her eyes, Kara stood scanning the room, until her eyes locked with his.

She gave him a nervous smile.

He winced at her unease.

Her forest-green below-the-knee fitted dress had a deep slash from her collarbone to the centre seam, and her hand rose to touch the exposed pale skin of her breastbone.

Her dress was perfect. She was perfect. With her irresistible wide smile and rose blushed cheeks she was what every royal bride was supposed to be.

The only problem was that she was a reluctant bride, only going through with a marriage of convenience in a selfless act of friendship.

Kara's description of her relationship with Nick Green had knocked him for six. He gritted his teeth, once again seething that he hadn't taken the time to unearth why he had never taken to Nick. Instead he had shrugged off that instinct that said there was something insidious about him and had put it down to him just being protective of Kara. He had tried to be chilled about their relationship, pleased for her, when in fact his skin had crawled at the thought of them being together.

But the truth of Nick's controlling personality wasn't the only reason he was so thrown—in Kara revealing the truth, for the first time it had dawned on him that Kara might want greater intimacy between them. What he had thought would be a simple marriage of convenience hadn't allowed for the needs and vulnerabilities that came with any relationship. What if Kara continued to confide in him and expected in return an emotional intimacy he wasn't capable of giving? Just because she had never looked for it as a friend didn't mean that would continue when they were husband and wife.

Michael would have freaked to see his little sister put in this position. Guilt and unease twisted inside him—he knew what he was asking of Kara, the huge sacrifices she was having to make in order to help him to the throne. *Dio*, he hated having to ask for her support—it was selfish, and it felt as though his world order was turned upside down. It was his role in their relationship to be the supporter, the one in control. He didn't want to be dependent on anyone, even Kara. He liked to be autonomous and detached from others. Emotional intimacy terrified him. It was the reason why all of his past relationships had ended. He had always backed away from letting anyone too close. He could never deal with the pain of losing someone he loved again.

Behind him his father called out, 'Maria, I told you not to delay us.'

While the rest of the room, including Kara, was startled at his father's barked reprimand, his aunt gave him one of her serene smiles and, ushering Kara into the room, said, 'The media can wait. Kara and I had some important matters to talk over, including selecting a dress created by a Monrosa designer for the engagement photos.

'What do you think, Edwin? Doesn't Kara look beautiful?' Not waiting, thankfully, for him to answer, his aunt spoke to her husband, Johan. 'Do you remember just how excited we were when we announced our engagement?' Looking back towards Kara and then him, she clapped her hands in excitement. 'Enjoy every moment of this very special time in your lives.'

His aunt, who knew nothing about the truth as to why they were marrying, waited for a response. Only his father, brothers and Kara's parents knew the true reason for their marriage. The fewer people who knew the truth, the better. Struggling to find an appropriate response, he obviously hesitated too long in giving a reaction because his aunt's expression shifted to one of confusion.

Before he had an opportunity to speak his father barked, 'We have much more important matters that need to be taken care of other than worrying about dresses.'

Kara stepped forwards with a conciliatory smile and addressed his father. 'I apologise for the delay, but I do agree with Princess Maria. My choice of dress will send out an important signal of my support for Monrosa.' She tilted her chin. 'It's inevitable, given the speed and nature of our engagement, that things will not always go according to plan one hundred per cent of the time, but I'm sure Your Highness will take that into consideration.'

His father reddened, not used to being challenged, even in such a polite way.

Edwin bit back a smile, proud of Kara's defiance.

Ever so subtly all of the others present in the room slipped to stand behind his father. Only he and Victor remained in the no-man's-land between Kara and his father.

Raúl, Director of Royal Communications, stepped

forward and addressed His Highness with a pained expression. 'Sir, the press are waiting.'

His father eyed Raúl with exasperation and growled, 'Well, what are you waiting for? Go out there and start proceedings.'

Raúl nodded, squared his shoulders. About to leave the room, he doubled back and whispered, 'Miss Duffy, please try to remember your answers from our rehearsal this morning.' Turning to regard Edwin, who had moved over to stand next to her, Raúl added, 'I would suggest His Royal Highness is the one who answers any unrehearsed questions that might arise.'

Kara gave Raúl an uncertain smile. Her job required her to speak in public frequently, but Edwin knew it was her least favourite part of her role and one she was overconscious and overly self-critical of. The last thing she needed now was somebody doubting her ability.

Edwin cleared his throat and stepped closer to Raúl. 'Miss Duffy is more than capable of answering any questions that might arise.' Edwin tried to eyeball Raúl but the other man's eyes shifted relentlessly in every direction but his. Biting back the temptation to sigh, Edwin added, 'I want some time with Kara alone before we speak to the media. Wait here for another ten minutes before you go out. We will be in the music room and will join you from there.'

Raúl, with a pained expression, peered back towards his father, who was now puce in the face.

'What's the delay now? Edwin, I command you to stop delaying proceedings.'

Edwin turned and approached his father. Those surrounding him remained where they were. A silence fell on the room. Edwin tilted his head and eyed each and every advisor one by one. They all understood he wanted to speak to his father in private. Was this their way of showing where their loyalty lay? Their concerns about his succession? Had he a rebellion on his hands? Seconds passed. He stood his ground. His father went to speak. Edwin shot him a look of warning. This was his battle. Eventually, no doubt realising that Edwin was prepared to wait for the rest of the day for them to retreat, the advisors slowly peeled away towards the back of the room. Edwin could only hope this was the start of the royal court accepting his authority.

Lowering his head, he addressed his father. 'Apart from a brief meeting earlier, I've spent no time alone with Kara since she arrived from London this morning. We need time to speak. I ask you to respect that.'

His father gestured out towards the courtyard. 'The media are waiting and we have important state matters to discuss. You can talk to Salma later.'

Edwin let out an impatient breath. 'You know damn well her name is Kara. And I don't care that you think I should have married someone with better connections and background. We are marrying because you have left me with no other option. But I will not cause any harm or distress to my bride.' As he held his father's gaze, years of frustration with his father's belligerence and uninterest in his family spilled out. 'Kara will soon be part of this family and, whether you like it or not, from now on we're going to act like one—this family has been dysfunctional for far too long. You are to respect Kara and her position. Never force me into a position where I have to choose between her and the crown.'

Whipping around, he guided Kara out of the room, a hand to her back, the need to protect her, to make sure she was okay, thudding through him like some primal beat.

Beneath his hand, her hips swayed as her high heels

hit the marble floor of the anteroom. 'What did you say to your father? He looked even more hacked off than usual.'

She didn't know of his father's unhappiness at his choice of bride and he wanted to keep it that way. 'I apologise for his foul mood. He's anxious about tomorrow.'

Glancing behind her to the silent room, as all those gathered there watched their departure, she frowned. 'Is it always this tense around here?'

'At times.'

'I hope you'll instil a more positive atmosphere when you are in charge.'

'I aim to,' he hit her with a teasing smile, 'but then, you did say that my father and I are alike, so maybe I'll end up just as grumpy as him.'

'Not under my watch you won't.'

He laughed at her warning but there was something in her expression that had him realise that not only would she have his back in her role as his consort, but she would also push him to do the right thing, even if it was not what he always wanted to do. He wasn't quite sure whether to be comforted or alarmed by that.

Moving into the music room, he led her towards the terraced doors, where they were able to watch the media unobserved, thanks to the immense size of the Fountain of Bulls at the centre of the courtyard.

She sighed on spotting the assembled media, a hand unconsciously kneading the side of her neck. She was nervous.

'We'll be okay.'

She turned and studied him. 'Will we?'

His gaze shifted back to the media, remembering the morning after his mother's death. He had joined his father out in the courtyard for his address to the world's media. He had been bewildered and scared, barely able to comprehend that his mother was dead. He had pleaded with his father not to make him accompany him, but his response had been a brief lecture on his duty to the crown and country. To this day he could still feel the force of his need for his mother in that moment, for her words of encouragement and the hug she would give him whenever he had to perform a public duty.

Living your life so publicly was grindingly tough.

'I'll protect you from the media.'

Her hand dropped from her throat to hang by her side. 'It's not the media I'm worried about. It's us.'

Where had that come from?

'What do you mean?'

'For the past few days my calls to my local taxi company have lasted longer than our telephone conversations.'

'As I explained, I've been tied up with legal issues around the succession, and Aunt Maria has been tying me up in knots with her elaborate ideas for the wedding.'

Her pink-glossed mouth flatlined. 'Not *the* wedding, *our* wedding—we should be planning it together.'

'I didn't want to bother you with the details. I knew you'd be busy with your own work.'

That earned him a disbelieving look.

'This may only be a short-term marriage but I want an equal say.'

'Of course you'll have an equal say.'

'So why are you shutting me out?' she asked.

'I'm not shutting you out.' He wasn't, was he? Okay, so maybe he had been distracted in their phone calls over the past few days, but in his defence he was snowed under with things to organise…and there was also the small fact that he wasn't sure how to negotiate their new relationship as an engaged couple.

She raised an unconvinced eyebrow and turned to stare back out towards the media.

He ran a hand along his jaw and grimaced. 'The media will expect us to kiss.'

Her head whipped around.

Her eyes a startled blue, a blush crept up her throat and onto her cheeks.

He should reach out for her, draw her into a hug, tell her everything would be okay…but would it? No matter how much he would like to deny it, them kissing, the physical intimacy of it, was about to shift their relationship from straightforward friendship to a whole lot more complicated.

Kara kneaded her exposed collarbone. 'You don't have to kiss me if you don't want to.'

'I don't have a problem kissing you.'

She gave a tiny snort. 'Are you sure? You certainly don't sound too enthusiastic.'

'I don't want to put you in any situation you are uncomfortable with.' Despite himself he couldn't stop staring at Kara's mouth, the cupid's bow shape of her lips.

What would it be like to kiss her?

He arched his neck, a much too pleasant physical sensation trickling through his body.

Dios! *What was he thinking?*

She backed away from him, her expression flustered. 'I'm sure we can handle a quick chaste kiss.'

'Who said anything about it being chaste?'

She eyed him warily for a moment but then with a laugh, obviously deciding he was teasing her, she added, 'You're all talk—knowing how you like to keep your interactions with the media as brief as is humanly possible, I bet it will be a quick peck.'

'Is that a challenge?'

'No! Just an educated guess. Anyway, based on how badly I fumbled my answers when I had a practice run of questions with Raúl earlier, maybe us kissing will be a whole lot safer than having to answer questions. I have the real potential of putting my foot in it—you know how much I can prattle on when I'm nervous.'

'Be yourself. I don't want you to ever change or feel the pressure to change. You're perfect as you are.'

She gave him an uncertain smile. *Dio!* That had come out all wrong. It sounded like an intimate, flirtatious compliment when it should have been just a statement of fact.

She turned her head to gaze around the room, taking in the antique musical instruments including a piano-forte and harp. 'I can't imagine myself roaming around here dressed in my pyjamas, eating a bowl of cereal any morning.'

'In our apartments you can do what you want.' He paused, and before he could stop himself he added, 'You can even roam around naked if it takes your fancy.'

Where the hell had that come from?

He raked a hand through his hair. Not only was he staring at her mouth in a whole new and inappropriate way, but now he was also inviting her to roam about their apartment naked. What was the matter with him?

She stared at him with her mouth open, but then rolled her eyes. 'I'd just put you off your breakfast.'

'Well, it'd certainly brighten up my day.'

Kara laughed but then, sobering, asked, 'What's going on? Are you trying to flirt with me in case I'm having second thoughts and might back out?'

Was she actually serious? 'Please tell me that you don't believe I could be so manipulative.' Pausing, he added, 'Are *you* having second thoughts?'

'No, but stop acting so weird. It's freaking me out. It's the kind of trick Nick would have tried on. I want to marry you. And how can I possibly not go ahead at this stage anyway, knowing I'd break your aunt's heart if I did? I had thought when she said she wanted to speak to me that it might turn out all Shakespearian and she'd try to persuade me not to marry you in a bid to gain the throne herself, but the complete opposite was true.'

Shaking his head at her vivid imagination, he pointed out, 'There are two important facts you need to know about my aunt—firstly, she hates public life and much prefers to spend her time attending to her gardens on her estate in the north of the island. And secondly, she is an incurable romantic. Planning a wedding is her idea of heaven. I haven't seen her so enthusiastic about anything in a very long time.'

'So I gathered. She also mentioned that your father's planning on moving to the north of the island also after he abdicates. Are you happy about that?'

That was a good question. 'I'll be able to stamp my authority more easily…'

She regarded him and then softly asked, 'But you'd like him to stay here?'

Was he naïve to think he would be able to drag his family back together? 'I know he might be a nightmare to have around but I want us to be a family, work together as a team.' There was a softness, a tender understanding in her eyes. She understood what it was like to have a family blown apart. 'It's what my mother would have wanted.'

Kara nodded and then, leaning against the terrace door, turning her back on what was going on outside, she studied him, her gaze drifting down over his navy suit. Nodding to his gold and purple tie, she said, 'The royal colours for the occasion.' Reaching out, she adjusted his tie a fraction. 'You're looking very handsome today. Your mother would be very proud of the man you have become.'

He swallowed at her words. *Dio*, he could only hope his mother would be proud of the man he was. When she had been alive he had always tried to make her proud and in death that hadn't changed. He wanted to emulate her care for Monrosa and its people. He wanted to keep her alive by his actions.

Out in the courtyard, Raúl hurried towards the media. No doubt under orders from his father to get the proceedings over and done with so that they could continue focusing on all of the issues arising from the impending abdication. 'The announcement is about to get underway.'

Twisting around, Kara watched Raúl. Her hand rubbed against her throat. Her fingernails were painted in a pale pink shade, the sapphire engagement ring he had presented to her earlier shimmering on her finger and disconcerting him with its unfamiliarity. With a wistful smile she said, 'I'm so glad you're going to try to get your family to be closer.'

With a sigh he pulled her in to him. As ever she held herself rigidly. 'I'm sorry your parents wouldn't be here today.' They had invited Kara's parents to be present at the announcement but both had declined, unhappy that Kara had agreed to a marriage of convenience.

She tilted her head so that her forehead rested lightly against his chest, the movement telling him everything he needed to know as to just how disappointed she was, and against her hair he whispered, 'I'll be your family now.'

She pulled back, her eyes glistening with tears. He touched his finger against her cheek, his heart pounding in his chest, emotion catching in his throat, at just how much he really meant those words.

But then with a shake of her head Kara pulled back. 'Please don't say things like that, not when this isn't a real marriage.'

Taken aback by the vehemence in her voice, he asked, 'Why not?'

She twisted away, walked into the centre of the room, as though gathering herself. Whipping around, she answered, 'Because…because I've already lost one family…'

He inhaled deeply, the feeling of being way in over his head hitting him. 'You're not going to lose me.'

'Neither of us can pretend that our marriage is going to be easy. I don't think either of us can say that we'll come out of it unscathed. We need to be careful as to what we promise each other.'

A wave of frustration pushed through him. Kara was right. Wanting to kiss her, thinking they could be family… what was he thinking of? Raising his hands, he sighed. 'You're right.'

'What have you told Luis and Ivo?'

'Luis is in Australia at the moment and Ivo's in Budapest, competing, so I spoke to them both in a conference call this morning.' He paused and frowned. It had not been an easy call. 'Let's just say that once they got over the shock of learning that our father was going to abdicate, they were livid with him for forcing my hand and even more livid with me for dragging you into this mess.' Over the years Luis and Ivo had got to know Kara when they met in both London and Monrosa. Kara and Luis spoke regularly by text, their relationship one of endless teasing and banter, while Ivo was a goodwill ambassador for the charity, promoting its work within the sporting community.

'Wait, are you saying that they didn't know about your father's abdication until you told them?'

'He wanted to wait until tomorrow morning to inform them. I couldn't persuade him to tell them earlier. Things are as tense between him and my brothers as they have ever been.'

'Why won't he accept that they are both professional sports people who compete at an international level?'

'In his eyes they are wasting their time, when they should be here in Monrosa fulfilling their duties.'

She swept her hands over her dress, wriggling to smooth out the material clinging to her hips.

'Don't be nervous,' he reassured. 'You look incredible and I know you'll do great.'

'Aren't you nervous?'

From a young age he had been taught to present a public persona, one that was polite and composed and detached. That persona got him through so many aspects of his public life and was a shield behind which he could hide his true self. 'Why would I be nervous when I'm ready to celebrate my engagement with the world?'

She gave a disbelieving huff. 'Now you just sound corny.'

'Think of all the positives that can come from this—we can run together every morning and we can go hiking into the mountains without having to schedule it months in advance. We can watch movies together rather than just chat about them. And I can finally teach you how to sail.'

'You almost had me until you mentioned sailing. And what of the old adage, familiarity breeds discontent?'

'I think it's contempt, not discontent.'

Kara hit him with a teasing smile. 'I know, but I wouldn't go that far.'

'I want to marry you. And I hope that I'll be a good husband.' His chest tightened, a wave of emotion catching him unawares. 'I want to make you happy. If you are ever unhappy in the marriage then we can end it.'

'Even before the two years?'

Dio! What if she did walk away? Walked away because their marriage had gone horribly wrong? Their friendship destroyed. What if he had hurt Kara when he swore he would only ever protect her?

He clenched his hands. 'If that's what you want.' Opening the terrace door, he asked, 'Are you ready?'

She gave him a nervous smile. 'With you at my side, what can go wrong?' And she stepped out onto the covered terrace.

A lot was the answer to that particularly hopeful question, as Kara soon found out.

As she stepped from the shade and obscurity of the courtyard gallery into the bright spring day and the glare of the world's media, her legs began to shake. All those eyes and cameras. Assessing. Already formulating words and images to describe her, to pass judgement on her.

And Edwin wasn't helping matters with his long stride. Through a clenched smile, she muttered, 'Will you please slow down? And shouldn't we be acting more coupley?'

Edwin came to a complete stop, his expression unreadable. Then, giving her that serious public smile of his that always swelled her heart with pride and affection for this honourable man who took his responsibilities so seriously, he tucked a strand of hair behind her ear and murmured, 'Is this "coupley" enough?'

At the periphery of her vision, reporters jostled each other for a better view of them, one reporter actually pushing another into a flower bed. She nodded frantically, worried Edwin might decide he should do something even more in his pretence of devotion.

He took her hand in his and they resumed their approach towards the reporters, her toes tingling from the sensation of his warm hand enclosing hers with an unnerving gentleness. Keen to distract herself from the endless walk across the vast courtyard, she whispered, 'My dad promised he'd try to watch the announcement on a livestream.'

Not breaking his gaze away from the media, Edwin whispered back, 'Once the abdication is over, we'll go and visit both of your parents. I'm sure we can persuade them to come to the wedding.'

'I've tried endless times during the past few days to talk them round.' Now was probably not the moment for this conversation but the need to offload her worry was too great—especially as she had been storing it up for several days, expecting to share it with Edwin on the phone, but his calls had always been cut short by some crisis or another. 'You know how private they both are—being in the public eye is their idea of a nightmare. And they think what we're doing is crazy—that it will never work. I've tried to tell them about all of the positives that can come from our marriage—raising the profile of the charity, your plans for Monrosa. But they won't listen to me. We'll need to find a suitable explanation as to why they won't be at the wedding ceremony.'

With one easy movement, Edwin pulled them to a stop again.

Standing in front of her, blocking her from the media, he studied her while a silence descended on the courtyard, the assembled media holding their breath at the prospect of a sensational story unfolding.

'The media are waiting,' she whispered.

'Your parents have been through so much—I don't

want to cause them any further distress. We really don't have to go through with this.'

For a brief moment, she was tempted to agree with him. God knew, she didn't want to create even more tension with her parents than already existed, but this marriage and all the publicity it would bring to the work of Young Adults Together was the most fitting way to make sense of Michael's death. She was doing the right thing. And in time, maybe her parents would come to understand that Michael, so passionate about helping others, would have wanted her to do everything possible to help those in need. Seeing the tension in Edwin's eyes, she tilted her head back. 'As I remember it, you've promised me a spectacular honeymoon—you can't back out of that now.'

Edwin studied her for a moment and then with a hint of a smile he turned around and led her towards the waiting media.

In his earlier briefing, Raúl had given her a thorough run-through of the engagement announcement procedure that had included showing her a photograph of each correspondent who would be permitted to ask questions. Sofia Belluci, the royal correspondent for the main state broadcaster, would be the first to speak to them.

'Congratulations, Your Highness.' Pausing, Sofia turned her attention to Kara with a hint of bafflement, and said, 'And to you, Miss Duffy.'

Beside her Edwin said in a clear, neutral voice with no hint of emotion, 'Thank you.'

'Your Highness, after so many years of knowing each other, why have you and Miss Duffy decided to marry now?'

'We've come to realise what we mean to one another.'

Sofia narrowed her gaze, clearly wanting a much more elaborate answer. 'Which is?'

Without missing a beat, Edwin answered, 'Kara is my best friend.'

God, he was good at this. To the point. Unemotional.

'And for you, Miss Duffy?'

She had practised her answer with Raúl endlessly this morning, but, opening her mouth to say all those practised lines, she paused and stared blankly at the media, whose sceptical stares were hardening by the second.

What were her lines...what had she agreed to say?

Tumbleweed moseyed through her brain. And then she blurted out, 'Edwin's my world.'

Oh, what? Why did you say that?

She'd sounded like a gushing teen fan who had just met her boyband idol.

Edwin, looked at her with a bewildered expression for a moment, but to his credit managed to somehow gather himself enough to place his hand tenderly on her cheek and gaze into her eyes, playing the in-love fiancé perfectly.

It was all pretence, of course, but to be gazed at with such unbridled affection had her struggling to breathe.

Edwin turned back to the media, his arm resting on her waist.

The microphone was passed from Sofia to a man in his late sixties, impeccably dressed. Óscar Collado, the major news correspondent from Monrosa's largest selling newspaper. And, according to Raúl, a man with a hound dog's scent for a story. 'How does His Royal Highness your father feel about your announcement...is he as surprised as the rest of us?'

Edwin stiffened beside her. 'Surprised? No. In fact he's pleased that finally one of his sons is settling down.'

Óscar reflected on that answer for a while, clearly sizing up Edwin's tense demeanour and trying to decide if he should repeat the first part of his question, but instead he changed tack and asked, 'And how about your family, Miss Duffy?' Here Óscar paused as though searching for the right words. 'They must be truly amazed.'

It was clear what Óscar was insinuating. Edwin went to speak but she got there before him. With a gracious smile in Óscar's direction she decided to tackle this issue head-on. 'Edwin and I may come from very different backgrounds but our ideologies and outlook on life are very similar. We both value loyalty and friendship and serving others. It's our hope that people will be open-minded and supportive of us.'

Óscar gave an unconvinced smile to her answer. 'How do you think your late mother would have reacted to your engagement, Your Highness?'

Edwin's hold tightened, and he edged her in even closer to him. She swung her gaze towards him, tempted to whisper to him that he should refuse to answer a question that was so unfairly personal and intrusive.

Seconds passed as the media waited for Edwin to answer. Her heart flipped over to see Edwin's jaw working. She placed a hand on his, which was resting on her waist, and threaded her fingers between his. 'I believe my mother would have been delighted to have a daughter-in-law like Kara.'

He spoke with raw emotion in his voice. Taken aback by the sincerity of his answer, she had to force herself to concentrate on Óscar's next question. 'And the engagement ring—is it part of the royal collection?'

'No, it was especially commissioned,' Edwin answered.

She looked down at the sapphire ring Edwin had presented to her earlier that day. It was a stunning ring, an intense violet-blue stone mounted on platinum and surrounded by a cluster of diamonds.

At the media's beckoning she lifted her hand to display the sapphire.

And forced herself to smile.

Don't let the media see you're thrown. So what that he's given you a brand-new ring and not one from the royal collection? It was the sensible thing to do. For a marriage of convenience. Thinking he might not trust you with a ring from the historic royal collection or believe you aren't worthy of one...well, they're just silly thoughts. Aren't they?

When the media had finally had their fill of photographs, it was the turn of another journalist to speak, asking with a bright smile, 'Have you any message for the people of Monrosa, Your Highness?'

'I hope they will enjoy the wedding celebrations, which are currently being planned and will be announced in full in the coming week,' Edwin answered.

The female journalist swept her bright smile in Kara's direction. 'And you, Miss Duffy—do you have a message for the people?'

Oh, just that I'm terrified and not to judge me too harshly when we divorce. Oh, and, yeah—sorry to all of you who will be heartbroken to hear that one of the world's most eligible men is no longer available. Don't hate me for it—it wasn't my idea, honestly. At least you have the consolation that this has nothing to do with love or passion or any of those normal things.

'My message is that I very much look forward to living here in Monrosa and getting to know this beautiful country.'

The woman, in her early thirties, asked enthusiastically, 'And what will your role be when you marry?'

The journalist seemed genuinely interested in her role, and, seeing an opportunity to talk about the charity, she answered, 'I will continue with my work for my charity, Young Adults Together, focusing on expanding its efforts internationally to promote the advocacy and support of positive mental health in young adults. But I also see my role as supporting Edwin at all times…' she paused there, at the point to which she had rehearsed with Raúl, but, seeing the journalist's encouraging nodding, as though willing Kara to say more, Kara found herself saying, 'especially during the transition…'

She stopped, her eyes widening, hot panic making her pulse thud wildly.

I almost gave away the abdication.

She stared blankly at the media as they all shifted forward in their seats with interest, that sixth sense of theirs intuiting a story. What was she supposed to do now? They were waiting for an answer. How on earth did Edwin think she was capable of taking on the role of princess?

Laying his hands on her shoulders, Edwin calmly finished her sentence, 'During our transition to married life. We have both led independent lives but we are looking forward to living together. I know Kara is excited to settle into palace life…' Pausing, his eyes alive with devilment, a smile tugging at the corners of his mouth, he added, 'She has a lot of intriguing plans for life in our private apartments.'

Kara reddened, a nervous giggle escaping.

The journalists gave each other a quizzical look as though wondering if anyone else got the joke.

With a pinched expression, Raúl swept in from where

he had been watching proceedings at the side of the courtyard and spoke to the media. 'Thank you all for attending today's announcement. His Highness and Miss Duffy will now pose for more photographs.'

Edwin pulled her in closer to him. They embraced and smiled.

Maybe this was all they would want. No kissing required.

But no sooner had she had that thought than a chorus of, 'How about a kiss?' rang out from the assembled photographers.

Edwin turned her towards him.

Her stomach took a nosedive.

He leant down to her ear and whispered, 'Do you still think my kiss will be chaste?'

He drew back. She smiled at him nervously. And in return he gave her a wicked grin.

What had she started?

The teasing look on his face disappeared and suddenly he was looking at her with a heart-stopping intensity. This was no longer a game.

Time slowed down.

She fell into the golden depths of his eyes, only now realising there was a solid single fleck of brown in his right eye. What other secrets did he hold? A hunger to know him better swept through her.

Oh, help.

She needed to get a grip. He was her friend, her pretend fiancé.

Stop getting caught up in the crazy pretence of it all. This is not real.

His mouth lingered over hers.

His hands ran down the length of her arms, coming

to rest at her elbows. The warmth of his touch had her sigh ever so lightly.

Something shifted in his eyes. A heat. A masculine heat.

His lips brushed against hers.

Firm and warm.

Light-headed, she swayed against him. Oh…oh…his heat, the hardness of his body, the electrifying rightness of all of him.

This is so wrong, but so right.

He pulled her closer, deepening the kiss, his arms wrapping around her, tilting her backwards.

This wasn't a polite kiss. It was personal. Intimate. His taste, his scent, the heat of his skin against hers was perfectly wrong.

Every cell in her body dissolved to nothing and fire burnt along her veins.

No man had ever had this effect on her.

Oh, please…this can't be happening.

Her pretend fiancé seriously couldn't be the hottest kisser ever. This wasn't fair!

She willed him to keep on kissing her and he obliged by twisting her so that she was hidden from the media, his back to them, and he deepened the kiss even more, exploring her mouth.

Her hands clasped the hard muscle of his neck. Any moment now she was going to burst into flames. They should stop. This was crazy. Beyond madness to be doing this in the glare of the media. But she just couldn't pull away. One more second. One more spine-tingling, head-spinning, belly-warming second. One more thrilling, life-affirming second of hot craving zipping along the length of her body.

Edwin ended the kiss. And studied her up close for a moment, his pupils dilated, heat on his cheeks.

Dazed, she stared at him. Why did he look so different? More handsome, more male...he had always been gorgeous but now there was a raw edge to him that spoke of danger...of lust. Of... Crikey, what was happening to her?

Turning to the media, Edwin gave them a nod before he led her away, much too quickly, across the courtyard.

When they were out of earshot he said, 'You're trembling.' His mouth tightened. 'Forgive me, I got a little carried away proving that I don't do chaste kisses.'

She had to downplay this. She couldn't let him know just how disconcerted she was, how he had just blown her mind.

So tell me, Kara, are you still convinced that you can walk away from this pretend marriage unscathed?

She withdrew her hand from his, gave him a disapproving tap on his forearm, and in the best blasé voice she could muster, answered, 'I could hardly breathe. Thank goodness we won't need to do that too often.'

CHAPTER FOUR

STANDING IN THE hall lined with mirrors, overlooking the formal gardens of the palace, spotting the telltale claret-red patches appearing on her dad's neck, Kara edged closer to him. 'I wonder what Aunt Joan will be wearing today?'

For a brief moment her dad smiled. 'Whatever it is, I'm sure they'll be able to spot it from outer space.'

Aunt Joan liked to wear colour, the brighter the better in her view, to counteract the greyness of so many Irish days. Unfortunately she didn't seem to understand the concept of clashing colours or that sometimes, less was more. Keen to keep her dad distracted in their long wait for Edwin to appear, and in truth looking for something to focus on other than her annoyance with her fiancé, she said, 'It's great that the entire family could make the wedding.'

When had the deep grooves in his cheeks appeared, the greyness in his hair? She hadn't seen him in over two years. Had it been during that time or had they been accumulating for ever and she had just been too preoccupied to notice? Her dad tugged at his shirt collar. 'Sure, wild horses wouldn't have kept that lot at home—this is the most exciting thing to have ever hit the Duffy family.'

Yesterday lunchtime they had finally managed to

squeeze in the wedding rehearsal. Not only had the logistics team had to contend with Edwin's father's schedule, which had him out of the country on a tour to Sweden and Norway from which he had only returned yesterday morning, but also Edwin's ever-changing travel plans.

She had found the rehearsal in the cathedral exhausting. It had taken all of her will not to stare at Edwin, as was her wont recently. Since their engagement kiss she was constantly finding herself staring at him, daydreaming about him in all types of inappropriate ways that certainly didn't belong in a place of worship.

At the rehearsal her dad had trembled as he had escorted her down the aisle. In the hope of relaxing him she had said she and Edwin would join him and the rest of her relatives for dinner that night in the nearby hotel the palace had booked out in entirety to house the Irish Duffy contingent for dinner. She had also invited along her bridesmaids—Siza, her old rugby teammate, and Triona, who was the first employee to join her in Young Adults Together, and was now one of her closest friends—who were also staying in nearby hotels.

She had ended up going for dinner without Edwin. His weekly meeting with the cabinet had apparently become heated when he introduced his plans for designating land zoned for tourist accommodation into a financial centre and nature reserve.

During the dinner she had tried to hide her frustration with Edwin's non-appearance, but when her dad had asked her for a chat after dinner she had expected yet another awkward conversation as to the wisdom of her deciding to agree to a marriage of convenience.

But instead, when they reached his room her dad had shyly plucked out the lightweight suits and crisp shirts he had bought for the wedding weekend. Her heart had melted to see how proud he was of his purchases, and how eagerly he had wanted her approval. He had asked for her advice as to what he should wear for today's garden party and had proudly modelled the grey trousers and pale pink shirt she had picked out. He had self-consciously studied himself in the full-length mirror of the wardrobe and it had hit her once again what it was she was asking of this private man, whose confidence and identity had taken such a battering, to have to step into the glare of the world.

Now with a grimace her dad admitted, 'I think you should know that your aunts gave an interview to one of the main Irish newspapers. I saw it online earlier in the special supplement they've published in advance of the wedding tomorrow.'

Kara groaned.

'It's all very complimentary…honestly, just photos of you growing up and how proud they are of you and how they knew you'd do great in life because you were such a headstrong child.'

Oh, please, someone tell me they didn't use the photos of me on the beach close to Aunt Nina's house with a battalion of cousins.

The photos where her hair was twisted into tight curls and stood on end like hundreds of startled question marks, thanks to a day spent in the sea.

So much for asking that family members wouldn't speak to the media. She didn't want her family or friends to be invested in this marriage. Unfortunately she had forgotten just how much her dad's side of the family liked a wedding, not to mention a royal one featuring their very own niece.

She couldn't even bear to think about just how crushed they'd all be when her divorce was announced. 'Am I right in guessing it was my aunts who eventually persuaded you to come to the wedding?' It was only last week that her dad had finally said he would attend, a fortnight after the rest of their Irish family's acceptances had started rolling in.

Her dad gave a resigned sigh. 'Five badgering sisters would be hard for any man to fight.'

She twisted Edwin's engagement ring, its weight still feeling alien on her finger, regret punching her stomach that her dad was only here because of family persuasion and not to support her in her decision, even if it was not one he approved of. But at least he was here…which was more than could be said for her mum.

'I blame myself,' he said.

'Blame yourself for what?'

He looked her in the eye, the intimacy of it swiping like a blade to her heart. How she missed his easy nature and love of teasing that had used to have her giggling endlessly as a child. 'If we were closer…' He paused, shrugged. 'We've drifted apart, haven't we?' He nodded unhappily towards their opulent surroundings, and then in the direction of Edwin's father and brothers and the various other members of the royal court standing to their side. 'If I knew what was going on in your life then maybe I could have persuaded you not to do this before it all got so out of hand.'

Kara rolled her shoulders and placed her bunched hands in the pockets of her summer cocktail dress.

This morning she had hopped out of bed, thrilled that she had finally persuaded Edwin last night, when he had eventually turned up at her dad's hotel, two hours late, to take an early morning trek with her into the mountains. She had hoped some time alone together would restore the equilibrium that had used to exist between them, that some teasing and banter would fix Edwin back into her world order of regarding him as a friend. But her hope and excitement had soon disappeared when she had gone in search for him. Unable to locate him, she had been forced to interrupt Victor, who had been in a meeting with many of the senior members of the household, to enquire as to Edwin's whereabouts. Curious eyes had studied her, everyone present clearly wondering why she did not know that her fiancé had left Monrosa earlier that morning. She had tried not to let her embarrassment, her disappointment, her confusion show but had backed out of the room, her cheeks stinging with hurt.

And after her make-up and hair had been completed by her team and she had pulled on the strapless dress she had fallen in love with the moment Ettie, a recent design-school graduate and native Monrosian had shown it to her, and stared at her reflection in the mirror, taking in the material printed in layers of pinks and purples and yellows, designed to resemble the colours and pattern of a butterfly's wings, she had stared at the stranger in the mirror and wondered if she could go through with the wedding. But what choice did she have? How could she back out now with most of their guests already here? And on what basis—that Edwin was never around, and even when he was he was constantly distracted by work? With a sigh she faintly said, 'Let's not go over all this again, Dad. You know the reasons why I want to marry Edwin.'

'A marriage without love destroys people.'

She did not want to hear this right now. She had enough on her plate without her dad prophesying doom and gloom for their marriage. She had enough of those niggling doubts herself. 'We might not have romantic love, but there's no one in the world I trust more than Edwin. He has always had my back.' Shifting her head even closer to her dad, she whispered with a fury that rose suddenly and fiercely from somewhere deep inside of her, 'He has never let me down. I owe him this.'

Her dad blinked. And just as quickly as it had risen within her, Kara's fury was quenched, to be replaced with those nagging doubts that had been germinating like a deadly virus inside of her following weeks of Edwin's distraction and distance.

Her dad reddened. 'I wish your mother were here to speak to you. She might be able to get you to see sense.'

Kara shrugged. It hurt like hell that her mum was refusing to take the short plane trip from the south of Spain to Monrosa to attend her wedding, but she was *not* going to admit that to anyone. 'Maybe it's for the best—the last time you two were in the same room it wasn't exactly a pleasant experience for anyone.'

Her dad cleared his throat, stuffed his hands into his trouser pockets, his gaze on the closed double doors out to the gardens. 'You can't spend your days and nights with someone and remain detached. Edwin is a good-looking man… I don't want you getting hurt.'

Her mouth dropped open. Was her dad actually warning her not to sleep with Edwin? Heat ignited in her belly as she remembered their kiss. A few weeks ago she would have been able to laugh off her father's warning, but now she became a physical wreck of hormones whenever she saw him. She fancied him. She really, really fancied him. He was that good a kisser. 'I wouldn't worry if I were you—if the past few weeks are anything to go by, we'll rarely see one another.'

'Victor, where is Edwin? Our guests are waiting for us.'

Both she and her dad jumped at Edwin's father's barked

question that echoed around the cavernous double-height hall ceiling like a helter-skelter in motion.

Victor stepped away from the marble pillar beside which he had been standing and calmly answered, 'His plane landed ten minutes ago, Your Highness. He should be arriving very soon.'

Eyeing Kara as though it was her fault Edwin was late for his own pre-wedding garden party, Edwin's father asked, 'Just how urgent was the business that took him out of Monrosa? Doesn't he realise he's getting married tomorrow and is needed here?'

For a moment Kara was tempted to fire back, *Don't look to me for answers. I've no clue as to what's going on in your son's head. All we've talked about in recent weeks is wedding logistics and succession planning. Heaven knows he's never been good at talking about anything of even a slightly personal nature, but since our engagement he's taken it to a whole different level.*

But instead she gave him a polite smile and answered, 'I'm sure it must be of great importance, as he would not have wanted to keep our guests waiting.'

His Highness muttered something before turning his attention on Luis, who was leaning against the wall, his shoulder touching the gilt frame of a no doubt priceless still-life, flicking through his phone, and snapped, 'Please focus on our important guests this afternoon.'

A grin formed on Luis's mouth. He got the poorly disguised insinuation of his father's words—not to get sidetracked by pretty female faces, as was his wont. 'Don't take your bad mood out on me.' His grin dropping, Luis eyed his father, the roguish prince with a reputation for short-lived affairs with some of the most beautiful women in the world now replaced with the astute professional sportsman who had come close to winning the World

Powerboat Series on several occasions. 'This whole mess is of your own making—no wonder Edwin doesn't want to play ball.'

Every eye in the room swung in Luis's direction, everyone clearly trying to understand the meaning of his words.

Tight-lipped, His Highness stared at his middle son furiously. 'Your constant absence from palace life has caused you to forget the importance of decorum.'

Luis held his father's gaze for long seconds, the heat in his cheekbones in stark contrast to the coldness of his expression. He shot his gaze in her direction. Kara gave him a supportive smile, all the while hoping he wouldn't start an argument that would add even more tension to the day. With a reluctant shrug Luis lowered his head and once again flicked a finger over the screen of his phone.

His Highness let out an irritated breath before turning his attention towards Ivo. 'I've scheduled time in my diary on Monday morning for us to meet.'

Ivo, with his tall, muscular physique, short-cropped hair and sharp features, on the surface appeared confidently aloof, but his low voice told the truth of his gentle nature. 'I'm flying out on Sunday morning.'

'Well, change your plans,' His Highness countered.

With zero emotion showing, Ivo studied his father for a moment. Kara expected him to refuse to change his plans. Ivo might be gentle but he had a stubborn and single-minded streak, which had served him well, no doubt, in his journey to becoming an Olympic rower. After a quick glance in her direction, rather surprisingly, he shrugged in agreement.

Walking towards a window overlooking the gardens, Kara studied their waiting guests down at the waterfront, her eyes brimming with tears. Edwin's distance stung even harder in the face of his brothers' understated support.

There were over five hundred guests mingling at the waterfront awaiting their arrival. Along with heads of state and prime ministers, local people and Young Adults Together staff were among the invited guests. She had had to fight hard the resistance of the wedding logistics team to have them invited ahead of corporate presidents and European politicians.

She had had to fight too for her idea to hold this garden party in the afternoon before the wedding. The logistics team had argued that many of the guests, especially those designated as dignitaries, would not arrive until the morning of the wedding and therefore the garden party was unnecessary and would only complicate preparations for the following day. Time and time again, Kara had had to remind them as to why she wanted to host the garden party in the first place—it was Kara's way of including as many Monrosians in the wedding celebrations as possible and her way of thanking those who had taken the time and expense to travel from all over the globe for the long weekend of celebrations.

As it had turned out, many of the dignitaries had opted to travel to the wedding early, and who could blame them for starting their weekend early on a sun-kissed Mediterranean island ablaze with colour, thanks to the springtime blooming of its native wild plants and flowers?

A number of guests had been unable to accept their invitation due to work commitments or personal issues. Only one had not sent an apology, however: her mum.

Kara had spoken to her only once since their engagement photos had been splashed across the front page of every newspaper worldwide. The pain in her mum's voice when she had begged Kara not to ask her again to attend the wedding had torn through her like a sharp blade. Kara knew just how private her mum was but had hoped she would have put that aside for her sake. In the reporting of their engagement, the media had referenced Michael's death, more often than not as a small aside paragraph at the end of an article, as though his death had been nothing but a blip in their lives.

She had gasped when she had seen the photos herself, grown all hot and bothered at the ones showing Edwin passionately kissing her. But it had been one photo—a fluke, a misinterpretation due to the angle at which it had been taken, but unfortunately the photo used by most of the media outlets—that still cut her to the quick. The photo had been taken in the seconds after Edwin had drawn back from their kiss, and the media had chosen to deduce from the intensity of his expression that it portrayed a man deeply in love.

When in truth it was nothing more than the portrayal of a man deeply irritated with himself. He regretted that kiss. He hadn't even been able to look her in the eye since. Which was mortifying, considering the lust it had unleashed in her. And any fears she had had about them sharing an apartment were a joke. Edwin had been away on business most nights since she had moved to Monrosa a fortnight ago. She had tried to shrug off his constant work and royal commitments abroad, burying herself in wedding preparations and in managing the transition of the day-to-day operations management of Young Adults Together in the UK to Marion Parry, her Head of Charity Services, so that she could focus instead on forming an international branch of the charity.

But despite her busyness, and how excited she was at the prospect of helping even more young adults, deep down she was lonely.

Was this how the next two years were going to pan out? Edwin consumed by work, their relationship nothing more than work colleagues who saw each other occasionally? Her spending her nights alone, rattling around their enormous apartment trying not to have sexual fantasies about her indifferent husband? Their friendship lost to the careful dance they needed to perform every time they stepped out to fulfil a public duty, lost to the exhausting toll of keeping up the pretence of being a couple in love, lost to Edwin's ceaseless drive to prove wrong all of the commentators who proclaimed that his succession was happening a decade too early?

His father's abdication announcement had been received with shock and disquiet, the media and public unsettled by what the change in leadership would mean to the country. Ever since, Edwin had been waging a campaign, both at home and abroad, to bring people on board with his succession.

'Edwin, about time.'

Her neck snapped back at His Highness's snarled chastisement. Whipping her head around, she felt her heart leap to see Edwin filling the entranceway, dressed in navy trousers and a white shirt, the top button undone to reveal the smooth, tanned skin of his chest.

His gaze swept towards her. She wanted to look away, to convey her annoyance at his lateness. But instead a rush of relief flooded her body, making her feel weak and light-headed. And then a charge of connection ran between them. A hunger for his company boiled in her stomach and blasted onto her skin.

It's as though he's a different person to the man I saw as my best friend.

She was noticing things about him she'd avoided seeing before—the powerful physicality of his body, the sharp height of his cheekbones, the firmness of his mouth.

He gave her a brief nod of acknowledgement and stepped to the side of the doorway, gesturing towards someone out in the corridor to join him.

And then he was protectively placing his arm around the woman who stood beside him.

Kara swallowed, disbelief punching away all thoughts. In a daze she moved across the room. Her light-headedness worsened. She swayed, her legs threatening to buckle beneath her. The outer edges of her vision darkened. Within seconds Edwin was at her side. Placing his arm around her, he pulled her against the strength of his body.

Together they faced her mother. Kara swallowed air greedily, drawing on Edwin's steadiness.

Her mum remained in the doorway, staring at her with an intensity that stripped her soul bare. Her mum gave a tentative smile that spoke of a bucketload of anxiety and uncertainty. And the years of fighting and disappointments and isolation suddenly didn't compare to the tight emotion in her chest at the joy in seeing her mum.

She held her arms out nervously, wondering how her mum would react.

Her mum drew back on her heels.

Kara winced.

Her mum took a hesitant step forward.

And then another.

They hugged, her mum's embrace so familiar and yet uncomfortable due to its long absence. Kara drew back, the intensity of it all too much to bear.

She turned to Edwin. He had done this for her, had known, without her saying anything, that she wanted her mum at her side when she married. She held his gaze, this man who knew her so well, and blinked back tears.

'Kara?'

She turned back at her mum's soft whisper.

Her mum moved towards her and for a moment Kara was transported to her childhood bedroom and her mum's whispered wake-up call that was always accompanied with a soft stroke of her hair. 'Edwin is right, you know: you *are* going to need me, not just this weekend, but also when this is all over. Divorce is awful. No matter what the circumstances.'

Kara's heart sank. She tried not to wince. On the eve of their wedding Edwin wasn't thinking of their marriage. Instead, he was planning for their separation and divorce.

As one soon-to-be extended family they walked down through the terraced gardens towards their waiting guests. Edwin could feel a headache coming on. They were a family in name at least, but, given the tensions that existed within both his and Kara's families, using the term 'family' was probably an infringement of the Trade Descriptions Act.

This morning he had had to spend way too long persuading Kara's mother to join him on the return flight to Monrosa, telling her that Kara deserved her support even if she didn't agree with her decision to marry him.

That damned engagement kiss.

It had thrown a curve ball into his life, as powerful as a cricket ball whacking him on the head, and had sent him into a month-long dazed existence.

What had been supposed to be a staged kiss had transformed into a primal urge for more...more heat, more connection, more bodily contact.

But the after-effects—seeing how upset Kara had been, the speculative calculation in his father's eyes when they had gone back into the palace, hating his constant urge, even weeks later, to pick up that kiss where they had left off, the conjecture in some of the media that a royal baby was bound to soon make an appearance after such an inflamed public display of passion, the texted messages demanding to know what the hell he was playing at from his brothers…all had led to him withdrawing into himself.

His behaviour was unsettling Kara. He had heard the disappointment in her voice every time he had called to cancel a planned trip to visit her in Brighton, and in more recent days, since her move to Monrosa, her attempts to appear unconcerned when he announced yet another long day of local meetings or another trip abroad.

But the constant questioning of his succession and its impact on Monrosa, the knowledge he had not only dragged Kara into this marriage of convenience but was also in danger of wrecking their friendship irreparably by having senseless fantasies of kissing her—and okay, he'd admit it, those fantasies contained a lot more detail than just kissing her—was spooking him. Fantasies that would wipe out a decade's history of a friendship built on trust and respect. As much as he wanted a more physical relationship with Kara, he knew taking that step would unravel a whole lot of emotions he was incapable of dealing with. He didn't want to compromise their friendship and most important of all he didn't want to hurt Kara. And right now he was trying to walk the exhausting and head-wrecking tightrope balance of not spending too much time with Kara while trying to continue to support her.

Last night, he had arrived late to her dad's hotel and she had bristled with irritation. But when her cousin Alice had sung a duet with her mother, Hilary, that irritation had melted away. The song had been upbeat and funny, the rest of the family howling with laughter, but despite Kara's forced smiles he had seen her loneliness in witnessing Alice and Hilary's close bond.

Now, as he led the party down towards the waterfront, given Kara's monosyllabic answers to his questions enquiring how everything was with her, he wasn't certain that persuading her mother to attend the wedding was the best idea after all.

Her hair was tied in a loose chignon, exposing her bare shoulders. A fragile chain hung around her neck. She was refusing to wear any jewellery from the royal collection and to date hadn't given him a satisfactory reason why.

As had become a recent habit of hers, her thumb was twisting her engagement ring around her finger. *Why does she do that?* Was it to remind herself of its presence? Did it annoy her? He had spent hours with a jeweller commissioning it, wanting to create a ring that was uniquely hers, that spoke of his admiration for her.

Her make-up was soft and subtle, a sweep of mascara on her long lashes, shimmering pink on her lips, but there was a tension emanating from her that said she'd happily tear him limb from limb.

They were only minutes away from their guests. He needed to sort out whatever was irritating her. Now. Before their guests picked up on it.

Keeping his voice low, he leant in to her. 'I thought you'd like having your mother here.'

'Are you trying to offload me onto her?'

Where had that come from?

'I have no idea what you're talking about.'

She tilted her chin. 'My mother told me you believe I'll need her in the coming years—are you frightened I'll go to pieces when our marriage is over? Is that why you went and fetched her this morning?'

'Of course not.'

She gave him a disbelieving look. 'Then why did you?'

'Because a mother should be at her daughter's wedding. And I told your mother that you deserved her attention, not just for the wedding but all of the time.'

She shook her head and as they approached their guests she placed her hand on his elbow, the smile on her mouth not reaching her eyes, 'I'm going to pretend to believe you but I'll tell you this much: I'm certainly not prepared to spend this marriage with you avoiding not only me but also your family. I've no idea what's been bugging you recently but you need to get a grip before you turn into a grumpy emotional hermit.' She paused and grimaced, and on a low sigh she leant even closer to him. 'We both know the consequences of people shutting down.' Bruised, pained eyes met his. 'We have to learn from Michael…'

She walked away from him towards her charity team. His skin tingled with shame and guilt. She was right, of course. Isolating yourself rarely did any good for normal people in normal circumstances, but in the craziness of this pretend marriage keeping a healthy emotional distance was going to protect them in the long run. Yes, there would be short-term pain, but the long-term gains would far outweigh them.

Kara's team embraced her with excited exclamations, bringing her into their fold, until she disappeared from view.

Kara had insisted the garden party was to be an informal affair, much to the disquiet of his father's advisors. But she had stood her ground against their arguments, firm that the party should be a relaxed afternoon where the guests got to wear casual clothes and to mingle informally in a bid to be as inclusive and accessible as possible for *all* those attending, without the pressures dictated by royal protocol.

So without the necessity of formal introductions, his family filed away from him, his father approaching the President of the European Union, almost unrecognisable now in his short-sleeved shirt over linen trousers rather than his usual conservative suits. Luis went and greeted the US ambassador fondly, their old rivalry forgotten now that the ambassador had retired from powerboat racing. Ivo joined Princess Maria and Johan, who were in conversation with a young group of Monrosians all wearing the Monrosa Environmental Protection Agency T-shirts, the charity his mother had founded before her death.

Not only was he getting things wrong with Kara but all of his intentions to force his family to be a tighter unit weren't happening, thanks to the others' uninterest and frankly his own lack of effort. On a number of occasions he had suggested they all meet, but he hadn't pushed the issue when he only got excuses as to why they weren't available in response, or, in Ivo's case, no response at all.

He could blame his workload. His office was tantalisingly close to attracting a major German bank to locate in Monrosa and he was having to lead the final negotiations. And on top of that, there was the management of the wedding and succession planning, diplomatic phone calls that had to be made to international leaders, and daily briefings with the cabinet alongside his father where he was trying to stamp his authority, much to the reluctance of his father's loyalists. And his father's belligerence wasn't helping either.

He had told Edwin he wanted him to take over the day-to-day decision-making in the run-up to the succession, but then proceeded to question every directive he made.

So, yes, his workload was insane. But in truth he

had been avoiding any personal interactions, even turning down Luis's and friends' attempts to persuade him to hold a bachelor party, needing time to get his head straight.

Kara's parents stood beside him, both glancing in the direction of her dad's side of the family, who weren't doing a particularly good job at hiding their surprise at Kara's mother, Susan's arrival. Kara's mother coloured and she turned as if to join Kara and her team but pulled back when the group erupted in laughter. Kara's father stepped towards her, gesturing towards his family. Kara's mother gave a pained smile but, straightening her shoulders, followed him as he led her towards his extended family. Could this weekend be the start of a reconciliation between Kara's parents? He sure hoped so. He was fed up with watching Kara's family letting her down. If they reconciled their differences then maybe they would give her the support and love she deserved.

He had *thought* Kara would be grateful to him for persuading her mother to come to Monrosa. But instead she had twisted his efforts to make it seem as though he had done so for reasons of pure self-interest. And as for Kara's contention that he was heading towards being a grumpy hermit—how was that even possible when he spent almost every waking hour in the company of others?

He stifled a groan.

His old work colleague from London, Laurent Bonneval, carrying his baby son, Arthur in his arms, his beaming wife, Hannah, at his side, was making a beeline in his direction.

After quick hugs, Laurent thrust Arthur into his arms, ignoring Hannah's protests to be careful. Arthur gave him a toothy grin.

Laurent chuckled. 'After all the babies you must have

held in the line of duty, I'd have thought you'd have mastered the art of holding one at this stage.'

Laurent pushed against his arm, forcing him to relax and to allow Arthur's tiny frame to curl against his chest. Arthur chortled and reached for his shirtfront, clinging to him. Edwin stared down at Arthur's tiny hand gripping his shirt, a loneliness, a longing unravelling in his soul.

'Kara, it's so good to see you again.'

His head jerked up at Laurent's greeting.

Kara hugged Laurent—they had met on several occasions in London before Laurent had returned to France to take over his family business in Cognac—and then shook Hannah's hand when Laurent introduced his wife to her. Edwin had attended Laurent and Hannah's wedding last year.

'I always knew you two should be together,' Laurent said, looking at them both with an expansive grin. He threw his arm around Hannah and kissed the top of her head. With a grin that was frankly a little sickening in its serenity he added, 'I'm glad you've finally found your way to one another. Just like Hannah and myself after I almost messed everything up between us by breaking up with her and leaving London for France. It goes to prove that love will eventually win out, no matter how much we fight it!'

Three hours later, and an hour later than scheduled, Edwin marched back up to the palace, his family and Kara trailing behind him.

At the Statue of Hera, he muttered a curse. His father and Princess Maria were still on the lower terrace, studying the wide swathe of agapanthus that grew there and from a distance resembled a stream of ice-blue water.

Had his family lost all sense of urgency?

Luis, idly climbing the wide steps of the terrace below, said something that had Ivo grin and Kara cover her mouth to hide a smile, before all three contemplated him and laughed once again.

When they eventually joined him, Luis gave him a wink before he and Ivo continued their climb back up to the palace.

Kara remained at his side and with a curious look she asked, 'What's the matter? Didn't you enjoy the party?'

'Three times I had to tell Luis it was time to leave.' Edwin blew out an impatient breath. He had had to insist that his family and Kara leave the garden party so that the guests could be encouraged to make their way back to their hotels and homes. Ricardo, the Master of the Household, had personally pleaded with him to bring the party to a close, explaining he desperately needed his serving staff to prepare for tomorrow's wedding banquet.

Kara backed away from him, giving a shrug. 'We were all enjoying ourselves.'

Her eyes were sparkling, her skin glowing, her pleasure at the success of the party twisting inside him so much that he was desperately tempted to push her against the granite plinth of Hera and kiss her happiness, touch his fingertips against the tender skin where her dress skimmed across her breasts.

Her breasts that swelled so perfectly.

Dammit, for years he had successfully ignored them. Even the times when they had gone sailing together and his eyes would burn with the effort of not staring at her when she'd stripped off to reveal a testosterone-surging bikini.

That kiss, and the fact that she was about to become his wife, were messing with his ability to see her as a friend only.

In silence they walked up the steps and into the hall of mirrors, where his brothers were waiting for them.

Luis was fixing his hair in the reflection of one of the mirrors. 'Ivo and I are taking you out for a drink tonight.'

Watching his father and aunt amble up the last set of steps to the palace, willing them to get a move on so that he could say his goodbyes to them, Edwin answered, 'I have other plans.'

Angling his head to better inspect his newly grown beard, Luis responded, 'Well, change them. You can't get married without some form of a bachelor party. Even if it's not a real wedding.'

Their father, now standing at the doorway from the terrace, growled, 'At least Edwin understands the meaning of duty.'

Luis cocked an eyebrow. 'You more or less put a gun to his head. Edwin doesn't want to marry. We all know that. You've given him a life sentence.' Turning, he gave Kara one of his trademark cheeky smiles. 'No offence, Kara, but you know what I mean.'

Kara gave him a half-hearted smile.

Right. He'd had enough. Luis's constant rebuking and bickering with his father was one thing, but this was just plain offensive to Kara.

'Cut it out, Luis.'

Luis twisted around, his arms shifting outwards in question. 'Are you seriously taking his side now?'

Edwin looked from Luis to his father, both angling for an argument, and then to Ivo, who had turned his back on them all to stare out of the window in the direction of the harbour. Aunt Maria appeared from the terrace, cradling a bunch of purple irises in her arms, frowning as she picked up the tension in the air. It was time they all went their separate ways before things kicked off.

He shifted towards the doorway. 'I have work to do.' Then, looking in Kara's direction, taking in once again the sexy slope of her exposed shoulders, imagining his lips on her skin, imagining releasing her hair and coiling it around his fingers, imagining her wearing nothing but the pink sandals on her feet, he backed even further away, his body temperature surging. 'I'll see you tomorrow...at the cathedral. Enjoy your meal with your parents tonight.'

Kara's gaze narrowed. And then she was stalking towards him. Chin tilted, a defiant gleam in her eye, she spoke loudly enough to include everyone in the room. 'I've decided we should have a change of plan. Both your family and mine will dine together tonight.'

She had to be kidding. Did she really want to subject her mother and father to a dinner where his father and Luis would constantly quarrel and Ivo be so detached he may as well be back in Lucerne training for whatever regatta that was currently preoccupying him? Not to mention his own plans for the evening. 'I'm not available.'

Her eyes narrowed even more at his words.

'I've already organised for a private room in the yacht club for myself, Edwin and Ivo to have dinner and drinks,' Luis protested.

Kara whirled around. 'Well, ring and cancel. We're having a family dinner.' And with that she moved towards the door, saying she would go and find Ricardo on her way to check on her parents, who were both staying in the palace tonight in advance of tomorrow's ceremony, to inform him of the change of plan. Before she left the room she glanced in his direction, her arched eyebrows and challenging stare silently reminding him of her earlier accusation that he was hurtling towards being an isolated grump. *Dio!* She really wasn't going to give him an easy time over this. Well, tough. He knew what he was doing. He needed to keep his distance from her. It was for her own protection. He just couldn't tell her that.

His Highness soon followed her, muttering that he had been planning on having a quiet night alone.

Only Princess Maria seemed pleased. Clapping her hands, she exclaimed, 'I'm looking forward to having Kara in the family—it's about time you men were whipped into shape!'

CHAPTER FIVE

A RAP ON her bedroom door had Kara quickly applying her lipstick, spraying on some perfume, standing from the dressing-table stool to make sure her wrap-around dress wasn't revealing anything it shouldn't be, and sitting back down.

Twisting her loose hair behind her shoulders and picking up her mascara bottle, she said, 'Come in.'

Pushing the door open, Edwin propped a shoulder against the door frame and studied her reflection in the Art Deco dressing table's mirror. Pretending to be applying some mascara, Kara waited for him to speak… while trying not to poke herself in the eye.

Would he stop staring at her? And what was with the dark mood?

Wearing a pale blue shirt over navy trousers, he angled his long body as though to deliberately blockade the entire door. 'It's considered bad luck for the bride and groom to see each other the night before the wedding.'

Picking up her hairbrush, she tried to ignore just how deflated she felt that once again he was preferring to spend time anywhere but in her company. 'I think a special dispensation can be awarded to us, considering our circumstances and the fleeting amount of time we've spent together over the past month.'

Moving across the room, Edwin came to a stand behind her, his bulk filling the delicate dressing-table mirror. A wave of awareness spread up her spine. She shifted forward on her seat.

'You're still angry I went and got your mum?'

Kara lifted one shoulder up and then the other, their separate movements indicative of her mixed feelings on Susan's arrival. At least now there wouldn't be endless speculation on her absence, and it just felt right to have her here. But how she wished that she had come of her own volition…and that Edwin hadn't persuaded her by pointing out the fact that this particular bride would need her mum even more than any other bride because of the fallout that was invariably on the cards for this unconventional marriage that would test even the best of relationships. A fallout that was steamrolling towards them at a faster, more intense rate than Kara had ever thought possible when she had agreed to the marriage, thanks to Edwin's continuing disappearing acts and avoidance of all things personal. 'Why don't you want to have dinner with us tonight?'

'As I said earlier, I have other plans.'

She ducked her head to catch his gaze, her heart in her mouth, the horror of his elusive answer stripping away any final pretence of being indifferent to his behaviour. 'A woman?' Nick had never been unfaithful but had subtly, and never favourably, compared her to his past girlfriends and work colleagues. It had seriously rattled her trust that men didn't have wandering eyes.

He rocked back on his heels and came to stand to the side of the dressing table, his eyes ablaze. 'Seriously?'

He was furious. For a moment she felt compelled to apologise but then anger rose in her—it was his evasiveness that was driving these questions and she sure as hell was not going to back down. 'Well, what, then?'

His mouth tightened.

Kara smoothed her hand against her hair, certain it was lifting because of the static tension filling the room.

His eyes narrowed as they honed in on her hand. 'Where's your engagement ring?'

Kara pulled open one of the two walnut inlaid drawers on the top of the table and pulled out her ring. 'I take it off when I'm showering.'

He watched her pull it on.

She grimaced at its weight.

'Don't you like it?'

She studied the sapphire. How could she feel nothing for something so beautiful?

Raising her gaze, she studied the man she was about to marry and answered, 'You're not the only one struggling at the idea of marrying, you know.'

With a sigh Edwin dropped to his haunches beside her. 'There is no other woman. I might be struggling with the whole concept of marrying and how on earth to be an even half-decent husband, but there's no other person in this world I'd rather marry. Please believe me on that.' His serious expression gave way to a light smile, his eyes scanning her for a reaction like a lighthouse beam scanning the oceans.

Well, prove just how important I am...spend time with me. Remind me of all the reasons why I agreed to this in the first place.

She eyed him, her poorly constructed defences crumbling in the face of his now keen attention, at the way his shirt pulled tight across his chest, at the smile on his face inviting her to believe in him, to forgive him.

Am I being too needy? Has Nick's stifling devotion

warped my understanding as to what a relationship should look like? Am I expecting too much?

'It's not going to be easy dealing with my mum and dad—they're both acting like stressed-out quarrelling Tasmanian devils.'

His mouth quivered.

She crossed her arms. 'What?'

He raised his hands defensively. 'Nothing.'

'Well, they are—at the garden party they refused to be photographed together and matters didn't improve when they found out their luggage had been brought to the same bedroom in the apartment they're sharing.'

Standing with a sigh, he said, 'I'm sorry—that should never have happened.'

'It's okay. The apartment has two other bedrooms. My dad moved into one.'

'I'll organise for another apartment to be allocated to him.'

'I suggested that but they both agreed it would be useful to have someone to navigate the palace with. They're both so anxious and intimidated by everything this weekend. I need your help with dealing with them—that's why I suggested we all have dinner together.'

'Maybe you should have left my family out of the mix—they're all like a powder keg waiting to go off.'

She stood and reminded him, 'It was you who had said you wanted for you all to be closer as a family.'

He rolled his eyes and shifted away towards the doorway. 'Sometimes I don't think things through enough.'

'Like our marriage?'

He came to a stop in the centre of the room. 'Not that…' he paused his gaze sweeping down over her '…but I shouldn't.' Again he hesitated, his gaze settling on her mouth. Reaching down, he plucked her silver and gold sandals from where she had earlier placed them on one of the two gilt stools sitting at the base of her bed. Well, her bed for now. Tomorrow her items would be moved to Edwin's bedroom next door.

Passing the sandals to her, he said in a rush, 'We'd better go down for dinner.'

Kara grabbed her sandals. Right, she'd had enough. Skirting around Edwin, she darted across the room and, banging the door shut, she leant against it with all of her weight. 'Right, we're sorting this out now once and for all. What is going on? Why are you shutting me out?'

Edwin moved across the room and, standing in front of her, placed his hand on the door handle and twisted it. 'Let's go—my father is going to be livid if I'm late again today.'

She pushed her weight even harder against the door. 'Not until we discuss this.'

He snapped his hand off the door handle. 'Fine. Give me some examples.'

'Today you arrived late for the garden party—'

'I was collecting your mother—'

'Why leave it till the day before the wedding? And this afternoon at the party, not once did you come to my side. What groom does that? It was embarrassing. And tonight you have some mysterious plans you're refusing to talk about.'

'You know how much I have to deal with right now, with the succession and persuading that German bank to locate here, not to mention all of the changes to the government structures I want to hammer out in advance of my enthronement.'

'There's nothing in that list that would stop you actually talking to me.'

God, how was she going to get through to him?

The urge to touch him, to be close to him once again, had her reach out her index finger to give a single light tap to his temple. 'I have no idea what's going on in there,' a tightness in her throat replacing the burn of anger in her belly, she tapped her finger against his chest, 'or in your heart.'

For a moment his shoulders flexed tight as though he was about to leap away from her. But then they dropped and, bowing his head, he stood silently in front of her. His hair was damp. Citrus mingled with his usual clean woody scent. She pushed herself even tighter against the door, her shoulder blades digging into the wood, for fear of giving in to the temptation of running her hands through the damp silkiness of his hair or cupping her hand against the vulnerable strength of his neck or, most compelling of all, the pull to move towards him and take shelter against his body.

Bruised golden eyes met hers. 'You deserve to have your mother here at your wedding. I wanted to make you happy. That's the only reason why I went and brought her here. But I obviously made a mistake.'

She closed her eyes against the softness of his voice. 'What would make me happy is if we could go back to how we were before all of this—where has our friendship disappeared to?'

She opened her eyes on his sigh.

He shifted to stand squarely in front of her.

Bare inches separating them, he studied her for long moments, a denseness entering the air between them. 'I'm struggling…'

His eyes shifted down to her lips.

Pinpricks of temptation tingled across her skin.

Her hips snaked outwards towards him. She slammed

them back against the door, her tailbone colliding with the wood, making her already unsteady legs tremble.

His head tilted, his eyes remaining fixed on her mouth as though it was a complex problem he was trying to understand.

With a distracted air, he repeated in another whisper, 'I'm struggling,' again he paused, and then his head lifted and his eyes blazed into hers.

Unable to breathe, unable to look away from the intensity of his gaze, hormones washing through her body like a lethal overdose, Kara felt her heart cry out for him to say something, something that would make everything okay, that would destroy the fear inside of her.

'I'm struggling…' he blinked and blinked again and, just like that, the passion, the hunger in his eyes was gone, traded for a wary defensiveness '…I'm struggling with the idea of being a husband.'

The feeling of being robbed of something she didn't even understand had her duck away from him and move into the centre of the room.

'Well, you'd better get used to it because this time tomorrow you'll be my husband—if you still want to go through with it.'

'Don't you?'

How many times had she asked herself that question over the past few weeks, her heart and instinct warning her to tread carefully? But her pride, her need to stick to her word and promises, seeing already the benefit her new position was bringing to Young Adults Together, her desire to help Edwin despite his recent infuriating behaviour, all had her want to see this through. 'On a number of conditions.'

She ignored Edwin's grimace and, holding up her hand counted off with her fingers, 'First condition is that we're going to have breakfast together every morning from now on. Second, we are trekking in the mountains and watching a movie together at least once a week. Third, you promised me a nice honeymoon. I'll accept your schedule is too crazy to allow for one right now, but at some point in this two years of marriage, I expect a holiday, and a spectacular one at that.'

Throwing his hands in the air, Edwin answered, 'Fine.' Opening the door, he added, 'Now can we please go to dinner?'

Coming to a stop where he was standing holding the door open for her, she attempted to hide just how vulnerable she was feeling inside with even more bravado. 'It's not too late to pull out of the wedding, you know—I won't take it personally.'

He smiled at that. His hand lightly touched her forearm. 'Getting married is way more complex than I ever anticipated...' he tilted his head, the tenderness in his eyes melting her heart '...but you're still the only person in the world for me.'

Their main course finished, Edwin caught her eye from the opposite side of the dining table and, looking in the direction of his father and her mother, who were seated to her right, he raised an eyebrow. Kara smiled. Who would have predicted his father and her mother would bond over a shared passion for olives?

Her mother lived alone in a two-bedroom *cortijo*, surrounded by olive groves, in the hills north of Málaga City. Throughout the meal she had described in vivid detail her new life tending to her olive trees, talking about her hopes and fears for this season's harvest. For the first time in years her mother was talking about the future.

The waiting staff reappeared, all five of them in a

gracefully coordinated dance placing a tiny but exquisitely formed trio of chocolate desserts before each diner.

As they backed out of the room, her dad stood up.

Kara held her breath. Her poor father's hands were trembling so badly the red wine in his glass was sloshing about.

He directed his attention towards Edwin's father. 'I would like to thank you for your welcome and hospitality, Your Highness.'

He raised his glass even higher, and the rest of the people at the table reached for their glasses to join in with the toast, but her dad wasn't finished.

Clearing his throat loudly, he added, 'I ask that you and your family take good care of my…' his voice cracked and it took him a few seconds to add, 'my little girl.'

Little girl. God, it was corny and sentimental but she could not help the feeling of delight and belonging that filled her heart at her dad's description. For so many years she had believed he had forgotten that—that she was his daughter, that she was the same person he'd given piggy-back rides to around their garden, jumping over sweeping brushes, pretending they were taking part in the Cheltenham Gold Cup.

She waited for her father to look in her direction, but instead his focus remained on Edwin's father. He was waiting for a response. He had thrown down a gauntlet. Her dad, a small-time builder, was challenging the sovereign of a small but powerful country. Kara wanted to burst with pride.

His Highness's frown deepened to a bottomless ravine transecting his forehead. Kara swallowed. He had done nothing in the weeks since their engagement to indicate he was shedding any of his misgivings as to Edwin's choice of bride.

Sitting back in his chair, he studied her father, then her mother and then finally her, taking his time, a monarch accustomed to people waiting for his considered judgement. Her palms started to sweat.

Edwin said, 'You have our word—'

With an annoyed shake of his head, His Highness interrupted Edwin, his attention now fully on his eldest son. 'My marriage was arranged.' He stopped and chuckled. Kara gave a nervous smile, uncertain what direction this conversation was going in. 'At first my wife and I argued. She actually said I was too arrogant and had to accept that the marriage was one of equals. Of course, she was right, and after a while we became friends. And with time we grew to love one another.' His gaze shifting towards her, he added, 'From the most inauspicious starts, miracles can happen.'

What did he mean by that?

Edwin's father did not wait for her to work that question out. Instead he stood and raised his glass in salute to her father, who was still standing and waiting for a response to his question. 'I will give you my word that we will take care of your daughter as long as she's a member of our family.'

Her father frowned. Kara reddened.

Shooting out of his seat, Edwin raised his own glass, his expression pinched. 'Please be assured, Mr Duffy, that we will take care of Kara *always*.'

Her father's gaze moved from Edwin to his father and back again before he said quietly, 'Thank you, Edwin,' and then took his seat.

Edwin remained standing. He rolled his shoulders and raised his wine glass again. 'To my mother and Michael. We miss you dearly but you will live on for ever in our memories and actions.'

A tangle of emotions lodged in her throat at Edwin's softly spoken and unexpected words. The entire table just stared at him, nobody raising their glasses. A twitch began to beat in Edwin's cheek.

Her mother stood up.

Oh, God, was she about to walk out of the room at the mention of Michael's name?

Raising her glass, her mother waited with a quiet dignity and slowly the rest of the table rose to join her. Only then did she say, 'To Princess Cristina and Michael.'

They all sat down. They had no sooner done so when His Highness added, raising his glass again, 'And here's to many grandchildren in the future.'

Edwin sighed.

Her parents stared open-mouthed at His Highness.

Her mother was the first to gather herself enough to splutter, 'I really don't think so.' Sending a glare in her and Edwin's direction, she added, 'Please tell me you aren't going to be so foolish as to bring a child into this?'

'Of course not,' Kara answered.

In a disgruntled tone, Edwin's father demanded, 'Why ever not?'

Her mother huffed. 'I am not having my daughter left to raise a child on her own.'

Princess Maria, who was seated next to her father, asked with a bewildered expression, 'Why would Kara raise a child on her own?'

'Exactly my question,' His Highness added, staring in Edwin's direction.

Luis gave a cynical laugh and asked his father, 'Are you happy with the mess you've caused?'

'You never specified I have to marry for ever,' Edwin pointed out, lifting his wine glass to his mouth but then lowering it to the table, not having taken a drink from it.

He pushed it away from him as though irritated by the golden-hued wine.

Princess Maria gasped. 'Are you saying—?'

His Highness interrupted with a flick of his hand, 'Of course this is a marriage of convenience. Did you really think Edwin had changed his opinion on ever committing himself to a relationship? I had no choice but to force his hand. This country needs successors. This family needs a new generation.'

With a horrified expression, Princess Maria asked her brother, 'Have you lost all sense?'

His Highness grimaced, but then sat back in his chair, a smile forming on his lips. He glanced in her direction and then Edwin's.

A queasy feeling formed in her belly.

'You saw the engagement photos for yourself. Are you seriously telling me that I was wrong in pushing Edwin to make a choice in his bride?' Edwin's father demanded.

Across the table, her father, red in the face, growled, 'Can I remind you that they are divorcing in two years' time?'

His Highness blanched. And then, leaning forward, he yelled at Edwin, 'Two years? Are you serious? Two years is nothing. You're not even prepared to give the marriage a chance.'

That twitch in his cheek now on overdrive, Edwin answered with poorly disguised fury, 'You do not have a say in this.' With that he stood and muttered, 'I need some air.'

Kara stood and followed him.

Edwin's father called out, 'You can't divorce. We've never had a divorce in this family and we're not having one now.'

CHAPTER SIX

IN THE FAST approaching twilight, a figure ran out onto the road. Slamming on the brakes, Edwin cursed, his motorbike skidding on the gravel surface. The figure, about to be pelted with incoming stones, leapt out of the way.

Tugging off his helmet, he muttered a low curse. Kara was barefoot, her sandals in her hand, her dress, a fine layer of gold and yellow silk material, skimming over the gentle curves of her body. Thoughts on Kara's body, no matter how delectable they were, were not where his focus needed to be right now. 'Being mowed down by a motorbike is a drastic way to get out of our wedding tomorrow.'

She stepped off the grass verge. 'I'm coming with you.'

He pulled on his helmet. 'Stay with your parents. I'm sure they have plenty of things to discuss with you after that get-together.'

Oh, for crying out loud.

Kara went to get on behind him. He reached out to stop her but she slapped his hand away and climbed on. Muttering, he turned the motorbike back in the direction of the palace's garage.

Inside the garage, which had once been part of the palace's own flour mill, he climbed off. And waited for

Kara to follow. But instead she sat there and pretended to ignore him.

He walked out of the garage.

Kara chased after him.

He followed the path towards the pool house and then made a quick divert away towards the sea. Still Kara followed him. 'Are you going to follow me all night?'

'Yes, until you at least tell me where you were going.'

Okay, so he was acting crazily. This was not the behaviour of a grown man, never mind one about to succeed to the throne. But his head was about to explode *and* there was no way he could be around Kara right now. 'Look, I want some time alone—is that too much to ask?'

Gesturing in the direction of the palace, she said, 'Well, you're certainly not leaving me here to face *that* lot alone.' Popping a hand on her hip she added, 'And actually, yes, it *is* too much for you to ask of your fiancée. You should want to be with me.'

Want to be with her…that was the problem: he wanted to be with her, but for all the wrong reasons. And it was eating him up inside. 'What do you want from me?'

Her mouth set hard, her eyes blazing, she answered, 'To not wreck our friendship. We need to talk. Properly. We can't keep burying our heads in the sand and pretending that marrying, your succession, the craziness that's going on around us isn't impacting on us as individuals but also as a couple.' Then with an exasperated gesture with her hands she added, 'At least Nick blew hot and cold…right now you're just blowing cold constantly.'

For long moments she stared at him defiantly but then her mouth wobbled and she blinked hard. His heart sank. There were tears in her eyes. 'I'm really messing up here, aren't I?'

'I can't survive the next two years if you're going to

be this remote. I need your friendship, your support. I need to understand what's going on inside your head,' on a sigh her shoulders lifted, her eyes sad pools of blue, 'because when I don't I feel so sad and lonely. And I didn't sign up for those things. And I know you didn't either.'

He wasn't sad or lonely. Was he?

An uneasiness spread through his bones, bringing a pressing need to end this conversation. But how was he supposed to walk away from those bruised blue eyes holding him to account?

His throat tightened when he realised what it was he needed to do. He had to stop running away into the safety of his own thoughts and isolation. He had to give Kara what she needed and deserved from him. Yes, it might mess with his head, make him deeply uncomfortable and frustrated, but that was his problem, not Kara's. 'I was going for a bike ride into the mountains to clear my head. And, given that you previously said you'd never ride with me again, I assumed you wouldn't want to come.'

She bit back a grin, rightly knowing he was giving in to her. 'I'll try not to scream this time.'

Back in the garage he gave Kara the smallest bike leathers he could find, probably a relic from the time Luis was a mountain-bike fanatic, much to his father's disapproval. For the teenage Luis, the faster and more dangerous the sport, the better.

Then he searched out a suitable-size helmet and boots. He waited outside the garage while Kara pulled on all of the gear.

She emerged a sensual mix of silk and leather. He grinned. 'Great look.' He ducked his head, pretending to be checking the hand clutch. His comment had been supposed to come out as a tease but instead had sounded way too familiar and suggestively carnal. He fired up the engine, trying to ignore the blush on Kara's cheeks.

He drove out of the palace and through the narrow streets of Monrosa City before they began their long climb up into the mountains, the road a series of endless hairpin turns. The sky was rapidly turning from a pink breath of fire to inky blackness. There was little traffic out at this time of the evening, so he was able to drive hard, needing the surge of the breeze against his skin to counterbalance the sweet warmth of Kara's body behind him.

After half an hour they reached their destination. The viewpoint was set high up in the mountain, allowing a clear view of Monrosa City below them. On a headland to the east, the San Gabriel lighthouse flickered.

Kara removed her helmet and threw her head backwards. 'Wow, so many stars.'

Leading her away through the forest, using a torch to guide their way, he brought her to the opposite side of the mountain to a clearing with picnic tables. She gasped and turned around in a slow circle, her neck stretched back to take in the endless night sky that hung over them like a glittering dark blanket just out of their reach.

'It's stunning.'

'There's no light pollution on this side of the mountain. Locally this area is called Angels' Reach. People say it's the closest point to heaven on the island.'

Balancing against the edge of a picnic table, Kara asked, 'It's a special place for you?'

'It used to be, when I was younger.'

'And now?'

Now he wasn't certain what he felt for Angels' Reach. He hadn't visited the mountain for years. 'Are you certain it's not bad luck to see each other the night before the wedding?'

Kara studied him for a moment. 'I'm not sure you can bring bad luck to a marriage of convenience.' She gave a light laugh. 'It's not as though we have to worry about falling out of love or anything like that.'

Silence stretched out between them. Kara tilted her head again to stargaze, eventually asking in a soft voice, 'Is this where you had been planning to visit before I stopped you?'

'Yes.'

'Why here?'

'I like the view. And, as I said, I needed space to think.'

She raised an eyebrow. 'And you couldn't find some space to think in a seventy-room palace?'

He scuffed his boot along the dry earth, remembering what it was like to lie down on it and hear his mother whisper tales from the folklore of her native Aragon. 'I should have brought something for us to drink.'

'You're shutting me out again.'

He started at the anger in her voice. Exasperation, frustration at his own avoidance, his inability to articulate the feelings that were tightly sewn into the fabric of his being and Kara's impossible desire for him to unpick those feelings thread by thread had him respond just as angrily, 'I don't know how to let you in.'

She turned away from him. Went and sat on the bench of the picnic table and stared out into the darkness in the direction of the Mediterranean that the waning crescent moon did little to illuminate.

He went and sat beside her.

She shuffled away, leaning back against the tabletop. Waves of irritation pulsated in his direction. 'Start with the small things—it doesn't have to be anything profound. Tell me about the first time you came here, for instance.'

He tossed the flashlight between his hands, a jittery energy entering his bloodstream. 'I can't remember the first time—it was decades ago.'

Those waves of irritation from her moved across to him in even quicker pulses.

Dio*, this was so hard. Why did he find it near impossible to speak? Why did it feel like torture?*

'My mother used to bring me here to celebrate my birthday. We'd sneak out before midnight and we'd sit here counting down the minutes until it was my birthday.' Something caught in his throat, but he could tell that Kara expected more, so he forced himself to find the words that described memories he had deliberately ignored for years. 'She used to say that she wanted to be the first to whisper *happy birthday* to me.'

Kara sighed. And whispered, 'She sounds wonderful.'

Something large and significant twisted in his chest at the soft wistfulness, the respect in Kara's voice. He held her gaze, his heart tumbling, tumbling, tumbling again and again and again at not just the understanding in her eyes but also the eagerness there, the eagerness to know more about his mother. 'Yes, she was.'

'Tell me more.'

An image of his mother, down on all fours on the palace lawn, chasing after him and his two brothers, pretending to be a grizzly bear, had him smile. 'She was playful, constantly thinking up new things for us all to do, new adventures for us to undertake. One summer we created our own pirate island on the palace's private beach—we even made our own lookout tower using old wine barrels she found in the cellar. And she used to dream up ways to trick the media into not following us, which of course was like something out of a spy movie for us.' He rolled his shoulders, his heart clogged with emotions he didn't want to have to process. 'It's hard to describe but somehow she just managed to make me feel secure, certain about the world.'

Kara twisted towards him. 'You wanted to remember your mum tonight.'

He shrugged.

'I'm sorry she's not going to be there tomorrow.'

A fissure opened up in his heart. 'Me too.'

'I'm sure she wouldn't be impressed with your dad forcing you into a marriage of convenience.'

He laughed at that, imagining his mother's reaction. 'She would have gone crazy.' Then, catching Kara's eye, he admitted, 'But she'd have liked you.'

Kara gave a snort. 'I'm sure she'd have wanted a more suitable bride for you, someone who understands royal protocol and doesn't constantly ruffle feathers, which I seem to be making my speciality.' She let out a sigh. 'Victor isn't happy that I'm refusing to back down on my tour of Europe to raise awareness for Young Adults Together. He wants me to dedicate more time to attending events with you instead. And the chamberlain is putting every obstacle possible in the way of my plans to open up parts of the palace to the public. And as for my proposal to start an apprenticeship programme within the palace for disadvantaged young school leavers… I've never heard so many reasons as to why something won't work. I get that there's a tradition of roles being passed within families—but nepotism like that is just plain unfair.'

He grinned and bumped his shoulder against hers playfully. 'Please don't stop questioning everything. The household needs a shake-up and you're also taking the heat off me.'

Kara pursed her lips and eyed him suspiciously. 'Are you saying I'm your fall guy?'

Did she really have to draw his attention to her mouth like that? It wasn't as though he was ignoring it in the first place. And why was he so damn distracted by her knee touching his thigh?

Her leather jacket was moulded to her curves like a second skin, its zip hanging just at the valley of her breasts like an agent provocateur. Blood pumping through him in hard beats, he placed an arm behind her back. 'Never a guy.'

Her eyes widened. She gave him an uncertain smile.

His hand touched her arm.

She jumped but then settled, leaning ever so slightly towards him, allowing his fingers to curl even more around the soft leather of her jacket. Soft leather. Soft lips. Soft skin.

Silence, darkness, unfinished business.

He eased her closer. She didn't resist.

Her loose hair tickled the back of his hand.

Memories of her scent, floral with an undertone of something earthier, wiped out the forest scent surrounding them.

Her shoulder slotted under his arm, the softness of her body pressed close to where his heart was hammering.

He touched a finger to her chin, tilting her head so that their gazes married. He breathed deep at the heat in her eyes, the parting of her lips. He inched towards her mouth, all thought wiped out by pure physical need. Their lips touched, her mouth even more sensual and lush than before. He tried to hold himself back but that lasted all of five seconds before he was deepening the kiss, wanting to taste, inhale every part of her.

And her hand on his neck pulled him even deeper into the kiss.

Kara was moving.

Panicked, he jerked away, worried he had read this all wrong and Kara was trying to get away.

She pulled him back, her bottom landing on his lap. He chuckled into their kiss and he could feel her lips draw up into a smile. But they didn't stop.

He pulled her hip in against his belly, fire raging through him, her hands raking through his hair.

He fumbled for the zip of her jacket and lowered it, his thumb tracing down over the smooth skin of her breasts.

He groaned again. Her bottom wriggled on his lap.

He wanted to part the material of her dress, expose the lace bra he could feel beneath the silk. He wanted to twist her fully towards him and have her wrap her legs around his waist. He eased away, his head swimming with crazy, destructive thoughts.

But only seconds after he broke their kiss, less than an inch away from her, with a sound of protest she pulled him back, both hands clasping his neck.

Burning, urgent, unthinking need yelled at him to stay there. To lose himself in her. But he had to stop. Before the mess of their impending marriage became an even more tangled chaos of emotions.

He unclasped her hands. Drew back from her mouth.

She stared into his eyes, dazed.

And then with a sound of disbelief she flew off his lap, gawked at him and rocked on her heels before collapsing back down on the bench.

She yanked her jacket zip back up, clamping the skirt of her dress between her legs. 'I hope there's no paparazzi with night-vision cameras hiding in the woods.'

He laughed, glad she was making light of the frenetic intensity of what had just happened.

'Our kisses…they're kind of confusing, aren't they?' she said quietly.

His laughter died. He had no way of explaining them other than as the result of human desire. 'I guess we're both young and healthy and it's been a while since either of us were in a relationship.'

She nodded eagerly. 'And the craziness of our situation isn't helping—maybe subconsciously we think we should be finding each other attractive.' She stopped, her expression growing horrified. 'Not that I'm saying you find me attractive—'

He interrupted her, 'I think we can at least admit to each other the chemistry between us.'

Did she really think their subconscious could be fooling them to that extent? But who was he to argue? If she was happy to believe that, then so was he.

'So what do we do about this attraction?'

Her brow furrowed. 'I don't know. Not beat ourselves up too much when it happens, I guess. And, more importantly, not ascribe too much significance to it…the survival of our friendship is what's important.'

He inhaled deeply. 'I don't ever want to hurt you.'

She nodded. 'I guess it's down to both of us individually to keep everything in perspective—to remember that this is a marriage of convenience thrust upon two people who have no interest in marrying and no desire to marry.'

He pulled his heel along the soft earth, a deep channel forming in its wake. 'Before Nick, did you see yourself marrying?'

She shrugged and scrunched her nose in thought. 'What happened with my parents put me off…but Nick definitely put a solid nail in the coffin of love and marriage for me.' She gave a light shiver. 'I struggle with the idea of trusting someone enough to commit myself to them for ever. I'd hate the vulnerability of that. I'd constantly be watching for a time when they'd try to manipulate me, hurt me. And that's not fair, is it?' Pausing, she considered him. 'You know what, you've never really given me a good reason why you're not interested in marriage?'

He flattened the channel of earth with the sole of his shoe. 'I like my own company. I don't think I'm husband material—I prefer to give my energy to my work.' Then, standing up, he held out his hand to her. 'I'd better get you home.'

She looked at his hand and then looked him straight in the eye. 'Being single suits some people…but only if it's for the right reasons.' Then, standing up too, she tugged him towards the wooden barrier at the edge of the picnic area. 'I think I can hear the sea.'

He leant forward, twisting his head. 'I think I can too. I've never heard it before, even in all the times I came here with my mother.'

She smiled at him, her hand touching his cheek. 'Thank you for bringing me here, for telling me about your mum. It's good to know you better.'

It did feel good to have spoken about his mother. He smiled at how Kara's eyes were dancing with pleasure, a connection, a spark, a sense of place making him intensely happy. But then, just as quickly as that happiness arrived, it disappeared, the intimacy of the moment making him uneasy. Was he making himself vulnerable by being this open? Was he setting them up for a whole load of heartache when this marriage ended by their being too close to one another?

CHAPTER SEVEN

MONICA, THE PALACE'S head florist, moved from table to table, adjusting a fraction the elaborate floral arrangements sitting in tall, clear vases at the centre of every table in the ballroom.

On seeing him, she went to leave, but Edwin gestured for her to stay and finish her work.

The doors out to the terrace were opened back, the heat of the day drifting into the coolness of the room.

Beyond the terrace, on the shimmering water, boats in full sail glided through the rolling white-topped waves.

In two hours he would be married. A husband.

He turned away from the golden dome of the cathedral.

The ballroom was a reflection of the view across the harbour. The vast gold chandeliers towering over the tables laden down with gold cutlery and gold-rimmed plates bearing the royal crest mirrored the cathedral's dome, the olive branches in the floral arrangements the green and silver glimmer of the Mediterranean, the pink blush roses the narrow buildings of the old town.

Ricardo bustled into the room. Did a double-take when he spotted Edwin.

'Is everything okay, Your Highness?'

He nodded. 'I want to ensure everything is in place for

the wedding meal later.' From the moment he had woken this morning he had been feeling off balance. Tetchy and nervous, with a side dollop of a tightness in his throat. Was he coming down with something?

Last night, talking beneath the stars, kissing…it had all felt too good, too exhilarating. He hadn't dated for close to two years. No wonder kissing Kara was igniting a fire inside him.

He needed to get through today. Not overthink it. Which was why he was here, unnecessarily inspecting the ballroom like a nervous housekeeper. Anything to distract him. Kara had left their apartment early this morning, as arranged, to get ready for the ceremony in her parents' apartment. Unable to stomach breakfast, he had paced the apartment, ready for the ceremony way too early, and even he couldn't bring himself to work on his wedding day.

Ricardo cleared his throat. 'Is everything to your satisfaction?'

Eucalyptus leaves wound their way up all seven layers of their wedding cake. On top two simple figures crafted from wood stood beneath an arch of intertwined leaves. Kara had asked him if he wanted an input into the cake. He hadn't. The tightness in his throat intensified. The cake perfectly symbolised their treks into the mountains of Monrosa. He turned to Ricardo. 'Everything is perfect.'

Relief washed over Ricardo's expression. 'We want to ensure you and Miss Duffy have a wonderful wedding day. We're all so happy for you. Miss Duffy has been very supportive in the preparations and it will be a pleasure to work for her in the coming years.'

Behind Ricardo, Luis walked into the room and chuckled. 'I'm sure Kara will be a dream to work for in comparison to our father.'

Ricardo flinched, made a non-committal sound and fled from the room.

Edwin sighed. 'There was no need for that.'

Luis shrugged. 'We've been looking everywhere for you. It's time to go.'

Ivo and his father were waiting for them on the central steps out in the courtyard. Ivo was dressed in the same navy-blue officer dress uniform of the Monrosian army as Luis, their father in the red dress uniform of the Commander of the Forces. Today he was wearing the black officer tunic of the Marines, gold cuffs on the sleeves, gold braiding on the shoulders. Across the tunic he wore the red and white sash representing the Order of St Philip, and pinned to the fabric the gold insignia of the two other Monrosian orders.

Without preamble they lined up, equidistantly apart. Edwin stood in the centre beside his father, Ivo to his right, Luis to his father's left.

At the western apartments, horses and carriages were awaiting Kara and her entourage. He closed his eyes, a wave of gratitude, of affection, of respect for her making him dizzy. How many friends would agree to something this enormous, this public, this life-altering? He *had* to make this marriage work.

With a call from their commander, the twelve soldiers flanking them on either side, all in their Sixth Infantry khaki uniforms, led them towards the closed fifteenth-century wooden gates that led out onto the cobbled streets of the city.

It took four of the household guard to open the gates.

A wave of sound rolled towards them. The waiting

crowd cheered and waved their purple and gold Monrosa flags, aided by the warm summer breeze.

The clamour, the close scrutiny, the fevered elation of the crowd sent a sickening sensation through him but he continued to walk at the steady beat that had been drilled into him from the moment he could walk, falling in behind the rest of the Sixth Infantry regiment already waiting outside the palace walls, the Second Regiment falling in behind them.

They walked down the incline that would take them to the narrow streets of the old town and then on to the harbour front towards Monrosa Cathedral, the cheering swelling.

He clenched his hands, the happy calls so at odds with the low weeping and murmuring that had accompanied them the last time they had marched together to the cathedral.

That time, with every step he had taken, his frustration with his father had inched ever higher. Why had he forced them to walk through the crowds to their mother's funeral? Why had he thought it was the duty of three bereaved children to march, just so the public would have the opportunity to express their grief at the passing of their beloved Princess Cristina?

The morning of the funeral, he had held Ivo in his arms and had promised that he would not be forced to march. But, despite his arguing fiercely with his father, his father had refused to relent, forcing Ivo to join them.

That was the day they had lost Ivo to his own impenetrable thoughts.

For his part, Edwin had been so full of anger and disbelief that he soon realised that to survive he would have to detach himself. Shut down all his emotions. Not react when his father had angrily demanded to know why he and Luis had refused to accompany their mother when she had gone out riding that day with Ivo. Not admit his own anger towards Ivo for insisting they go riding even though their mother had complained of vertigo earlier that day.

Now they swept through Plaza Nueva, the thunderous applause startling pigeons from the roof of the Tufail Observatory Tower. A dark-haired girl of five or six, perched on her father's shoulders, waved a cut-out of him and Kara on their engagement day. He smiled at her. She dropped the cut-out, her eyes wide, her mouth a perfect circle of surprise.

His mother would have loved every moment of this. She wouldn't have even tried to hide her pride in her husband and three sons' marching together as one seemingly united family.

How they had all failed her.

They turned a sharp right, the open harbour bringing a strong sea breeze and the sight of waves lapping against the quay walls. People hung from the upstairs windows of the quayside cafes, filming the procession on their phones.

A girl called out her love for Luis. His father sighed loudly.

At Plaza Santa Ana, the Cardinal of Monrosa was waiting for them on the cathedral steps.

Inside came welcome near silence apart from the low whispering from the already assembled guests. Edwin's nose twitched thanks to the heavy scent of incense.

He was about to follow the cardinal when his father placed a hand on his arm. 'You can make this work if you want to.'

He bit back the temptation to laugh.

Did his father seriously think this forced marriage,

already fraying at the edges, could be made to work just to serve his egotistical desire to ensure a future heir?

He walked away, smiled and nodded his way down the aisle, the beaming grins of Kara's family, friends and colleagues punching him in the stomach. How many lies had she had to tell on his behalf?

He took a seat at the top pew.

Tried to breathe.

His mother's casket had sat only feet away from where he sat now.

He had refused to look at it. Instead he had tilted his head and tried to count the number of flowers on the triptych of stained-glass windows behind the altar. But the disbelief kept dragging him back—to the fact that only four days prior his mother had left to take Ivo horse-riding. He and Luis had been supposed to go too but they had become caught up in a battle to win a game of tennis and had refused to leave. He had vaguely waved his mother goodbye. Hadn't replied to her departing call to be kind to one another. Her horse had startled and thrown her off, causing a catastrophic head injury.

Ivo, alone on the isolated trail they had been following within the palace grounds, had raised the alarm on her mobile phone and had frantically carried out the emergency services' instructions on how to help her, a ten-year-old child, alone, carrying the responsibility for saving his mother.

Losing her had destroyed them.

He placed his hands on his knees. Light-headed.

Time stretched out. His father grumbled at Kara's lateness.

Kara was going to walk down the aisle, wasn't she? What if she had changed her mind?

His heart boomed in his chest. Only one person, since

his mother had died, had settled him—Kara. Her acceptance of him as well as astute challenges to his ways of thinking and behaving, her energy, had freed him.

Dammit, where was she?

Cold terror ran through his veins.

Had he blown it? Had he thrown away their friendship for this farce?

Standing at the bottom of the aisle, while Triona and Siza brought her long train under control, her hands resting on both of her parents' arms, Kara felt her legs buckle.

And for a moment a crazy thought passed through her mind at lightning speed.

What if she spoke out? Right here? Right now? Explained that she couldn't be the answer to what the media were terming a new era of optimism in Monrosa? Explained she understood the marriage was creating an unprecedented feel-good factor and was being hailed as an example of hope triumphing after the tragedy of the country losing Princess Cristina, but the media's new near adoration of her, lauding her charity work, describing her relationship with Edwin as the ultimate love story that saw friendship blossom into enduring love, was so far from the truth that she felt as if she was going to burn up in shame?

What if she explained there definitely would be no babies born to them?

What if she made it clear this was only a marriage between friends? One that would end one day, but until that happened she would have Edwin's back and would try her very best to be the princess Monrosa deserved?

What would happen if she said all that, cleared the air?

Chaos probably.

'Are you ready?'

She wanted to say no to her father's question but instead she nodded *yes*. Which was a good thing because there was no way she was going to be heard anyway. The cathedral practically shook as the Bridal Chorus boomed from the pipes of the organ positioned on the gallery overhead, the notes flinging themselves against the vast roof of the even vaster cathedral.

Edwin jerked in his seat, music booming against the stone pillars as the organist began to play. The cardinal and his fellow celebrants on the altar looked down the aisle, a smile transforming each of their up-till-now serious expressions.

Kara had that effect on people.

He shouldn't look back. Not yet.

But he didn't give a damn.

He needed to see her. He needed to see her with a desperation that burned through him and scorched his heart.

He breathed in deeply, stepped even further out into the aisle. Desperate to have her look in his direction, desperate for a connection.

Flanked by her mother and father, her bridesmaids carrying her train, Kara walked towards him, her gaze sweeping to either side of the aisle but not once looking in his direction.

A veil was the only adornment in her tied-up hair. His aunt hadn't persuaded her to wear a tiara after all.

Her full-skirted satin dress with its sweetheart neckline was overlaid with delicate lace that skimmed her shoulders and the length of her arms.

In her hands she carried the same blush-pink roses interlaced with olive and eucalyptus leaves as the displays in the palace ballroom.

There was heat on her cheeks.

She was beautiful.

Look at me.

Her head dipped as though studying the blue and white mosaic tiles on the floor.

Look at me, Kara. Let me know you're okay. I need you...and I don't understand why, but I'm panicking here.

And then finally, only a few steps away, she looked towards him.

Her gaze was heavy with emotion.

His heart pounded.

She gave him a tentative smile.

He blinked away the stinging sensation in his eyes.

She was here.

Standing in the centre of the aisle, powerful, intent, Edwin held her gaze with a burning intensity. Kara's heart turned inside out.

His hair was newly cut. His black, heavily adorned military uniform suited the hard planes of his face, the seriousness and loyalty of his personality.

Her parents peeled away to awkwardly shake Edwin's hand before they took their seats. From the corner of her eye she saw the fond smiles from their guests taking in the fact both her mother and father had guided her down the aisle to their future son-in-law, a family united in their joy of the ceremony about to take place, when the sad reality was that they had only announced this morning that they were both going to escort her down the aisle, united in their ongoing objections to the wedding.

Well, at least they were finally agreeing on something for the first time in a decade.

The music disappeared and silence fell on the cathedral.

This was about to happen. She was about to marry

this man. Her best friend, her saviour, the person who kept her sane, who got her, and with whom she had the most uncomplicated relationship in her life—she was about to marry him and step into a very complicated world.

Edwin continued to stare at her.

She smiled, not certain what to do, not certain how to react to his intensity. 'Hi.'

She waited for him to say something in response.

At the altar the cardinal cleared his throat, and made a gesture for them to approach the altar steps, as they had rehearsed.

But Edwin didn't budge.

He leant down and whispered, 'You're here.'

She swayed at the low tenderness of his voice.

He took her hand in his and led her to the altar.

The cardinal smiled but then frowned in the direction of their joined hands. The joining of hands was supposed to come later in the ceremony.

But Edwin's grasp only tightened around her trembling hand.

She needed to pull herself together.

She was *not* going to crash and burn under the pressure of all this expectation. It was messing with her head and distorting her feelings for Edwin, and she needed to get a grip. She had to stop struggling to keep her emotions in check around him, and as for her body—well, that was off in a la-la world of misguided sexual attraction. As was witnessed last night. She would have happily slept with him. Her legs threatened to buckle under her again. But this time it wasn't terror but a lick of heat in her belly, remembering the dominance of his mouth, the sweep of his hand against her breast.

This was so wrong. She shouldn't be having these

thoughts standing in front of a cardinal, being watched by millions worldwide.

She needed to hold on to the cold, hard fact that this was nothing more than a theatrical performance. A performance that would allow her to champion the work of Young Adults Together.

She dropped her gaze, a stab of loneliness emptying her lungs. Michael would have understood her reasoning. He would have agreed to subvert an institution like marriage to further a good cause. Wouldn't he?

When it came to the exchanging of vows, vows she had written, agonising over every word, not wanting to publicly commit to anything with which they would never follow through, she held her breath and willed herself to remain detached.

But Edwin's intense golden gaze shredded any hopes of her remaining indifferent.

'I promise you my friendship, loyalty, trust and understanding regardless of the obstacles we may face together.' His voice danced along her spine. She tightened her fingers around his, needing an anchor as she made the same simple vows, praying they would survive all the obstacles that littered their future.

And then the cardinal invited them to kiss.

Edwin touched his fingers to her jawline. Her heart kicked hard at the tenderness of his touch. She was doing it again…confusing acting with reality. She straightened, trying to regain some backbone.

She wished he would stop gazing at her as though she was the love of his life and just kiss her. He didn't need to over-egg this. The guests wouldn't suspect this was anything but a love marriage.

But he stayed there, touching her face, reverently, gently.

People began to shuffle in their seats.

His father muttered something.

This was torture. Unfair. Wrecking her heart.

And, fool that she was, she wished they could stay in this moment for eternity. A moment when the past and future didn't matter.

Something cracked inside of her.

I want closeness and intimacy with you. I want to be my true self. I want the freedom, just for a while, to have my heart soar and not be racked by doubts and guilt. I want to be wild and not give a damn.

Inch by inch he edged towards her.

His kiss was gentle. Caring.

Her heart fluttered in her chest.

She leant in for more. But he pulled away.

She wanted to scream. She wanted heat. More of him.

He was smiling when he pulled back.

But frowned as his gaze followed the big, fat tear that rolled down her cheek.

CHAPTER EIGHT

THEY STEPPED OUT onto the cathedral steps to thunderous applause. Kara blinked in the bright daylight, a gust of wind whipping her veil over her face. She scrambled to push it back, heard a chuckle, and then Edwin's strong, capable hands were helping, pushing the fine lace away, his gaze holding hers fondly, his fingertips settling wisps of her hair that had broken free.

Brace yourself, Kara. You can't cry again. Remember this is only all pretend. Don't get caught up in it. Know what is real and what isn't, for the sake of your sanity when this is all over and you have to walk away.

A chorus of 'Kiss! Kiss! Kiss!' rolled through the crowd. Edwin gave a teasing smile and the crowd reacted with good-natured laughter and then even more insistent calls for them to kiss.

Edwin turned to her, those golden eyes burning a path to her soul. An utterly convincing newlywed husband.

He's way too good at this pretence. But then, he was raised to present the image of utterly charming prince to the world. This is all second nature to him. Remember none of this is real.

His mouth touched hers. Her eyes closed, a deep shiver running down her spine.

The crowd erupted, their cheers echoing the boom in her heart.

Dammit. His kisses were perfection.

He pulled away, took her hand in his and led her to their awaiting carriage.

When they pulled away, Edwin took her hand in his and whispered against her ear, 'You look amazing and you're doing a fantastic job. The hard bit is over—try to relax and enjoy the rest of the day.'

How was she supposed to relax with the eyes of the world on her…and when he made her head spin with those kisses? 'You sound as if you're carrying out a work appraisal.'

He raised an eyebrow. 'I must make sure to give you a good bonus at the end of all this.'

Despite everything she felt herself blush, his flirting tone catching her by surprise.

All along their procession back to the palace they were greeted with shouts of goodwill and blessings for their marriage.

At the palace they and their families posed for formal photographs in the Oriental Room, Edwin's steadying hand on the small of her back all the time.

And when they joined their guests for the pre-reception drinks he stayed at her side throughout, and she so wanted to allow herself to drift into a tantalising fantasy world where all of this was real.

A fantasy world that became even more entrancing when, during the intervals between the various wedding banquet courses, acts that Edwin had especially organised for her entertainment appeared on the ballroom stage.

A world-famous contemporary dancer perfectly enacted the words of one of Kara's favourite songs. And before the main course was served a legendary 1970s singer took to the stage. Kara, deep in shock, stared open-mouthed as the backing music to her most famous disco track began to play. Within seconds the entire room were out of their seats, dancing.

After the singer had finally left the stage, having performed three encores, Edwin hugged her, his thumb gently wiping the tears of happiness Kara couldn't hold back.

And then, before the dessert, Edwin stood to make his speech. He formally thanked the guests for their attendance and spoke for a few minutes on his plans for Monrosa, paying special attention to praising the impressive legacy he was inheriting from his father, who gave a brief satisfied nod in acknowledgement.

Then, folding the sheet of paper he was reading from, he waved it briefly in the air before saying, 'I've decided to deviate from the rest of my speech.' Turning, he addressed Kara directly. 'Today, in the cathedral, while I was waiting for your arrival, I began to panic. I thought that you might have changed your mind and wouldn't come.'

She shook her head—that had never been a consideration. Her arrival had been delayed thanks to a dog startling one of the horses along the route.

Edwin shrugged. 'I guess sometimes we need to face the worst possible scenario to fully appreciate what it is we have. You're my best friend. Kara, your loyalty, your intelligence, your humour all ground me. I know we're going to have an incredible partnership.' He paused and those golden eyes melted her heart. 'Thank you for being my wife.'

Then, turning to their guests, he raised his glass and said, 'Please join me in toasting my incredible wife, Kara, Princess of Monrosa.'

She smiled and smiled and acknowledged with a nod all those who rose and toasted her, her cheeks hurting, confusion, disappointment she had no right to feel making her heart thud in her chest.

Friendship…partnership…all the right words to describe their relationship. Had anyone noticed the absence of any mention of love in all of that? Or was it just her?

Changed into a blue trouser suit and white plimsolls, Triona at her side, Kara did a double-take of the now deserted ballroom.

Walking out onto the dance floor where earlier they had danced together, that disturbing chemistry rising between them and causing his heart to thud wildly, Kara said to Edwin, 'Please tell me you didn't end the party early? My dad's side of the family will never forgive you. They don't think it's a proper wedding if they don't get to see sunrise.'

Not waiting to draw breath, she planted her hands on her hips, her jacket parting to reveal an ivory silk camisole tucked into her trousers, her gaze shooting between him and Triona. 'What's going on? Why did I need to change out of my wedding dress?' She lifted her feet. 'And why the plimsolls?'

Triona gave him a look that said this was all on him, muttering she needed some air, and slipped out to the terrace, closing the door behind her.

Kara's suspicious gaze took in the open-necked dark blue shirt and lightweight navy trousers he had changed into.

He needed to make this marriage work. And the only way he knew how to do that was by trying to recapture what they had before he'd ever suggested marriage—a light, fun friendship with laughter and adventure and no complications or expectations.

He followed in Triona's footsteps, coming to a stop by the terrace door. 'I have a surprise for you.'

Her hands dropped from her hips. She edged up onto her toes to try to get a better glimpse out onto the terrace.

He opened the door and stepped outside, gesturing for her to follow.

She squinted out into the darkness and then eyed him with a frown.

But her curiosity obviously got the better of her because she walked towards him with an expression that said this surprise had better be good.

The moment she stepped outside a cheer went up from the awaiting guests who were lining both sides of the walkway down to the waterfront. And, as planned, the guests activated their light sticks in sequence, so that two rows of blue lights flowed all the way from the terrace down to the sea.

Kara screamed, gasped, and finally, thankfully, laughed.

She allowed him to guide her down the cobbled walkway, the guests swaying in time to the band's rendition of Kara's favourite song, 'Sunset Love'.

Kara's hand tightened around his as they made their way down the path of goodwill and celebration of their union. He smiled at Kara's laughter, relieved that so far he had made the right call in planning this goodbye to their guests.

The walkway led them to the palace's private marina and their awaiting families.

Kara dropped her hand from his and stared at *Mistral*, the royal yacht, and its crew, all lined up dockside in order to welcome them aboard. 'Please tell me they're not waiting for us.'

'I did promise you a honeymoon.'

'You said you were too busy.'

'I changed my mind.'

She glanced at all those around them, gave a faint smile towards the crew, and, edging closer to him, whispered, 'You know I get seasick.'

He laughed and gestured to the thirty-three metre boat with its five staterooms. 'I defy even you to get sick aboard *Mistral.* A superyacht is a very different experience to being on a racing yacht. Trust me, you'll be fine, and it's only three days' sailing on the Med.'

She blanched. 'Three days!' She stepped closer to the marina's edge, frowning at the waves. 'Those waves look big…why the hell couldn't we just have gone to some nice hotel or beach? Not that we needed to go away in the first place.'

The sea was choppier than he would have liked, but there was no way he was going to worry her by admitting that. 'You won't feel much movement on board *Mistral.*'

For that he received a disbelieving scowl.

He stepped closer to her. 'I know just how stressful the past few weeks have been for you. You deserve time away, a break.' He held her gaze, his heart swelling with his affection for her, his throat catching. 'It's time we hung out together like we used to, away from the glare of the palace staff and the media.' His throat tightened even more. 'It's time we recaptured our friendship.'

She let out a shaky breath. 'You're right…things have got so confusing.' She swung away to berate Triona, Siza and her parents for keeping the honeymoon secret from her.

Luis was attempting to charm one of Kara's cousins, who rightly was having none of it, so he went over to where his father and Ivo were standing together, not a word passing between them.

His joining them didn't help matters and all three eyed each other warily.

'Best of luck in…' He grimaced, trying to remember where Ivo's next major competitive regatta was to be held. He should have made more time to talk with him.

Ivo studied him and then his father, as though waiting to see if his father knew where his next regatta was.

His father simply shrugged.

'Plovdiv,' Ivo finally answered in a hacked-off tone before he walked away from them.

Edwin eyed his father, who held his gaze unapologetically, a faint tic working in his jaw the only sign of any emotion. He turned away. This whole mess was his fault. He had turned his and Kara's lives upside down.

He went and waited for Kara to join him by the gangway.

She hugged her parents a brief goodbye, but with Triona and Siza she giggled and hung on to them for the longest time.

Why could he never be like that with people? What must it be like to be your true self? Not to feel apart and different?

As heir to the throne, he was always destined to be different. People looked at him differently. Behaved differently around him. People were more of everything around him—more nervous, more gushing, more reserved, more self-conscious. And he had known, for as long as he could remember, that he had to behave appropriately—an inner critic constantly telling him to be careful and proper. An inner critic that over the years had escalated to tight inner control in the aftermath of his mother's death, where he was able to shut himself off from feeling too much for other people.

Kara turned away from her friends.

Rolled her shoulders as though bracing herself.

He rocked back on his heels. A realisation side-sweeping him. With him, Kara *did* hold herself back. It was as though an invisible wall existed between them. Even when they kissed there was a slight reservation, a hesitancy that was right and normal and proper. But it was also the most vulnerable place in the world.

Mistral eased away from the marina wall. Their guests cheered and waved, their blue lights dancing in the air like fireflies.

An explosion filled the air.

Kara jolted and grabbed hold of Edwin.

Gold and purple light filled the air.

Edwin chuckled.

She slapped him on the arm. 'You could have warned me.'

He raised an amused eyebrow. 'Come on, we'll see the display better on the opposite side.' He led her across the upper deck of the yacht, explosions of colours dancing overhead, the gold and purple of Monrosa giving way to the blue and red of the Union flag, and for a while she forgot just how cross she was with Edwin.

But that all changed once they left the natural protection of the harbour and hit the swell.

The boat pitched.

She grabbed the rail. Oh, God, it was only going to get worse once they were really out in open sea.

'I can't believe you thought a sailing holiday would be my idea of fun.' The boat pitched again as they rounded a headland, the swell growing higher. Exhausted from trying not to let the emotion of the day get to her, terrified she was going to spend the night throwing up, she added, 'I thought you knew me better.'

Edwin considered her for a moment, clearly trying to understand where her anger had come from.

Well, good. He could have at least talked this through with her.

'You're scared. That's understandable.' His mouth tightened. 'But will you please just trust me on this?' With that he walked back across the deck and peered towards the building and street lights of the island, which were increasingly growing dimmer and dimmer.

Her anger deflated like a popped balloon. She felt herself redden. Now she just felt stupid.

Swallowing down her pride, she knew she had to do the right thing and show some gratitude. She went and stood next to him. 'How long have you been planning all of this?' she asked, pushing back the material of her suit jacket's lapel that had blown forward in the breeze. The suit was beautifully handcrafted, the silk lining soft against her skin. 'Who selected this suit? The shoes? Was it Princess Maria?'

His gaze trained out to sea, he answered, 'I did—it's that same shade as your eyes. The shoes were the most practical solution for our journey.' His tone was distracted.

He chose the suit? *Really?* A shiver ran down her spine. Here she was worrying about being seasick when in truth she really should be worried about the prospect of spending time alone with her new husband. He seemed to want it to be about them reconnecting as friends, which she was all up for. But what if they did something stupid like kiss again? Going away together, especially after last night, was like dancing with the devil. And it didn't help when he went and did something so cute and adorable and kind as select an outfit for her. One that he obviously had put thought and consideration into. Was he doing all of this just to keep her on-side? She winced at that thought, hating how cynical and wary she had become since Nick. God, she really did have trust issues. Staying well away from relationships really was the best thing for her.

She studied Edwin. What was he scanning the horizon for?

The engine of the yacht cut out. A whirring sound was followed by a splash. Was that the anchor being dropped?

Pointing in the direction of the silhouetted high cliff edges of Monrosa, Edwin said, 'This is where we disembark.'

Disembark? Already? They were miles away from land.

Squinting, she stared in the direction he had pointed in and realised a tiny dot of light was getting ever closer.

She followed Edwin down to the lower deck and then down to the platform at the rear of the boat.

That dot of light turned out to be Domenico and Lucas on board a small boat.

Pulling alongside, Lucas threw a rope to an awaiting crew member, who held the boat tight against the yacht's platform. Domenico held his hand out, gesturing for her to transfer across.

Memories of the blood-curdling heat that had assaulted her insides the time she had been seasick had her hesitate.

A wave hit, pulling the boat away from *Mistral*, a huge gap of black sea opening up just beyond her feet. She stepped back. She was going nowhere.

The crew member and Lucas brought the boat back alongside.

Edwin leapt over onto the boat and held his hand out to her.

'There's no way you're getting me on that inflatable.'

He gave her a bemused look. 'Rib—not an inflatable. And a rib that's used for military patrols worldwide, so it's more than up to the job of transferring us back to Monrosa. When have *you* ever walked with lead feet?'

They were going back to Monrosa? That was a good thing, wasn't it? Was all of this just a hoax? Had he pretended they were going on a honeymoon to avoid speculation as to why they hadn't? Was he playing mind-games with her? Dread knotted in her stomach. Nick had once pretended to be taking her on a trip to Paris, only to cancel it after they had had an argument. She had only learnt he had never even booked their flights when she had broken up with him.

Edwin reached his hand out even further. 'Come on, I'll take care of you. Trust me.'

She studied his hand, both boats rocking in the swell. She trusted him. Of course she did.

'Kara?'

His voice was baffled. He was her friend. She had to trust him. Her feet refused to budge. But he wasn't just her friend any more…he was her husband. And trusting him now took on a whole different perspective. Could she trust him while still protecting her heart, her sanity, her grip on reality?

Enough.

She had to focus on the end game—raising the profile of Young Adults Together and helping Edwin to the throne.

She was allowing herself to get caught up in the emotion and drama of the day again, caught up in the concept of going on honeymoon with her new husband—which didn't look as though it was going to happen anyway, so why was she being such a drama queen?

She grabbed hold of Edwin's hand and leapt, colliding with him, her chest bumping against his. He steadied her, one warm and solid hand on her waist, the other on her back. The heat of his body fused with her limbs. His hold on her tightened. Without thinking she responded by edging her hips against his. The heat of longing fired in her stomach.

He dipped his head, his eyes narrowing as he slowly and silently studied her.

Undone by his nearness, feeling vulnerable under his gaze, she pulled away and attempted to act as though he had no effect on her pulse, which was racing so hard she was struggling to think straight. It felt as though every cell in her body was turned on by him. 'Where should I sit?'

He pointed to a seat at the centre of the boat alongside the cockpit.

Edwin took control of the wheel. She had thought Lucas would resume that duty. He pulled away from *Mistral* at an incredibly slow speed. At this rate they wouldn't reach Monrosa until daybreak.

'You do know what you're doing, right?'

He grinned. 'It was part of my training.'

Got him! 'Your special-forces training, you mean.'

His grin widened and he eased the throttle forward, pulling the rib into a wide arc.

The boat soared over the water. The wind rushed against her, making it difficult to breathe. She gasped. And laughed. The rush of water beneath them, the speed, watching Edwin expertly handle the rib, was exhilarating.

In no time they were slowing as they approached a slipway in an isolated cove.

Two SUVs were waiting for them.

Domenico and Lucas went in one, she and Edwin in the other.

The unpaved road out of the cove was steep and narrow; only a SUV would be capable of accessing the slipway.

At the main road, instead of turning left back towards Monrosa City Edwin turned right. Domenico and Lucas followed behind them.

'Aren't we going back to the palace?'

Edwin threw her a confused look. 'I told you we were going on a honeymoon.'

'Oh, I thought…'

'That I was going back on my word?' He worked his jaw, clearly annoyed. Tense seconds passed, and he shot a look towards her, his expression a horrible mix of disappointment and irritation. But then, with a shrug of his shoulder, he smiled. 'Sorry, but you're stuck with me for three whole days. I'll try to make it as painless as possible for you.'

Forty minutes later, having followed a hairpin-bend-laden road up into the mountains, they passed through the gates of Edwin's family's mountain villa, the sentries on duty saluting.

So this was where they would honeymoon.

She laid her head against the headrest and gave an internal sigh. She was a mountain girl. Walking amongst the towering pines and eucalyptus trees, the only sound coming from the breeze swooping through the valleys, trickling streams, and hidden birds happy to share their voices with the world, restored her. Being surrounded by this landscape that had existed for millennia before her always pulled her up to a sharp stop, grounding her in the reminder of just how transient life was and to be grateful for every day she got to enjoy it. But this would be different. They would be staying in a royal residence with all of its reminders of protocol. What she wouldn't give not to have to be on her best behaviour, to not have to act as if they were a loved-up couple on their honeymoon.

On a turn in the road, the vast royal residence in the distance, Edwin shot off the lit road and onto a narrow lane she had never spotted before.

Studying the side mirror, she said, 'You need to stop—we've lost Domenico and Lucas.'

'That was the plan. We're going to be on our own for the next three days.'

On their own? That was what she had just been longing for. Why, then, did it fill her with terror rather than relief? 'Please tell me we aren't going camping.'

He shook his head. 'Why are you being so cranky?'

She gave an indignant huff. But then did a mental eye roll. He was right. She was being cranky...and crabby and grouchy. She hated this side of herself. But being around Edwin nowadays she just felt this defensive force field around herself and it just seemed natural to be surly.

She needed to snap out of it. She held up her hand, her fingers in the Girl Guide pledge position she had learnt years ago. 'I promise to try harder and not moan even when I wake from dreaming of drinking cocktails on some tropical beach, only to find myself in a bug-infested tent.'

He grinned. 'That's more like it—it's good to see the old Kara back: good-humoured with an undertone of sarcasm.'

She snorted.

Edwin's eyes twinkled, and his grin grew even wider. She grinned back, heat infusing her limbs.

They climbed even further up into the mountain. Kara opened her window, the trees of the forest zipping by, and a perturbing mix of fear and exhilaration filled her bones at not only their crazy speed but also at the prospect of being alone with Edwin for three whole days.

The road ended at a set of wooden gates.

Edwin zapped them open.

Beyond the gates the road dipped down in a curve that brought them to a circular driveway.

Edwin killed the engine.

A light shone over a solitary wooden door of a flat-roofed, metal-panelled structure.

'We're staying in a shed?'

He opened his door. 'Well, that promise didn't last long.'

She climbed out of the car and joined Edwin on the gravelled driveway. He pressed a button on his phone. The door popped open.

Inside, the shed was in darkness. Edwin gestured for her to step inside. She folded her arms and refused to budge. 'This isn't where you turn out to be a psycho husband who holds me captive against my will in a shed in an isolated forest, is it?'

He raised an eyebrow, his smile suddenly as sexy as hell. 'It can be arranged if that's a fantasy of yours.' A look of pure masculine heat she had never seen before entered his eyes, setting alight a wild longing in her belly. 'I'm sure there are some ropes in the shed.'

Something very carnal and dangerous melted inside her. She sprang towards the door and leapt inside.

A row of internal lights, domino-style, lit up down the length of the building.

She gasped.

This was no shed.

She walked further into the long and narrow interior, agog at the gorgeous ultra-modern open-plan space. The walls, with the exception of the narrow entrance, were made of huge floor-to-ceiling glass doors. The modern kitchen was made from pale wood, the counter tops the same poured light-grey concrete as the floors. In the living area, two sofas covered in duckling-yellow fabric surrounded a wood-burning stove.

Edwin opened up a row of doors that folded back to reveal decking made from the same wood as the kitchen.

Walking out onto the deck, running the entire length of the building, she said, 'I can't believe that I thought this was a shed! It's absolutely stunning.'

The building was stretched like a bridge between two rocky banks, a stream running beneath the house.

Before them, the forest tumbled down the mountain-side. Kara inhaled deeply, greedily sucking in the heavily pine-scented air.

'Do you like it?'

She turned at Edwin's question. She gestured around her and laughed. 'This is my idea of heaven. Of course I love it.'

'Good. It's my wedding present to you.'

Kara watched him turn away and walk inside, her mouth open.

She rushed after him as he walked towards the far end of the house, which they had not yet explored.

She caught up with him at a bedroom door. 'But all I got you was a set of cufflinks.'

He leant against the door frame. 'You're forgetting the *How To Be a Good Husband* guide that came with them.'

'I hope you took note of point five—"Let her know you realise how lucky you are to have her as your wife".'

'Duly noted. My legal team have the paperwork ready for you to sign to give you full ownership of Villa Kara.'

She swung her arms up into the air in horror. 'Villa Kara! Are you serious? You have to change that name and I can't accept a villa from you. This was never mentioned in the pre-nup. You know I don't want anything when we divorce.'

'You just said you love it here—as I had hoped you would.' He folded his arms. 'Are you saying you're refusing my wedding present to you?'

How did he manage to make it sound as though she was being thoroughly unreasonable and ungrateful? When it was he who was at fault here? 'It's way too generous, and what happens when we split up? I can hardly drive through your family's property to get here.'

'Why not?'

'Because it'll be as awkward as hell.'

His amused expression disappeared. He straightened from his relaxed leaning against the door frame. 'When we divorce…if we divorce—that's still your decision to make—you'll still be an important part of my life.'

She sagged against the opposite wall, suddenly feeling exhausted. She dipped her head, uncertainty and fear sweeping through her, causing her heart to contract as though it was under attack. She should let this go. She knew she should. Just continue pretending they'd resume life as before, pretending their friendship was not already damaged by this whole experience. 'Do you really think we will be able to part so amicably—without any hurt or complications?'

Those golden eyes considered her for long silent seconds. She resisted the urge to cry, to laugh. How had she ended up in the position where she was being torn between the desire to kiss this man and to punch him for not feeling the same confusion and turmoil as she did? Had their kisses had any emotional impact on him?

'It's up to us to make sure we part amicably.' With that he turned and walked into the bedroom.

Like the living area it had floor-to-ceiling windows overlooking the forest. Edwin went and opened one of the two doors either side of the king-size bed, draped in crisp white cotton linen and accented with a green throw and cushions. 'This is your dressing room—your bathroom is on the other side. Your luggage was brought here earlier.'

It was disconcerting to see the faded black jeans she had bought in a shop in Brighton hanging from the rail, a solid crease line running the length of both legs showing that someone had carefully ironed them.

Her gaze moved to the bed. And then back to Edwin.

He cleared his throat. 'My bedroom is across the corridor.'

So they wouldn't be sleeping in the same bed on their wedding night after all. It made sense and would eliminate any awkwardness. Why, then, did it feel like a rejection?

She breathed in deeply. Stepped back to make space for him to leave. Smiled. 'It's been a long day—I need a shower and sleep. A lot of sleep. I'm exhausted. Worn out.'

She stopped. He had probably got the point the first time.

He nodded and moved towards the door.

She breathed in hard when he passed her. Was about to exhale, but he came to a stop a footstep beyond her. He turned. 'Please tell me you'll accept Villa Kara? It's important to me.'

Her entire body tingled from having him stand so

close by, by the appeal of his gaze that was utterly focused and determined. 'Why?'

'Because it will mean that you'll still want to be in my life.'

She closed her eyes, uncertainty, confusion, sheer bewilderment over the beautiful intention of his words clashing with her fears for the future of their relationship.

She opened her eyes. 'The first thing I'm going to do is change its name—Villa Kara is one hundred per cent cringe.'

CHAPTER NINE

SITTING ON THE stone ledge, her feet dangling in the stream, Kara tossed her head back to catch the rays of sunlight breaking through the overhead tree canopy. Her denim cut-offs suited her perfectly and her white halter-neck… well, as much as he hated to admit it, it was troublingly sexy. It was just a piece of simple white cotton after all, but the way it pulled on her chest, its cut exposing all but a few inches of her shoulders, got to him in a way it shouldn't.

The sun caught the platinum shades in her hair, the ends brushing against the dusty surface of the ledge.

How was he going to cope with sharing a bed with her when back in the city? When they returned to the reality of their lives away from this oasis of escape?

They had spent three days trekking in the mountains by day, cooking meals together and playing poker at night, Kara cheekily refusing to admit she tried to cheat every single time. Three days of conversation and teasing. Three days of pretending she wasn't getting under his skin. Yesterday he had become obsessed at the idea of undoing the pearl buttons of the blue embroidered blouse she had been wearing and had even burnt himself when distracted as they had been preparing dinner, scorching the tip of his finger on a hot pan. Three days of resisting the urge to kiss her, of averting his gaze from her bottom when she trekked ahead of him. Three days of resisting the urge to hunker down to retie her laces, which she never knotted properly, knowing that if he knelt before her his fingers would trail against the now lightly tanned skin of her legs, trace over the small brown birthmark at the back of her right knee. Three days of his heart dancing to hear her laughter, to see her blue eyes widen in amazement when a red kite swooped close to where they had been picnicking, her hand reaching for his. Three days of quickly ending their celebratory hugs when they reached the summit of their climbs.

And two nights of her closing her bedroom door to him.

Two nights of sitting out on the terrace staring at the stars, unable to sleep, listening to a nightjar filling the air with its constant song.

Two nights of journeying through that labyrinth of hopes and fears and thoughts in the middle of the night, of wondering if the chemistry, those fleeting looks that electrified him, were all in his imagination or if she bore their curse too.

Dio! To think that a week ago he had actually considered cancelling his tour to Asia. Now it was his lifeline. In two days' time they would make their first appearance together as a married couple when they attended the opening of a new conservation centre in Monrosa's protected wetlands, named in honour of his mother. And the day after, he would leave for Asia. Ten days away would clear his head, give him the space to get back on track with this marriage of convenience.

They had one more night alone before they returned to the city. He *had* to continue keeping his distance from her.

He dropped the picnic blanket to the ground. Her eyes popped open and she smiled. 'Hi.'

He nodded back, unfurling a picnic blanket beside her, trying to steady his pulse. When she was so obviously delighted to see him it did crazy things to his heart.

Kara edged onto the blanket and he sat beside her, dipping his own bare feet into the stream. Maybe the icy water would cool the heat in his body.

Lifting her feet from the water, she wriggled her toes. 'You'll be glad to hear my feet are no longer aching.'

Her toes were long, her feet narrow with a delicate arch. She lifted her feet even higher, circling them. Her ankles were slim, her calf muscles toned.

What would it be like to have her legs wrapped around his?

He grabbed the champagne bottle from the basket, popped it open. He passed her a glass.

She sighed. 'This is heaven.'

For the next half an hour they drank the champagne and nibbled on the fresh bread they had baked together that morning, using an olive-oil-based recipe Kara swore by. The sun was gentle, the birdsong and sound of the water pressing over the boulders in the stream hypnotic. A lazy sense of calm had his body grow increasingly heavy, his thoughts drowsy.

Champagne finished, Kara lay back on the blanket with a sigh and he joined her, the hard stone beneath him a welcome solidness. They lay with their feet side by side, drying them on the edge of the rock ledge.

Kara swayed her bent knees side to side, her hands on her belly, her gaze in his direction, a wide smile on her mouth. 'I think the champagne has gone to my head.'

'Mine too,' he admitted. 'I guess the long trek and lack of lunch probably didn't help.'

Above them a buzzard soared in the thermals.

His heart rate upped a gear. Without looking he knew Kara was staring at him. He closed his eyes. He was *not* going to look in her direction. He should make some excuse and leave.

'I'm very jealous of your long eyelashes, you know.'

He opened his eyes and turned to her. Her eyes held a soft, dewy tone. Her lips glistened as though the champagne had seeped into them. Gentle heat infused her cheeks.

Her hand shifted off her belly and onto the blanket between them. 'I'll miss you when you're away.'

He sucked in some air. *Dio!* He really should head back to the villa. 'And I'll miss you.'

Why had he said that? Because it was true.

Qualify it... Don't go down a road that will be hard to come back from.

'Touring can be boring—it would be nice to have you there for company.'

She looked away from him but not before he saw the disappointment that dispatched her smile.

She bit her lip for a moment before saying, 'And I have the Pink Heart's charity ball to attend. It will be my first official duty on my own.' She looked back at him, gave a shrug. 'I'll miss having your guidance.'

'I've asked Princess Maria to travel with you to the ball and sit at the same table.'

She gave a fleeting smile. 'Thank you.'

His hand found hers on the blanket.

Her eyes widened. He held his breath, waiting for her reaction. Her fingers threaded through his.

A question appeared in her gaze.

'I guess it's understandable that things might get a

little muddled between us at the start of the marriage,' he said.

'Muddled?'

'The emotion of the wedding, being alone, neither of us having been in a relationship for a long time…our hormones, our feelings, are getting muddled up.'

She nodded eagerly. 'And the champagne isn't helping either.'

Why is this...this...? Dio! *Call it what it is. Why is this flirting so damn enjoyable?*

He cleared his throat, his eyes glued to her mouth, memories of what it was like to kiss her heading straight to his groin. 'I want to kiss you.'

She shifted onto her side. 'Good.'

He released her hand. Moved onto his side too, edged up to her. Ran his hand through her hair. It was warm. As was her cotton top. Even the denim of her shorts held the heat of the day. He placed his hand on her bottom. Pulled her even closer. Found her mouth with a groan.

They kept it soft and exploratory for the whole of ten seconds.

Then her hand clasped against his skull, her mouth opening for him.

He rolled onto his back, taking her with him. And saw stars when her body rocked against his. He held tight, his arms on her back, one hand cupping her bottom, the other a sharp shoulder blade, wanting to meld her to him.

Within a minute things were seriously getting out of control. Kara was moaning against his mouth, her legs twisted around his. Her chest pressed against his was the sweetest, most dangerous, most tempting thing that had ever entered his life.

His thumb stroked the side of her breast. Her body shuddered.

Her mouth shifted away from his and began to trail down his throat, her lips scorching the skin beneath his open-neck T-shirt.

Her hands trailed even further south.

Pleasure blasted through him. With a groan he pulled her back up towards him, cradling her face in his hands. 'We can't.'

Her expression shifted from unseeing desire to frustration to disappointment and finally acceptance on a long inhale of breath.

She rolled off him.

He held her hand. 'Are you okay?'

'In a few minutes I will be.' She rolled her eyes. 'These blasted hormones—they have a lot to answer for.'

He sat up, allowed his blood pressure to settle and stood up.

He yanked off his T-shirt and then his shorts.

Kara gawked at him, a hand covering her mouth.

He spun around and jumped into the deep pool of water beyond a large boulder, a spray soaring upwards as he plunged beneath the cold water.

Even submerged, he heard Kara's shriek.

CHAPTER TEN

THE CENTRAL COURTYARD of the Senator Hotel had been transformed into a Viennese ballroom. Chandeliers hung from invisible wires, and a full orchestra played on the temporary stage. Dancing with Javier Ventosa, a paediatrician consultant at Monrosa's University Hospital, Kara tried to focus on her steps and turns, her head spinning at the quick rotations, only too aware Princess Maria was following her every move, just as she had done all week when she had supervised Kara's dance lessons.

Mastering the steps of the Viennese waltz had been excruciatingly slow, she had tripped over her dance teacher, Horacio, more times than she could count and she had used the feeble excuse that she was more of a rugby girl to explain to Princess Maria her lack of progress when in truth it was her nephew who had stolen her concentration away.

They had been so close to making love. And a week on, her focus was still shot and a throb of unfulfilled lust was making her rubber-boned. A week on and she still couldn't strip him from her mind, that image of him yanking off his top and shorts and plunging into the stream, soaking her in the process, playing on a constant loop. He had emerged all wet, glistening muscle, frustration etched on his face.

In silence he had walked away from her and she had collapsed back onto the ledge, weak with the need for more.

Dinner that night had been tense. Their conversation had been halting and awkward and full of things unsaid.

When he had left for Vietnam, his hug goodbye had been brief and she had watched him get into the car taking him to the airport and had winced at the relief that had swept over his expression.

He had wanted to get away.

Mortified by his relief, she had thrown herself into work, into settling into her new life in Monrosa, taken dance lessons in advance of tonight, and spent her evenings walking the interior of the palace and grounds, trying to familiarise herself with her new home.

A few times she had considered travelling to Villa Kara, driven by the need to find some antidote to the constant confusion settling into her bones. Confusion driven by his infrequent calls to her, which were full of facts but absent of any real truth between them.

The mountains usually brought her peace and in the private isolation of Villa Kara she might have been able to eke out some calmness. But memories of their stay there had kept her away. Memories of how Edwin had looked every morning when she had opened her bedroom door to find him freshly showered and preparing breakfast in the kitchen, his good-morning smile managing to ignite a furnace of happiness inside of her. Memories of his deep laughter when she had got stuck when rock climbing, but then his calm words of encouragement in guiding her back down.

Trying to create a new life in a new country, the pressures of royal life, trying to map out precisely how she was going to turn Young Adults Together into an effective global charity, were all making her vulnerable… and if her past history was anything to go by, when she was stressed and confused she was prone to making bad decisions. Very bad decisions. Decisions like sleeping with Edwin even though it would torpedo any hopes of their maintaining their friendship when this was all over. Some people managed to remain friends with their exes but there was no way she could do it. She simply didn't have the emotional toughness for it. She would find it impossible not to feel exposed and heart-sore knowing what once had been there.

See, this was why she wasn't cut out for relationships—she just became an emotional mess when embroiled in them. She was better off in the safety of singledom. She needed time to adjust to her new reality. Time to let the emotional fever inflamed by what the media had called a fairy-tale wedding ceremony and the promises they had made in public, die away.

The music came to a stop.

Javier bowed his thanks to her for accepting his invitation to dance. He was an incredibly attractive man… and single too. But not one cell in her body seemed capable of responding to his dark looks and charming smile.

She accepted his hand and offer to escort her back to her table.

But then she dropped his hand, the hairs on the back of her neck standing to attention.

Javier stepped back and bowed to someone behind her.

And backed away.

A dovecote-full of fluttering exploded in her stomach.

'I never knew my wife could dance so well.'

Longing pure and unadulterated flushed through her body at his low whisper.

She swung around. She wanted to throw herself into his arms but caught herself in time.

Instead she smiled at him goofily, heat blasting her cheeks. 'You're home.'

All through her dance with Javier, whom he had first met when opening the new children's wing of MUH, Edwin had stayed in the shadows of the courtyard watching Kara as she glided across the floor in Javier's arms. Lust and jealousy had him barely clinging to his sanity. He had wanted to march onto the dance floor and interrupt the dance midway, demand the right to dance with his wife.

His wife. His beautiful wife. *Dio!* Her ballgown was the sexiest thing he had ever seen. It was a dress that summed up her personality—the pale blue, close to silver tulle skirt overlaid with floral appliqué, cute and lovely just as she was, the plunging front and back the hidden side of her that was all heat and passion.

'You're home.'

Had words ever seemed so sweet, so right, so layered with danger?

He searched for some light-hearted response, but the delight shining in Kara's eyes stole every word away.

He held out his hand and invited her to dance with him.

Around them, other couples who had already begun to circle the dance floor smiled fondly at their reunion.

She stepped into his arms. He longed to be able to pull her close, anchor her to him, but the waltz demanded an exasperating distance be kept between their bodies.

'Why are you home early?' she asked.

'There's still a lot of work that has to be done in preparation for my succession.'

And I missed you.

'How was Hanoi?'

'Hot and chaotic but very beautiful. I loved it there.'

He *had* loved Hanoi, but he had felt flat there. He had longed to have Kara by his side, experiencing the infectious chaos of the city and the stunning beauty of the surrounding countryside. He had missed her laughter, the appraising sweep of her blue gaze, the way his body tingled when she was in the same room. *Dio*, he was so sick of pretending his feelings for Kara had not changed, when they had. She was no longer just a friend. She was his wife. Lying in his hotel bedroom two nights ago, he had finally admitted to himself that he wanted her. As a husband wanted a wife. He wanted to sleep with her, mouth against mouth, breath against breath, skin against skin.

The pretending had to stop.

'I missed you,' he said.

Her gaze shot up to meet his. She frowned as though she was trying to decipher the true meaning of his words.

Her lips parted. Those glorious soft lips… Thoughts of what they were capable of had tormented his dreams for the past week.

The music came to an end. Instead of stepping back, Kara touched her fingers against the skin above his shirt collar, an intimate move that had relief and raw need buckling his knees. 'I missed you too.'

He gathered her closer. Placed a kiss on her neck, just below her ear.

They stayed on the dance floor until the orchestra played the final song of the night. They said their goodbyes to the event organisers and he led her out of the private exit, where Álvaro and Marco, their assigned protection officers, were waiting for them. Domenico and Lucas had made a poor attempt at disguising their delight when he had announced he was cutting his trip short. Their eagerness to get home to their families had sent his head into a spin. Why was he jealous of something he didn't want?

He had told them to take the next three days off work.

They drove in silence through the streets of Monrosa. Tourists and locals, leaving the restaurants of the old town, stopped to stare as the outriders passed them by, grabbing their phones to snatch a photo as their SUV driven by Álvaro swept past.

He held Kara's hand, her fingers clasping his tight.

Back at their apartment, he instructed both Simone his valet and Cecilia, Kara's dresser, who were awaiting their return, that their services weren't needed.

He brought her into the drawing room, knowing he was at a fork in the road that was his life.

He gestured towards the drinks cabinet but Kara shook her head.

This would be their first night of needing to share a bed.

The decisions he would take, *they* would take, in the next few minutes could alter their lives for ever.

But they were both adults. Capable of handling uncharted territory.

He cleared his throat. Lost for words.

Kara touched her hand to her breastbone, giving him an uncertain and fleeting smile.

'Tonight…' he faltered.

She moved forward from where she had been balancing her fingertips against the side table filled with gold and silver framed family photographs towards the marble fireplace. 'Yes?'

There was a new framed photograph on the side table. He went and lifted the heavy silver frame. It was a signed photograph from their wedding photographer, Patrizia

Mauro, of them waving to the crowd as they had emerged from the cathedral. Kara's eyes were sparkling. The perfect image of a bride overcome with emotion. He cleared his throat again. 'Tonight…we'll be sharing a bed.'

Kara inhaled deeply. 'Yes.'

He winced at the dread in her voice. 'I can sleep on the floor…'

'No! Of course not.'

It really was time for the pretending to stop. He bunched his hands.

But would the truth destroy everything?

'If we sleep in the same bed…'

He lowered the frame to the table, catching a glimpse of his parents' wedding photograph. They had had a good marriage despite its having been arranged. Could Kara and he come to some sort of arrangement that would work for them?

'I'm attracted to you and I've missed you. I want to kiss you again. And I'd prefer for it not to stop there.' Unsteadied by his admission, he paused. Had he just made the biggest, most embarrassing blunder of his life?

He waited for Kara to say something, but instead she walked past him and out into the corridor.

He followed her, unsure what was happening.

In their bedroom, she stood at the near edge of the bed, her back to him. 'Cecilia was going to help me undress, so I'll need you to unbutton my gown for me.'

A lick of desire travelled the length of his body at the huskiness of her voice. He fumbled with the button holding the material tight to her waist, his fingers beating like nervous bats against her lower back. The button, once he got his fingers under control, gave way easily. He shifted his head down to her ear. 'I'm guessing you could have easily undone that yourself.'

She shivered, her neck tilting away from his breath. 'Yes, but there would have been no fun in that, would there?'

He touched a finger to her spine. She arched her back.

'I've spent the entire week away thinking about you.'

She twisted her head. Her eyes, even in the faint light cast by the single lamp in the corner, glittered. 'In a good way, I hope.'

'I'm afraid not.' He liked her groaned response. A lot. His fingertip bumped over the knots of her spine and then his whole hand fanned out to sweep across the edge of her shoulder blade, his skin tingling at the soft warmth of her body.

He edged the material of her dress off her shoulders. She drew her head back and whispered, 'Tell me what you've been thinking.'

He touched his lips to her collarbone. 'Our kiss, the pattern of your ribs,' he edged closer to her neck, he nipped her skin between his teeth, chuckled to hear her moan, 'your sighs of pleasure when I touch somewhere tender.'

She turned to him, her hands holding the material of her dress from falling down. Fire and energy radiated from her. 'Tell me what you want.'

'I want to make love to you.'

She nodded. Dropped her hands. Her dress fell to the floor.

She stood before him, naked except for pale blue panties.

He drew in a breath. She was more beautiful than he had ever imagined.

She arched her back and, reaching up, released her hair from its coil. It tumbled down over her shoulders.

He undid his bow tie. Pointed to the buttons of his dress shirt. 'Your turn.'

CHAPTER ELEVEN

CRUSHED SHEETS. Aching and deliciously heavy bones.

Kara grinned and twisted onto her side. Sleep called to her, but just out of reach gorgeous memories wound their way through her dazed brain.

She sighed.

'Your sighs of pleasure when I touch somewhere tender...'

Her eyes shot open. The room was in darkness. Water was running in the bathroom.

She curled the top sheet over her head and groaned.

What had she done?

Had she really done those things with Edwin? She flung the sheet back, struggling for air.

Everything was going to be okay.

This was still a marriage of convenience. Their relationship might have shifted off centre from friendship but the roller coaster of emotions, the power play, the constant threat of heartache that came with a full-blown relationship wouldn't apply to them.

The water was switched off. Shadows moved on the white marble floor of the bathroom.

She sat up in the bed, yanking the sheet up to her shoulders. Would she have time to dash into the dressing room? No! She couldn't bear the thought of him seeing her naked.

Why didn't you care last night, when it mattered? Because you were lost to the joy of seeing him again? Lost in the intimacy of his words, his touch? Lost to the chemistry that experiencing the powerful act of marrying had unleashed on you?

She had to play it cool. Not freak out. Not overthink all of this.

The bathroom door swung fully open.

Edwin stood there, a towel tight on his narrow hips, beads of moisture on his chest.

He gave her a devastating, satisfied smile that slowly morphed into a tender, almost bashful grin. He tilted his head, ran a towel over his hair and walked towards the bed. 'Good morning, my lovely wife.'

A storm of panic passed through her.

'We made a mistake.'

His smile evaporated.

'What?'

His hair was all tousled and sexy. But his expression was one hundred per cent perplexed.

She shivered despite the fact that her insides were scorching, churning chaos.

'We shouldn't have slept together.'

He flicked a hand over his hair, fixing it into position, his mouth tightening. 'Why?'

She didn't know why. She just knew she was drowning in panic. What was the matter with her? Why was she saying these things? Her panic rose like a tide that would never recede. 'You know why. It's just going to make our divorce more complicated.'

He flung the towel towards the bathroom. It hit the door frame and smacked onto the wooden floor of the bedroom. 'Are you saying you regret sleeping with me?'

She closed her eyes. 'No.'

'So what are you saying?'

Put some clothes on. I can't think straight, remembering how my hands, my lips, touched every inch of you. How I refused to stop even when you begged me to. I needed to know every inch of you. I wanted to know you... I've spent a decade wanting to know you. I've spent a decade wanting to love you.

Unable to breathe, she blinked.

I love you. Oh, God, I love you. This can't be happening. I'm messing everything up. And if you find out I'll just want to die. Will you feel sorry for me? Will you find excuses to walk away? Or will you, like Nick, use it against me?

She lifted the sheet even higher, gathering the edges around her neck. 'Don't you think it was a mistake?'

His mouth tightened even more. He turned away, grabbed the towel from the floor, disappeared into the bathroom for a moment, returned and then went into his dressing room.

An agonising time later he emerged, flicked on her bedside lamp and studied her. He had changed into a dark grey suit, silver tie and white shirt. Brooding and hacked off.

He knows! Her cheeks flamed. 'I'm sorry.'

His mouth tightened. And then with a sigh he sat down on the bed beside her.

She wanted to leap out of the bed, escape from him, but she was naked, and she and her shredded dignity couldn't handle the thought of him analysing every imperfection of her body as she wobbled towards the bathroom.

He dipped his head, his hand moved as though to touch her leg beneath the sheet but he grabbed it back. They had made love endless times during the night, drunk on physical release. Drunk on whispered words of discovery, of tenderness between two people who knew each other but whose souls, whose secret internal selves were a mystery they were just discovering.

He looked back up, his expression closed. 'Last night wasn't a mistake. We're attracted to one another.' He paused and shrugged as though that fact was of little significance. 'These things happen when two people are in close proximity. Let's keep it in perspective. It was one night.' He stood up, his expression emotionless. 'It doesn't have to happen again.'

She faked a smile, while her heart was on the floor. 'I guess we got it out of our systems.'

He shrugged again, and, taking his phone from his pocket, he checked the screen and frowned. 'I have a cabinet meeting I need to attend.'

Halfway towards the bedroom door, he turned around. 'Will you be okay?'

She heard the concern in his voice. She nodded. 'Of course.'

He left the room and she closed her eyes, curling onto her side, inhaling his scent on the sheets.

She was in love with him. She was in love with her husband.

She closed her eyes, hating the vulnerability of that. Hating that it weakened her, made her susceptible to so much pain and humiliation and disappointment.

She jerked the sheet back, sprang out of the bed and in the bathroom switched on the shower. Her diary was full for the day. If Edwin could walk away from last night so easily, then she sure as hell was going to do the same thing. How many times had she seen her dad reach out to her mum, only to be rejected and humiliated? How many times had she tried to please Nick, only to encounter a snide comment or whatever mind game he had decided to indulge in that day?

She was not going to humiliate herself. She was going to behave with dignity and pride both within this marriage and when it was time for them to separate.

And just maybe, with the passage of time and aided by Edwin's interpretation of last night as having been of no particular consequence, she might be able to stuff her feelings for him so deep inside of her, even she would be able to disregard them.

Edwin's father glared at the organisation chart he had just distributed to the cabinet so intently Edwin wouldn't have been surprised if it spontaneously combusted.

'These changes aren't necessary. You're overcomplicating things. Why on earth do we need a social-media team, a technology minister?' His voice growing ever louder, his father added, 'A diversity and equality minister? What on earth will *his* contribution be?'

'*Her* contribution, you mean. I have already selected a candidate for the role—Sofia Dati, Professor of Equality Studies at Monrosa University.'

Pausing, he studied the cabinet he was inheriting from his father, the majority of whom were men who had been in their roles for far too long.

'It's my intention to reshuffle this cabinet too. Reassign roles. Change the nature of each department's responsibilities to reflect the challenges we face as a country—our need to be more responsive and responsible to the environment, the changing diversity of our population and the need for a more advanced communication infrastructure that will attract even more companies to our business hubs.'

His patience thin, his ability to concentrate even thinner, he cut across his father before he could utter a word of objection, 'We've covered enough ground for today. I'm calling an end to this cabinet session.'

The ministers were regarding him with a variety of expressions from nervous to aghast and outraged. He couldn't afford to alienate them, not with their experience and influence within the country, which he would need in the coming months. He had to bring them with him on this journey of change, even if it meant dragging some of them kicking and screaming into the twenty-first century. 'I will meet with each of you individually to discuss aligning your experience and interests with the new structure. Change can be daunting, but we have to embrace it to ensure we are meeting the needs of our people. We have an exciting future ahead of us.'

At least a few of those around the table smiled at his words—albeit nervously.

He left the cabinet room, his footsteps the only sound. Even his father seemed to have been stunned into silence.

He walked in the direction of his offices. He had a call with the Swedish Trade Minister in an hour. Then a meeting with his own Finance Minister and his team, where discussions on budget reallocations would undoubtedly get heated. A meeting after that with the succession-ceremony logistics team.

He needed to remain focused and present. And not give in to the disbelief pounding through him.

He entered his outer offices, Victor's team all turning in his direction. Maribel, his travel coordinator, stood up, holding a pile of documentation in her grasp.

He couldn't do this. He couldn't discuss his trip next month to Washington.

He backed out of the room.

Out in the corridor he flung open the nearest door into the gardens.

He bolted down the terraces, ignoring the curious glances from the gardening team, until he came to the waterfront.

He sucked in air greedily but the tightness in his chest refused to give.

He cursed, the thin layer of denial that had got him through the cabinet meeting melting. To be replaced by the sharp kick of shame.

He had let himself down. He had let his country down. And, most importantly of all, he had let Kara down. She had agreed to their marriage in good faith. She hadn't signed up for him to seduce her.

No wonder she had immediately regretted it, considered it a mistake.

What had he expected? That she would have been happy with the fantasy he had imagined in the shower this morning of them sleeping in the same bed every night and fulfilling each other's needs?

He had walked out of the bathroom intending to wake Kara by kissing the length of her spine, and instead had faced her bruised eyes and horrified expression.

Maybe he should be grateful that at least one of them was thinking straight and saw it for the mistake that it was rather than feeling as though someone had punctured his ego and kicked it down the street like a rusty old can.

He had to make this right. Do the correct thing after a night of making the wrong decision over and over again.

He found her in her office, staring out of the window towards the internal courtyard.

Was she thinking of their engagement announcement out there? Their first kiss?

He called out her name.

She startled and whipped around. Wearing wide-legged pink trousers and a white blouse, her hair tied back in a ponytail, the crispness of her appearance was in sharp contrast to the tiredness in her eyes.

He worked his jaw, hating the unease between them. 'We can separate.'

Her head jerked back. 'Is that what you want?'

No, what I want is to kiss you, to bring you back to my bed and lose myself in you like I did last night. I want to go back in time to when our relationship was easy and straight forward. When I hadn't been pulled under into a world of chaos by the chemistry that our first kiss, out there in that courtyard, unleashed.

'What I want isn't of importance.'

Kara's expression tightened. 'I asked you a question Edwin, do you want to separate?'

'If it will make you happier.'

She folded her arms. 'It was a yes or no question.'

He cleared his throat, frustration bubbling up inside of him. Why was she making this so hard? He should lie, make all of this easier. But the least she deserved was his honesty. 'No I don't want us to separate but after last night—'

'Why?'

He swallowed and blurted out, 'Because I want to somehow make this right, and if we separate now it probably won't ever be right between us again.'

She winced and on a long sigh she considered him. Her eyes were so terribly sad.

He had really got this all so wrong.

'What do you mean by "make this right"?'

'I want things to go back to where they were, when we were friends.'

Seconds passed. She studied him with a perplexed

expression. She went and stared down to an open diary on her desk. 'I have a teleconference call in ten minutes with a Greek mental health charity who are interested in rolling out the Young Adults Together model as part of their work.' Her gaze swept up to meet his, her expression cool. 'I'd like to think we are both mature enough to put the importance of our work before any regrets.'

CHAPTER TWELVE

THE SCRAPE OF a door handle turning. Silence. Eyes closed, she waited for the mattress to compress. But there was only a stillness. She opened her eyes. The bed beside her was empty. She darted a look at the door, listened for a sound from the bathroom. Nothing. Had she imagined the door opening?

Her hand moved out, patting the cool sheets, the vast emptiness.

Where was he?

Disorientated but knowing it was some time in the early hours of the morning, she grappled to turn on the bedside lamp. Then fumbled for her phone in the bedside locker drawer.

Her hands shook. He had *never* not come to bed in the two weeks since they'd slept together.

She typed out a message.

Where are you?

Waiting, desperate for the phone to ping, she imagined him in an accident. Had he gone out on his motorbike? What if he was with another woman? No. He wouldn't do that.

Her phone pinged. She jolted, the chime an invasion of the silence of the room.

I'm in my office.

She hurled the phone across the bed. The bed where they had explored each other's bodies. She sprang off the mattress and, pulling on her dressing gown, she bolted out of the bedroom and across the corridor.

Her dress, on a silk padded clothes hanger, hung from the dark wood freestanding mirror of her old bedroom, which nowadays functioned as her hair and make-up room. Later this morning a team would once again magically transform her from Kara Duffy to Her Serene Highness, Princess of Monrosa.

Transform her on the outside. Inside she knew she was a fraud. Pretending to be a princess. Acting out, in an ever so careful and measured way her love and devotion for her new husband, desperately hiding the truth of her real, visceral love for him. Especially from him.

And today was what it was all about. His enthronement. The first day he would reign as Monarch of Monrosa.

She eyed her dress for the ceremony again. It was a dress that simply was. It made no demands. No statement. Below-the-knee length with cap sleeves, the ivory cotton tweed shot with threads of gold, it was elegant and understated. It conformed. It was a grown-up's dress in the serious world of power and politics and duty and service.

It represented everything she had to become.

She touched the soft tweed, tiredness washing over her. She should go back to bed. Today was going to be exhausting with both the enthronement and the celebration ball afterwards to attend. An entire day of public scrutiny where she had to act the dutiful and proud wife and hide her constant heartache, her real, authentic, frantic, soul-destroying love for her husband.

She turned, her steps immediately faltering.

Edwin was standing at the door.

She pulled the lace edges of her dressing gown together, feeling exposed in her nightwear while Edwin was dressed in black trousers and a lightweight black cashmere jumper. Gorgeous in a tired and crumpled way.

For a nanosecond she felt tenderness for him. She wanted to hold his hand and lead him to their bed. Hold him while he slept.

But then a wave of anger, of fear, of raw vulnerability swept through her. 'If you decide not to come home, at least have the courtesy to tell me.'

He blinked at her fury. 'We need to talk.'

He wasn't only exhausted, he was also nervous. Was he about to end their marriage? Their friendship? Was he too worn out by the pretence of their marriage?

She lifted her chin. Determined to be dignified. She would *never* let him even glimpse her devastation.

He held up the ivory sheet of paper in his hand, the crown's gold insignia on the top. 'My enthronement pledge. I'd like to read it to you.'

Where was this conversation going? She wanted to say no. She was in no mood to talk about his enthronement but, seeing how his hand trembled as he held out the heavy page towards her, appealing for her to say yes, she nodded.

'I do here solemnly swear to govern the people of Monrosa in accordance with the laws and customs of our country. I promise to rule with fairness and integrity, serving to the best of my ability, always with the utmost honesty.'

With a sigh he lowered the paper. 'With the utmost honesty.' He grimaced and inhaled another breath as though starved of oxygen. 'How can I promise to serve with honesty when I'm not honest with either you or myself?'

His voice was husky, as though it was taking a huge effort even for him to speak.

She swallowed hard, her fingernails biting into her closed fists. It was all over, then.

She moved towards the door, her gaze focused on the dark corridor behind him. The media would camp outside her Brighton apartment. 'I need to call my dad.'

His hand reached out as she neared him. 'It's five in the morning.'

She pulled her arm away so that he couldn't touch her. 'I can slip out of Monrosa before everyone wakes. We can go to my Aunt Nina's house—it's in the middle of nowhere. The media will have a hard time tracking me down there.'

His hand shot further out, blocking her from leaving the room. 'Hold on. Why would you go and stay with your aunt?'

Remain dignified. Don't cry, don't plead. Don't think you can change his mind. Don't do any of the things that stripped Dad of his pride and self-worth.

'You can say I'm ill...or whatever excuse you want to use for me not attending the enthronement. I'm guessing there's nothing your father can do once you've acceded to the throne.'

Edwin stood squarely in front of her. Pale and horrified. 'You're leaving?'

She winced at the distress in his whisper, her threatening tears turning to ones of pure confusion and anger. 'Isn't that what you want?'

He stepped back, and then strode into the room, raking a hand through his hair. 'Of course I don't want you to leave. *Dio*, Kara!' His voice was rising all of the time, his horror replaced by dismay. 'I have told you time and time again that I would never want to separate from you. Why won't you believe me?'

'Why won't I believe you? Oh, give me a break, Edwin. We both know you're only in this marriage to succeed to the throne.' She threw her hands up into the air.

Stop it. You said you wanted to leave with dignity.

Well, I don't care now. I want to lash out. I want to be angry. I'm so fed up with pretending and being nice. I'm too upset and heartbroken to shut up.

'We both know it makes you deeply uncomfortable—we barely speak, you can't bear to look at me and at night you turn your back on me.'

Turning away, she ran into their bedroom and then into her dressing room next to it. She flung back the sliding door of the wardrobe where her weekend bag was stored, wincing at the sight of her wedding dress, which was being stored there temporarily. The national museum wanted it for a special display to celebrate their wedding. They wouldn't now.

'It's not the marriage that's the problem, it's me.'

The bitterest, most cynical laugh she had ever made erupted from deep inside of her. She whirled around to face him. 'Oh, please—not the *It's not you, it's me* line.'

Why was he looking so upset? He had no right to be. She grabbed some T-shirts and bundled them into her weekend bag, burning humiliation torching her skin. She was failing everyone. Failing the charity. Failing Michael's memory. Failing all of the people who relied on the charity. Failing everyone who had come to their wedding in good faith.

'I never wanted to fall in love with you.'

Her hand stalled where she had grabbed a pile of underwear. The white, pastel, bright red and pink colours of her underwear blurred together. He had never seen her wear any of them. How many wives could say that of their husband? She closed her eyes. Pushed down on the hope that stirred somewhere deep in her stomach, disappointment making her feel faint and nauseous. She placed a hand on the frame of the wardrobe to steady herself, reality and memories fortifying her. 'I'm sorry to tell you that I'm well versed in *I love you* being used as a get-out-of-jail-free card. It was a speciality of Nick's any time I tried to break up with him. He would suddenly transform from being indifferently cruel to being the most loving and thoughtful boyfriend a girl could wish for. He was a master of manipulation. What had you expected, that you would waltz in here this morning and we would have a nice little chat about being honest and I would just say okay and agree to staying in a marriage that was destroying me?'

White noise crowded his head. Panic crawled beneath his skin. Why did it physically hurt so much to talk, to express everything that was swarming inside of him?

Making an angry sound, Kara hurled some underwear into her suitcase, the light cotton landing like confetti. Then, yanking at her hand, she shoved her engagement ring towards him. 'Here.'

Dio! She really was serious about leaving.

'No…it's yours.'

The brilliance of the blue stone caught in the sharp light of the recessed lighting. He had spent hours working with Alberto Enciso, the head designer at the royal jewellers, Frechilla & Rouet, designing the ring and picking the exact shade of stone to match Kara's eyes.

'It will never belong to anyone else.'

Her mouth tightened, her eyes blazed with disdain.

'Oh, yeah, I'd forgotten that it would never be part of the royal collection. A fake ring for a fake marriage.'

'It's an eight-carat sapphire! There's nothing fake about it.'

Her nose wrinkled, her mouth twisted. 'That's not what I meant. My point is it's not from the royal collection.'

Lost, he stared down at the ring she was still thrusting towards him. Her hand was shaking, her fingertips white where she was grasping the ring. He had thought his choice of ring would symbolise to Kara his desire to create something unique just for her. Instead she had clearly seen it as a form of rebuttal. *Dio*, he had got so many things wrong. 'Why did you refuse to wear jewellery from the royal collection?'

Her nose wrinkled even more, her cheeks grew hot. 'Because I thought you wouldn't want me to.'

Aghast, he leant against the door frame, ran a hand against the screaming tightness in his temples. 'You don't believe that I see you as part of this family now, do you?' It was as much a question to her as a realisation to him.

Her bottom lip trembled for a split second before she whipped around and tugged open another drawer in her wardrobe. This time, sweaters in her favourite colours of cobalt blue, bright red and pure black hit the suitcase.

He was so tired of living a lie. Tired of being terrified of losing her. So tired of being terrified by emotional intimacy because of the potential pain of growing close to a person and losing them. So tired of closing his heart, of hiding himself from her in fear of appearing foolish, of failing in his promise to protect her.

He opened his mouth, a hot sensation running through his body. 'I have things I need to say to you,' he paused, lost for words, 'things about me and my life I've never shared with you before. Or with anyone else.' He gave a mirthless laugh. 'You see, that's the problem—there hasn't really been anyone else in my life except you for the past decade. You have been the star around which my life has revolved.'

She turned with a sneer, folding her arms.

She wasn't buying it. And he couldn't blame her. Not after Nick's games. And especially given just how closed he had been with her throughout their friendship and especially since they had made love.

He ran a hand through his hair, frustrated and scared he was going to get this wrong. 'I swear I'm not trying to manipulate you. I've been living a lie for so long, and I'm tired of it.'

She made an impatient sound before brushing past him. Out in the bedroom she pulled back the curtains to the early morning sky and went and sat on the sofa in the sitting area. She crossed one leg over the other, her dressing gown parting to reveal her thigh. Seeing his gaze, she tugged the material back in place. Folded her arms and waited for him to speak with a cynical eyebrow raised.

He sat beside her but after a few seconds stood again, needing to move.

He paced the room, his shoulders on fire from tension. He rolled them but found no relief. His skin burnt. He came to a stop, forcing himself to sit and talk to her at the same level, eye to eye, even though he felt sick with the thought of having to open himself up to her. 'I'm in love with you. Not as a friend. As your husband.'

She winced. 'Why should I believe you?'

He glanced at their bed, his chest tightening. 'The night we made love...' He paused, the horror, the slamming disappointment of her words the following morning, coming back to him. He cleared his throat. 'I thought we spoke then, not in words but in our lovemaking. But the day after, you said it was a mistake.'

Kara shifted forward in her seat, her arms dropping to her sides. Stared at him.

Dio*, she had seen his tears.*

He wanted the ground to swallow him up.

'Edwin.' She said his name as a sigh. She ran a hand down her cheek, closing her eyes for long moments before opening them again. 'It *was* a mistake because it shifted my love for you from being a friend to being your wife.' She sighed deeply, shook her head. 'I don't know why I'm saying these things, but I get it when you say you're tired of lying. So am I.'

What was she saying? Was she saying she was in love with him? He worked his jaw, the adrenaline of panic sending his pulse into a frenzy. He opened his mouth, closed it again.

Dammit, just ask her.

'Are you saying you love me?'

Her hand, trembling, moved against her mouth, her cheeks flaming. 'I'm in love with you…' his heart soared, but crashed to the floor at the pain etched in her eyes '…but I can't stay in this marriage.'

'Why…if you love me and I love you?'

'But they're just words. I love you, Edwin. I love your honour, your sense of duty, your drive to do the best for your country, your inherent decency. But I'm lonely. I'm lonelier in our marriage than I have ever been in my entire life. You feel so distant from me.' A large tear dropped along her cheek, and she gave an unhappy laugh. 'I swore I wouldn't do this. I can't live in a marriage where I don't feel safe, and I don't feel safe with you because you shut me out.'

Her words cut him in two, their honesty searing his

heart. His throat was on fire. It felt like a monumental task to even open his mouth to speak. Years of silence and denial had made him psychologically mute. But he *had* to speak. Or else he was going to lose her. 'I'm terrified of losing you, but the crazy thing is I shut you out because I'm scared of the pain that would come if I did lose you—it's this crazy circle of avoidance that feeds itself and it's out of control.'

Her hand trailed over the soft lace edges of her dressing gown. 'You won't lose me.'

He smiled at that. 'You were just packing your bags.'

She gave a guilty smile. 'I was running away, embarrassed by my feelings for you. I wasn't really thinking, but deep down I was hoping we'd stay friends…that maybe with time and a small miracle we'd be able to go back to where we were.'

He held her gaze. The blue-eyed gaze that had spat fire all those years ago when he had plucked her off a muddy pitch. 'I don't want to be your friend. I want to be your husband. And not just in name.'

Such beautiful words. Words that could turn a world upside down. But meaningless if they weren't backed up by action and truth and real connection. Her parents' marriage had been destroyed by a lack of truth and connection.

If their marriage had any hope of surviving then they both needed to speak the truth, expose what was really in their hearts. She felt faint and, no matter how hard she tried to breathe in, she wasn't capable of dragging in enough air to feed the panic pushing her heart to near exploding point. 'I'm in love with you, but relationships, marriage, terrify me.' She wanted to stop but knew she needed to continue and blurted out without drawing breath, 'Losing Michael, my parents' marriage imploding, my relationship with Nick have all made me wary of trusting that people will be there, will be truthful and honest with me. And so far in our marriage it doesn't feel like we've had any of that.'

Grimacing, Edwin shifted his gaze away from her. He bowed his head. Studied his clasped hands. A long silence followed. Her heart raged in her chest. He was doing it again, closing down on her. She wanted to weep with frustration. He had spoken his oath to her, saying he wanted to be honest with her. And yet he kept shutting her out, as though he didn't trust himself, or simply want, to fully open his heart to her.

'I learned at a very young age that I have to present a mask to the world. When my mother died I was scared and angry, I wanted to rebel, to walk away from everything. But how could I? I was the heir to the throne, the oldest son. I *had* to be responsible. I had to be the one who remained in control while Luis went crazy and Ivo went silent.' He clasped and unclasped his hands, tension radiating from him. 'And the mask I had learned to pull on when in public soon became a private mask too.' He cleared his throat and stared unseeingly at a point beyond her shoulder. 'I used to think I could hear her footsteps outside my bedroom door. I was certain I caught glimpses of her walking around corners of the palace. I thought I was going crazy. I felt so weak. I could barely function. Princess Maria tried to help me, but I couldn't bear to talk. I was afraid that if I did start talking everything I was holding in would spiral out of control.'

Her heart broke to hear his bewildered pain. He looked at her and inhaled a long, deep breath full of remorse. 'With Michael, I should have helped him. I should have been a better friend but I was so closed to my own emotions I just panicked. I didn't know how to help him.'

A tight band squeezed her chest. 'You did help. You spoke to the university authorities and my parents.'

He shrugged away her comment.

Her stomach churned and her throat was raw. She dug her nails into the palms of her hands.

Ask him! For God's sake, ask him!

'Was it because of Michael that you stayed friends with me?'

Those golden eyes burnt into hers. 'No, you had already got under my skin.'

Her heart tumbled, emotion clogged her throat. She dipped her head to meet his gaze and whispered, 'We all feel guilt. We all wish we could have done more for him. I don't think that regret will ever leave us.' She paused, struggling to find the right words. 'You haven't been the only one hiding. I have too. I've been hiding even from myself.'

His hand reached out to rest on the cushion between them. 'What do you mean?'

'For far too long I've been too terrified to accept my feelings for you because I thought it would destroy our friendship. I was too proud to be honest about my feelings because I never wanted to be humiliated. I guess I need to learn from that. And the best way we can honour Michael is by trying to lead truthful lives ourselves, where we don't hide our pain.'

'Losing my mother, witnessing Ivo's pain, the way my family has floundered ever since…shutting down was the easiest way to cope.'

She nodded in understanding. 'Before our engagement, I thought I was okay with the fact that you were so private and closed off. It suited me that we had distance between us. But being married, being around you all of the time, the intimacy of it all, that distance went from being okay to just being very alone and uncertain and insecure.'

He shifted closer to her, those golden eyes searing into hers. He was only inches away from her, both of their heads bowed as though in confession. 'Do you believe me when I say I love you?'

'I don't know… It's so strange to hear you saying you love me after all these years,' she whispered back.

He moved even closer, his mouth close to her ear. 'But it feels completely natural for me to say it. I love you. I love you, Kara Duffy, with your sexy laugh and glittering blue eyes. I love that you always try to beat me to the peak of every mountain we climb. I love your chatter all the way up and down that mountain. I love you for your optimism and humour and imagination. I love that you treat me like a normal human being, never pandering to me.'

She tilted her head, dizzy with the intimacy of his whispers, dizzy with the desire to believe him.

His hand touched against the silk material covering her leg. She pulled away from him, doubts suddenly crowding in.

He moved back towards her, a quiet determination in his eyes. 'When we slept together, it was the most right and real night of my life.' His voice was low, tender. She wanted to weep in relief. 'There was a truthfulness and honesty there that I desperately wanted to ignore, desperately wanted to pretend I didn't crave. That's why, despite it feeling like a kick in the teeth, I tried to pretend to myself that I agreed with you that it was all a mistake, when in fact it felt like the best thing that would ever happen in my life.'

'Are you really saying all of this because you love me—or is it due to the enthronement?'

He studied her with a quiet determination. 'I won't succeed to the throne in order to prove to you my love. Princess Maria can succeed instead.'

She leapt out of her chair, her mouth working like a goldfish's before she finally managed to spit out, 'You're kidding me. You're not about to give up the throne, the role you were born for.'

Edwin shrugged, his expression deadly serious. 'I want you in my life. I want to be your husband. I want to spend every single day proving to you just how much I love you.' His voice cracked. Pinched lines appeared at the corners of his eyes. 'I will walk away from the crown to prove that to you.' Taking his phone from his pocket, he added, 'I can call my father now and tell him of my decision.'

'No!' She took the phone from him, threw it onto their bed. Faced him and said in low voice, 'You do love me.' She whispered those words as much for herself as him. Needing to hear the most amazing realisation of her life out loud.

His expression transformed into gentle delight and tenderness.

She blinked and said, 'Love is pretty terrifying, isn't it?'

'Yes, that's why I think we should ease into this.'

'What do you mean?' she asked.

'We skipped a whole lot of important stuff, like date nights.'

She eyed him. 'We've known each other for more than a decade.'

He took her hand. 'A decade where I've been trying to deny my feelings for you. I've stood on the sidelines and watched you become this incredible woman with endless passion and empathy. A woman I hugely admire. A woman who makes every day worthwhile.'

Her heart about to beat its way out of her chest, she softly whispered, 'I love you. And I want to be your consort.'

Leading her to their bed, kicking off his shoes, he lay down on the mattress and opened his arms to her. She placed her head against his chest, his hand stroked her hair, and he told her a story of a misguided prince, too scared to love his wife until he found the courage to let her into his heart.

And later that day she stood at his side when he was crowned Sovereign Prince of Monrosa, her heart overflowing with pride and love.

EPILOGUE

GABRIELA'S TINY NOSE WRINKLED. She let out a mewl of protest as the cold holy water trickled down her forehead. But she immediately settled back into her deep sleep the moment Edwin drew her against his chest, a small smile lifting on her pink Cupid lips.

Kara reached out, laid a finger against her daughter's cheek. How could skin be so soft, so perfect? She shared a look with Edwin, the wonder in his eyes matching her own amazement. After three long years they finally had their much longed-for baby. At times, she had thought it would never happen for them, her arms aching with the need to hold Edwin's baby.

The cardinal blessed Gabriela and walked away towards the main altar of the palace's private chapel. Handing Gabriela to her godfather, Ivo, who studied his niece with intense pride and adoration, Edwin took her hand and lead her towards the altar too.

Confused, she turned and looked behind to their families. But they were following behind them. Her mother and father walking side by side, their annual trips to visit her in Monrosa for Christmas and during the summer helping to heal the wounds between all three of them. And now they were united in their adulation for their firstborn grandchild. In front of them, Edwin's father seemed to be swallowing back tears. He too knew just how desperately they had wanted Gabriela. Retirement hadn't suited him, but now that Edwin had convinced him to be the island's environmental ambassador he was thriving in his new role.

Edwin brought her to stand before the cardinal.

Touching his hand to her cheek, he said quietly, 'I thought this would be a good time to renew our vows.'

Really? She still looked pregnant, her boobs were sore and she sobbed at the drop of a hat. She eyed her husband, her rock, her life, her calm reassurance when yet another blue line would fail to appear, and nodded *yes*.

He smiled, his eyes pulling her into that private, intimate space they disappeared to when alone.

Then, handing her a white card, his looping handwriting on one side, he said, 'I thought I should write our vows this time.'

At the cardinal's invitation he spoke his vows first. Not once did he look down at the card. Not once did he falter in his delivery. He knew the words as though they were etched onto his brain.

When it was her turn, she laughed when Edwin handed her a clean handkerchief embroidered with his initials—he knew her so well—and, swiping away her tears, through a voice choked with love and hope, she spoke the words her husband had written for them both. 'You are my best friend, my ally, my safe harbour in life. I promise to give you my trust and honesty, my truthful love. I promise to take risks for you. I promise to be always there for you. You are my heart. Dance and laugh and love with me for ever.'

* * * * *

[illegible]

Nor did he look down at [illegible]

[illegible]

Where [illegible]

THE BEST INTENTIONS

MICHELLE MAJOR

To Lana. I couldn't do it without you.

Chapter One

"To Daniel's memory."

Finn Samuelson raised his beer bottle and clinked it against Parker Johnson's before throwing an expectant look toward Nick Dunlap.

Nick shook his head, the flames from the firepit in his backyard crackling in the silence.

It had been ten years since Finn had been together with his two best friends from high school in their hometown, a decade in which he hadn't once returned to Starlight, Washington. He hated that it had taken the death of another former classmate to finally lure him back, top on his long list of current regrets.

"Come on, Nick," Parker urged. "Daniel's gone, and despite what's come to light, no one deserves that. You can honor his memory and still be loyal to Brynn."

Finn watched Nick's knuckles tighten around his beer, but finally he lifted it in a half-hearted salute. "Whatever," he muttered. "I know too much to believe there was anything honorable about Daniel Hale at this point."

"Have you talked to Brynn?" Finn asked.

"Other than knocking on her door in the middle of the night to deliver the news that her husband lost control of his truck out at Devil's Landing leaving her a widow and single mother?" Nick gave a sharp shake of his head. "Uh, no. That was about the extent of it."

Finn had driven the switchback road through the nearby Cascade Mountains dozens of times in high school. He pictured the hairpin turn where Daniel had gone over and inwardly cringed. He didn't envy his friend, who was Starlight's police chief, having to make that kind of visit to anyone, let alone the woman who'd once been his best friend. "Do you think she knew about the affair?" Daniel had died in the crash, along with the truck's passenger, who'd turned out to be his mistress.

Nick sighed. "It wasn't his first. She might not

have known about this one, but she understood the type of guy she'd married."

"It's still hard to believe the two of you aren't friends anymore." Finn took a pull of his beer. "She was like your shadow back in high school."

"We're friends, but things change," Nick answered, his voice tight. "Neither of you has bothered to come back here in way too long."

"Everything feels the same to me," Parker muttered. "My dad has been gone for years, but as soon as I pull into town I start to sweat. I can still feel the force of his disapproval like he's waiting for me to come home so he can tell me what a screwup I am."

"Except you're not," Finn reminded him.

"Somehow that's hard to remember in Starlight."

Finn could relate to his friend's sentiment. No one from his life in Seattle would believe that Finn Samuelson, prominent investment banker about to make partner at his prestigious firm, was a huge disappointment to his own father. Finn's decision to leave his hometown instead of remaining heir apparent to the local bank his family had owned for decades had caused a seemingly irreparable rift in his already strained relationship with his dad.

He knew Parker's situation had been even worse. Although Jeff Johnson had been Starlight's mayor for several terms, Parker's dad had been cruel and abusive to his wife behind closed doors. Even after he'd died of a sudden heart attack their senior year, Parker had been as desperate to leave his childhood behind as Finn. In fact, Nick was the only one of the three to stay in Starlight.

Returning caused an itch under Finn's skin that he couldn't manage to scratch. Sure, a part of him missed the quiet and the beauty of the valley. Seattle was gorgeous, but between the crowded city and the frenetic pace of his job, Finn rarely found time to take a moment to appreciate it. Even the air in Starlight seemed fresher, pine-scented and tangy. Every breath brought memories of his childhood, both good and bad.

"Have you seen your dad?" Nick glanced at him over the rim of his bottle.

"I'd hoped he'd be at the funeral," Finn admitted, shaking his head. "Hoped and dreaded in equal measure, I guess. I figured if I talked to him there and he said something to set me off, I could leave again with a clear conscience."

Nick raised a thick brow. "No such luck?"

"He didn't show. Back in the day I remember him making the whole family go to every funeral of a bank customer. He told us it was part of his role in the community."

Parker let out a humorless laugh. "If I had a

nickel for all the times my dad force-marched us out to solidify his loving family-man mayor routine, I'd be rich."

"You're already rich," Finn reminded his friend.

"The divorce business has been good to me," Parker conceded. "I like making people happy."

"You're delusional." Nick laughed. "Divorce doesn't make people happy."

"It does if those people are miserable in their marriages."

"Speaking of…" Finn placed his empty beer bottle on the patio, leaning back in the Adirondack chair where he sat. Nick had bought this house from his grandparents a few years ago and it backed up to one of the local fishing lakes. Water lapped rhythmically against the rocky shoreline at the bottom of the hill.

"Don't tell us you're getting married," Nick interrupted.

Finn laughed when both his friends shot him equally horrified glances. "No," he assured them. "Although it's expected at the firm. Marry a socially appropriate wife, have a couple of adorable kids and join the country club."

Nick made a gagging sound in the back of his throat. "That sounds like the life my parents wanted for me. I still think they believe law enforcement is a passing fancy."

"You just need to explain that you've got a thing for handcuffs," Finn said, earning a one-finger salute from Nick. "Marriage might not be your choice but once I make partner, it's part of the deal. Which is why I want to talk about the pact."

Parker let out a low whistle and picked up the bottle of whiskey that sat next to his chair. "I need something stronger than craft beer for this conversation."

"It's not complicated," Finn said as his friend poured the liquor and passed a shot glass to each of them. "Have you fallen in love?"

"Of course not," Parker scoffed.

"You?" Finn transferred his gaze to Nick.

"We know Tricky Nicky hasn't given away his heart," Parker answered before Nick had a chance to speak. "He's still hung up on Brynn."

"I'm not hung up on her," Nick said through gritted teeth. "We never even dated."

"Yeah," Parker agreed, running a hand through his blond hair. "Thanks to the fact that you set her up with Daniel. If you hadn't been too busy working your way through the cheerleading squad—"

"That's not what I was doing." Nick pushed out of the chair, fists clenched tight as he took a step around the firepit toward Parker. "Brynn and I were friends. Nothing more, then or now."

Parker looked like he wanted to argue but Finn reached out and swatted his arm. "Give it a rest.

She buried her husband today. Nothing's going to change right now."

"Or ever," Nick added, a razor-sharp edge to his voice.

"Fine," Parker agreed after a moment. "Sorry for bringing up a sensitive subject. I've been in the courtroom too long. It's second nature to push people's buttons."

"Apology accepted." Nick flexed his hands, then crossed his arms over his chest. "Just leave my buttons alone." He turned toward Finn. "I haven't fallen in love or even come close, although I think that has less to do with our pact and more to do with the fact that I'm happy not being tied down to one woman."

Parker leaned forward in his chair. "I spend most of my life seeing the worst about falling in love. There's no way in hell I'm getting tangled up like that."

"But the pact doesn't rule out marriage, right?" Finn asked quietly.

"You're a grown man," Nick pointed out. "Some stupid, drunken promise we made after high school shouldn't stop you from falling in love if that's what floats your boat."

"I'm not talking about love," Finn clarified. "I'm expected to get married. While it would be great if the woman I choose is a decent human being, I'm not planning on going all romance hero at this point."

"I like it," Parker said with a nod. "Very eighteenth century of you. It's like a business contract. That could actually work a hell of a lot better than leading with your heart."

"Exactly." Finn waited for relief to fill him that someone else understood his plan. It had been a night much like this one when the three of them had made their pact. After making the rounds of graduation parties, they'd gone out to one of the Forest Service campgrounds with a bottle of cheap whiskey. They'd survived high school, but not without their individual scars.

Finn had just revealed to his father that he wanted no part of the family business. His dad had reacted with angry threats and a convincing promise that Finn's mom would have been sorely disappointed in her only son if she'd lived to see him break his father's heart. Finn's own chest had ached at the knowledge that his father wanted nothing to do with him if he wasn't contributing to the bank's bottom line.

As committed to leaving Starlight as Finn, Parker had been struggling with guilt over the death of his dad. Guilt because a big part of him was relieved to finally have his family free of the emotional abuse they'd endured for years. But

Finn knew his friend also harbored a secret fear that he'd inherited not only his late father's eye color but also his temper and the darkness that had seeped from his soul. Finn didn't believe it for a minute, but Parker wouldn't be convinced otherwise.

Nick's heartbreak had been the most straightforward. He'd pushed the girl who'd had a crush on him for years into the arms of another guy, only to realize the depth of his feelings for her once she was gone. But Brynn was pregnant and she and Daniel had just announced their engagement, cutting off any future Nick might have had with her.

They'd been a pathetic trio, committed to never suffering from disappointment, rejection or heartbreak again. Parker had been the one to suggest the pact against falling in love. He was convinced that if they eliminated that sort of deep emotion, they'd stay safe from future pain.

At the time, it had seemed like a joke to Finn, but he'd played along. Through the years, the drunken promise had become an excuse he'd used whenever a girlfriend got too close or wanted more than he was willing to give. No falling in love. Easy enough, and if he kept that oath clear in his mind, maybe he could do what was expected by his boss and still keep his heart out of the mix.

"I wouldn't bother with marriage in the first place," Nick announced into the silence. "But at least you've got Parker's number when things don't work out."

"You never know how things are going to work out," Finn answered, dread pooling in his gut at the thought of facing his father.

Even in the dim light cast by the fire, he could see the pain that shadowed Nick's gaze.

"To the unknown," Parker said, raising his glass.

Finn lifted his in response, then downed the amber liquid, hissing softly as the whiskey burned his throat. "To the unknown."

Kaitlin Carmody reached for her coffee mug, sighing when she found it empty. She had a strict personal rule about limiting her caffeine intake to one cup a day, although she could use another jolt of energy. She'd already been at her desk three hours, and it wasn't even ten in the morning.

Her ex-boyfriend would have snickered at her attempt at restraint. When she and Robbie had been together, *excess* had been the word best used to describe their bond. Alcohol, drugs, sex… Often all three at the same time. That had been rock bottom, and Kaitlin was proud of how far she'd come. How much she'd abandoned—basically everything—to start over in Starlight.

Two years ago, she'd been working as a barista in one of Seattle's ubiquitous coffee shops when a customer had left behind a Washington State map. While refolding the slick paper, her gaze had snagged on a dot east of the city, the name Starlight printed next to it.

Something tiny and almost unrecognizable had begun to unfurl inside her as she traced her fingers over the shiny letters. Kaitlin didn't have much experience with hope, but she recognized it just the same. That night, she'd loaded her meager belongings into a backpack and the next morning set off out of the city and toward her new beginning, leaving a note for Robbie not to look for her.

"Earth to the woman in the gray dress."

She glanced up as the deep voice invaded her meandering thoughts. Her breath caught in her throat at the sight of the imposing man frowning down at her. Dark hair, piercing blue eyes and broad shoulders that looked almost out of place contained in the expensive suit he wore.

"Sorry," she said automatically, then inwardly cringed. Jack had told her she needed to stop saying sorry for everything, that it showed a weakness and self-doubt she shouldn't let people see. But apologies still rolled off her tongue like a snowball down an alpine ski slope. "I was daydreaming," she continued with a half smile, as if that wasn't totally obvious. As if she owed this tense stranger an explanation.

"Right," he agreed. "You get what you pay for."

Ouch. So much for the pleasantries of casual conversation. Kaitlin straightened her shoulders. "Can I help you?"

"Is he in?" The man inclined his head toward Jack's office.

"Do you have an appointment?"

One side of the stranger's full mouth curved up. "Not exactly."

"Mr. Samuelson has a busy calendar," she lied. Despite her resolve to be different than she used to be, lying still came naturally to Kaitlin. A fact that had worked in her favor the past six months. "If you leave your name and number, I can get you added to his schedule."

"He'll see me now," the man insisted, his gaze locked on the closed oak door.

Kaitlin might be good at apologies, but she was even better at standing her ground when the situation called for it. This situation called for it.

"I don't think that's a good idea." She stood, moving quickly to block the man's progress.

He blinked, as if he'd never had anyone deny him a request before. She could well imagine that no woman had ever denied him.

One smoldering glance from those blue eyes

framed by heavy brows and model-sharp cheekbones and most of the women she knew would melt in a puddle at his feet.

Good thing Kaitlin wasn't much of a melter any longer.

"Are you going to step aside?" he asked, one dark brow arching. "Or shall I move you?"

"I'm going with door number three," she told him with her phoniest smile. "Leave your name and number. I'll put you on Mr. Samuelson's schedule." Out of the corner of her eye she could see that one of the personal bankers, Missy, had come out of her office and was waving at Kaitlin as if to warn her of something.

Kaitlin didn't melt and she refused to back down. Not after everything Jack Samuelson had done for her. No one in the office might understand why the bank's owner needed her protection, but it didn't change the fact that he did.

The stranger took a step toward her. "I'm seeing him now."

She narrowed her eyes. "You lay a hand on me, and I'll call the police so fast it will make your smug head spin."

"I have Nick Dunlap's cell number," he said evenly. "Would you like me to dial?"

Why would this guy know Starlight's police chief so well? She studied him for a moment longer, then stifled a gasp. Those bright blue eyes and thick brows… She knew another man who had them.

"Who are you?" she whispered.

"Finn Samuelson," he answered. "And if you'll excuse me, I'm going to see my dad."

Jack's estranged son was back. Heart hammering in her chest, Kaitlin automatically took a step away and watched Jack's estranged son walk past her and enter his father's office. The door closed behind him with a decisive click.

Chapter Two

Finn drew a shallow breath as he stepped into his father's inner sanctum. The office still smelled of polished wood and judgment, as if the cherry bookshelves and executive desk held him up for appraisal, only to find him lacking.

He gave a small shake of his head, the thought that the bank held any sway over him after so many years preposterous. He sniffed again and caught the faint scent of vanilla, like the woman who was his father's gatekeeper had tried to infuse the space with a bit of warmth.

Good luck with that.

His father hadn't turned around in the oversize leather chair that sat behind the desk. Finn glanced out at the view of downtown Starlight. The main lobby of the bank operated on the ground level, with executive offices and private banking handled from the second floor.

Finn had worked summers and holidays in the bank all through high school, but he'd avoided his dad's office. There were too many reminders of the past and the legacy he never believed was his due. Photos of his relatives lined the bookshelves, including several of his great-great-grandparents at the bank's grand opening. Starlight had been little more than a pit stop for pioneers back then. First Trust had seen the town through booms and busts and remained an institution he'd always link with his past.

He cleared his throat, but his father still didn't turn. Had the far-too-pretty assistant somehow warned him about Finn's arrival? She seemed pit bull protective, but he couldn't imagine her as a master of mental telepathy. Unfortunately, he easily imagined her as the master of every one of his fantasies.

He couldn't pinpoint what it was about the beautiful blonde with the milk-chocolate eyes and curves for miles, but his immediate awareness of her had gone way beyond sensible. If she was on Team Jack Samuelson, clearly Finn needed to keep his distance.

"Hey, Dad," he said, frowning when he got no response.

He stepped around the desk and his heart froze. His father's head was bent forward, eyes closed and hands in prayer position over his chest. His hair was almost pure white, deep lines fanning from his eyes. Somehow he'd aged a lifetime in the decade Finn had been gone.

There was no way…

"Dad!"

Finn sucked in a breath as his father startled at hearing his name shouted. He blinked several times, then glanced up at Finn. For a moment it was as if he didn't recognize his own son. Yes, it had been over ten years, but Finn had always resembled his dad's side of the family. Plus, this was his dad. What the hell…

"Finneas?" the older man whispered after a moment.

"Yeah." Finn concentrated on keeping his voice steady. "I'm in town for Daniel's funeral so I thought—"

Suddenly his father stood and wrapped his arms around Finn's shoulders. "Son. I've missed you."

"Um…okay." Finn swallowed back the ball of emotion welling in his throat. This certainly wasn't the reception he'd expected. He couldn't remember ever being hugged by his dad. A hearty clap on the shoulders was the most he'd gotten and that was after being named valedictorian of his senior class.

"Are you returning to Starlight?"

Now it was Finn's turn to blink. "No, Dad. My life is in Seattle. You know that." The delivery might be softer than before, but his father could still land an emotional punch like a prizefighter.

Jack stared at him for a moment, his eyes clear and far too familiar, searching for something Finn didn't know how to offer. Then he nodded and let out a long breath. "You always had bigger dreams than Starlight could make come true."

Finn gave a startled laugh. That was one of the nicest things his dad had ever said to him. Back in high school, Jack had seemed to take great pleasure in making Finn feel like there was something wrong with him for wanting more.

He stepped back, putting the desk between himself and his father. He needed some kind of a buffer. He'd imagined talking to his dad a million times since leaving Starlight. Never would he have guessed he'd feel anything but anger and bitterness. Where had this version of his father been when Finn needed him most?

"You're a big success in Seattle," Jack said, lowering himself back into the chair.

It was a statement, not a question, and the pride in his father's voice shocked Finn to the core.

"I'm on target to be named partner this year."

"Congratulations. We should have dinner tonight as an early celebration. Will you come to the house?"

"Sure," Finn answered, still dumbfounded. "I didn't think you'd—"

"Jack?"

Finn turned as his father's assistant entered the office. She darted a worried glance between the two of them, and he wondered how much she knew about his relationship with his dad.

"Kaitlin, have you met my son?" His father leaned forward in his chair. "He's a big-shot banker in Seattle."

"You've mentioned that," she said, walking forward. She shoved her hand toward Finn, her gaze trained on the middle of his chest instead of looking him in the eye. He was oddly disappointed. "I'm Kaitlin Carmody. I work for your dad. Obviously."

"Finn Samuelson," he replied, trying not to notice the softness of her skin as he shook her hand. "You're not from Starlight."

"No," she confirmed, snatching back her hand. He couldn't figure out why she seemed so nervous.

"Jack, you have an appointment with Ernie in the mayor's office."

"Right," his father agreed. "I guess Finn isn't the only big shot around here. The bank is underwriting the Starlight Art Festival."

Finn frowned at the comparison, then noticed Kaitlin's mouth thin. "You haven't committed to anything yet," she told Jack. "You wanted to ensure they were going to have appropriate marketing and signage."

He waved a hand as he stood. "I don't need reminding," he snapped. "This is my bank and I can still make the best decisions for its future."

There was the Jack Samuelson that Finn remembered.

"Of course," Kaitlin said softly.

"I could show you a thing or two about the art of a deal." Jack pointed to Finn, then straightened his tie. "We'll compare notes over dinner. Kaitlin will have the food ready at seven. Don't be late."

Without another word for either of them, Finn's dad left the office, his gait slow and measured.

"You cook for him?" Finn asked, his mind reeling.

"Um..." Color flooded Kaitlin's cheeks. "Sometimes."

What was he missing about this woman's relationship with his dad? He couldn't put a finger on it, but some instinct made him certain there was more to it than she was admitting. "But you're his assistant at the bank," he prompted.

She nodded.

"Are you his girlfriend, too?" he forced himself to ask.

Her mouth dropped open before she snapped it shut. "Of course not. He's old enough to be my dad."

He didn't bother to point out that plenty of women dated older men. The second wife of AmeriNat's North American CEO, a man in his early sixties, was younger than Finn.

"How long have you been at the bank?"

She crossed her arms over her chest. "Two years," she mumbled.

"Your background is in finance?"

She started to shake her head, then stopped, her shoulders going stiff. "Is there a reason for this interrogation?"

Finn ran a hand through his hair. "I haven't seen my dad for over ten years, but he's different than he used to be. I'm trying to figure out why."

"I don't know what you're talking about," she muttered. "Jack is exactly the same as he's always been."

"Then you don't know Jack," he whispered.

She huffed out a small laugh at his pitiful joke, and the sound reverberated through him. He didn't want to have that kind of visceral response to Kaitlin Carmody but couldn't seem to stop himself.

"I need to get back to work," she said with a pointed look.

"Sure," he agreed, thoughts and emotions pinging through his mind. The physical changes were to be expected, but it was the transformation of his father's personality that shocked him. Maybe the change in his dad had nothing to do with Kaitlin, but Finn remained unconvinced.

With a last look around the office, he slowly walked out, aware that Kaitlin followed like she was herding a recalcitrant child.

"I'll see you tonight," he said, studying her classically beautiful features for a hint of…something. She flashed a tight grin and her dark eyes gave nothing away.

"Tonight," she agreed.

Feeling summarily dismissed, he started down the hall, stopping to chat with several people who had worked at the bank for as long as he could remember.

The atmosphere was so different than his Seattle office. He got hugs and a few cheek pinches, made congratulatory remarks about graduations, weddings and grandchildren. Despite his absence, people treated him like he'd only been away for a short time instead of a decade.

In Seattle, his coworkers kept to themselves. Finn was management and had been pegged as the future of the division. That put a wall between him and everyone below him on the company totem pole, and until this moment he hadn't realized how much it bothered him.

He might not have wanted the First Trust of Starlight as his future, but could appreciate the warm and welcoming atmosphere he associated with everyone except his dad. Now he was starting to doubt his own memories. Maybe his father hadn't been as bad as he'd once thought. Jack might not have made updating the decor a priority, but he certainly engendered loyalty from his staff.

Was it possible the problem had actually been with Finn the whole time? As he walked out into the bright morning sunshine, he shook off the thought. He needed to call his sister. The last he'd heard from her, Ella was working at a hospital in a speck of a town somewhere in Argentina. She hadn't put down roots since leaving Starlight, constantly traveling and spending months in remote parts of the world.

They managed to keep in touch whenever she

had internet or cell service but could go long stretches without any type of communication. That didn't change the bond they shared, and Ella would gladly remind him of all of their father's faults.

He glanced up and down Starlight's main street. There was a stoplight on the north end of downtown that hadn't been there when he'd left. The mountains loomed in the distance as the light turned from red to green. Otherwise, the town looked much the same as he remembered. Some of the businesses had changed, but otherwise he felt as though he'd stepped back into a scene from his youth.

A gang of kids on mountain bikes rode by, happy voices and laughter trailing on the air in their wake. It reminded him of so many summer days when he, Parker and Nick had ridden for miles, exploring the trails and back roads surrounding the town.

Would his hypothetical children have that kind of freedom? Most of his coworkers' kids seemed overscheduled and often glued to their devices, a sad shell of a childhood in Finn's opinion.

He massaged a hand along the back of his neck. He was getting ahead of himself. He didn't even have a wife, let alone kids. This trip to his hometown was supposed to clear out his emotional roadblocks so he could move ahead on both fronts. Right on schedule.

It was funny, actually. He'd bristled against his dad's expectations and what he considered the proverbial prison of First Trust, but he was chained to his job in a way that would have horrified his younger self.

As he headed toward his BMW sedan, he told himself he'd chosen his life, which made all the difference. Too bad he was having trouble believing that at the moment.

"You're Finn Samuelson, right?"

Finn turned as a middle-aged man approached from the entrance of the bank.

"That's right."

"Doug Meyer," the man said, holding out a hand. "I'm your dad's vice president."

"Nice to meet you," Finn said with a practiced smile. Doug had the job that would have been Finn's at this point if he hadn't left. He had no right to be annoyed, but he was anyway.

"I was wondering if I could bend your ear for a few minutes about a situation at the bank?"

Finn grimaced. "You must know I have no involvement at First Trust."

"Of course," Doug agreed quickly. "But it involves

your father. I'm concerned about his recent behavior. Some things have changed."

Like Jack Samuelson had grown a heart?

"Your dad won't discuss the issues, and Kaitlin goes into dragon mode whenever I approach, so—"

"What does Kaitlin have to do with this?" Finn asked, his gut tightening.

"I'm not exactly certain, but things aren't good. Someone has to do something. Maybe you can help."

Hell, no.

Finn should walk away right now. He wanted nothing to do with the bank or any suspected problems in his father's life, especially not if they had to do with Kaitlin Carmody.

"I have some time," he answered, unable to stop himself.

Doug nodded. "Let's grab a cup of coffee." He pointed down the street toward the sign that said Main Street Perk. "I'd rather not get tongues wagging at the office."

"Fine." Finn fell in step with the shorter man, willing away the tension that crowded his shoulders. Whatever Doug had to say, Finn would listen, then politely explain he didn't want to be involved. No problem.

* * *

Kaitlin dragged in a shuddery breath as the doorbell at Jack's sprawling ranch-style house rang later that night.

She glanced out the kitchen window to where her boss practiced his putt on the tightly mowed green he'd had installed last year. Okay, she was answering the door.

Easy enough.

She dried her hands on a nearby dish towel and headed through the kitchen and down the hall toward the foyer. She should have known Finn immediately. Jack didn't have many photos on display, but there were enough of a young Finn, his sister, Ella, and Jack's late wife, Katie, to recognize the man the boy had grown into.

She'd been caught off guard. That never would have happened before life in Starlight turned her soft and trusting. Bouncing in and out of foster care as a kid, Kaitlin had learned always to be on the alert for threats.

Although it made no sense, every instinct for danger she had gave off warning lights when she thought about Finn.

Plastering on a bright smile, she opened the door.

For a moment, he appeared nonplussed before

his features tightened into a flat mask. “Playing lady of the manor?” he asked with that irritating brow lift.

She let her smile fade. If Jack’s son didn’t want to play nice, why should she? “Don’t look shocked. He told you I was helping with dinner.”

“I just wonder what else you’re helping with,” he said as he followed her through the house. “Or maybe ‘helping yourself to’ is more accurate.”

She spun on her heel so fast he practically plowed into her. This close, she could see the gray flecks in his blue eyes and feel the heat coming off him. He’d changed into a polo shirt and faded jeans, but the casual dress did nothing to make him less intimidating.

Kaitlin hated being intimidated.

“What does that mean?” she demanded.

“I think you know.”

“You’re wrong.” Wrong on so many levels, she wanted to add. Her track record with morals and good judgment was spotty at best, but she’d changed since coming to Starlight. Jack had given her a chance, and she’d never take advantage of that, no matter what vague insinuations his son made.

“What the hell’s going on here?”

She turned at the sound of Jack’s booming voice.

"Your *assistant* and I are getting to know each other," Finn answered, and she heard a thread of temper lacing his tone.

She glanced over her shoulder. "Tell me you didn't use air quotes."

He shot her a quelling glare. "Do I look like I need hand gestures to convey my distaste?"

"You look like you need a swift kick in the back end," Jack called. "Both of you get in the kitchen."

"There's the dad I remember," Finn said under his breath as he stalked after her.

"You obviously bring out the best in him," she shot back, then pressed her lips together. Why was she engaging in this verbal sparring with Finn? She'd have better luck waving a stick at an angry mountain lion.

"I asked Kaitlin to make your mother's shepherd's pie recipe," Jack announced as they entered the kitchen. "We'll eat and then talk."

"I'm not really hungry," Finn muttered.

"You were always hungry," Jack countered. "It's been a lot of years since you've been in the house, but I can't imagine that's changed."

She heard something that sounded like a stomach growling, and Jack let out a satisfied chuckle. "There's a bottle of wine on the dining room table," he told Finn. "You open it while Kaitlin finishes with the food. I'll be right back."

She glanced toward Jack, but he waved off her obvious concern. “I’m fine. Just need to check something in my office.”

Kaitlin grabbed two pot holders from the counter and moved toward the stove. Maybe she should have refused to make a dish that had been one of Finn’s mother’s signatures. Honestly, she hadn’t thought about Finn’s reaction. She simply liked cooking in the homey kitchen and using the recipes that Katie Samuelson had written on index cards in her precise cursive.

Carrying the casserole into the dining room, she purposely avoided eye contact with Finn. She set the dish on the trivet she’d placed on the table and turned back toward the kitchen to retrieve the side dishes.

“There are three places set,” Finn announced from the head of the table, his voice a low growl.

“Jack invited me to stay for dinner.”

“You called him Mr. Samuelson at the bank earlier today.”

“What’s your point?” Finn’s attitude caused every one of her hackles to rise.

“Leave the girl alone,” Jack said as he entered the dining room from the far door.

Finn popped the cork on the wine. “I think it’s time she left you alone.”

Kaitlin felt a blush stain her cheeks. She knew

there were questions about the nature of her relationship with Jack but mainly ignored the gossip. It bothered her that Finn had so quickly heard the rumors, even if most of what was said wasn't true.

"You have no idea what you're talking about," Jack said with a shake of his head.

"Why don't you fill me in?"

As Finn poured the wine, Kaitlin met Jack's gaze across the table. For a moment he let down his guard, and she saw both fear and frustration in his tired eyes. She gave him a small smile and nodded, as if her opinion of how he should handle this conversation would matter.

His mouth thinned as he looked away, and she sighed. If Jack didn't tell Finn the whole truth of his situation, it would only cause more trouble for all of them.

She moved to the kitchen and picked up the salad bowl and basket of bread still sitting on the counter. When she returned, both Jack and Finn stood next to their chairs, clearly waiting for her to sit first. The reminder that both of these men were gentlemen despite the tension between them was like a slap in the face.

Kaitlin didn't belong here, even if Jack wanted her to. "I'm going to the guesthouse," she announced.

"We haven't even started dinner," Jack told her.

"You need to eat after all the time it took to make the food."

"Wait." Finn held up a hand. "You live here?"

"Don't go there," she warned.

"I'll go wherever I want," he shot back.

Kaitlin opened her mouth to deliver a snappy retort, but Jack's howling laughter stopped her. Finn seemed just as surprised at the sound, and they both turned to the older man.

"I remember all the times you and Ella squabbled over the dinner table," he said, swiping a hand across his cheek. "It used to annoy me to no end. I'd get home after a long day at the bank, and there was no peace and quiet to be found."

"Kaitlin isn't my sister," Finn ground out.

No doubt, Kaitlin thought to herself. As much of a pompous jerk as she found Finn to be, her awareness of him was anything but brotherly.

"I still can't believe I miss the arguing," Jack said, more to himself than either of them. "Kaitlin, sit down. Let's have a civil dinner."

Jack had given her a chance to make a new life in Starlight, and she owed him her loyalty but also knew he was using her as a buffer. "Not tonight," she told him gently. "You two have some catching up to do. I'll only get in the way."

"Amen," Finn said at the same time Jack answered, "You won't."

"I'll see you in the morning," she told her boss, doing her best to ignore the weight of Finn's stare. Jack looked like he wanted to argue but finally nodded, and Kaitlin walked away, hoping the two men could manage to get through the meal without killing each other.

Chapter Three

The knock came at close to midnight, according to the clock on her nightstand.

Kaitlin struggled to wake, then shot up in bed, her first thought that something had happened to Jack.

The guesthouse was more of a tiny apartment, with a cozy living area on one side and a small bedroom situated off the kitchen. She stumbled to the floor, the sheet still wrapped around her legs.

"I'm coming," she shouted, flipping on a light before hurrying across the wide-plank floor and—ouch—stubbing her toe on an uneven strip of oak.

When she wrenched open the door, Finn stood on the other side, tall and brooding and staring at her like she'd just made her escape from some kind of circus sideshow.

"Is your dad okay?" she whispered, worry clawing at her chest. She and Jack had been through some rough nights together, and although she knew he was healthy now, those times were difficult not to revisit.

"My guess is he's sleeping," Finn told her with a scowl. "Sorry I woke you."

She took a deep breath to calm herself and studied him, standing on the porch with only moonlight to reveal his handsome features. She'd been sleeping fitfully, unwelcome visions of the man standing at her door causing her to toss and turn. "I doubt that," she murmured. "People don't normally knock on someone's door in the middle of the night without the intent to wake them."

"True," he agreed with a little half smile that suddenly reminded her she was standing in front of him in pajama shorts and a loose tank top with no bra.

As if reading her mind, his gaze trailed down the front of her, then quickly back to her face. A faint hint of pink tinged his cheeks. Was Finn Samuelson blushing? A strangled giggle escaped her lips at the thought.

"Can I come in?" he asked, a husky note to his voice that had goose bumps erupting along her skin.

Oh, yes, her body squealed.

"Nope," she breathed.

"Kaitlin."

Her name whispered in that deep tone made her feel far too hot and bothered even though the temperature had cooled off considerably from earlier in the day.

"Finn, why are you here?" She kept her arms at her sides, tamping down every feminine desire she had. She was no longer held captive by her impulses. Those had led to nothing for her but circling the drain.

"I couldn't sleep."

"They have pills and late-night movies for that."

"My dad has cancer."

Right. She sucked in a breath, his quiet words slamming into her with the force of a sledgehammer, and then took a step back so he could enter the small space.

"Tea or liquor?" she asked, gesturing for him to have a seat on the overstuffed sofa.

"Your choice."

She moved to the kitchen, plucking the teakettle from where it sat on the stove top and then filling it with water. After turning on the burner, she took her terry-cloth robe from the bathroom door and slipped into it. She couldn't figure out how to subtly put on a bra, so adding the shapeless layer over her tank top was the best she could do.

The noise from her movements seemed to echo in the quiet. A glance at Finn showed that he was staring in front of him, as if some invisible movie played that captured every bit of his attention.

She unwrapped two tea bags while waiting for the kettle to boil, then poured the steaming water into the mugs. She'd developed a taste for herbal tea since limiting caffeine, and there was no doubt this was a much safer choice than alcohol. The last thing she needed was her defenses softening when it came to this conversation and the man invading her tiny home.

"Cream or sugar?" she asked as she set the tray on the coffee table in front of Finn, like she was some kind of British duchess serving high tea at midnight to one of her upper-crust friends.

"No, thanks."

"So..." she began, lowering herself onto the cushion next to Finn and curling her legs under her. She made sure to keep as much distance as possible between them but imagined she could still feel the warmth coming off his body. He'd make a darn good personal space heater on a cold winter night.

"He said you're the only one who knows." Finn took a small sip of the tea, then muttered a curse.

"It's hot," she belatedly warned.

Up went that eyebrow again. "Trying to burn my tongue to shut me up?"

"No, actually," she said with a soft laugh. "I don't enjoy being the keeper of your father's secret."

"Why did he trust you with it and what made you agree?"

Kaitlin reached for her mug, wrapping her fingers around the warmth of the porcelain. "I came to Starlight on a whim with no idea of what the future held. Your dad and I met in a coffee shop. I was reading an old copy of *On the Road*, looking for inspiration, I guess."

"He lived his entire life in this town, but that was always his favorite book."

"Didn't do much for me," Kaitlin admitted, "and Jack and I had a lively discussion about my error in opinion."

That comment earned a real smile from Finn, transforming his face from brooding to boyish in an instant. "I can imagine."

She nodded. "I'm sure you can. He asked some questions and when I told him I'd come to Starlight to start over, he offered me a job as his assistant. Mary had retired a few weeks earlier."

"That woman terrified me most of my childhood," Finn said. "She and my dad were a great match."

"I've done okay filling her shoes," Kaitlin said. Then she amended, "Or at least I've tried. I noticed Jack getting tired more easily about a year after I started, and he was having some hip and chest pain that the doctor chalked up to old age, but obviously it was way more than that."

"Stage-three melanoma," Finn murmured.

"The doctors in Seattle gave him a few months, so I found an oncologist in San Francisco who was conducting a human trial called tumor targeting. I'm sure he told you he's officially in remission. But he missed a lot of time at the bank, traveling for treatment."

"You've gone with him on every trip?"

She nodded. "Without the chance your father gave me, I'm not sure where I'd be right now. I owe him a lot."

"What do you get for your loyalty?"

She tightened her grip on the mug. "I don't understand what you mean."

"What's in it for you? Are you hoping to be the next Mrs. Jack Samuelson?"

"No offense to your dad," she said through clenched teeth, "but gross."

"Think he'll change his will?"

She shook her head, strangely disappointed that he continued to think the worst of her. "It isn't like that, Finn. Why do you need to make me the bad guy in all this?"

He stared at her for several long seconds, flummoxed by the question. He hadn't actually come here tonight to accuse her of anything. After his father's big revelation, Finn had been numb.

He'd returned to Nick's house, where he was staying, but hadn't shared with his friend what he'd learned about his dad. He needed more time to process things, or so he told himself.

Parker had already gone back to Seattle, and Finn had planned to drive back tomorrow morning. But between the information Doug at the bank had shared and the news about his father, he didn't see how he could leave just yet.

"Why doesn't he seem to understand that the bank is failing?" he asked instead of answering the question.

She shrugged. "He knows but believes he can fix it. Your father has quite the streak of optimism after the cancer treatments worked so well."

"Doug believes the problems started after you came on board," Finn said, studying her.

She snorted, and the indelicate sound was strangely appealing. "He thinks I'm smart enough to take down a hundred-year-old banking institution? That's actually a compliment."

"Your past isn't exactly spotless."

Color stained her cheeks as she narrowed her eyes at him. "You researched me?"

"I had Nick plug in your name to a few law enforcement databases this afternoon."

"I wasn't a saint, but nothing in my past should make you believe I could manage what you're insinuating."

She said the words calmly, and he liked that she didn't make excuses for her mistakes. She was right, too. She'd been in and out of foster care, had a misdemeanor for vandalism on her record, but nothing serious.

"Maybe you should take a closer look at ol' Dougie-boy." She made a face. "That guy's a weasel in a bad suit."

Finn chuckled. Doug definitely wasn't a paragon of fashion, and Finn hadn't particularly liked him after hearing everything he had to say.

"My dad trusts you," he told her, "obviously with his life. I don't want to feel guilty for not having been here with him through the treatments, but what's happening at First Trust is more complicated than fraud. At this point, the depositors are at risk. I need to figure out what the hell is going on and make it right."

"It would be simple if you could place the blame on me," she answered, lifting the ceramic mug to her lips.

He should not be focusing on her lips. Or her sleep-tousled hair. Or the way the robe she'd put on kept gaping at the center to reveal the lacy edge of her thin tank top.

"True," he managed, shifting on the sofa and commanding his body to behave.

"Life is rarely simple."

"Also true."

She leaned forward to place her mug back on the coffee table, giving him a tantalizing glimpse of the swell of her breast. He needed to get back to Nick's and take a cold shower or maybe a dip in the mountain-runoff-fed lake behind the house.

"Why is it your responsibility to make this right?" she asked, worrying the sash of the robe between two fingers. "You haven't spoken to Jack in years."

"He's my dad," Finn said, still not quite able to believe the depth of his emotion around his father's illness.

"He loves you and your sister," Kaitlin said gently. "We talked a lot on the flights back and forth to San Francisco. He has so many regrets about how he behaved after your mother died."

"Regrets are a family tradition for the Samuelsons." Finn rubbed a hand over his eyes. "I'm hoping to let go of some of mine if I fix this."

"Does Jack want your help?"

"What do you think?"

"He's proud, and cancer has taken a lot out of him."

"Yeah." Finn sighed. "But I have to do it."

She didn't say anything, but the quiet way she watched him, her brown eyes gentle, made his heart hammer in his chest.

"I want you to help me," he blurted.

"You don't trust me," she said with a laugh.

"My dad does, and that's a start."

She looked down, and a stray lock of hair fell forward to brush her cheek. He couldn't help himself. He reached out and tucked the soft strands behind her ear. His fingers grazed her cheek and it was all he could do to resist leaning in to claim her mouth with his.

Earlier today this woman seemed like a threat to his father and the bank. Now it felt like she was the only true ally Finn could rely on. How the hell had that happened, and was it his libido leading?

He snatched back his hand and stood.

"We don't have to be friends," he said, more for himself than her. "But if you truly care about my father, you'll help me figure out what's going on at the bank. It would kill him to lose it."

She stood, pulling the robe tight over her chest. "Okay," she whispered, and the breathless note to her voice sent all of Finn's blood south.

"Then I'll see you tomorrow."

"Tomorrow," she repeated, tugging her lower lip between her teeth.

Finn swallowed a groan. "Good night, Kaitlin," he said in a rush of breath.

Before she could answer or he could do something stupid like drag her into his arms, he turned and walked out into the night.

Chapter Four

"I put in an extra shot because you look like you're coming off a long night."

Kaitlin smiled gratefully as she took the paper cup from her friend Mara Reed, who also happened to be the best barista at Main Street Perk, Starlight's local coffee shop.

She didn't bother to mention that the extra caffeine would negate her one-cup limit. Kaitlin had suffered enough hard knocks that she knew the value of appreciating an unexpected kindness.

This whole town was filled with kindness and generosity, at least compared to the life she'd left behind in Seattle. She thanked Mara, then looked away when tears sprang to her eyes.

How embarrassing. She needed to pull herself together. She'd dealt with far worse than the mistrust she saw in Finn Samuelson's movie-star-handsome gaze. Why was having her motives and morals called into question affecting her so strongly?

"Hey, Jana," Mara called to the teenager filling the napkin dispenser next to the coffee bar. "I need five minutes. Can you cover the register?"

"Sure," the girl said, smacking her gum and tossing a thick braid over one shoulder.

"I'm fine," Kaitlin protested as Mara came around the counter and placed a hand on her shoulder.

"Scone or brownie?" the willowy brunette asked.

"Brownie."

Mara released Kaitlin long enough to pluck a cellophane-wrapped square from the basket next to the cash register, then led her to a high-top table in the corner.

"If you need chocolate this early, *fine* doesn't cut it."

Kaitlin didn't bother to argue even though it would make her late to work. Mara was the closest friend she had in town so Kaitlin wouldn't pretend everything was great.

She opened her mouth, unsure of how to explain the situation, but Mara held up a hand. "This is a two-bite story. I can tell."

"What does that mean?"

Elegant fingers unwrapped the brownie. "Two bites of chocolate and then you can start talking. It's emotional fortification. Trust me. I've been there."

With a soft laugh, Kaitlin took the hunk of brownie Mara handed to her. Although the dessert had been baked the previous day, it was still moist. She closed her eyes as she chewed, savoring the rich sweetness.

"This is your recipe," she said after swallowing. "It's way better than the brownies your aunt bakes."

Mara looked almost embarrassed at having her talent called out. "You don't even want to know how many late-night baking sessions I had after my divorce."

"I would have gained a hundred pounds," Kaitlin admitted.

Mara flashed a grin. "I took everything into Evie's day care. Those ladies were actually disappointed when I started to get myself together."

"I doubt that," Kaitlin said as she took a second

bite. "Okay, maybe I believe it," she amended as the chocolate hit her taste buds once again.

She'd met Mara almost a year ago, when the single mother had moved to Starlight and started working at Perk, as the locals called it. Kaitlin loved the fact that she'd become a part of this small community, even if a few people remained standoffish due to her close relationship with Jack.

Mara's aunt, Nanci Morgan, owned Main Street Perk and had taken in Mara and her adorable daughter when they'd moved to town. Apparently she'd gone through a nasty divorce that had decimated her, both emotionally and financially.

Kaitlin had immediately liked the snarky, sarcastic barista, as she had a sixth sense for recognizing another wounded soul. Most people in Starlight had grown up in town or lived there for years, and she was grateful for a connection with someone who was also starting over.

Kaitlin was an only child and had found it difficult to make close friends as a kid when she and her mom moved around so often. Cindi Carmody had a habit of falling fast and hard for whichever man caught her eye. Since she typically stuck to run-down, month-to-month rental apartments, she was always happy to shack up with a boyfriend as soon as he'd invite her into his home. The older Kaitlin got, the more her mom seemed to be scraping the bottom of the barrel with the men she chose. She had a penchant for pills and had been to rehab three times before Kaitlin had graduated high school.

Each time Kaitlin had been thrust into a different foster care family, and she'd hated and resented every experience.

She doubted Mara had ever sunk to the depths she'd experienced. Despite her reduced circumstances since the divorce, her friend retained a level of polish and class that came from having experienced a privileged life. Mara might be standoffish with people who didn't know her well, but she wasn't a snob, and she seemed to appreciate that Kaitlin didn't judge her for how far down in life she'd presumably tumbled.

"Okay, the chocolate should be hitting your system," Mara said with a wink as Kaitlin wiped one corner of her mouth with a paper napkin. "What's going on?"

"Trouble at work," Kaitlin said with a sigh and watched her friend blow out a relieved breath. "What did you think?"

"Your ex-boyfriend," Mara admitted. She was the only person in Starlight who knew about what a scumbag Robbie had been.

"No more man trouble for me," Kaitlin said, then bit her lip. "Well, not exactly."

"That sounds intriguing."

One word to describe Finn. *Irritating*, *irresistible* and *irate* also came to mind.

"Jack's son is in town," Kaitlin explained. "He found out about the cancer and the trouble at the bank. He blames me."

"For cancer?" Mara sounded outraged.

"No. Of course not. For what's happening at the bank." Over drinks at Mara's tiny bungalow a few weeks ago, Kaitlin had confided her fear that Jack's focus on his cancer treatment was compromising his ability to run the bank. She understood Jack didn't want anyone to know about his illness but had needed to share her worry with someone she trusted.

"Why would that be your fault?"

Kaitlin shrugged. "He had Nick Dunlap run a background check on me."

"You were wild but not exactly a white-collar criminal," Mara pointed out, her pert nose wrinkling.

"No doubt." Kaitlin sipped her coffee, the sweetness of the smoky caramel flavor soothing her like she was a child who'd been given a lollipop after skinning her knee on the playground.

"But it still has nothing to do with you."

"He also wants me to help him figure out a solution."

"He thinks you're part of the problem *and* he wants you on his team?" Mara glanced over her shoulder at the line forming around the side of the coffee bar.

"I'm guessing it's his version of 'keep your friends close but your enemies closer.'"

"You've done nothing wrong," Mara reminded her. "In fact, Finn has you to thank for his dad's recovery. Your research discovered the doctor working on the successful treatment."

The bells over the entrance tinkled, and like a moth to a flame, Kaitlin's attention was drawn to the tall, devastatingly handsome man entering the coffee shop.

Mara gave an appreciative whistle under her breath. "Tell me that's not Finn Samuelson."

Finn glanced toward their table, his blue eyes darkening when his gaze met Kaitlin's. She thought about the warmth of his finger on her cheek. The answering heat that had pooled low in her belly. Goose bumps pricked along her skin, and she dug her fingernails into the fleshy part of her palm, willing herself not to react. Finn's dark brows furrowed slightly. Then he nodded in greeting and headed to the back of the line.

"You see my problem, right?"

Kaitlin shifted her gaze across the table toward

her friend. Mara was fanning herself with one hand, a smile curving her lips.

"I saw the way he looked at you."

"Like I'm a criminal," Kaitlin muttered.

"Like he wants to do things to you that are probably illegal in a number of states," Mara answered with a laugh. "What happened to your self-imposed dry spell with dating?"

"It's still in effect."

Mara shook her head. "Then you'd better hope Finn's stay in Starlight is a short one. I'm not sure how anyone would resist that guy for long."

"It's not a matter of resisting," Kaitlin insisted. "He doesn't trust me."

"But he wants you," Mara told her, "and that's either better or worse depending on your perspective."

Kaitlin darted another glance at the way the tailored suit jacket stretched across Finn's broad shoulders as he waited in line. "Definitely worse," she whispered.

Mara stood and reached across to give her a quick hug. "I need to get back. Just remember that this is your home now. Don't let Finn Samuelson, or anyone, make you feel like you don't deserve the life you've created here."

"I didn't even tell you my fear," Kaitlin said with a strangled laugh, "and you knew it anyway."

"It's my gift," Mara said. She pointed a finger at Kaitlin. "And don't have sex with him. No complications."

"I would never in a million years..." Kaitlin trailed off. She absolutely would have taken Finn to bed, and not that long ago. In her old life she had a penchant for making bad decisions and self-sabotaging, often with bad choices in men. "I'm not planning to do anything with Finn."

"Stick to the plan," Mara said with a nod, then headed back to work.

Kaitlin popped one last bite of brownie into her mouth, then rewrapped the leftover bit and shoved it into her purse. She felt both calmer after talking to Mara and kind of jittery from the extra shot of caffeine.

Those jitters turned into a full-blown swarm of butterflies flitting across her stomach when she turned to find Finn waiting for her at Perk's entrance.

"Good morning," she said as she approached, proud of how calm her voice sounded. "You got through the line in record time."

He held up his cup. "Black coffee is an easy order. How did you sleep?" he asked, and she immediately choked on a swallow of coffee.

"Fine." She wiped at her mouth with the back of her hand.

He gave her a look like he knew she was lying. She'd always been a terrible liar, something that had probably kept her from getting into more trouble back in the day. It was difficult to take too many risks when she had no confidence in her ability to not get caught.

She imagined the amount of fun she could have getting caught by Finn.

"Your dad was still at the house when I left," she said, reminding them both of the connection between them. Not her physical reaction, which she needed to ignore.

"What time does he usually get to the office?"

"By nine."

He let out a disbelieving snort. "Some things never change. When we were kids, he was gone by sunup and often back late at night after a business dinner."

"He's not the same as he used to be," she said, widening her steps to match his as they crossed the street.

"I get it."

"Do you?" The entrance to the bank was two storefronts away, and Kaitlin took hold of Finn's muscled arm, moving to block his progress, much as she had when he'd shown up to see Jack yesterday.

"It's not just about the cancer," she clarified.

"You've been gone for years, Finn. I understand that you had problems with your father when you were younger, but he's not a villain. Whatever perceived grievances you have, I know he regrets not being closer to you and your sister."

"Perceived?" he repeated, temper turning his voice razor sharp. "You have no idea what my childhood was like or how he closed himself off after Mom died. It was like living with a ghost. He just faded away, only materializing when he wanted to yell at Ella or tell me how I needed to work harder to live up to the Samuelson legacy. The pressure of…" His eyes narrowed. "What is that?"

"You don't recognize it?" She'd raised her hands in front of her chest and cocked her head like she was playing a musical instrument. "It's the tiniest violin in the world with a song of great pity for your horrible childhood."

"You can't understand—"

"Give me a break." She stepped closer until the toes of her black high-heeled shoes just touched the fronts of his expensive-looking leather wingtips. "Look at this town." She spread her hands wide, careful not to spill her coffee. "It's like Washington's version of Pleasantville. It's tragic that your mom died and awful that your dad had trouble dealing with it." She dropped her arms. "But you can't convince me you didn't have it pretty good. Let's play a little game of 'have you ever,' Finnie-boy."

He looked at once annoyed and amused by the endearment.

Kaitlin drew in a deep breath, then asked, "Did you ever have to sneak food from the cafeteria trash can because there were no groceries in the house?"

He blinked. "Of course not."

"Ever get put into foster care when your parent went to rehab?"

"You know I didn't."

Old anger and bitterness swelled in her. She should push it down but instead let it wash over her like a wave, losing herself in all she'd endured even though it still hurt. "Have you ever sneaked out of your bedroom window and slept a night under the playground slide in your neighborhood park because your mom's lousy boyfriend of the week got that look in his eye when you were brushing your teeth?" A tremor went through her at the memory. "The look that said he was coming into your bedroom late that night and nothing was going to stop him."

"Kaitlin."

She shook off the sympathy in his tone. "You don't know hard."

His full mouth thinned and a crease appeared between his brows. "When I was fourteen, my mom had a seizure while driving me to football practice. I'd been in the middle of a teenage rant complaining because we were running five minutes late. She ran off the road and crashed into a tree. I was ejected from the car but sustained only minor injuries."

"I'm sorry for your loss," she whispered, "but—"

He held up a hand. "You said your piece. It's my turn." He ran the same hand through his hair and she noticed his fingers trembled. "The front of the car was like an accordion, collapsing into my mother and damaging her inner organs. I couldn't free her no matter how hard I tried. Another driver dialed 911 but she died before the ambulance arrived. I was holding her hand when she let go."

Reaching out, he traced a finger along the tears streaming down her cheeks. Kaitlin hadn't realized she was crying. "I don't think you want to weigh our respective situations and tally who had it worse. We both went through something terrible."

She gave a shaky nod, embarrassed that she'd gone down this road with him in the first place.

"It's great that you and my father are friends." Finn drew back his hand. "I appreciate everything you've done for him. But don't tell me I'm not entitled to my own feelings about my childhood. They're none of your business."

"Your dad has talked about you a lot in the past few months. He has a lot of regrets, Finn. I just wanted you to know that." Even to her own ears the rationale sounded weak.

"Duly noted. Now, stay out of my life."

Finn turned on his heel and stalked toward the bank, and Kaitlin felt like the biggest jerk on the planet.

Chapter Five

Two hours later, Finn massaged a hand along the back of his neck, still feeling like a colossal jerk for how he'd spoken to Kaitlin.

He also couldn't believe he'd shared so much detail of his mother's death. He hadn't talked about the accident for years. Of course, everyone who'd been in Starlight at the time knew what happened.

But if his family ever came up in conversation in Seattle, he said as little as possible. A few people knew his mother had died when he was in high school but no one knew the circumstances.

He hated the sharp ache in his gut that accompanied his memories. He hated himself for trying to one-up Kaitlin in the crappy-childhood department. She'd revealed a lot about herself with those "have you ever" questions, and the vulnerability in her melty brown eyes had triggered something in him. Something ugly and small that caused him to lash out.

He knew his childhood wasn't the worst. The car wreck that had claimed his mother's life was unthinkably tragic and an event no child—no person—should ever have to endure. But he'd known she loved him. Hell, she'd spent the last minutes of her life whispering words of comfort to him, telling him he was brave and strong and how proud she already was of the man she knew he'd become.

Despite the way his father had closed himself off emotionally after her death, he'd taken care of Finn and Ella. They might have wanted for affection but little else. There were a hell of a lot of levels on the hierarchy of need they'd had met, unlike Kaitlin.

No, Finn had endured tragedy but his life hadn't been tragic.

Maybe that was why he'd reacted so harshly. As much as he would have liked to blame his father or use the excuse of his mom's death for the vague discontent he couldn't shake, he understood deep inside that he was the one lacking. He was to blame. He'd been given so much more than most. Way more than Kaitlin with her laundry list of childhood horrors.

Yet he couldn't find happiness. His heart refused to settle. The longer he remained alone, the more certain he became that his heart was the real problem. Was he a real-life happiness grinch? The organ that beat inside his rib cage didn't exactly feel two sizes too small, more like frozen or stunted in its development.

Returning to Starlight seemed to highlight that fact. This town, with memories around every corner, made him feel in a way he'd forgotten he was capable of, and he hated that most of all.

It was safer on his own. His ordered, compartmentalized life suited him and the amount he was able to give. His plan had been to confront his father and gain confirmation that Finn could move on with his life. That he had a good reason for his hindered emotions. But the changes in his father and Kaitlin's affection for the old man prevented such an easy out.

Finn would never admit it, but he was jealous of Kaitlin's relationship with his dad, of her easy loyalty and the way Jack seemed to rely on her. The old man had been an emotional island since Finn's mom died, or at least that was Finn's impression. What if Finn had spent a decade stoking the fires of his anger and bitterness for no good reason?

He pushed away from the computer and stood. He'd been given space in an empty office now being used for storage. When Kaitlin arrived at the office, a few minutes after him and refusing to make eye contact, she'd introduced him to the personal bankers and tellers, explaining that he was working on a new investment project with his dad.

It had further embarrassed him when the bank's staff, both new and old, gave him an enthusiastic welcome. Several people mentioned that they felt like he was already a part of First Trust because of how proudly Jack spoke of him.

He'd seen Kaitlin's shoulders go stiff, as if she expected him to lash out at the suggestion that his father cared about him, the way he had with her.

She'd disappeared soon after, and he couldn't help but wonder if she'd purposely set him up with the space farthest from his dad's because she wanted to avoid him. That would be the smart choice for both of them, but Finn wasn't feeling wise at the moment.

The morning hadn't produced the proverbial smoking gun he'd expected, something that would clarify why the bank was struggling. Instead he'd discovered a simple but bleak explanation, a series of risky decisions and unfortunate circumstances combining in a perfect storm of plunging profits and excessive losses.

It seemed unfathomable that his dad had mismanaged the business so catastrophically. With a ball of unease festering in his gut, he left the office, making polite conversation with a few people as he headed down the hall.

Kaitlin gave him a tight nod as he passed her desk, and it was on the tip of his tongue to apologize. Then the door to his father's office opened, Jack emerging with a smile for his assistant that faded when he caught sight of Finn.

Typical.

"Satisfied your curiosity?" he demanded.

Finn shook his head. "The bank is headed for big problems if you don't address your overly aggressive lending and risky credit portfolio."

"Keep your voice down." Kaitlin leaned forward over her desk, checking the empty hallway to make sure no one had overheard him. "You know how fast gossip travels in a town like Starlight."

He did his best to ignore the way her breasts strained against the fabric of her thin sweater. He hadn't had this kind of uncontrolled reaction to a woman in…well…ever, that he remembered.

"It's fact," he told her, "not gossip."

"Then you and Jack will fix it."

His father scoffed. "There's nothing to fix. We've been doing business the same way for decades. Our model is solid and will see us through."

Could it be as simple as that? Was it possible his dad's unwillingness to modernize and his insistence on funding every loan application submitted by someone in the community had caused all of the issues he saw with the bottom line?

He refocused his attention as his dad pointed at him. "First Trust made it through the Great Depression and the banking crisis of 1933. We're still standing strong. Things can't be as bad as you're making them seem. We've had ups and downs before and we'll weather whatever comes our way."

Finn glanced at Kaitlin, who flashed the barest hint of a pleading smile, as if silently asking him to ignore his father's rant and help make things right.

"I'm driving over to Seattle," he announced, earning a frown from Kaitlin. "I'll be late tonight," he added. "I have a friend who's a banking analyst. I'd like him to check out the debt-to-income ratio and see if he has any ideas."

"You can't share our information with a stranger," his dad protested immediately.

"I have to if we're going to turn things around." He ran a hand through his hair. "Dad, the bank is your legacy. Even though I'm not involved, I can respect that. I don't want it to fail, and I know you don't, either. Too many people in Starlight depend on you. Please let me help."

His father's thick silver brows drew together. "Take Kaitlin with you," he said instead of responding directly to Finn's comments.

"What?" both he and Kaitlin asked at once.

Jack gestured toward Kaitlin. "I trust her."

"But not me?" Finn demanded.

"Finn can handle this," Kaitlin added.

Jack looked between the two of them. "I trust you both, and I want you working together."

"Dad, I don't think—"

"Besides," his father interrupted, "she works too much. Kaitlin could use a night out on the town in the big city."

"I don't like the city," she whispered, and Finn noticed the color had drained from her face.

"Use the corporate card. Dinner's on me."

"I'm not going to Seattle for fun," Finn protested.

"Would it kill you to have some?" Jack pointed to Kaitlin. "*You* definitely need some fun in your life."

"My life is plenty fun," she argued weakly.

Jack laughed. "The only way I'll agree to Finn continuing to have access to bank data is if the two of you become a team."

"I'm supposed to meet with the mayor's office to talk over the signage for the art fair."

"I'll handle it," Jack said. "I mean it about the access, Finn."

"Fine," he muttered.

"Not fine," Kaitlin shot back.

"Work it out," Jack said with a wave of his hand before disappearing back into this office.

"I'm not going to Seattle with you," Kaitlin said, her wide mouth pulled into a mulish line.

"You have to. You know my dad. He'll shut me out if I don't meet his terms."

"Why do those terms have to involve me?"

He shrugged. "Not a question I can answer." He checked the silver Rolex that encircled his wrist. "But it doesn't surprise me. It's why I asked you to help in the first place. We need to get going. I told Roger I'd be at his office by noon."

When she didn't move, he stepped forward. "It's one afternoon, Kaitlin. It won't be that bad. I promise."

She sat as still as stone for a moment longer, then reached into a desk drawer and yanked out her purse. "I'll drive along for the meeting, but dinner is unnecessary. We can come right back after you finish with your friend."

"Whatever you want," he said. "And, Kaitlin?"

She looked at him. "Yes?"

"I'm sorry about earlier and even sorrier about everything you went through as a kid."

Color bloomed in her cheeks. "I shouldn't have shared any of that."

"I'm glad you did," he said, surprised to find the statement so true. "It was good for me to have a reminder that as sad as my mom's death was, I was lucky to have her and to know she loved me."

She gave a small nod and then they headed out of the bank. Finn opened the passenger door to the BMW, taking a deep breath as she slipped in. This return trip to Starlight was becoming more complicated by the second.

Especially his feelings for Kaitlin.

As shocked as he'd been by his dad's suggestion that she join him in Seattle, he liked the idea of spending the afternoon with her. That could lead to nothing good for either of them.

"A town like Starlight is a big change after living in Seattle," Finn said as the landscape on either side of the highway changed from rugged to pastoral to urban.

"I needed the change." Kaitlin grasped her hands tightly in her lap.

They'd been driving close to an hour, and she had yet to relax. She'd made a clean break when she left Seattle. Although Finn was meeting his friend in the heart of downtown, nowhere near her old stomping grounds on the south side, nerves still danced across her stomach. Seattle was a great city, but her life there had been a mess. She didn't want any reminders of that this afternoon.

"Do you miss any part of it?"

"The water," she answered automatically. She had to give Finn credit for trying.

She understood he was as unhappy having her riding shotgun on this drive as she was to be with him. But he'd tried to keep up the guise of friendly conversation for most of the trip, although her anxiety prevented her from giving him more than basic answers to his questions.

She drew in a breath and forced her body to relax. "I used to save my money to take the ferry to Bainbridge Island. The lakes around Starlight are nice, but it's not the same."

He nodded. "I bought a boat with my first bonus check."

"Of course you did," she said with a soft laugh, as if she needed another reminder of how different their lives were.

"It was small," he added, almost sheepishly. "The first time I took it out, the engine died and I couldn't figure out how to fix it. The coast guard had to come and tow me back to the dock."

She grinned and couldn't help but appreciate

that he'd shared the memory with her. "At least tell me you weren't wearing a captain's hat and an ascot."

"Only in my mind."

"I assume you got better at the whole sea-captain vibe."

He shrugged, and she noticed his fingers tighten on the steering wheel. "I sold it a couple of years ago. I didn't have the time for it."

"You're a classic workaholic."

"There are expectations when you're on the senior management track."

"Expectations are the worst," she said softly, and Finn laughed. The sound landed like a fist to her chest, stealing her breath.

She could tell herself all day long that she hadn't wanted to go to Seattle because of her past, but a part of her was afraid of spending time with him. Terrified of the way he made her feel and the unexpected connection joining them when they were together.

More quality time was exactly what she didn't need with this man.

"My dad said you were overdue for some fun." He glanced over at her before exiting the interstate toward downtown. "Does that mean you're a workaholic?"

"I'm just boring," she admitted.

He laughed again. "I doubt that."

"Don't get me wrong. I like it that way. Starlight is a good fit for me. The town rolls up the sidewalks early most nights, and I'm already home and tucked into bed with a good book."

"Just a book?" The car pulled to a stop at a red light, and Finn lifted a brow as he looked at her again. "No boyfriend to help you turn the pages?"

"I can turn the pages just fine on my own," she told him, color flooding her cheeks when she realized the not-so-subtle innuendo of their conversation.

"Duly noted," he said, his voice taking on a hoarse tone.

"It must be difficult for you to be away from work. I get the impression it doesn't happen often."

"I have a client I take skiing down in Lake Tahoe over the holidays. That's the only vacation I've had in years."

"Entertaining a client isn't vacation."

"It's me not in the office."

"Still doesn't count," she insisted, reaching over to poke his arm.

"Ouch."

A giggle bubbled up in her throat, and she clamped her mouth shut. "You're a baby."

"Am not." He squeezed her leg just above her knee and she squirmed. "You're boy crazy."

"Oh, heck, no." She grabbed his hand, smiling at the old childhood test. "Used to be, but not anymore."

But when she went to release him, he turned his hand, lacing his fingers with hers. "I'm glad you came with me."

"Why?" she couldn't help but ask.

"I don't want to be alone right now," he said, his fingers tightening on hers.

Kaitlin swallowed as emotion washed through her. Sometimes it felt like she'd been alone most of her life. For this man to want her with him meant something, even if she desperately didn't want it to.

"What do you think your friend will tell you?"

Finn gave a slight shake of his head. "I don't know. My hope is that he sees something that I'm missing in the financials I emailed. Something that offers an easy explanation for how to fix things."

"And if the answer isn't an easy one?"

He released her hand. "Another question I can't answer."

"The bank means the world to your father."

"It became his whole life after Mom died, even more than it was before."

"You and your sister mean more."

He let out a snort as he maneuvered into a parking space on a busy street a few blocks from the water.

Although she'd grown up in Seattle, Kaitlin hadn't spent much time in this part of the city. Businesspeople and trendy hipsters crowded the street. Even though she wore an outfit that was totally professional in Starlight, here she felt underdressed and out of place.

She got out of Finn's sleek car and waited while he fed the meter. When he glanced up at her, all the teasing from a few minutes earlier had disappeared from his blue gaze. Although he and his father were estranged, she could tell how much he wanted to get the bank back on track as a way to potentially mend his relationship with Jack.

She followed him into the modern office building, hoping for good news for both him and his dad.

Chapter Six

"This can't come as a surprise. We see it far too often in community banks. First Trust has been overly aggressive in lending, and now the debt-to-income ratio is way off." Roger Franks removed his reading glasses and leveled a sympathetic look toward Finn. "You didn't really think there was a smoking gun in these financials?"

Finn forced his reeling mind to focus. Roger might be confirming what Finn already knew, but he'd held out some slim hope that there was another explanation. He could feel the weight of Kaitlin's shocked stare on him but didn't turn toward her.

"No," he admitted quietly. "But I hoped you'd find something I missed."

Roger let out a small laugh. "When was the last time you missed something, Samuelson?"

Finn pressed two fingers to his temple. His head was pounding. "Never."

"Your family's bank is nearing the verge of failure."

"Can it be saved?"

Roger put his glasses on again and turned his attention back to the computer screen. "Maybe," he said after a moment. "But it would be easier to find a buyer. First Trust has one of two bank charters issued in Starlight. You know how valuable that is, Finn. AmeriNat specializes in this sort of deal. Your division specifically. If you got in touch with—"

"No," Finn interrupted. "I know my dad won't agree to sell."

"It would kill him," Kaitlin whispered.

Finn wanted her to be wrong. His father had survived the death of his soul mate and estrangement from both of his kids and had just kicked cancer's butt to the curb. But the bank was different. It wasn't just something his father loved. First Trust was a big part of who his dad was. His identity. His legacy.

And it was failing.

"I need a plan," Finn said, more to himself than to either Roger or Kaitlin.

Roger leaned back in his chair. "This isn't your wheelhouse, Finn. You're a regional director with one of the largest financial institutions in the country. Your focus is growth metrics, not running a family bank."

Finn had met Roger Franks his senior year of college, when he'd interned at the company where Roger was a senior partner. The older man had become both a mentor and a friend over the years, as well as a cautionary tale. Roger was a genius when it came to banking, but he'd also just finalized a divorce from his third wife. Finn had known walking down the aisle again was a mistake, but Roger insisted on chasing his own happily-ever-after even though his true love remained his career. No one and nothing could take its place.

The two of them had a lot in common, but Finn didn't want to believe that single-minded focus on work was something they shared. He had very few examples of happy marriages in his life. His parents' union had been one of them. His dad had always worked long hours, but he'd loved Finn's mother with his whole heart. And that had made it all the more difficult when his dad closed down so completely after her death. It was as if Finn and Ella weren't worthy of love with their mother gone.

Now the one love Jack had left was in jeopardy.

Finn shook his head, unsure why he felt such a desire to fix this but needing to do it just the same. "It doesn't matter. Tell me what to do."

Roger's bushy brows drew down over his eyes. "The bank needs to modernize. Draw in new customers while keeping the old ones happy with the personalized service they offer. Most important, they need to be more cautious with lending and minimize the risk for the bank's credit portfolio."

"How long will it take?"

"You need to implement some of these strategies immediately. Sooner if possible. If the bank can bring in new depositors quickly, you may have a chance at righting things."

Panic and resignation battled deep inside him. He didn't have six months, or even six weeks, to devote to his family's bank. How was he supposed to put his life on hold? But if he didn't, would his dad lose everything?

As if sensing his mounting anxiety, Roger gave him an encouraging smile. "I have a plan we put together for a community bank outside Portland. They didn't have quite the same set of issues but close enough that it may help." He looked from Finn to Kaitlin. "Maybe there's someone you trust in Starlight to spearhead this for you."

Finn heard a soft scoff and kept his gaze on Roger. "I'll figure it out. Thanks for everything."

He stood, still not willing to look at Kaitlin. He couldn't stand it if he saw doubt in her eyes. Even with Roger's ideas, Finn knew his bid to turn things around was a long shot.

"I hear wedding bells might be in your future," Roger said, almost as an afterthought, as he walked them toward the door.

Finn stopped so suddenly that Kaitlin bumped into him. She quickly stepped away as he turned toward Roger. "I'm not even dating anyone at the moment."

The older man clapped him on the shoulder. "I golfed last week with Peter. We saw Chelsea's father in the clubhouse. Ray said the two of you were taking a break."

Another sharp pain erupted behind Finn's right eye. He'd met his ex-girlfriend, Chelsea Davidson, at a charity event he'd attended with a client. Her dad was a prominent attorney in Seattle and close friends with Peter Henry, his bank's chief operating officer. On paper she was his perfect match and they'd dated for almost a year. He never should have let it go on that long, but she made it too easy for him. Chelsea had never seemed to expect anything from him until he realized the one thing she did want was an engagement ring. He couldn't give her that, even though he knew it would help his bid for a promotion.

"We aren't together," he told Roger but somehow knew it was Kaitlin he wanted to hear those words. "The relationship ended for good."

Roger rolled his eyes. "Not if Peter and Ray have anything to say about it. Those two were plotting like a couple of matchmaking mamas."

"No wedding bells," Finn insisted, the words coming out a low growl.

"Whatever you say." Roger turned to Kaitlin. "It was lovely to meet you."

As the two shook hands, Finn darted a glance in her direction. If the news of his ex-girlfriend affected her in any way, she hid it well. Not that she should be affected. Or that he wanted her to be. Except…

He left the office and strode toward his car, leaving Kaitlin to catch up to his long strides. He clicked the button on his key fob to unlock the BMW's doors and slid behind the wheel. As soon as the passenger door closed, he pulled away from the curb, focusing all his energy on maneuvering through downtown traffic.

He turned after a few blocks and entered the parking garage under the building that housed his condo. He waited for Kaitlin to speak, but she remained silent, as if she somehow understood he was at his breaking point right now. He never imagined being in this position with his father.

She followed as he got out after parking, and the sound of their shoes on the concrete echoed through the cool, quiet space. He punched the elevator button, and the doors slid open. It could be any normal day, although he wouldn't usually return home in the early afternoon. But the action of pulling out his keys and heading down the hall on the seventh floor, where his condo was located felt so routine. If he concentrated only on the moment, he could almost pretend his life hadn't been turned upside down.

But pretending wouldn't help anyone.

"Nice place," Kaitlin said quietly, and Finn glanced around his condo like he was seeing it for the first time.

He'd bought it for the location and because the address fit with his image. He hadn't given much thought to the decor. Any thought, really, since he'd hired an interior designer the firm used to buy all of his furniture. She'd gone for a typical bachelor look of sleek leather couches and contemporary accents.

It had seemed fine at the time, but he had to admit he didn't have one comfortable place to sit other than his king-size bed. Best not to think about his bed and Kaitlin at the same time.

He loosened his tie as he walked into the kitchen. “You really think so?” he asked, pulling two glasses out of a cabinet.

“If you’re into sterile waiting rooms as design inspiration,” she said dryly, “this place is the bomb.”

Despite the tension rolling through him, Finn smiled at her smart-aleck comment. Kaitlin Carmody didn’t pull any punches, and her refreshing honesty was damn attractive.

“Let me guess.” He turned and placed the glasses on the island that now separated them, then reached into a lower cabinet for a bottle of liquor. “You’re into lace doilies and embroidered throw pillows?”

One side of her mouth kicked up. “You might benefit from a needlepoint pillow around here. Maybe with the message ‘Trust me. I’m a banker.’”

“I’ll keep that in mind the next time I’m out shopping.”

He poured a finger of liquor into each glass, then pushed one toward her.

“Liquid lunch?”

“Liquid and then lunch,” he clarified. “It’s been that kind of a morning.”

She picked up the glass, grimacing as she sniffed the scotch.

“That’s an eighteen-year-old single-malt scotch.”

"Still smells like lighter fluid if you ask me," she told him but took a tiny sip as he downed his.

"Not much of a drinker," he said when they'd both placed their glasses back on the counter, his empty and hers still filled.

"Not anymore." She hugged her arms around her waist. "Back in the day I could have drunk you under the table." She tapped one finger on the rim of the glass. "Even then I didn't like the taste. But temporarily obliterating reality made downing copious amounts of cheap booze worth it."

The more time he spent with Kaitlin, the more difficult it was to imagine her as a hard-partying wild child. Her presence grounded him, and he couldn't imagine her ever losing control. He had to admit he would have liked to see her lose control. Not with alcohol but from his touch.

Shaking his head, he undid the top two buttons of his shirt, then grabbed two water bottles from the refrigerator.

"This might be more your speed," he said as he handed her one.

She nodded and took it from him, her fingers grazing his.

"What are we doing here, Finn?"

"I need to pack," he answered simply.

She took a drink of water, then pressed her lips together. "How long will you stay in Starlight?"

He liked that she didn't pretend not to understand his intention. "Like I said, I haven't taken a real vacation in years. I can get some time off. My boss won't like it, but I'll be able to manage most of the day-to-day business remotely."

"How long?"

He blew out a breath. "A couple of weeks."

She closed her eyes for a moment. "Thank you," she whispered.

"I don't know if it will be enough," he admitted. "But if I can manage to implement some of the initiatives Roger mentioned..."

"I'll help in whatever way you need. Everyone at First Trust will pitch in. No one wants to see the bank fail."

Finn eyed the bottle of whiskey. Of course it wouldn't help the situation to get totally drunk, but it would certainly feel good in the moment. He grabbed the bottle and shoved it back into the cabinet before he made a decision he'd certainly regret. "What about my father?"

"Jack wants the bank to do well. You can't think otherwise."

"I know he's dedicated, but you have to understand that First Trust is in this situation because he wouldn't modernize and he won't say no to anyone who needs money. As much as I wanted there to be a smoking gun or a villain—"

"Me," she interrupted.

He inclined his head. "I apologize for that. But yes, I wanted you… Doug, who smells like onions… Anyone to blame for all of the problems. A bad guy is easier to vanquish than an old man so stuck in his ways that he runs his own business into the ground."

"Doug *always* smells like onions," she said, wrinkling her nose. "No matter what time of day it is. That's weird, right?"

He laughed again. "It's kind of nasty."

Her features softened, as if it made her happy to hear him laugh. God help him, he liked the idea of making this woman happy.

"We can convince your father to make the changes," she promised. "I know it." She reached across the island and squeezed his hand. Her fingers were warm, her touch comforting. When was the last time someone had comforted him? When had he ever allowed it?

He looked down at her small hand covering his. Emotion gathered in the back of his throat and he pulled away.

"I was a jerk to you."

She flashed a crooked smile. "I understand why Doug had suspicions. I became pretty protective of your dad during the cancer treatments, and no one understood the reason. Of course, I also figured you were a jerk in general."

"That could be."

"It doesn't matter." She waved her hand as if dismissing his rudeness, which bothered him. He got the impression she'd dealt with more than her fair share of disrespect and managed it far too easily.

"I'm sorry."

"Oh." Her mouth formed the syllable on a small puff of breath. Clearly she also wasn't accustomed to hearing those words. "Okay. Well, it's fine. Really."

He wanted to argue but could tell his attention to this detail bothered her. That was the last thing he wanted. To be honest, he needed Kaitlin's belief that the mess at the bank could be fixed. Even if she was faking her faith in him, it meant something. More than was smart for either of them.

"I'm going to change clothes and pack a couple of suitcases. I need more than I brought for the funeral." He pointed to the flat-screen TV that dominated the far wall of the condo. "Feel free to watch a show or whatever."

"Whatever," she echoed.

"We can get something to eat on the way back if you want."

"You don't need to do that," she told him. "I know your dad said I need to have more fun, but—"

"I need fun." He shrugged. "And food. You don't want to see me when I don't get three squares a day."

"Then you're a meal behind," she said, glancing at her watch.

"Exactly." He placed a hand to his stomach. "I'll be ready in five."

Running a hand through his hair, he walked toward his bedroom. He grabbed two oversize suitcases from the corner of the closet and began tossing in clothes. No need to bother with his best suits. Even at the bank, he'd be overdressed in Starlight. He shoved in as many clothes as he could fit, a few pairs of shoes, including his old and recently underused hiking boots, then pulled the two pieces of luggage back toward the main living area of the condo.

Kaitlin stood to one side of the sink, using a dish towel to dry the whiskey glasses. As he watched, she returned the clean glasses to the cabinet, folded the towel and set it on the counter.

"You didn't have to do that." He felt oddly touched by the small display of domesticity.

"I have an idea for our late lunch," she told him. "Or early dinner. Whatever you want to call it."

"Is it fun?"

"Yes, unless you're a stodgy, sanctimonious stick-in-the-mud."

He barked out a surprised laugh. “No pressure.”

“Exactly,” she agreed. She walked forward and wrapped her fingers around the handle of his smaller suitcase. “Let’s go.”

The small gesture of solidarity caused a faint pinch in his chest, somewhere in the vicinity of his heart. They walked to the parking garage in companionable silence and loaded the trunk with his luggage.

“You’re confident you can get the time off from work?”

He shrugged and hit the button to turn on the car. “Yes, but it wouldn’t change my decision if not. I have to do this. We both know it.”

She punched something into her phone, then hit a button, and the GPS gave him instructions for which way to turn out of the parking lot.

“Are you going to tell me where we’re headed?”

“On an adventure,” she said, brown eyes dancing.

Adventure. Finn rolled the word around in his head for a moment. It felt unfamiliar and slightly terrifying. His life was about order and stability, and he was heading back into the murky waters of life in Starlight. He wasn’t sure that counted as adventure or if his nerves could handle anything more right now. But Kaitlin was beautiful and smiling at him like she really wanted to spend this afternoon together, despite what an ass he'd been.

She was giving him a second chance, and he might not be the sharpest knife in the drawer but he was smart enough not to turn it away.

"Where you lead," he told her as he pulled out into the shockingly sunshiny Seattle day, "I'll follow."

Chapter Seven

Nerves danced across Kaitlin's stomach as Finn turned his fancy car onto the dusty gravel driveway twenty minutes later. They weren't far from downtown, but it might have been a different planet.

"Since when is there an amusement park in Seattle?" he asked, leaning over the steering wheel to take in the tall Ferris wheel, twisty roller coaster and various other festival rides.

"It's a traveling fair," Kaitlin said and bit down on her lower lip. "They've been open in this location every June for as long as I can remember."

"Seriously?" He glanced over at her. "I had no idea. Is this the part of town where you grew up?"

She swallowed. "Mostly," she admitted, knowing how shabby this area must seem compared to his upscale building or the sprawling rancher that was the Samuelson family home in Starlight. "I moved around a lot. Foster care and all that. But this was close enough that my friends and I could ride our bikes here on summer afternoons."

"That must have been awesome," Finn said, maneuvering the car over a deep rut in the pasture to park between two Ford trucks. "The most we had was a dunk booth at the town Independence Day festival."

"Your life in Starlight was perfect," she chided. "Don't try to tell me any different."

"Would you believe I've never been on a Ferris wheel?"

"Come on. What about the one on the waterfront downtown?"

"Not once."

"Then I'm glad we're here."

She unclipped her seat belt and reached for the door handle.

Finn placed a gentle hand on her arm, and she turned to find him grinning from ear to ear. "Me, too."

Warmth spread through Kaitlin, and she forced

herself to climb out of the car before she did something really stupid like launch herself across the console and into his lap.

She had no idea why she'd thought to bring him here in the first place. But ever since Jack had said she needed to have fun, Kaitlin had been thinking about the last time she'd associated that word with her life. The MegaFun Amusement Park had sprung to her mind. No matter what had been going on in her life during any given year, summer nights spent stuffing her face with cotton candy and running from ride to ride with her friends always made her forget.

Finn needed to forget everything going wrong in his life, at least for a few hours.

And the fact that he'd never been on a Ferris wheel confirmed that she'd made the right decision. As much as she wanted to keep her distance from him, even more she wanted to see him patch up his relationship with Jack. Maybe he'd even choose to stay in Starlight. She knew that was his father's dearest wish.

One step at time.

"I haven't been here for a few years," she told him as they approached the ticket booth. "But if it's the same as it used to be, we can start with a few ride tickets or get an all-access band. Either way—"

"Kaitlin."

She turned, frowning as Finn stared at her in disbelief, his muscular arms crossed over his chest. He'd changed from his suit into a casual olive green collared shirt and loose jeans, but he still looked out of place amid the couples and families walking past. With his expensive haircut, chunky designer watch on his wrist and general air of superiority, he clearly wasn't part of this world. Her world. The one she'd belonged to for so long.

"What's wrong?"

"Do I look like the kind of guy who'd be satisfied with a few tickets?"

"Um…is that a trick question?"

He chuckled. "Sweetheart, I'm all access all the time."

The way his mouth curved up, she could tell he was joking, but heat still gathered low in her belly at his gentle teasing. She could easily imagine what it would be like to give all access to a man like Finn.

All night long.

They ordered corn dogs and slushies as they walked around the fair, and then purchased wristbands and headed toward the first ride. The park wasn't as crowded as it would be later, but a few groups still stood in line in front of the brightly colored Ferris wheel.

"Why do they keep stopping with people at the top?" Finn rubbed a hand along the back of his neck as he gazed up at the ride.

"It's part of the fun," she told him, laughing when he gave her a look like she might be crazy. "Don't tell me you're afraid of heights."

"Of course not," he said too quickly.

"Right," she agreed. "A man like you isn't afraid of anything."

"Oh, I'm afraid of plenty," he answered, still studying the Ferris wheel. They shuffled forward in line as the older man operating the controls loaded groups on and off. "Going back to Starlight. Losing my family's bank. Torpedoing my career with this extended vacation. The potential fallout from wanting to kiss you so badly I can hardly think of anything else."

She drew in a sharp breath, shocked by both his honesty and what he'd said about wanting to kiss her.

"You're trying to distract me."

"Or myself," he countered.

Suddenly the ride operator motioned them to load into the empty passenger car.

When Finn didn't move, Kaitlin took his hand and led him forward. "One step at a time."

"This isn't so bad," he whispered as they rose

about twenty feet off the ground, then stopped while another car loaded below them.

"I used to love the Ferris wheel most of all." She started to release her grip on his hand when she realized she still held it. But Finn tugged her closer, draping an arm over her shoulder.

"Why?" he asked.

"Because for a few minutes I was on top of the world."

"Quite a sensation." His voice sounded slightly strangled as the Ferris wheel gave a shudder and they began to spin.

"You can see downtown from here," she said, pointing north. "Maybe you can pick out your building."

When Finn didn't answer, Kaitlin glanced toward him, then grimaced. His eyes were closed, his shoulders rigid, and his free hand gripped the metal bar like he was holding on for dear life.

"Are you okay?"

"I lied," he said through clenched teeth. "I'm totally afraid of heights."

She brushed the hair away from her face as the Ferris wheel rose and fell again. She loved the breeze and the view and everything about the ride.

"I can get the guy to stop it so we can get off."

Finn gave a sharp shake of his head. "I'm not admitting that to anyone but you."

She pressed two fingers to her chest when it pinched. Something about seeing this strong alpha male's vulnerable side made every one of her defenses start to disintegrate.

Inching closer, she wrapped her arm around his waist. "I've got you," she told him. "It's all going to be just fine."

That teased a bit of a smile from him. A smile that disappeared when they abruptly stopped at the very top of the ride.

"What the hell…" he muttered.

"Remember, it's part of the fun," she promised. "Look around."

He kept his gaze fixed on hers. "No way."

"Finn, it's amazing." She turned to look behind her, where she knew she'd be able to see Puget Sound in the distance. Her movement caused the car to sway.

Finn muttered a hoarse curse as he gripped her shoulders. "Don't move."

"We're fine," she assured him with a confident smile. "I told you I'd give you an adventure."

"You're going to give me a heart attack," he countered, closing his eyes again.

His chest hitched in shallow breaths and she could see a thin sheen of sweat along his hairline. *Oh, gah.* Kaitlin had planned to take his mind off his troubles and instead she was serving up a different kind of stress.

"I'm sorry," she whispered, placing her hand on his cheek. "I didn't know..."

"It's a stupid fear," he said through gritted teeth. "I can manage a ski lift so I figured I'd be okay on this thing. I *am* okay. Seriously."

He didn't look anywhere near okay to Kaitlin. The Ferris wheel jerked and they moved one car length forward, rocking gently as the ride stopped again.

A muscle in Finn's jaw clenched, and without letting herself think about what she was going to do, Kaitlin leaned in and brushed her lips over his. He didn't react for a moment but then angled his head so that their mouths joined more fully. Even with the breeze picking up, she could smell the scent of him—shampoo and some spicy cologne. It had been a long time since her body had reacted to a man the way it did to Finn. A long time since she'd allowed herself to act on any sort of physical attraction.

In truth, she doubted she could have prevented this moment. She'd wanted to kiss Finn Samuelson since the moment she'd looked up from her desk to find him glaring down at her. Which was stupid and self-destructive, two things Kaitlin hadn't allowed herself to be since moving to Starlight.

He deepened the kiss, seeming not to notice when the ride started, then stopped again. At least she was distracting him. And herself. This was safe, she rationalized. An innocent kiss out in public. She could get it out of her system, then go back to ignoring him. Her reaction probably had more to do with a two-year dry spell in the bedroom department than something specific to this man. Sure. That was the ticket. A couple minutes of kissing and she'd be done.

As Finn's grip on her shoulders gentled, he made a soft sound low in his throat, or maybe the noise came from her. Either way it lit her insides on fire, like a spark to a dry field. His kiss was incendiary and she'd never felt so willing to go up in flames.

She pressed closer and his fingers trailed along her collarbone, the touch featherlight but affecting her to her core.

Suddenly a chorus of wolf whistles and applause broke out around them. Kaitlin drew back, color flooding her cheeks when she realized they'd come to the end of the ride. The Ferris wheel operator stared at them, tapping an impatient foot on the metal stairs.

"You two didn't get it out of your systems in high school?" he asked with a dismissive snicker.

"Sorry," Kaitlin mumbled, scrambling out of

the car. She straightened her thin sweater as she walked off the platform, not making eye contact with anyone waiting in line.

As soon as they were around the corner, she glanced back at Finn, and they both dissolved into fits of laughter.

"Totally busted," Finn said, shaking his head.

"Did you see the mom with the two little girls?" Kaitlin grimaced. "She was sending me death glares. Her kids are probably scarred for life."

"It was a kiss," he answered. "More likely the mom was jealous."

"No doubt," she agreed. "That was a heck of a kiss."

Finn grinned, then made a show of looking around at the other rides. "I need to find something else really high up. I like how you distract me."

She gave him a playful shove. "That was a one-time deal."

He took her hand and drew her closer, winding his arms around her waist. "I hope not."

"Finn." She bit down on her lower lip. "We can't. You know we can't."

His expression turned mulish. "Why not?"

"It will overcomplicate an already complicated situation."

He leaned in, pressing his forehead to hers. "For a few minutes when I was scared of plummeting to my death in a freak amusement park accident, I actually forgot about everything else."

"That was the point of this."

"I thought you were just looking for an excuse to have your merry way with me."

She choked out a laugh. "I don't have a *merry* way."

"Liar," he whispered but stepped back from her. "What's next?"

"We're keeping you close to the ground," she told him, earning an eye roll.

"How about bumper cars?"

"Perfect."

He reached out and smoothed a stray lock of hair from her face. "Yeah, it is."

Her breath caught in her throat. The way he was looking at her made her feel…everything.

"I'm going to kick your butt in the bumper cars," she said, forcing a light tone. She had to keep this casual. It was a fun afternoon of blowing off steam. Nothing more.

"We'll see about that," he said as they headed toward the next ride.

They went on the bumper cars, the scrambler and then the merry-go-round. Finn won her a stuffed elephant at a game booth along the midway, and then they ate a dessert of sweet funnel cakes.

As the sun began to set, the fairgrounds glowed with thousands of twinkle lights. Kaitlin felt grimy and stuffed and happier than she could remember in ages.

Finn was like a little boy making up for lost time. Although they stayed away from a second ride on the Ferris wheel, he insisted on trying everything else. He was playful and flirty, and while they didn't kiss again, attraction continued to simmer between them.

By the time they were heading toward the exit, Kaitlin felt dizzy, both from the rides and the unexpected connection she felt with Finn. It was more than physical. She enjoyed him. She liked who she was with him, which was new for her with a man.

"I'm going to wash my hands before we leave," she said, holding them up, palms out. "I still feel sticky from the funnel cake sugar."

"Isn't sticky part of the fun?" he teased.

Oh, sure. It was going to be simple to go back to ignoring her feelings for him.

She made a show of rolling her eyes and shoved the elephant he'd won for her toward him. "Hold Josiah," she told him.

His brows furrowed. "Who names a stuffed elephant Josiah?"

"Me." She stuck out her tongue as he took the animal from her, then turned on her heel and flounced toward the bathroom. It had been years since Kaitlin had done any flouncing, but she couldn't help adding some extra swing in her hips. Finn's laughter echoed behind her as she entered the restroom.

She moved in front of the row of faucets, glancing up at herself as the water automatically began to flow.

Her cheeks were flushed and although her hair was messy and tangled and her makeup had given up the ghost hours earlier, she couldn't help but notice that she looked happy. Like she used to feel at the amusement park when she was a girl.

Why was happiness so underrated in adulthood?

Or perhaps just difficult to attain.

She concentrated on her hands as the door to the restroom opened.

"I thought that was you, Kait."

Kaitlin glanced up into the mirror to find Cammie Pruitt staring at her, a smile on her face more suited to a cat that'd just made a meal of the canary. All those happy memories dissolved like spun sugar on her tongue. Cammie had been a part of Kaitlin's life when the perception of popularity became more important than her true friends.

"It's me," she said, trying to sound casual. A quick check of her reflection as she turned for a paper towel showed her she was doing a terrible job of looking casual. "It's been a while. You look good, Cammie."

"Been a while?" The voluptuous blonde let out a shrill cackle. "You disappeared."

"I moved," Kaitlin corrected. "Not the same thing."

"Same result." Cammie sidled closer. "I saw the guy you're with tonight. Moving up in the world, huh?"

"He's a friend." Kaitlin crumpled the paper towel in her fist and commanded herself to get a grip. She could not show Cammie how rattled this impromptu reunion made her.

"With benefits, I hope."

"*Just* a friend." She turned and pasted a bland smile on her face. "What are you doing here? The rides always made you queasy."

Cammie nodded as she placed one hand on her hip. "My new guy has a kid who wanted to come. I'm auditioning for the role of loving stepmom."

"Good luck… I guess."

"Yeah, he's a rung up from the old neighborhood." She waggled her overly sculpted brows. "Not the colossal leap you made, but that's no surprise. You were always different from the rest of us. Better in some way."

Kaitlin swallowed. “I never thought I was better than anyone.”

“Robbie did. It’s why he picked you in the first place.” Her hip jutted out and Kaitlin could all but feel the attitude being sent her way. “He was so angry when you left.”

“We weren’t good for each other. Everyone knew it.”

“Not him.”

“It’s been two years,” Kaitlin said helplessly.

“Oh, he’s moved on,” Cammie said with a snarky little laugh. “Plenty of times.” She took a step closer. “But I’m sure he’d like to see you.”

Panic gripped Kaitlin. Robbie had never been abusive, but they were toxic together. That whole part of her life had been poison. A complete break was the only way she could have extricated herself from their self-destructive codependency. And she might be different now but she had no intention of testing her resolve.

She’d left Robbie and Cammie and the hot mess she’d been far behind.

“That’s not a great idea.”

“So, where are you living now?” Cammie asked, the calculating light in her eyes belying her casual tone.

“On the north end of town,” Kaitlin said, and it

wasn't totally a lie. The Samuelson property was on the north side of Starlight.

Cammie's eyes narrowed. "You're still in Seattle?"

"I'm in Seattle." That wasn't exactly a lie, either. She was in Seattle. At the moment. And planning to get the hell out of town as fast as possible. "It was great to see you." Now, that was a lie. "I hope things go well with your guy."

"Yours, too," Cammie said, moving aside so Kaitlin could pass.

"He's not mine," she said over her shoulder.

"In that case, you want to introduce me?" Cammie laughed at her own joke, but Kaitlin didn't bother to respond.

"Let's go," she said to Finn, who was waiting near the ticket booth.

She didn't wait for his answer but took long strides toward the parking lot, head down like someone else from her past might recognize her. She hadn't ever gone to the fair as an adult, so she wasn't expecting to see anyone she knew.

But if Cammie was here because of her boyfriend's kid, Kaitlin imagined others in her former circle of friends might have settled down. She'd only been gone two years, and this wasn't exactly the place for a baby or toddler, but still…

Finn caught up with her in a few steps. "What's the hurry?"

"Nothing. I just want to get back. An escape from reality is great, but tomorrow the real work starts. We can't be bleary-eyed for it."

"Are you worried about a funnel cake hangover?"

"That's not a thing."

It was easy to find the BMW in the sea of cars that filled the field. The sleek black sports car stuck out like a sore thumb, or more like a fine piece of silver on a table filled with plastic cutlery.

Just as she got to the passenger door, Finn placed a hand on her arm. "Kaitlin, what's going on?"

She spun toward him, ready to snap, but stopped abruptly when he held out the stuffed elephant.

"Josiah," she whispered, unable to prevent her smile. She wouldn't allow Cammie or anyone else to ruin this day. She'd spent so much of her life living in fear, doing nothing more than reacting to what other people did or said to set her off. It was easy to think she'd changed since her move to Starlight, but how much had she truly grown as a person if a few snide remarks from someone she used to know could put her back to square one?

"Terrible name for an elephant," Finn muttered but she could hear the amusement in his tone.

"I saw someone I used to know," she admitted. "From before I left Seattle."

"Not a friend, I take it."

"She had been a friend of a sort. We hung out in the same crowd." She swallowed, then said, "For a while, we dated guys who were best friends, so Cammie and I were together a lot."

"The boyfriend you left behind."

"Yeah." The word was no more than a whoosh of breath, a piece of dandelion fuzz carried along on the breeze.

"Regrets?"

"Too many to count," she admitted. "But none about walking away. It was just…disconcerting." She shrugged. "I grew up around here but forgot about the possibility of running into my past. I thought it would be fun. I didn't think much beyond that."

"I had fun," he said, and although his gaze darkened, he didn't move to touch her.

As much as she wanted him to, she appreciated that he held back. She wasn't sure her emotions could handle anything more at the moment.

"I'm glad. I did, too."

He nodded and opened the door for her. "Then it was a good day."

She smiled as she climbed into the car. A good day.

That would work for her.

Chapter Eight

"You're welcome here as long as you want."

Finn dropped his duffel bag to the tile floor of Nick's kitchen, then picked up the mug of coffee his friend had set on the counter for him. It had been three days since he and Kaitlin spent the afternoon in Seattle. He'd returned to his friend's house but didn't feel right bunking here for his entire stay in town.

"I appreciate that, but if part of the reason for returning to Starlight is making things better with my dad, it makes sense that I stay with him."

Nick studied him over the rim of his mug, which

read "Police officers do it with handcuffs." "Is that part of your reason?"

Finn grimaced as the bitter coffee hit his tongue. "I thought a cop would be able to make a better brew."

"I like it strong."

"There's strong…" Finn placed his mug back on the counter. "And then there's tar."

"Is that why I keep spotting you walking out of Main Street Perk?"

"You should try a decent cup once in a while."

Nick shook his head. "I don't do fancy coffee. I'm old-school that way. Now, stop trying to distract me from interrogating you about your prolonged return to Starlight. Will you and Jack survive a few weeks under the same roof?"

"I'll make it work," Finn answered. "My priority is making sure the bank survives."

"You're doing a good thing, Finn." It was strange to hear so much sincerity in his friend's voice. Nick normally kept things in his personal life light and on the sarcastic side. A defense mechanism, and it meant something to Finn to know he'd been deemed worthy of more than some easy banter.

"Why do I feel like I waited too long?" He pressed his thumb and index finger to his forehead.

"If I'd come back a year ago, maybe First Trust wouldn't be in this position."

"And if you hadn't come back, maybe Jack would have lost everything."

"I know my dad loves to wax poetic about respecting the bank's historical significance in town, but it's still difficult for me to believe he thought he could make it through this crisis without some enormous changes."

"It sounds like he had other priorities."

"He swears he's been given the all clear but I can't help but wonder if he'd even share with me if he was still sick."

"Kaitlin would tell you."

"The keeper of all when it comes to Jack Samuelson."

"I don't know her well," Nick said, draining his mug with a loud slurp. "But I like her. She's friendly without being pushy and seems genuinely dedicated to your dad and the bank."

"I guess." Why was it so hard to admit that he'd been wrong about her? Their time in Seattle had been the most fun he'd had in ages. Not the morning, of course. The meeting with Roger had left him close to shattered at the understanding of truly how much it would take to fix the mess at First Trust. Somehow Kaitlin had sensed it and managed to shore up his tattered emotions with an afternoon at the pop-up amusement park, something Finn had never considered doing in his adult life.

"The town needs the bank, Finn. It's a local institution. So many families and small businesses rely on the support they get there."

He sighed. "No pressure."

"It's an unbelievable amount of pressure. I can't think of anyone better equipped to handle it than you."

"This is not how I imagined adulthood when we were younger."

Nick chuckled. "It was going to be fast cars and no one telling you to clean up after yourself."

"Exactly," Finn agreed, his chest aching for the naive kids they'd been. "Now I'm cleaning up after my dad and you're the one giving tickets to the speeding drivers."

"And I can tell you the exact number of tickets my department has issued over the past five years."

Finn shook his head. "We're pathetic."

"You're rolling out the plan today at the bank, right?"

"Yep."

"Text me later and let me know how it goes. I'm on duty until seven but if you need someone to buy you a beer later…"

"Thanks."

Finn left his friend's house and headed toward downtown Starlight. The sun glinted through the canopy of pine trees as he drove the familiar mountain roads. This valley was still relatively sleepy, even with a steady stream of summer tourists and city dwellers looking to escape to nature for a few days. Growing up, he hadn't appreciated the quiet the way he could now.

He parked next to his dad's Lexus SUV in the parking lot behind the bank, reminding himself that he was here to help. He had no idea how his plan would be received by anyone at the bank, but that didn't make him less committed to carrying it out. There was no other way to turn the ship around.

"I've called a staff meeting for ten," his father announced as Finn entered his office. "Kaitlin tells me I'm not allowed to fight you on any of the silly newfangled stuff you've come up with. I have to *support* you." The words came out almost as a growl, and Finn wasn't sure whether to smile or grimace.

He glanced over his shoulder as Kaitlin walked in behind him, carrying two cups of coffee, and cleared her throat.

"I appreciate what you're doing to help the bank," his father said quietly. "To help me."

"Coffee?" Kaitlin asked, handing Finn a cup.

She didn't make eye contact, which irritated him on some visceral level.

But he focused on his father. Even if Kaitlin had put him up to agreeing, the fact that his father was willing to meant something. He'd talked to his dad the morning after his meeting with Roger, and although Jack had been reluctant to admit how dire the situation truly was, he'd eventually agreed to let Finn implement a new strategic plan for First Trust. It had taken him a couple of days to iron out the details. Now all he needed to do was wrap his mind around the idea of working with his father again.

"I'd like to go over some of the *newfangled stuff*," he said, taking a sip from the cup as he stepped forward. He almost groaned in pleasure at how much better it was than the swill at Nick's. He hadn't stopped at the coffee shop, so he needed the jolt of caffeine in a bad way. "The key is going to be to roll it out quickly."

"I don't like change," Jack grumbled. "Do you know I've eaten the same thing for breakfast every day for the past four decades?"

"Yogurt, granola and half a banana." Finn nodded. "I know. But this isn't like a meal preference, Dad. It's progress."

His father scoffed.

Finn pointed to a device sitting on the desk. "You use a cell phone."

"He likes to text," Kaitlin added.

"I don't *like* to text," Jack grumbled. "It's convenient."

Finn hid a smile as Kaitlin rolled her eyes. "So are some of the changes I'm proposing," he told his father.

"Our customers want to come into the bank, either here or the branch out near the high school."

"Not everyone likes to do their banking on-site these days."

"People are disconnected in the real world. Everything's about apps and social media."

"You can't ignore it." Finn placed his coffee cup on the edge of the desk and pulled a laptop out of his briefcase.

"I'm not ignoring anything."

Except the fact that you're running the family business into the ground, Finn wanted to argue.

"We're going to have a Facebook page," Kaitlin said brightly, clearly doing her best to ignore the tension between the two men. "You love Facebook, Jack."

It was Finn's turn to scoff.

His father's bushy eyebrows drew down over his familiar blue eyes. "I enjoy the quizzes," he said as if that explained everything.

Kaitlin gave Finn a pointed look.

Right. He was supposed to be placating his father so that he'd lend his support to the changes Finn wanted to implement. Antagonizing him would do no good, but old habits and all that.

"I'll friend you," he offered.

"You do that." His father moved a few things from the middle of the desk to make room for Finn's computer. It was a tiny gesture but Finn knew it meant something significant. This desk represented his father's power, and he was making room for Finn.

Finn swallowed against the emotion rising in his throat. Would it have made a difference in how he'd felt about First Trust if his father had made him feel more welcome here when he was younger? Even though it had been clear his dad expected him to take his place at the bank, it had been just as evident that Jack would never relinquish any sort of real power.

Or had that been just an excuse—a rationale Finn had told himself so that he wouldn't feel guilty for walking away from the family business?

"I have a question for you before we get started," his dad said, steepling his hands, elbows on the desk.

"What's that?" Finn lowered himself into one of the chairs positioned in front of the desk. He wanted Kaitlin to take a seat next to him, but she remained standing just behind his father's left shoulder. Finn didn't like it. It made him feel like they were on opposite sides and he wanted—needed—her in his corner.

She hadn't given him a reason to doubt her, despite some of his less-than-chivalrous behavior toward her. She'd made herself scarce since that kiss on the Ferris wheel, but he knew she wanted the best for him, his father and First Trust. Although that should make him happy, he wished her loyalty was only to him. The shadow of the bank had loomed large over every part of his life. It had been his dad's greatest love, often at the expense of his wife and children. No wonder Finn hadn't wanted to dedicate himself to the institution that he'd so often resented during his childhood.

Although here he was, taking an inconvenient absence from his own life to do just that.

"Who's going to manage all of these new initiatives when you trot back to Seattle?"

Finn felt his eyes narrow at the derision in his father's tone. As if he'd be deserting First Trust for something frivolous.

"The staff will handle it," he said, hating the gnawing tightness in his voice.

"Most of them aren't equipped to handle the sort of programs you want to implement."

"They can be trained," Finn insisted. So much for his father supporting what he was trying to do here. He glanced at Kaitlin to see if she realized what was happening. Jack might give lip service to accepting the change, but Finn realized his doubts about his dad had been well-founded, as usual.

Jack leaned forward and pinned Finn with his assessing stare. "Who's going to train them?"

"I will," Kaitlin offered as she came around the desk.

She took the seat next to Finn, just as he'd hoped she would. And as he'd hoped, her presence instantly calmed him. This woman was like his own personal aromatherapy diffuser.

"You don't know anything about marketing at a bank," his father told her, his tone considerably gentler than the one he'd used with Finn.

"Finn will show me." She nodded. "Train the trainer. I've been up late the past couple of nights researching the strategies that other community banks our size have started and the ones that have seen success. I've made some calls to institutions within the region." She held up one hand as she ticked off a list. "There are a few in Washington and a couple others in Oregon. I've scheduled an appointment with the marketing director at Willamette Community Bank. It's only a three-hour drive."

Finn glanced at his dad and found Jack's mouth hanging open much the way he figured his own might be. A moment later, Jack snapped it shut, returning his gaze to Finn. "Did you know about all that?"

"I…um…"

"It was his idea," Kaitlin said without even so much as an eyebrow twitch. "Finn has this under control, Jack. We'll get the staff on board, keep the current customers happy and attract new ones. It's going to work. I know it."

She turned to Finn, and he wasn't sure whether to be buoyed or terrified by the quiet confidence in her dark gaze.

"It's going to work," he repeated. Somehow with Kaitlin in his corner, he believed it.

Kaitlin heard the voices drifting from the break room at the back of the bank's first floor as she walked down the hall.

"I don't know who she thinks she is."

"I've been at the bank for almost twenty years now. Why don't I get to be in charge of this new plan?"

Kaitlin recognized the voices. Liz Martin, the customer service manager, and Cassie Pope, one of First Trust's personal bankers. Both of the women had been kind, if a bit condescending, in the way ladies who considered themselves town mavens could be. But she'd liked them. Cassie had tried to set up Kaitlin with her single nephew. So she was good enough to date a relative but not to take on any real responsibility at the bank?

"She's not even a true local. She shows up in town one day and Jack practically adopts her—"

"As a stand-in since he messed up things with his flesh-and-blood kids, no doubt."

"Do we know who her people are?"

"Does she even *have* people?"

A titter of laughter followed that rhetorical question.

But the casual and crass words weren't funny to Kaitlin. She placed a hand on the wall, needing something to steady herself from the avalanche of emotions pounding through her.

"Don't listen to those two old biddies," a voice said at her shoulder.

She whirled around to find Meg Anderson, one of the young tellers, offering a sympathetic smile. "It's how they deal with change. Those two are like dinosaurs that refuse to see the meteor coming even when fiery rocks start hitting them on the head. Liz is convinced I'm a secret drug addict because of this." She touched the tiny diamond that flashed in her pierced nose.

"I thought they liked me," Kaitlin whispered, somehow unable to pretend the words didn't hurt. More evidence that she'd let herself go soft since she'd come to Starlight. She'd dealt with far worse criticisms than the ones Liz and Cassie were bandying about.

"They do." Meg touched her arm. "I'm not sure why it took Mr. Samuelson so long to start implementing changes around here. Or how the old-timers at the bank managed to convince themselves that business was great. I've only been here six months, but I could see we were heading for disaster."

"I'm not sure it's that bad," Kaitlin said, feeling as though she needed to be loyal to Jack.

Meg shrugged. "I want to keep my job. My boyfriend works for the Forest Service outside town, so we're in Starlight for the foreseeable future. I like eating at restaurants too much to be a waitress. I hate waiting tables."

Kaitlin smiled. "Me, too."

"The ladies will get used to you being part of the management team."

"I'm not management," Kaitlin protested immediately.

"You will be if you do a good job with this." She winked. "No pressure."

"Thanks—I think—for the vote of confidence."

Meg gave her an exaggerated thumbs-up, then continued down the hall and disappeared around a corner.

Kaitlin inched closer to the break room.

"I bet she's sleeping with one of them," Liz said.

"Maybe both of them," Cassie added with a whoop of laughter.

"You've been reading too many of those *Fifty Shades* knockoffs," Liz admonished the other woman.

All the confidence Kaitlin felt talking to Meg vanished in an instant. How could they reduce her to some sort of office stereotype that way? She wasn't sure why she expected better from other women, but she did.

She pressed a hand to her stomach. Suddenly the fruit and yogurt she'd put in the staff refrigerator this morning held no appeal. She turned and headed back toward the front of the bank, through the main lobby and out the antique cherry doors without making eye contact with another soul.

If she had, there was no way she'd be able to hide her embarrassment and shame. She crossed Main Street and hurried into the park that made up a full square block in the center of town. The voices of children in the playground situated in one corner filtered through the air, but she turned in the other direction. There were a few quiet corners in the park, despite its year-round popularity.

Her breathing began to return to normal as she walked along a narrow dirt path canopied by sprawling branches of mature oak trees. At the end of the lesser-used path was a weathered park bench. Sometimes Kaitlin brought her lunch to this spot, but today she just sat.

Closing her eyes, she focused on pushing air in and out of her lungs and releasing the negative emotions that plagued her. Meg was right. The women's petty gibes had less to do with Kaitlin than they did with their own insecurities. She didn't have to take it personally. She wondered if this was how Finn felt when Jack expressed doubt about the plan to save the bank.

If two insulting coworkers hurt her, imagine how much worse it would be for Finn with his own father.

She blinked and glanced up as heavy footsteps sounded on the gravel. As if her thoughts had drawn him to her, Finn walked toward her and then sat down on the empty side of the bench.

"I grew up in this town and I don't think I've ever walked down this particular path until today. I never even noticed it."

"The literal path less taken," Kaitlin said, trying to make her voice light. "I'm all about it."

"I like that about you." His voice sounded even deeper than normal in the quiet of the shady clearing.

She hummed an acknowledgment of his words in the back of her throat, not trusting herself to speak.

"This morning went well," he commented.

"Sure." She swallowed back any other response.

He shifted next to her on the bench, turning so he was facing her. Kaitlin kept her gaze straight ahead.

"You rushed out of the bank just now. What's wrong?"

"I'm fine, Finn. Really."

"What's wrong?" he asked again in the same tone, patient and slow as if he had all the time in the world to wait for an answer.

It practically undid her.

"I heard some of the longtime staff talking about me in the break room. It's stupid and not at all your concern. I need a few minutes to myself. Nothing more."

"Tell me about this talking."

She shrugged. "Petty gossip about how I don't deserve to be leading the charge on any of the new initiatives." She flicked her gaze toward him. "About how I'm probably sleeping with you or your dad as job security."

He let out a breath that sounded more like a hiss. "I hope you marched in there and told them—"

"I ran away. Out here."

"Kaitlin."

She hated the soft admonishment in his voice.

"It makes sense that they'd believe the worst of me."

"Why?"

"Why not?" Now she turned to fully face him. "You did."

His full lips thinned into a tight line. "I didn't know you."

"You still don't trust me."

"I do."

She let out a little snort of disbelief.

He reached out and slowly traced the curve of her ear before his hand lowered to the back of her neck. She didn't realize how much tension she held there until Finn's warm fingers began to gently massage it away.

"I want to trust you, and I appreciate everything you've done to help my dad and support me. Turning things around isn't going to be easy, but you've made me believe it's possible."

"It is," she whispered, letting her eyes drift close and trying not to embarrass herself by moaning out loud.

"How do you know?"

"You may have gone off to do your own thing in the world, but you love your dad and this town. You're going to make things right."

"You'll be a big part of that. Don't let what other people think define you."

She breathed out a small chuckle. "That line should be on a poster with some stylized photo of a rock climber gripping the side of a cliff."

"If I'm the guy in that poster, will you hang it above your desk?"

Her smile widened and she opened her eyes. "Only if you're shirtless."

His laughter rang out in the quiet, and a bird seemed to warble in response. "It's a deal."

She shook her head. "That won't make me any more popular with the ladies at the bank."

He inclined his head, his blue eyes dancing. "You could sell copies."

"Good to know you have a healthy sense of yourself."

"Would you like to confirm my 'sense of self'?" he asked, loosening his tie and unbuttoning the top button of his tailored shirt. She couldn't decide whether she liked him better in his business attire or more casual like he'd been on their afternoon in Seattle.

The truth was, she liked him both ways and

could imagine she'd appreciate him even more with no clothes.

"I'll take your word for it," she said even as her body screamed a silent protest.

"Come on," he coaxed, his voice a sexy growl. "Seeing is believing."

"You're trying to distract me from being upset."

"I'm trying to seduce you," he countered and leaned in to kiss her.

Chapter Nine

He hadn't planned on kissing her again. He wasn't even sure why he'd followed her out of the bank. Finn didn't consider himself either intuitive or a guy who was sensitive to other people's moods.

He was a dealmaker. He managed facts, figures and, most important, profit margins. Rarely did emotion play into his work, and he definitely hadn't become the youngest person to be named a regional director by acting on his emotions. Starlight was messing with him, with who he was on a cellular level. As if the fresh air and slower pace of life had seeped into him, recalibrating everything he knew to be true about himself.

Or maybe it was Kaitlin and the strange, visceral connection he felt with her.

He shouldn't have kissed her but could resist her about as much as he could stop himself from breathing.

The urge was almost involuntary.

Except he was choosing this. Choosing her.

As he slanted his mouth over hers, he heard her sigh. Resignation or desire—he couldn't tell which.

Then she threaded her fingers through his hair, her nails gently grazing his scalp. Lightning sparks of desire skipped along his neck and shoulders. As he was coming to expect with Kaitlin, his tension eased.

Another sort of agitation escalated through him as her tongue licked across the seam of his lips. He opened for her, beyond grateful that she deepened the kiss. There were no words for how much he wanted this.

Luckily, he didn't need words to tell her how he felt. He put all of his desire into kissing her, hoping she understood. Based on her reaction, she felt as much as he did.

Until suddenly she pulled away and stood, straightening her pale pink sweater with a sharp tug.

"I should get back." Her voice was shaky, breathless. "No need to give Liz and Cassie another reason to talk about me."

"I didn't mean for that to happen," he felt compelled to tell her.

"I know," she whispered and then hurried away.

What the hell was wrong with him? He rebuttoned his shirt and straightened his tie. Damn Daniel for dying and bringing him back here, he thought, then immediately regretted it. What kind of a selfish jerk had he turned into that he thought the changes in his life could hold a candle to what Brynn's family must be dealing with now?

In truth, Finn had been given a gift. He had a do-over with his father, a way to clean the slate so he could move forward in his own life without guilt.

This morning had been more difficult than he'd imagined. He was used to managing money. His division employed plenty of people, but he felt so much more of a personal responsibility to the people at First Trust, even though they weren't technically his employees. Chances were good that if his father was forced to sell the bank to a national institution, most employees would retain their positions. But there was no guarantee and, even so, it wouldn't be the same.

He retraced his steps down the path, pausing

to watch the children playing on the park's jungle gym. The equipment had been added since Finn left Starlight. He and his friends had largely roamed the town unsupervised from a young age, gangs of skinned-kneed kids riding bikes, climbing trees and building forts in the surrounding woods.

A woman with thick, dark hair falling over her slender shoulders waved to him. Finn's chest lurched. He hadn't seen Brynn since the funeral, and at that time she'd been surrounded by so many friends and family members he hadn't done much but give her a hug and whisper a few perfunctory words of comfort.

He lifted a hand in greeting and walked toward her. They'd been friends in high school, although unlike Nick, Finn had hung out more with Daniel. They'd played football together all four years of high school, which was as much of a bond as any to teenage boys.

"Hey, Brynn," he said as she met him at the edge of the mulched border that surrounded the rubber base of the play area. "How are you?"

She gave a small laugh. "I've had better months."

"Of course," he answered quickly, embarrassed that he'd asked the question. "Sorry." Shouldn't he know she wasn't doing well? She'd buried her husband a week earlier. How could she be? "I'm really sorry."

"Finn, it's fine." She placed a hand on his arm, her smile warm and comforting. It said a lot about Brynn Hale that her instinct was to make him feel better about shoving his foot in his mouth. "I was making a joke." She frowned. "There seems to be some rule about newly widowed women not being allowed to smile or laugh. I haven't gotten to that part in the instruction manual."

Finn felt his jaw go slack. "There's an instruct—" He inclined his head, studying Brynn. "That was another joke."

"You're catching on," she told him with a quick grin.

"I like that you're smiling."

"I have a son to raise." She turned to gaze toward ten-year-old Tyler, who was totally engrossed in shoveling sand in the oversize sandpit. "He has enough grief of his own without having to deal with mine, as well. I want him to know it's okay to still feel happy, even if he misses his daddy."

"He's a handsome kid," Finn said, at a loss for how to bridge the gap of a decade and their different lives.

"He looks like his father." Brynn's voice was soft, almost sad.

"I see you in him. He has your features."

She smiled, and this time it reached her eyes. "Thank you for saying that."

"You're one of the strongest people I know," he said quietly. "For a lot of reasons."

Her smile faded slightly. "You don't have to feel bad for me. Not for any of it. Tyler is my world, and everything that happened with Daniel pales in comparison to the joy my son gives me. I'd do it all again. Every last moment."

"Even the ones where you and Nick stopped being friends?" he couldn't help but ask.

He heard her audible breath and cursed himself once again. "I'm sorry. It's none of my business."

"Nick and I are still friends," she answered after a moment. Tyler looked up then, glancing around until his gaze landed on her. Finn saw the boy's small shoulders relax. Brynn waved and smiled, and the boy went back to digging. "We're just the kind of friends who don't talk much. But if he ever needed anything, I'd be there for him."

"He'd be there for you, too." He bent his knees until he was at eye level with her. "If you need him, all you have to do is—"

"I don't," she said quickly. "I'm fine."

"Brynn."

"Seriously, Finn." She wrapped her arms around herself, knuckles going white as she grasped the opposite elbows. "I *need* to be fine. For Tyler. For myself. So that I don't let anger and bitterness take over. I don't need Nick or anyone. I've got Tyler, and we're going to be fine."

"I know you will." Finn covered one of her hands with his, letting the warmth from his fingers seep into hers, which were unnaturally cold. "There's no doubt in my mind."

"Thank you," she whispered, nodding. A few of the other mothers sent furtive glances their way, and he was impressed at Brynn's ability to ignore the sidelong looks. "What are you still doing in town anyway?"

"Haven't you heard?" He gave her hand one final squeeze before dropping his. "I'm here to save the bank and become a local hero."

A laugh broke from her throat before she clasped a hand over her mouth. "That's the first time I've laughed out loud since the night he died."

"Glad I can be useful in some way."

"You never struck me as the hero type," she admitted sheepishly.

"That makes two of us."

She studied him for a moment, and he resisted the urge to fidget like a recalcitrant schoolboy under her soft gaze. "It's good you've come back," she said finally. "Life is too short to let the past rule your future."

"My father would appreciate hearing that."

"Also..." She leaned in, as if sharing a secret. "Maybe you could encourage Nick to settle down."

It was Finn's turn to stifle a laugh. "I'm not sure that's in the cards for any of us... I mean..." He cleared his throat. "Nick, Parker or me. Plenty of guys we knew back in the day settled down. Your husband was a perfect example."

Brynn lifted a brow. "Daniel married me, but he never settled. I ignored it for far too long because being the good wife was what people expected."

"I'm sorry that he's gone, but I'm also sorry he hurt you. You deserve better, Brynn."

"We deserve what we choose to accept in our lives," she countered. "I'm going to make sure I start living like I believe I'm worth more." She swiped a quick hand across her cheek. Finn hated the tears swimming in her eyes. "My son needs to see his mom that way."

"I agree," Finn told her, again amazed by her quiet strength. What a fool Nick had been back in high school not to recognize what a prize this woman was in his life. They'd all been fools and probably still were.

"Mommy," Tyler called as he ran toward the climbing wall. "Watch me."

Brynn's smile returned, brighter than ever. "I'm watching, sweetie."

"I should get back to the bank," Finn told her when she returned her gaze to him.

"You're not still honoring that stupid pact the three of you made after high school?" Brynn demanded.

"I...um... How do you know about the pact?"

"Daniel told me years ago. I thought it was just drunken silliness, but the fact that none of you have married and you claim that you aren't going to—"

Finn held up a hand. "The pact had nothing to do with marriage. It was about falling in love."

"So you plan to get married without love?" She shook her head. "Not reassuring me, buddy."

"There are reasons to marry that have nothing to do with love."

"Yeah," Brynn said in a quiet laugh. "I have one."

"I'm not talking about an unplanned pregnancy." Finn felt heat rise up the back of his neck, and suddenly he wanted to loosen his tie again. "Sometimes marriage is more of a partnership than a love match."

"Like a business arrangement?" Brynn asked, a delicate brow rising.

"In a manner of speaking."

She cuffed him on the ear so fast he didn't even see her reaching for him.

"Ouch. Jeez, Brynn, what was that about?"

"Maybe I was trying to knock some sense into you. You're a smart guy, or at least that's the rumor. I don't know what prompted the three of you to commit to not falling in love, but you can't still think it's a smart idea."

"It's worked so far."

"I don't believe that, for any of you. Daniel and I got married because I was pregnant, and things were never perfect. But I loved him as best as I could. It's the only way."

"I hope you find happiness on the other side of this loss," Finn told her. "I'm not built for the kind of love you seem to think is so important."

"You're selling yourself short. Nick and Parker, too, if they think the same way."

He shrugged.

"Go back to the bank," she told him, lifting a hand to gently rub the edge of his ear. "But keep your options and your heart open."

He opened his mouth to argue, but she held up a hand.

"You can't say no to a grieving widow."

"Wow. That's intense. Were you like this in high school?"

One side of her mouth curved. "No, but I like me better now."

Finn chuckled. "I do, too."

He walked back to the bank, trying not to think too much about love or expectations or whether or not his life as he'd created it really was working. These weeks in Starlight were a blip on the radar, and when he had things settled at the bank he'd return to his regular life.

Wouldn't he?

"You're the last one here."

Kaitlin glanced at the clock display in the corner of the computer screen, then quickly clicked the mouse to minimize the screen. She'd managed to avoid Finn since that kiss in the park a few days ago. Heat crept up her cheeks at the memory of his mouth on hers.

"Just finishing up some stuff," she said as she stood, placing a hand on the top of the monitor like she needed to guard it from Finn. "It's only seven."

"Haven't you heard about banker's hours?"

"You're still here, too," she pointed out, trying not to fidget as he looked from her to the computer. She didn't want to lie, but heat crept up her cheeks as she thought about explaining why she was working late tonight.

Of course Finn moved closer, curiosity clear in his eyes. "What are you working on?" he asked.

"Stuff," she muttered.

"Is that an official financial term?"

"I'm finished for tonight," she told him, hitting a few buttons to power off the monitor.

"That doesn't answer my question."

"Your dad is out on a date," she said, hoping to distract him from his irritating interest in what she was doing. "With Nanci, who owns the coffee shop."

Finn nodded. "He told me."

When she came around the side of the desk, he edged closer. "It's nothing," she said immediately.

"You're a terrible liar," he countered.

"I thought you were going to trust me."

"I'm curious as to what has you so ruffled. Tell me you're not trolling some online dating site."

"It's a class," she blurted. "For college."

He opened his mouth, shut it again. "College?"

"Community college," she clarified. "I'm working on my associate's degree in business. It's an online program for working adults."

She shrugged and grabbed her purse from the desk, embarrassed at sharing this bit of herself and irritated at her humiliation over trying to better herself. "I have bigger plans. But my grades in high school were pretty dismal, so I'm going this route and then I'll work on my bachelor's. It probably seems stupid to you." Her voice broke because what she meant was "I probably seem stupid" and she was pretty sure he knew it.

"Why would that seem stupid?" he asked, his voice as soft as fluffy cotton.

She started to move past him, but he stepped in front of her. "Kaitlin."

"I don't need a degree to be Jack's secretary or to wait tables or whatever stupid job I'm going to get when I'm finished here. The truth is, your dad felt sorry for me, and I take care of things. It works for now but I'm not fooling myself into thinking I have a real future. I get that doing these classes is probably just a waste of time."

"If you've got it all figured out, then why work so hard?"

She bit down on the inside of her cheek, willing herself not to answer. She didn't want to say the words out loud. They felt too vulnerable, like the finest blown glass that could shatter at any moment. But there was something about this moment and this man that made her unable to stop the confession. "I want more," she whispered, feeling at once both greedy and liberated from trying to hide her desire.

"Then you should have it," he answered without hesitation.

She glanced up at him through her lashes, unable to lift her head but needing to see his reaction. Her breath hitched as she realized those blue depths held admiration, not judgment. *Breathe in and out*, she inwardly counseled herself. The air goes into the lungs, then out again. Breathing might be an involuntary function, but it seemed that Kaitlin's body had forgotten how to manage it.

Clutching her purse to her stomach, she started to turn away, not sure where she was planning to go.

Finn wrapped his hands around her arms, holding her gently enough that she knew without hesitation he'd release her if that was what she wanted.

Instead she stepped into his arms, pressing her cheek against the warmth of his chest. The purse dropped to the ground as she gathered handfuls of his suit jacket between her fingers, squeezing hard. She did *not* want to cry. She wouldn't cry. Not for such a simple kindness.

Something a stranger would offer, but Kaitlin never expected it from Finn. From anyone. Life and the experiences that came with it had taught her to keep her dreams and desires well hidden. They were weaknesses that the people she thought should care about her would exploit for their benefit.

"Nothing I've seen you do has been a waste of time," Finn said into her hair. He stroked the back of her jersey-knit dress, his touch far too comforting.

"I don't know why it bothers me so much," she admitted. "It's not a big deal. Who cares if I get a degree?" She hiccuped, then continued, "I should be content with the life I have, which is more than I ever thought I'd get."

"Stop selling yourself short." The words were quiet but firm. "You came up with some great ideas for modernizing the way First Trust does business. It was amazing. There's no doubt you can handle more responsibility, and if a degree will give you more confidence, that's great."

"No one but Jack knows."

"Why?"

She forced herself to pull away, smoothing a hand over the wrinkled fabric of his suit jacket. "Because of what I heard Liz and Cassie saying about me. I don't want them to think I'm trying to be better than I am."

"Isn't the point of living—to keep working to become better than we are?" He placed a finger under her chin and tipped it up. "You have a place at the bank. Not waiting tables or whatever other job you think is in your future. You're good here."

She could get used to this…having this man in her corner. But she knew it wouldn't last, even if she allowed herself to raze her walls and open to him. "What about when you're gone?"

"Dad will need you more then," he answered without hesitation.

It wasn't what she wanted to hear. In her silly, stupid, vulnerable heart, she wished for him to tell her that she was changing things. That he could see himself in Starlight, making a life with her at his side.

No.

She wouldn't let herself entertain fantasies that could never come true. She hated how easily Finn had slipped past her defenses.

"He will, Kaitlin," Finn said, and she realized she'd spoken the word out loud.

"You're right, of course." She made her voice purposely light. "I don't know why I let those two get in my head. What do I care what they think? Jack is going to need all the help he can get, especially after you're gone." She picked up her purse. "I'll be here for him, Finn. We'll be fine without you."

He pressed a hand to his chest and flashed a lopsided grin. "Ouch. You don't need to suddenly sound so enthusiastic about the prospect."

"I thought that would make you happy."

"I'm not in a hurry," he said with a shrug, matching his strides to hers as they walked out of the bank.

"But you have your life with all your important plans for your career and a wife who will go perfectly with that."

"There's not exactly a plan for a wife. And my life will still be there when I get back." He held open the door for her, then locked it behind them.

"You like it here," she said with a wide grin. "Admit it. You missed this place."

He rolled his eyes, then hitched a thumb toward the far end of the street. "I might have missed the sweet potato fries at The Acorn Diner. Do you have dinner plans?"

Chapter Ten

Kaitlin's stomach picked that moment to let out a rumbling growl. "I do now," she said. "But I'll warn you, I can practically eat my weight in sweet potato fries."

Finn laughed. "I'd like to see that."

They walked along the sidewalk toward the restaurant, several people stopping to say hello or calling out greetings as they passed. She'd gotten used to the friendliness of small-town life, but she felt a different level of belonging with Finn at her side.

"How is it you've been gone ten years and it's like you never left?"

He grinned down at her. "Trust me, it's a blessing and a curse. Tell me about your associate's degree. How far along are you?"

Anxiety tied her stomach in knots. "I'll be finished at the end of this year."

"Have you thought about where you want to go for your undergraduate?"

They'd arrived at the restaurant, which was the perfect mix of cozy charm and contemporary flare. Kaitlin knew the restaurant had been a staple in Starlight for decades but the owners had managed to keep it fresh. Much of the menu changed seasonally and they always offered a fantastic selection of food and drink that highlighted the local area.

The young hostess showed them to a booth in the back. "You ask the question like it's a given that I'll go on to a four-year degree."

"Isn't that the plan?"

"Well, yes..." Kaitlin pressed her lips together to stop from adding a *but* to her response. "Yes," she repeated with more force. "It's the plan. I'd like to stay in Starlight, so I'll look for online undergraduate degree programs, as well."

"Can I start you two off with some drinks?" a waitress asked as she approached the table. "Oh, hey, Finn. I heard you were back in town."

"Hi, Lauren." Finn greeted the pretty blonde

with a strangely tight smile that Kaitlin didn't understand. She didn't know their waitress personally, although the woman seemed friendly enough. Her pale hair was pulled back into a low ponytail, and she wore a black T-shirt with the restaurant's name silk-screened across the front, a denim miniskirt that showed off a great pair of legs encased in patterned tights and stylish but comfortable-looking ankle boots. "I'll have a beer, please. Whatever you have on tap."

"There's a great IPA from a brewery over in Yakima."

"Sure."

"How are things in Seattle?"

"Fine." Finn's troubled gaze collided with Kaitlin's and she wished she could understand what had him so upset. "Would you like a drink?"

"We've got a real nice pinot grigio from Harvest Vineyards down in Oregon," the waitress offered.

"I'm great with water," Kaitlin said. "Did you two go to high school together?"

"Senior prom," Lauren said with a soft laugh. "Finn bought me the biggest corsage. It was like a weird growth hanging off my wrist."

"So you dated?"

"Not really," Finn said quickly.

"Neither of us were looking for anything serious back then," the other woman confirmed. "That changed for me when I met Seth." She smiled at Kaitlin. "He's my husband. Five years next week."

"Congratulations," Kaitlin said.

"I'm sure Seth was a big step-up from me," Finn said with a surprising amount of bite to his tone.

"Just a better fit," Lauren answered, her delicate brows furrowing. "Do you want to hear about today's specials?"

Finn shook his head. "We've decided."

Kaitlin hadn't even opened her menu, but she wasn't going to argue that point at the moment.

Lauren flashed an uncomfortable smile as she nodded. "What can I get for you?"

"I'll have the pork chop and a salad," Finn told her, keeping his gaze on the menu.

"How about you?" the woman asked Kaitlin.

"I'll do a burger, medium well, with sweet potato fries." Kaitlin handed her menu to the waitress once she finished scribbling the order on her small pad of paper. "Thank you so much. Right, Finn?"

"Yeah," he agreed, offering the waitress a sheepish smile. "Thanks, Lauren. It's been a long day."

"I totally understand that," Lauren told him. "Seth had a meeting at the bank this afternoon to get final approval for a loan to expand his welding shop."

Finn traced the condensation on the edge of his water glass with one finger. "You haven't spoken to him yet?"

Lauren shook her head. "I turn off my phone when I get to work, but he's been working on his presentation for weeks."

Finn looked like he wanted the floor to swallow him whole as the waitress smiled at him expectantly. Taking pity on him, Kaitlin got Lauren's attention and inclined her head. "I think the table across the way is trying to get your attention."

Lauren threw a glance over her shoulder. "Oh, right. I've taken too much of your time already. I'll get that order in right away and bring over your beer."

As she walked away, Finn pressed a finger and thumb to the bridge of his nose. "I should change that beer order to a straight shot of whiskey."

"The news her husband got today wasn't good," Kaitlin guessed.

"It was a fine presentation, but the business isn't a smart investment for the bank right now."

"Why?"

His full mouth tightened. "His credit score was off, and I wasn't confident he could meet the annual revenue threshold. I wish I could be like Mark Cuban on *Shark Tank* and give money to whatever business struck my fancy, but that isn't how things work at the bank."

"But banks are there to help people make their dreams come true."

"Banks are in business to make money."

She shrugged. One of the things that she'd first noticed about Jack was his dedication to not only his bank but also the community as a whole. "By helping people make their dreams come true."

"That's a fairy-tale version of a much harsher reality," he told her and she tried to ignore the sharp edge in his voice. She knew his irritation wasn't directed at her. "This isn't *It's a Wonderful Life*."

Why couldn't Finn see the value of giving someone a chance? "But if the business plan was solid, why can't you give him the money? You know Seth. He's a hard worker and has made a success of the welding company. I know you'd be making a great investment in him."

"It's more complicated than that," he said, then sat back and let out a breath when Lauren returned with his beer.

"Can I tell you a secret?" the pretty blonde asked as she slid the glass of amber-colored liquid in front of him.

"Please, no," Finn muttered at the same time Kaitlin said, "Of course."

"Seth and I are expecting." She placed a hand on her flat stomach. "We haven't even shared it with our families yet, but I had to tell someone."

"Congratulations." Kaitlin forced a smile despite the way her heart hurt at the thought of Seth sharing the bad news he'd received with his pregnant wife. "That's amazing." She kicked Finn under the booth.

"You'll be a great mom," Finn said, which seemed to be exactly what Lauren wanted to hear based on the enormous grin she gave him.

"I hope this doesn't affect anything about Seth's loan," she said, her smile suddenly fading. "I don't want you to think he'll be less dedicated to the business. It's the opposite, in fact. He's so excited to have a kind of legacy for our son or daughter."

"Everything will still be fine with the loan," he promised, then pulled his phone out of his pocket. "In fact, there was something I forgot to mention to Seth earlier today."

Kaitlin's breath caught in her throat as he shot her a pained look.

"I don't have his number in my personal contacts, and I'd like to talk to him tonight if I can. Could you put in his number for me?"

"Of course." Lauren took the phone and tapped the screen. "You're sure it's okay?"

"Better than," Finn assured her, sliding out of the booth. "I'm going to step outside for this call. I'll tell Seth you said hi."

"Awesome. Your food should be out shortly." She looked toward Kaitlin as Finn walked away. "You don't want anything besides water?"

"Water is perfect."

Finn still hadn't returned when Lauren brought their food, and Kaitlin wasn't sure whether to be nervous or optimistic at the length of his absence If he'd changed his mind about the loan… Jack usually had the final say in those types of transactions and couldn't imagine the older man denying Seth his loan if Finn supported it.

She picked up a fry and popped it into her mouth, savoring the way the smoky, sweet flavor complemented the crunchy texture.

"You started without me," Finn said, plucking a fry from her plate as he sat down again.

"What did you say to Seth?" she asked, pushing her plate away and leaning over the table.

Finn took his time cutting into his pork chop. He forked up a bite, his eyes drifting closed as he chewed. "The Acorn isn't fancy, but no one makes better comfort food."

He opened his eyes again, giving Kaitlin that half grin/half smirk she'd come to think of as his signature smile. "This is a first for me."

"What?"

"A woman so infatuated that she ignores an order of perfect sweet potato fries for the pleasure of watching me eat."

As his grin widened, Kaitlin picked up a fry

and flung it at him. It hit him square in the nose before dropping onto the table.

"Good aim," he told her.

"Finn." She narrowed her eyes. "Don't make me come over there."

He chuckled. "I'm not sharing my pork, if that's what you're after."

She kicked him again.

"You're like a professional soccer player. I'm going to have bruises." He made a show of looking under the tabletop. "Are you wearing steel-toed flats?"

"Tell me," she urged, beyond curious to know what had kept him away for so long.

He shrugged. "I talked to my dad, then called Seth. There are conditions he'll have to meet and the APR will be a bit higher than normal..."

"But you're giving him the loan?"

"Yeah. I'm going to help push through a Small Business Association–backed loan." He nudged her plate in front of her. "Now, eat before your food gets cold."

"You sound like somebody's mom." She drew in a relieved breath, happy to know he did care even if he had a difficult time admitting it.

"Like my own," he told her. "Ella and I used to mess around all the time at the dinner table. It was just the three of us when Dad would work late. We gave her a ton of trouble."

"I can imagine," Kaitlin murmured and bit into her burger. She wanted to ask him more questions about the loan, the terms and Seth's response, but she was afraid Finn would change his mind again. What if he redialed Seth and took away his dream because Kaitlin showed too much interest? Because she cared too much about what he'd done?

Stupid. She knew that line of thinking was stupid. Her mom had played those kind of emotional mind games when Kaitlin was a kid, taking her to the pound on a Saturday afternoon to choose a dog, then saying no to whichever one Kaitlin liked best. But Finn didn't operate that way. And besides, why would her opinion matter to him in the least?

Maybe he still had some sort of leftover crush on Lauren, an unrequited-love type of thing, and his giving her husband the loan was his way of trying to take care of her. All very Sydney Carton from *A Tale of Two Cities*, which Kaitlin had read for a world literature course she'd taken last semester.

"That burger must be pretty mesmerizing."

She blinked and glanced up, realizing she'd gotten caught up in her jumbled thoughts.

Finn held out a napkin. "Ketchup on your chin."

"Thanks," she mumbled and dabbed at it, feeling color rise to her cheeks. "The burger is good."

"Are you rushing to eat your food before it gets cold? Did I trigger some kind of childhood memory of your mom's dinner rules?"

She barked out a laugh. "My mom never cared when or what I ate. Dry cereal was a dinner staple in our house when she could be bothered to shop for groceries." She shook her head, refusing to let the emotions from her childhood weigh down on her. "I was wondering about Seth's loan."

Finn studied her for a moment, then shrugged. "I'm going to approve the loan against my better judgment," he admitted. "Dad was thrilled. He'd wanted to give the money to him all along. He'd give money to anyone with a great story and a firm handshake. But that's what's caused some of the problems in the first place. There has to be a balance between lending money to people who need it and becoming overleveraged. It's difficult on the community bank to separate the personal from the professional. At least for some people."

"Like your dad?"

He nodded.

"Maybe Seth will really make a go of it and the welding business will be a breakout success. He could become the star of some sort of welding reality television show."

"I hope so." Finn smiled, then took a drink of beer.

"Why did you change your mind?" she couldn't help but ask. "Was it Lauren? The baby?" She rapped the heel of her palm against her forehead. "Of course that was it. The baby. Babies get people every time."

"It was you," he said quietly, and Kaitlin felt her throat go dry.

"Me?" she asked after clearing her throat.

Lauren brought the check at that moment, and Finn pulled out his wallet to pay for their dinner.

"Tell Seth I expect a tour of his new shop when it opens," he told the waitress with a slight smile, and Kaitlin's stomach swooped and dipped as Lauren processed the simple words and what they meant for her small family.

"He's going to make you proud," she promised, her voice trembling slightly. "Thank you, Finn."

He nodded but focused his gaze on the check, seeming almost embarrassed by her gratitude.

"Are you finished?" he asked when Lauren walked away. "I need to get out of here."

"I'm ready." Kaitlin slipped from the booth and led the way out of the diner, waving to Lauren as they left.

Out on the sidewalk again, Finn started back toward the bank and she hurried to match his long strides.

"Finn, slow down. What's wrong?"

She placed a hand on his arm, tugging until he turned to face her. His blue eyes were dark with an emotion she couldn't name, and his whole body appeared fraught with tension. "I don't want people to look at me like I'm some kind of small-town savior. That isn't who I am. I'm here because…" He shook his head like he couldn't put the reason into words.

"Because you care," Kaitlin supplied. "You're a good man and you care."

"No, I'm a corporate banker. I don't save smaller institutions. I engulf them. Mergers and acquisitions—that's my specialty."

"What did you mean when you said I had something to do with giving Seth the loan?"

He lifted a hand to her face, cradling her jaw in his palm as his thumb traced a path across her cheek. "You were so fervent in your belief, and I wanted to see you look at me the way you are now."

"How am I looking at you?"

"Like you want to be kissed."

She breathed out a soft laugh. "I'm not sure that has anything to do with Seth's loan."

"But you aren't denying it?"

Her heart seemed to skip a beat at the mix of hope and vulnerability in his gaze. This man was so strong, so independent and so damn unwilling to admit that he cared. About his father, the bank and the entire town. But she could see beyond the mask he wore to the honorable core of the man he was meant to be.

He wouldn't push her for more than she could give, and that was just one more thing that made her want him. Kaitlin needed to show him that she was not only done denying her desire but more than willing to take a chance on him. On the two of them.

She might not trust her past with men, but she'd changed since coming to Starlight.

She raised up on tiptoe and pressed her mouth to his, the kiss at once a question and an invitation. One he immediately answered by wrapping his arms around her waist and pulling her closer.

It was different than the kiss they'd shared on the Ferris wheel. That had been a distraction, and this was a declaration. Kaitlin had buried the part of herself that craved physical closeness since coming to Starlight. So many of her bad decisions in life had their start with men, much like her mother. She hadn't wanted that in her new life but couldn't ignore the way she wanted Finn. She didn't want to anymore.

"Come home with me," she whispered against his full lips.

She felt him smile against her mouth. "Since I'm staying with my dad now, I'll be going home with you every night."

"You know what I mean."

He lifted his head, his gaze intense on hers. "Are you sure?"

No.

"Yes."

"Enough that you won't have second thoughts on the drive? We're both parked behind the bank."

"I want you," she said, allowing all of her desire to seep into those three little words.

He grabbed her hand and tugged her around the corner toward the parking lot and, after another lingering kiss, she climbed into her car and followed his taillights onto the darkened streets of Starlight.

He'd been right about her having second thoughts on the way back to the house. Second, third and fourth thoughts were more like it. Something about trailing his sleek BMW in her humble compact sedan reminded her of the differences between them. This town might be her home now, but they came from two different worlds, and she wasn't sure how they'd ever bridge that gap.

Desire was one thing. Reality quite another. Finn's reality was the upper echelons of Seattle society. Country clubs and fancy dinners and women who wore the right clothes and could talk about art or fashion or whatever moneyed women discussed.

Her past made her totally unfit for his world. Before leaving Seattle, she'd barely scraped by and had no ambition beyond tracking down the next party. The crowd she ran with was wild at best and oftentimes bordered on criminal in their crazy antics. While Starlight seemed to put them on a level playing field, she knew that would change as soon as he returned to his life in the city.

Her palms were sweaty on the steering wheel as she worked to keep her breathing steady. The town was steeped in shadows, but the golden light shining from the windows of the houses they passed reminded her of what it felt like to belong here. She'd spent most of her life on the outside looking in, wishing for security and warmth and a place to belong. Jack had given that to her—or at least a chance at it—when he'd hired her to work at the bank.

No one was going to take that from her now, and she wouldn't allow lust to make her forget her priorities.

Even if she wanted to with her entire being.

Chapter Eleven

Finn parked in front of his father's sprawling rancher and walked around back toward the guest-house, passing Kaitlin's small sedan on the way. No need to advertise his plans for the evening when his father returned home. Not that he wanted to keep whatever this was between Kaitlin and him secret. Unless she did.

Hell, he'd agree to just about anything she asked for the chance to kiss her again. To do more than kiss her. He'd never felt anything like the need pounding through him as he thought about Kaitlin.

He picked up the pace until he was practically

jogging across the lawn, then forced himself to slow down. He didn't want to seem desperate, despite the fact he felt exactly that. Fear flickered along his spine at the thought that she'd change her mind.

I want you.

Those three words had made his body grow instantly rigid with desire. He'd dated plenty of women, both casually and a few who'd ended up with more serious intentions. But he'd never wanted anyone the way he did Kaitlin.

He couldn't understand it. She was beautiful with her golden-blond hair and dark eyes framed by long lashes. But it was more. *She* was more. He had a feeling she could become everything to him if he let her. Which he wouldn't, of course. Couldn't. If he let her in all the way, she might see he actually didn't have enough to give.

He slowed his pace even more as he approached the small cottage. Kaitlin stood on the edge of the cobblestone porch. In the dim moonlight, it was difficult to tell whether she was acting as sentry or rolling out the welcome mat.

"Your dad can't know about this," she said, her voice carrying across the quiet night.

Hoop number one. "Okay."

"*No one* can know," she added.

So she did want to keep it a secret. He ignored

the disappointment that speared through him. This was simply hoop number two. "Fine."

"It ends when you leave town."

Hoop number three. "Why?" He couldn't help but ask, even though he understood the logic of it.

"I'm not part of your world in the city, and I'm building a life here. I don't want people to see me as Finn Samuelson's small-town castoff."

He stepped closer, trying to figure out why her rules for their relationship bothered him so much. Normally he was the one checking off boxes to make sure no one got too attached. He wouldn't let Kaitlin get close, so he should be thanking her for taking care of this aspect. It made him look like less of an unfeeling jerk. But that was the crux of the problem. His feelings for her. "Anyone who would think that isn't worth a moment of your time."

One corner of her mouth kicked up, but the almost smile seemed sad to him. "If that's part of your foreplay routine, you're pretty good."

"I'm better than good," he answered without hesitation. "But it's simply the truth."

"We have an expiration date," she insisted, crossing her arms over her chest.

"Like a gallon of milk," he muttered, then nodded. "It ends when I leave Starlight."

What if he stayed?

The question flitted across his chest like the flutter of butterfly wings, and he tamped it down. Of course he'd return to Seattle. That was his home.

He walked forward and climbed the first step, tall enough that they stood eye to eye even with her on the porch. "Anything else?"

A delicate brow rose. "I like the sound of 'better than good,'" she told him.

How could it be less than perfect with this woman?

She affected every cell of his being like she was an energy that flowed through his veins. The power she had without even knowing was at once heady and terrifying.

"I'm glad." He reached for her, twining his arms around her waist and lifting her into his arms. Her legs settled around his hips and all he could think was that there were too many layers of clothing separating them. "Because I'm done talking now."

As their mouths fused together, he maneuvered them through the front door, grateful she'd left it open. He wasn't sure he'd have the mental wherewithal to manage something as mundane as a doorknob at the moment. Not when all of his blood had rushed south at the promise in her eyes.

She laughed when he bumped into the back of the sofa. "You need directions?"

"I'll manage," he said and drew her lower lip between his teeth, eliciting a throaty groan from Kaitlin that nearly had him on his knees.

The guesthouse was tiny, and he and Ella had played there as kids, so Finn easily made his way into the only bedroom.

He slowly—reluctantly—lowered her to the thick carpet that covered the wide-plank floor.

"Tell me you didn't sneak your high school girlfriend in here," she said, making a horrified face as he took a back step.

He shook his head. "Not one," he assured her. "I wasn't that smart."

She gave a small nod, then started on the buttons of her burgundy-colored dress, the deep color a perfect complement to her dark eyes.

His mouth went dry as inch after gorgeous inch of pale skin was revealed to him.

She began to shrug out of it, then paused, clutching the fabric to her. "You can't just stand there and watch."

He tapped a finger against his chin, as if considering her comment. "I'm having so much fun."

"That isn't how it works." She shook her head. "Not for me."

There was something in her gaze he didn't understand, a kind of vulnerability he hadn't expected from her.

"Tell me what you want."

She bit her lip as her gaze wandered along the front of him. "You aren't wearing your suit jacket."

"It's in the car."

Still holding the fabric of her dress closed with one hand, she pointed at him with the other. "Your shirt and tie." She drew in a breath and added, "Please."

"The *please* is nice." He grinned. "I didn't know being polite could feel like foreplay."

"Before you get ahead of yourself with a bunch of 'nice girl' fantasies, don't go there. I'm going to disabuse you of the notion that I'm fit to star in any of them."

He drew the silk from around his neck and tossed it at her feet. "I'm game for any type of fantasy that involves you."

Pink tinged her cheeks as he unbuttoned his dress shirt, starting with the cuffs, then working his way down the front. The way she watched him was such a turn-on, he was half-tempted to rip the damn shirt apart and get on with things.

But he kept his movements measured, wanting to savor every moment. After yanking the shirt from his waistband, he finished with the buttons and pulled it off, dropping it to the floor.

Her brown eyes widened, and Finn was suddenly grateful for atrocious sleep habits that had him waking before five every morning. He'd made working out a regular part of his routine, not realizing all that sweat and fitness had been solely done so he could impress this woman.

"Your turn," he said, waggling his brows.

She waved a finger up and down in his direction. "I don't look like that."

"What a relief."

She rolled her eyes but loosened her hold on the dress, peeling it away from her body to reveal a lacy skin-colored bra and polka-dot panties.

"Damn," he muttered. "You're so beautiful."

She opened her mouth, then snapped it shut again as she tossed the dress onto a nearby chair. "I hate it when women can't take a compliment," she told him.

"Me, too." He took a step closer. "Especially since I plan to give you plenty of them." Her body was perfection, curvy in all the right places with smooth skin and a smattering of freckles along her chest and belly. He planned to kiss every one.

"I think I could spend the entire night looking at you and I'd be happier tomorrow morning than I have been in ages."

"That's kind of a waste of this bed," she said, hitching a thumb behind her.

"Ah, yes. The bed." He nodded as he moved toward her. "Wouldn't want it to go to waste."

She held up a hand, palm toward him. "Lose the pants."

"No *please* this time?" he asked as he slipped out of his shoes and undid his leather belt.

"I told you I wasn't a nice girl," she said. "You'll have to earn the next one."

"With pleasure," he said, pulling his wallet from a back pocket. He tossed it onto the nightstand before pushing his slacks over his hips and taking the boxers he wore with them for good measure.

He shucked off his socks and then straightened. "Now, who's wearing too many clothes?"

She swallowed audibly as her gaze traveled up the length of him. "I should turn off the light," she said quickly, reaching for the lamp on the nightstand.

"Leave it." He caught her wrist in his hand. "Please."

"*Please* really is quite a sexy word," she said with a small laugh. "But I don't really do this—" she gestured to the bed with her free hand "—with the lights on."

"Feels like the first time," he sang, tugging her to him.

She giggled. "I've definitely never laughed this much."

"I like how bright your eyes are when you laugh," he told her, then nipped at the corner of her mouth. "I like everything about you other than the fact that you aren't naked right now."

She hummed low in her throat as he trailed kisses along her jawline. "Let's do something about that then. Please."

It only took Finn a second to flick open the clasp of her bra. He lowered the straps from her shoulders and leaned back to look down at her as the thin piece of fabric fell to the floor.

His muttered curse was somehow the best compliment she'd ever heard, and her whole body went limp with liquid desire as he covered one puckered nipple with his mouth. He lowered her to the bed, yanking down the comforter and sheet as he did.

She couldn't help but arch into him as he continued his attention to her sensitive breasts. Heat built low in her body, like she was a slow-burning ember ready to explode into flames. Which was exactly what happened when Finn moved his attention lower, peeling her simple panties from her hips and down her legs. He opened her legs, all the while murmuring words of praise about her beauty and all the things he wanted to do to her.

He made her want to offer him every part of her.

Then he stopped talking as she felt his hot breath on her center, followed almost immediately by the gentle touch of his mouth. Not that she was about to admit it—or could even form the words at the moment—but Kaitlin had never allowed a man that kind of access to her body. It felt too vulnerable, and Kaitlin didn't do vulnerability. Not with her heart or her body.

Except now she knew what she'd been missing. Or maybe she hadn't because she couldn't imagine that anyone except Finn could make her feel this way. He'd taken her tamped embers and stoked them into bright, sparking flames. His tongue skimmed along her core and she almost bucked off the bed. It was like nothing she'd ever experienced and she didn't want it to end but felt like she might combust from the intensity of the pleasure tumbling through her entire being.

And when he whispered for her to let go, she had no choice but to obey, her body exploding into a million glimmering flashes all around her. It was as if light and fire rained down over them, consuming her even as it set her ablaze her from the inside out.

"More," she whispered as she returned to herself, because still it wasn't enough. "I want all of you, Finn."

She couldn't let him stop now because if she allowed reality back she was afraid she wouldn't be able to deny what a mistake this was. Yes, she'd been the one to put limits on what was between them but he'd effectively busted through every internal defense she'd created. She was teetering on the edge of fully losing her heart, and still she didn't want it to end.

"Nothing I want more," he said as he reached for his wallet.

She swallowed back a whimper of protest when he shifted away from her, but after sheathing himself with the condom, he returned. The weight of him felt glorious and she tried to remind herself that this feeling of security was an illusion. In a few weeks, his plan for retooling the bank would be in place, and he'd return to Seattle. She'd stay in Starlight and though only an hour separated them, their time together would be at an end.

That was how she wanted it.

Why was it so difficult to hold on to that thought?

"You okay?" Finn asked, his voice so gentle, tears pricked the back of her eyes. She could feel him at her center, but he didn't move, and she knew he would stop this here if that was what she wanted. He was allowing her to choose, willingly giving her the power to decide what happened next. Kaitlin had spent her life being forced into decisions based on fear or anxiety or a host of other unhealthy emotions.

This moment was hers.

She rolled her hips, bringing him closer. "I'm better than okay," she promised. "Please, Finn. Now."

He licked a path from the base of her throat up to her jaw. "You with the *please*," he said, then claimed her mouth.

A moment later he entered her, all heat and velvet strength. Kaitlin moaned, the feel of the two of them joined in this way so right. She knew she'd never be the same but welcomed the change. It was a reclaiming of sorts—of trusting herself to decide without an overarching fear of what would come next.

She wanted to be done with worry ruling her life, and Finn felt like a perfect way to forge a new path. Sensation bathed her in golden light, and she welcomed it. Welcomed everything she hadn't allowed herself to feel.

So what if it ended? This was her moment and as they found their release together, she knew that this moment was all that mattered.

Chapter Twelve

Finn blinked awake early the next morning, a slow grin spreading across his face at the sight of Kaitlin sleeping next to him. Her blond hair spread across the pillow like a slumbering wave. Last night had been…

Amazing. Mind-blowing. Scary as hell.

The last thought had him tensing, and he forced himself to relax again when she stirred with a soft humph. She turned her head but didn't seem to wake, a tiny gift for which he was eternally grateful.

He needed a minute to gather himself and his chaotic emotions. Mostly because the emotions were a shock.

In the throes of passion, it had been easy to rationalize them as a reaction to great sex. Mind-blowing sex. Even this morning, if he really wanted to pretend, he could allow himself to believe that the vague twinge in his chest was the waning afterglow.

But that was a lie.

His heart had shifted sometime in the night, or maybe the overarching pleasure of being with Kaitlin had finally shaken loose the emotions he'd been trying to control. She meant something to him. She made him feel things he hadn't allowed himself to in years.

Which gave her the power to wreck him.

After his mom died, it had been easy for Finn to close down his heart. What other choice did a motherless son have? His father had been too consumed by his own grief to shepherd Finn or Ella through theirs. Finn understood he was stunted by the loss but until now it hadn't mattered.

He'd made himself a success, which was important. More significantly, his two best friends had agreed that the complications of love weren't worth the trouble. He wasn't alone. He belonged to a trio of hard-hearted men, and although it might not be healthy, it worked for all of them.

In fact, he figured the walls he'd built around his heart were a benefit in the long run. When he left Starlight, he hadn't planned to ever marry, but when it became clear it was expected in the firm, he knew he'd be able to choose a wife based on practical criteria. Someone who could be a partner for him. His imagined wife would complement him and he'd support and make her happy to the best of his ability. He simply wouldn't fall in love.

Easy enough.

Only not with a woman like Kaitlin. Last night was proof that he had no defense she couldn't breach, no way to keep any part of himself from her. Or to keep himself from craving all of her.

That simply wouldn't work.

He quietly got out of the bed and gathered his clothes, carrying them out of the bedroom and into the main part of the house.

As he dressed, he tried a million different ways to convince himself he was overreacting. Maybe this was the proverbial sowing of his oats. After all, Kaitlin had made it crystal clear that she didn't want a future with him.

He thought her argument about coming from two different worlds a bunch of nonsense, but it might be the thing to keep them both safe.

Still, he needed time. Distance. A bit of perspective. He wasn't an inexperienced kid reading too much into a night of passion. He would have laughed at his rambling thoughts if they didn't make him feel so damn pathetic.

He started a pot of coffee and then left the guesthouse, lifting his head to the gray sky overhead. A fine mist hovered in the morning air, giving the property an odd, somber quality. A perfect match for his mood.

He let himself into his dad's rancher through the laundry room, remembering all the times he and his buddies had stopped up the utility sink with dirt or gravel they'd gathered from the woods that bordered the backyard for terraria or other boyhood projects. His house had been their central hangout, and looking back on things with the perspective of adulthood, he realized his father had done the best he could. He might not have been emotionally available, but Jack had allowed Finn and Ella to make messes and forts with friends, trashing the house and yard as long as it kept them busy and seemingly happy.

Not that any of them had found much happiness once they were without Finn's mom. He took the stairs two at a time and changed into a T-shirt and shorts before returning to the main floor. It wasn't even six in the morning, so he had time for a run before showering and getting ready for work. He hoped pounding the pavement, or at least the trail that wound through the forest, would help clear his head.

"Late night?" a voice asked as he entered the kitchen.

His father sat in one of the swivel chairs at the island, a newspaper open in front of him. He reminded Finn of some of the older partners at the regional office of his bank, who started every day with a cup of coffee and the *Wall Street Journal*, the same way they had for decades upon decades.

Back in the day, Finn's mom had been the one to gather the morning paper once his father left for work, shoving it into the recycling bin, muttering about how she was a glorified maid.

"Do you miss her?" Finn blurted, then felt color rise to his cheeks when his father's eyes widened.

"It's been almost twenty years," Jack answered, slowly folding the paper.

His plan for a run forgotten, Finn hurried toward the coffeepot next to the sink, both because he needed the caffeine and to give himself an excuse to avoid eye contact with his dad.

They hadn't discussed his mother in over a decade.

"I know," he said as he poured a cup. "But nothing has changed in this house since the day she died. Being back here makes me think of her more, so I can't imagine it's different for you."

"*I've* changed," Jack answered. "I don't need to get rid of frames or tchotchkes that belonged to her. I still regret how badly you and your sister were hurt by her death and how I handled it, but I could never regret the time we had with her."

"Tell me you're not lying about being in remission," Finn whispered.

As if sensing that Finn was on the precipice of losing it, his father stood. "It's the truth, son. I'm not going anywhere. It's good to have you back in Starlight. The bank is going to be okay with your help. I can't tell you how grateful I am that—"

"Wait." Finn held up a hand, a sick pit opening in his gut as instinct flared. "Did you purposely put First Trust in this position so I'd be forced to step in?"

His dad's gaze softened even further. "I haven't been able to force you to do anything since you were in elementary school, and barely even then. I love this town and the people who live here. I think I lost track of the fact that I have to balance running a business with my desire to help people who need it."

Finn studied his father, trying to decide if this was the truth or a master manipulation.

"Come on," his dad insisted. "I couldn't have predicted you'd be back here for Daniel's funeral or that Doug would talk to you about the current state of the bank."

"But I would have heard about it sooner rather than later anyway. You know part of what my division does is liquidating struggling financial institutions."

"The bank has been part of my life forever." His dad shook his head. "I wouldn't sabotage it."

"Fine," Finn answered, but part of him wasn't convinced. "I'm going for a run before I shower. I have a meeting with senior management at eight thirty."

"I'll see you at the office," his dad said as Finn turned for the door. "What made you change your mind about Seth's loan?"

Finn paused. "Nothing in particular," he lied as an image of Kaitlin's dark eyes flashed in his mind. He rubbed at his chest. "The more I thought about it, the more sense it made."

"I'm not sure I believe you," Jack said, "but I'm glad for it."

"Yeah," Finn agreed, not meeting his father's gaze. He wasn't sure when Jack Samuelson had gotten so damn insightful, but he didn't like it one bit.

"One more thing, son," his father called when Finn was almost to the hall. He stopped but didn't turn.

"Kaitlin is special, and not just to me. She deserves to be happy."

At that, Finn turned. “Are you implying that I can’t make her happy?”

“Not at all.” His father ran a fingertip over the empty ring finger on his left hand. “I’m warning you to leave her alone unless you *plan* to make her happy.”

Finn wanted to argue. He hadn’t liked being told what to do when he’d been a kid, and he sure as hell didn’t now. But he only gave a sharp nod and headed out of the house. Kaitlin deserved happiness, and if his dad wanted to advocate for her, so be it.

He hit the ground at a pace he hadn’t managed since he was on the cross-country team in high school. Maybe the physical punishment would clear his head and his heart.

At least it would hurt enough to help him ignore everything else for a time. That might have to be enough.

Main Street Perk had a line of people almost to the door when Kaitlin walked in the next morning on her way to the office. She’d been so baffled at waking to find no trace of Finn that she’d left her travel mug of coffee on the counter.

She struggled not to feel hurt that in the morning light it was as if their night together hadn’t even happened. Had it meant so little to him that he'd been eager to make his escape?

It counted in his favor that he'd made coffee for her before he sneaked out. Sort of. The coffee had been thoughtful, but it didn't change the fact that he'd left without a word or note.

She couldn't let herself read too much into either his tenderness while they were together or the unexpected disappearance this morning. She'd been the one to mandate the rules. For all Finn knew, she didn't want anything more than a fun night of passion with him.

Except it had been so much more than that—at least for her. Thank heavens she'd mandated the rules before they got naked. Those guidelines might be the only thing keeping her heart safe.

A few people left the line, grumbling about the wait, and she moved forward. She should really be at work already but her stomach turned to knots every time she thought of facing Finn.

So much for living in the moment as she had last night. Now that the moment was over, the one that had left her feeling satisfied in a way she hadn't realized was possible, all her doubts came flooding back. Doubts about her worth as a person and whether or not she deserved the happiness she'd found in Starlight. Impostor syndrome reared its nasty head like a venomous snake just waiting to strike.

The line moved again, and she tried to tamp down the anxiety that rose like a wave inside her. Maybe she should go for a cup of herbal tea instead of caffeine.

"Can I help you?"

Kaitlin blinked, realizing that she'd made it to the counter, so wrapped up in her own head she hadn't even registered the passing minutes.

A pretty but harried-looking brunette stood on the other side. She flashed Kaitlin a smile that was just this side of panicked.

Although the woman seemed familiar, Kaitlin was almost positive she'd never seen her in the coffee shop. "I'll have a grande skinny vanilla latte."

The woman stared at her for a moment, then grabbed a cup. "Can you repeat the order, but a little slower this time?" She met Kaitlin's gaze and grimaced. "It's my first day, and I'm not exactly up on the ordering lingo."

"I'll take over." A skinny kid plucked the cup and marker the woman held. "Brynn, you can wipe down tables."

The woman's mouth thinned. "Nanci wanted me taking orders," she protested weakly.

"Not when you keep getting them wrong," the

kid answered with a sneer. "You can come back to the counter after the morning rush."

"Sure," the woman agreed. "James will finish your order."

Kaitlin nodded and offered what she hoped was a reassuring smile.

She watched Brynn Hale walk away, shoulders slumped, as James quickly marked the cup with the shorthand for her order, which wasn't overly complicated as coffee drinks went. Still, she felt a huge wave of empathy for Brynn.

She'd only met the woman personally once or twice, but everyone in town knew the story of Brynn's recently deceased husband, whose body had been found in the wreckage of his truck with his alleged mistress. Brynn now had a son to raise on her own, and she imagined the widow had taken this job as a first step in her new life as a single mother.

She paid for her coffee and, after the barista handed it to her, headed for the door. But at the sight of Brynn swiping at her cheeks as she filled the napkin dispenser on the far counter, Kaitlin detoured toward the woman. "It won't be long until you get the hang of things around here," she said, making a show of taking a napkin like that was her main purpose.

Brynn let out a disbelieving laugh. "I drink

black coffee," she admitted. "I don't seem to know what customers are talking about half the time."

"You'll figure it out." She placed a hand on the woman's sleeve. "New beginnings can be hard."

"Harder than anything I've ever done," Brynn whispered, her gaze trained on Kaitlin's hand.

"I'm sorry about your husband," Kaitlin said, feeling like she needed to offer something in the way of a condolence.

Brynn's mouth tightened, but she nodded. "Thank you." She glanced up at Kaitlin. "You work for Jack Samuelson, right?"

It was Kaitlin's turn to nod. "I'm Kaitlin Carmody."

"Nice to officially meet you, Kaitlin. I'm glad Finn is staying in town to help with things at First Trust."

"It means a lot to his dad. I guess you and Finn were friends in high school?"

"We grew up together," Brynn said, her mouth gentling into a small smile. "We all hung around in the same crowd. It was a huge shock when he left town. Everyone assumed he'd take over the bank."

"I think he wanted to make his own way in the world."

"Yeah." Brynn sighed. "Neither Daniel nor I had that choice. I guess that's part of what made him so dissatisfied with his life. I held him back.

His future was determined with one reckless decision on prom night."

"Would you have left Starlight if you had the chance?"

Brynn's eyes widened for a moment, and Kaitlin immediately regretted the question. "I'm sorry. I don't mean to pry into your personal life. It's just that this community feels perfect to me. It's hard for me to imagine why anyone would want to leave."

"It's pretty great," Brynn agreed. "I don't mind the question. I wouldn't have changed anything because my son is the best thing I never imagined happening in my life. He's worth all of it. Now I just need to figure out how to support the two of us." She placed the box of napkins under the reclaimed-wood sideboard. "The woman who owns this place used to babysit me, so she offered me a job and was willing to be flexible with my hours. If possible, I want to work while Tyler is in school."

"I hope you're able to manage that."

"I might need to find something that I can actually handle. Mara Reed did my training and I thought I was ready, but this morning has been a rude wake-up call."

"Like I said, you'll catch on and be whipping up half-caff soy extra-shot lattes in no time."

Brynn laughed, some of the tension easing from her shoulders. “That sounds more like a rap song than a fancy drink.”

“Good luck.”

Brynn grimaced. “Thanks.”

As Kaitlin started for the front door, Brynn called her name. Kaitlin turned.

“Any chance you’d want to grab a drink tonight?” she asked in a rush of breath. She swallowed and added, “Tyler has Scouts on Thursday evenings. It doesn’t have to be this week. If you’re too busy…”

“I—”

“I’m sure you already have friends,” Brynn continued, the words coming more rapidly now. “You’ve been here a couple of years. I have friends, of course. Mostly from high school. And family. But…I just thought…”

“Tonight would be great,” Kaitlin told her. She reached into her purse and pulled out a scrap of paper, quickly jotting down her cell number. “Let’s invite Mara, too. She can give you tips on coffee orders. Text me about the time and your address. I’ll pick you up.”

“Great,” Brynn said, folding the small piece of paper and pocketing it.

“Brynn, will you grab the box of lids in the storage room?” the barista called.

She nodded but continued to smile at Kaitlin. "Thank you for the words of encouragement. I'm not sure I'll ever be able to rattle off a mocha, steamed, double-shot whatever, but I have the first inkling of hope that I'll find my new normal, whatever that ends up looking like."

"You will," Kaitlin promised, then headed for the bank. In truth, she owed Brynn a thank-you, as well. She'd let herself sink into a funk far too quickly this morning.

So what if Finn had taken off? He owed her nothing, and she wasn't going to let herself be some overly sentimental woman who made a night of great sex into more than it was.

By the time she walked through the bank's polished mahogany doors, she'd finished half her coffee, which also helped her confidence. A jolt of caffeine and female bonding were a powerful combination.

She waved to Meg at the teller window, then took the steps to the second-floor offices. She'd built in time to review some of the marketing initiatives before the executive management meeting Finn had called, but thanks to her coffee shop detour, she went straight to the conference room at the end of the hall.

Channing Cooper, the chief finance officer,

pumped a fist in the air as she entered. "You owe me a dollar, Finn," he shouted across the room.

Finn, who was speaking to his father near the head of the table, glanced up at Channing and then toward Kaitlin, his brows furrowing as he took in the coffee cup she carried.

"I told everyone you'd stop at Perk," Channing said as he approached Kaitlin. "Finn thought you'd bring something from home."

"My vote was that you'd get to the office early and make a fresh pot here," Jack called, one side of his mouth kicking up.

"But I was right." Channing tapped a bony finger against the side of her cup. "I know you so well."

"That sounds a little creepy," Martha Paige, the bank's operations and human resources manager, told Channing. "Leave Kaitlin alone."

"I don't mean it like that," Channing insisted. "Everyone knows Kaitlin doesn't have a personal life."

"Inappropriate," Martha said with an eye roll. "Go sit down, Channing."

Channing grumbled but did as he was told. That was another thing Kaitlin liked about life in a small town. Even in a business setting, there was a camaraderie that couldn't be faked. She knew there were plenty of mean people in any community, and those two women who'd derided her in the break room certainly proved that people could be jerks no matter what, but she had a place in Starlight.

"I know he was joking," she assured Martha anyway.

"Yeah," the woman agreed. Then she added under her breath, "He only looks like a creeper."

Kaitlin coughed to cover a laugh. "Is the HR manager allowed to say that?"

"Probably not." Martha shook her head. "Sorry. My toddler is teething so no one in the house is getting any sleep."

"We're ready to start the meeting," Jack announced to the room.

As Kaitlin slid into a chair at the far end of the table, her gaze caught on Finn's. His dropped to the cardboard cup, and he raised a brow.

She gave a small shake of her head, then opened her notebook, trying not to make it obvious how much it affected her to be in the same room as him.

Everything about Finn affected her, but she wasn't going to let him know it. Talking to Brynn had been a great reminder that Kaitlin had succeeded at starting over. She'd reinvented her life in this town, and she wouldn't let anything or anyone jeopardize the happiness she'd found there, no matter how good a particular anyone looked naked.

Chapter Thirteen

Finn bit back a growl of frustration as he watched Kaitlin duck from the conference room as soon as they finished the staff meeting.

He couldn't exactly fault her as he had no doubt she was heading for her desk to start on the new work he'd assigned her as he discussed various projects and initiatives for the staff to implement in the coming weeks.

In a short time they'd made decent progress, and he was impressed by the updates he'd been given, especially Kaitlin's headway on the marketing plan. Not that he'd told her that in front of everyone else.

He didn't want to do anything to attract attention to his feelings for her, although it was difficult to believe people didn't see the sparks flying between them.

Unless those sparks were only one-sided at this point.

Why hadn't he stayed with her this morning or woken her with the kiss he'd been dying to give her?

Could he follow her without being obvious? He wanted to find a way to pull her aside and smooth over whatever damage he'd caused by walking out.

He inwardly cursed himself even as he listened to Channing discuss the new risk assessment metrics Finn had suggested. He had no business with her outside the bedroom. She'd made the rules around what was between them abundantly clear. There was no reason he should want to change that, not after one night.

"Mr. Samuelson?"

He focused his attention on the young woman who'd approached him. "Meg, right?" he asked and she nodded with a small smile. "Call me Finn. What can I do for you?"

She glanced toward his father and Channing, then swallowed. "A man named Peter Henry is here to see you. He was asking a lot of questions about the health of the bank downstairs and I didn't want everyone to get anxious. When I asked him about his business at First Trust, he said he had an appointment with you. He's waiting in your office."

"What the hell, Finn?" his father muttered as a hush fell over the staff who remained in the conference room.

"He's here to go over some things on my accounts out of Seattle," Finn lied, knowing that whatever had brought Peter, the chief operating officer of AmeriNat's West Coast offices, to Starlight couldn't be that simple.

"We're getting things on track," Jack said, more to himself than Finn. "No one is going to swoop in and take over at this point."

"I know, Dad."

But Finn also knew that the bank wasn't on solid footing yet. He hadn't been specific at his office about why he was taking time off, allowing everyone to believe it had something to do with his dad's health.

True and not true.

Lies and not lies.

After last night it felt like the only real thing in his life was Kaitlin, but she didn't belong to him. He couldn't make her his true north because there was no scenario where that would lead to a happy ending.

"Thanks, Meg," he said with as much of a smile as he could muster. "It's not about First Trust," he told his dad.

Jack gave a curt nod. "Stop by my office later."

"I will." Before heading to his office, Finn walked at a normal pace down the hall toward his father's.

Kaitlin sat at her desk in the corner of the reception area, her eyes glued to the computer screen in front of her.

As he approached, she glanced up, her expression schooled even as one feathery brow rose in question. "I heard your boss is here."

"It's not about First Trust," he repeated. In response, her lips thinned. "We need to talk," he said quietly, massaging his hand along the back of his neck.

"The way you left this morning said everything."

"You made the rules," he snapped, then shook his head. "I can't leave Peter waiting. Can we talk later?"

She shrugged noncommittally. "I'll be working on the marketing materials for the booth at the art show. We'll talk about that."

"Kaitlin."

Her jaw tightened.

"Please," he whispered.

"That isn't playing fair," she muttered, eyes blazing.

"I don't—"

"There you are."

He fought back a groan as he turned toward the hallway. Peter Henry, chief operating officer of AmeriNat Bank, walked toward him, looking irritated and impatient.

"Hello, Peter. I wasn't expecting to see you in Starlight."

The older man inclined his head. "And I anticipated you'd be back in Seattle by now. I didn't realize the angle you were working here."

Finn squeezed shut his eyes as he heard Kaitlin's sharp intake of breath. "No angle, but we should talk in my office."

"I'm waiting," Peter agreed.

Finn didn't look at Kaitlin again. He couldn't stand to see the disappointment he knew he'd find in her gaze, even though he didn't deserve it.

"This bank's a hidden gem," Peter said without preamble as Finn followed him to the office at the end of the hall. "If they entertained multiple offers, it could start a bidding war. But I'd like to lock it down for AmeriNat before that happens. They have—"

"It's not for sale," Finn said, moving to stand behind his desk.

"Everything's for sale," Peter argued, his quiet tone laced with steel. "The Pacific division needs a win right now, and if you're the one to pull it off, there would be no question about your bid for the partner title."

"I didn't realize anyone had questions," Finn countered. He waited until Peter lowered himself into one of the winged armchairs before taking a seat in the leather desk chair.

"Nothing's set in stone until the board approves it." Peter rested his elbows on the arms of the chair, pressing his fingers together in a way that reminded Finn of his own father. It would be interesting to see Peter and Jack together. Two old-school bankers whose careers had taken very different trajectories. The thing they had in common was that both men were used to being top dog and neither liked to be challenged.

"This is my family's bank," Finn said, as if Peter didn't already know that. "I'm helping my dad return it to financial health."

Peter waved a dismissive hand. "Community banks are a dinosaur in the industry. We both know that, even if your father doesn't. I don't have to remind you that acquiring them is a big part of what your career is based on."

"You don't," Finn agreed, "although it sounds like you just did."

"AmeriNat wants to continue our expansion throughout the Pacific Northwest. I'm not sure why First Trust hasn't come up as a potential purchase before now. Having a bank charter in this part of the valley would be a huge coup for you, Finn. It would also make your dad and his board very wealthy."

"But he wouldn't have his family bank anymore."

"He might not anyway. We can make sure First Trust retains a decent percentage of the local employees and offers fair severance packages to those they let go."

Nausea rolled through Finn's stomach as the metallic taste of bile filled his mouth. Being back in Starlight had reminded him how important the bank was to this community. Not just for day-to-day operations but also because of the relationships his dad had formed and the lives he'd helped to change.

Finn thought about the deals he'd done over the years, and how the banks he'd bought and sold had been anonymous entities. It was simple to determine a bank's worth on paper. Spreadsheets and financial reports showed the facts and figures, but there was more to valuing a small-town business than what could be shown in black and white.

Anger plunged through his veins, mostly self-directed. He'd ignored the lessons he'd learned watching his father's dedication to the family business for so many years. He'd let his resentment and bitterness shadow everything in his life.

Hell, he'd willingly turned his back on his family legacy in order to make his life about the opposite.

"First Trust isn't for sale."

"Be realistic, Finn." Frustration edged his boss's words. "This bank isn't your dream or your future. I have no doubt you'll turn it around for a period of time, but what happens when you return to Seattle? There's no way to guarantee the kind of lucrative offer we can put together will still be on the table."

"I understand." Finn rolled his shoulders, trying and failing to dispel some of the tension weighing on them. "I made a promise to my father."

"You have a commitment to me and to AmeriNat," Peter countered.

"The numbers in my division have been top in the country for the past four years. I've done more than my part for you and for AmeriNat."

Peter looked around the office as if assessing the decor. "Needs updating," he said quietly. "Businesses either keep progressing or they fail. Nothing and no one is irreplaceable."

Finn ignored the implied threat in the words. "I'll be finished here and back in the office within the month. Until then, I'm keeping up with clients remotely. In fact, I have a conference call scheduled with Bay Bank."

"Not necessary," Peter answered immediately. "I'm sending Trent to San Francisco. He leaves tomorrow."

"That's my account."

"Not while you're in Starlight." Peter stood, the conversation effectively ended. "It's a pretty little town but way too quiet for men like you and me. We need the thrill of the chase." Peter smiled, and Finn wondered why he'd never realized how smarmy the older man was under his facade of polish and sophistication. "I saw Chelsea Davidson at the club last weekend. I don't know why you ever broke things off with that woman. She looked good, Finn. Very good."

He'd heard rumors of Peter's wandering eye for years although he'd never seen his boss with a woman other than his over-Botoxed wife. But when Peter spoke of thrills, Finn couldn't help but think he was talking about more than making business deals. Was that what happened when a man chose a wife based on whether she could host a decent party?

"I hope Chelsea's happy, and I'll get the files

over to Trent," Finn said quietly. He wasn't going to win a squabble over a client meeting with his boss, so why even bother?

The thought made him almost laugh. He'd never walked away from a fight in his life, but right now he couldn't muster the energy to care.

"Within the hour," Peter advised, then walked out of the office.

Finn pressed two fingers to his temples, which were practically throbbing with tension. He knew the senior banker's appearance in Starlight would raise all kinds of questions about Finn's intentions and master plan when it came to First Trust.

As much as he wanted people to trust him, he'd done little to earn it. He thought he was on sure footing at AmeriNat, but the fact that Peter would so quickly give away his client showed that there was no loyalty from that quarter. Although Finn was officially on vacation, he'd been working his accounts late at night, between meetings and planning at First Trust or in the early-morning hours.

Contrast that with his father, who'd been through months of secret cancer treatments and had taken his hands off the reins at the bank for so long it was in real jeopardy of failing. As far as Finn knew, every one of his employees still showed him respect and loyalty as if he were some benevolent business owner taking care of each of them personally.

Finn couldn't help but wonder what it would be like to lay his head on the pillow each night knowing he made that kind of difference in the lives of the people he employed.

Kaitlin knocked on the door of Finn's office several hours later, growing concerned when he didn't answer.

"Finn?" She knocked again. "At least grunt so I know your creepy boss didn't take an ax to you while he was here."

The door opened a crack, Finn glaring at her from the other side. "Don't you think you would have heard a struggle?"

"It was a joke," she said.

"I'm not in a mood to be funny."

"Lucky me." She held up a brown paper bag. "I brought you lunch."

His eyes narrowed.

"It's chicken salad," she continued. "From The Hole in the Wall Deli. It opened last year. Sal, the owner, smokes the chickens himself and adds the tiniest bit of curry to the recipe. It will ruin you for all other chicken salad."

"The way last night ruined me?" he said, his

voice low and rumbly and doing dangerous things to her insides.

"I doubt that," she answered, then gave a startled yelp as he hauled her into the office, slamming shut the door behind her.

"I made you coffee this morning," he said, and it sounded like an accusation.

"Right before you sneaked out." She couldn't help the words or the accusation that laced her tone. She'd brought him lunch because she cared, but a part of her hated that she cared.

He took the bag from her and turned for the desk. "I get up early. I didn't want to wake you."

"Liar."

"You seemed downright mad in the meeting this morning, but now you brought lunch. Did something change or do I need to worry about you trying to poison me with the chicken salad?"

She shrugged. "I've had some time to think about it, and I realized you were right not to stay." She'd worked hard to convince her heart of that.

"Because..."

"Last night was physical," she said, crossing her arms over her chest. She watched as he pulled the parchment-paper-wrapped sandwich from the bag. "I set up the guidelines, and you were honoring them."

"But this morning was different?"

"Not exactly," she lied. "I woke up ready for…"

He arched a thick brow. "For…?"

"You know." She could feel a blush rising to her cheeks. She hadn't meant to have this conversation but couldn't stand to think of him holed up alone in his office all day. She had no idea why Finn's boss from Seattle had come to Starlight, but it couldn't be good for anyone.

"I'd like to hear you say it."

She blinked. "For you," she blurted. "I woke up ready for you."

Her embarrassment faded as a slow, sexy smile spread across his face.

"I shouldn't have told you that." She shook her head. "We had one perfect night, and that's enough."

"Nope." He placed the sandwich on the desk, then moved toward her, so close that she could feel the heat radiating from him. But he didn't touch her, and she forced herself not to lean into him. "One night wasn't part of the agreement."

"But it would be the smart thing to do," she told him. He smelled like the perfect combination of soap and cologne. It made her want to press her nose to the crook of his neck and breathe him in. Which would be really weird and probably make her seem more obsessed with him than she already felt.

"I disagree." He leaned in and placed a feather-light kiss at the corner of her mouth.

Kaitlin swallowed back a whimper. She should walk—no, run—out of his office now. She needed to be smart. Prudent.

"I think an affair during my time in Starlight..." He drew his tongue across the seam of her lips "...is the perfect arrangement."

"Mmm..." was all she could manage as a thousand sparks zipped through her body like an electric current across a high wire.

"I'll be satisfied." His words vibrated against her mouth. "You'll be satisfied."

She wanted to protest that she could never be satisfied when she knew things with him were temporary. But no. That was the way it had to be. She'd made a vow to herself when she left Seattle that she'd get her life together before getting involved with a man again. She had too rocky a track record—bad decisions and putting her own needs aside to make someone else happy.

The problem was how happy Finn made her. Not just the physical aspect, either. She liked talking to him and the way he made her laugh. He took her seriously, her input at the bank and her dreams of making something more of her life. It was as if with Finn she could see herself as the woman she wanted to be. All of which made him far too dangerous to let herself get carried away.

She opened her mouth to protest but before she could form one word, he kissed her. Just like that she forgot every one of her objections. She could easily lose herself in Finn. She wouldn't, of course. But for the moment she let herself be carried away.

His mouth was warm and deliciously firm. He kissed her like they had all the time in the world to discover each other. That thought had her pulling away. She stumbled back a step, pressing two fingers to her lips.

"We can't do this here," she told him in a rush of breath. One kiss and she'd lost all good sense.

Finn ran a hand through his hair, and it helped to see his chest rising and falling like he couldn't quite get a hold of himself. At least she wasn't the only one affected.

"Sorry," he said. "I've been wanting to kiss you since I opened my eyes this morning. You're cute when you sleep."

She couldn't help but laugh. "I drool."

He grinned. "Cute."

"Right." She laughed again. "You don't need to take off or hide out in your office from me. I don't bite."

"Tell that to my shoulder." He made a show of rubbing it.

"You need to stop that." She leveled a finger at him. "I can't walk around here with a permanent blush. Everyone will notice."

"Your penchant for using your teeth in the throes of passion—" he crossed a finger over his heart "—is our secret. But know that I don't make morning coffee for everyone."

"I did appreciate the coffee," she admitted as he sat on one corner of the desk and then took a bite of the sandwich. "Although I'm glad I forgot my mug and went to the coffee shop. Brynn Hale is working there now."

Finn swallowed. "Seriously? I didn't know that."

"It was her first day."

"How's she doing?" He shook his head. "I ran into her in the park and we talked, but I haven't reached out to her since then. I'm a jerk."

"I doubt she thinks that." Kaitlin absently straightened a stack of papers on the desk. "She seems a little lost but determined to figure things out. I can't imagine having to start over from that kind of loss, especially when everyone in town knows the details surrounding it."

"You don't think she'll leave Starlight?"

Kaitlin shook her head. "Not with Tyler. She needs the support."

"It's a good town for that," he said, popping the last piece of sandwich into his mouth. "It's also a good town for chicken salad."

"You inhaled that thing." She handed him a napkin.

"I skipped breakfast. Lost my appetite once Peter showed up."

"You really didn't know he was coming?"

"I'm not trying to sell the bank," he said, his voice tight.

"People will talk. I think everyone has been trying to ignore that bank takeovers are what you're known for. They trust your father to take care of them…"

"But not me?"

She shrugged. "No one knows you well enough."

"What do you think?" He wadded up the parchment paper as he stood, shoving it in the carryout bag and tossing the whole thing in the trash can. "You know me pretty well after last night."

Did she know him? She wanted to believe that but had enough experience to understand sex and intimacy weren't necessarily the same thing.

"I trust you," she said quietly and watched him visibly relax. "You need to show your face out there." She pointed toward the door. "Go on with business as usual so people see they have nothing to worry about from AmeriNat."

"Do you mind if I sit in on the meeting with the volunteers from the art festival? I should probably try to prove that I'm taking an interest in the local scene and all that."

Kaitlin's heart stuttered as she watched pink bloom on Finn's angled cheeks. He made a show of clicking his keyboard and focusing his attention on the computer screen while he waited for her answer. But his blasé demeanor didn't fool her. He needed her, and although she could tell herself all day that didn't matter, it did. She wanted to be needed by him and not just at the office if she admitted the whole truth.

"It would be good if you're there. First Trust has a history of supporting the community. You can be part of that."

He nodded and flashed her an almost sheepish smile. "It's a plan, then."

She turned to leave.

"Kaitlin?" His eyes turned gentle when she met his gaze. "Thanks for lunch, and I'm sorry about how I left things this morning. One night with you isn't nearly enough."

"I feel the same way," she said softly.

They both glanced toward the door when a sharp knock sounded.

Kaitlin opened it to find Jack on the other side. "How did things go with Peter?"

Finn shrugged and tried to look nonchalant. Kaitlin didn't buy it and doubted his father did, either. "Fine. He had some questions about a deal I'm working on in Northern California."

"Always the power player," Jack said, a muscle ticking in his jaw. "It must feel like you're stuck in East Dullsville here compared with what you're used to."

"I never said that," Finn protested, his tone cool. Kaitlin wished she could make the two of them admit how much they cared about each other. It was so clear, but every time she thought Finn and Jack were making headway on their relationship, they'd slip into this strange, subtle dance for superiority.

"It seems as though there's plenty you haven't said," Jack countered. "But I'm heading out of town until Sunday morning." His shrewd gaze darted between the two of them. "I trust you can handle things while I'm gone."

"Gone where?" Kaitlin asked. "I thought you wanted to finalize your remarks for the opening of the art show."

He waved a hand. "Put something together. Finn will do the talking on Saturday, so you don't need me."

"Of course we do," she argued.

An emotion she couldn't name flashed in the older man's eyes, but he blinked and it was gone. "I'll be an hour away."

"Do you need a hotel?"

"Already arranged."

"Where are you going?" Finn asked.

Jack's shoulders stiffened. "Seattle. You're not the only one who can handle a big city."

Something passed between the two men, and Kaitlin wanted to shake them both.

"Why?" Finn demanded.

"I'm taking Nanci for a weekend in the city," Jack answered, as if it were the most normal thing in the world.

"You've only been on one date with her," Kaitlin pointed out. "Things are moving kind of quickly, don't you think?"

He chuckled. "At my age, time is a bit more relative. Besides..." He inclined his head and gave her a knowing look. "I'm not sure either of you are in a position to talk to me about moving quickly."

Kaitlin felt her mouth drop open.

"Well played," Finn said from behind her.

It wasn't exactly a surprise that Jack would have figured out what had happened between her and his son last night. But being confronted with his knowledge of it was an entirely different thing. It felt a bit like being called out by a parent. Not that her mom had ever cared much what Kaitlin had been doing with boys.

"I'll see you on Sunday," Jack said, patting her shoulder. He winked. "Have a good night."

Kaitlin glanced at Finn as his father walked away. "That was weird, right?"

"Extremely," he agreed, massaging a hand along the back of his neck. "I'm having flashbacks to high school and I just found out I'll have the house to myself."

"Are you planning a big kegger for all your friends?"

He grinned. "I'm planning on you and me and a bottle of wine."

The whisper of promise in his voice made her stomach dance and spin, and then she remembered her date with Brynn.

"I'm busy tonight," she said, grimacing. "Brynn and I are going for dinner and drinks while her son is at a meeting. My friend Mara was going to come with us, but she already has plans. I think Brynn needs some new friends."

"I'm glad she has you, then," Finn told her without missing a beat. "Just be sure to save room for dessert."

She swallowed hard at the promise in his eyes, anticipation already making her body tingle from head to toe.

Chapter Fourteen

"You won't believe who made me the worst cup of coffee I've ever had this morning."

Finn adjusted his baseball cap as he climbed into Nick's truck later that night. "Brynn Hale." He shut the door and reached for his seat belt. "And I highly doubt it was the worst. I've tried that swill you brew."

Nick's mouth fell open. "How did you know that?"

"Kaitlin mentioned that today was Brynn's first on the job at Main Street Perk."

"Are the two of them friends?" Nick turned onto the road that led into town.

Finn had planned to spend the evening alone, going over the bank's commercial loan portfolio and ideas for restructuring distribution within the branch. But neither task appealed and, more important, he didn't want to seem like he was waiting around for Kaitlin to get back from her girls' night.

Of course he'd checked his watch at least a dozen times once he'd changed from his suit and settled in at the table in his childhood kitchen. With his dad gone, the house felt weirdly empty, like he was rambling around with childhood memories as his only companions.

So he'd called Nick, who'd been on his way home from the station and offered to swing by for Finn before heading to Trophy Room, a longtime favorite bar of locals in Starlight.

"I guess." Finn shrugged. "Kaitlin didn't say much other than they were going to dinner tonight."

"She's probably going to Brynn's house." Nick fiddled with the radio dial. "Brynn is an amazing cook."

"But not that much of a barista?"

Nick cringed. "I hate that she's having to do that. Put herself out there in town when everyone knows the circumstances surrounding Daniel's death and what he was putting her through before that."

"Maybe she wants to get out there again. I feel like a schmuck even bringing this up, but it's not like he meant to crash," Finn felt compelled to point out. "It was an accident."

"He was cheating on her," Nick countered through clenched teeth. "I'm not saying that meant he deserved to die, but he wasn't doing right by her. This affair wasn't the first."

"You know that for sure?"

"I pulled him over a couple of times for speeding. Let's just say he was never alone and Brynn wasn't with him on either night."

"You've got to talk to her, Nick."

His friend's knuckles turned white. "I can't. I wouldn't know what to say."

"She was your best friend."

"Years ago, man. A lifetime."

"That doesn't change things. Look at us."

"It's different because we're guys."

"Sexist much?"

Nick thumped a hand on the steering wheel. "I don't mean it like that. Things changed for Brynn and me. We can't go back. We're different people now."

"I don't know," Finn said quietly, thinking of Kaitlin. She was different than any woman he'd ever known. His feelings for her were certainly unfamiliar territory. If he planned to stay in Starlight or if he thought she'd be willing to come to Seattle, would that change things between them?

"I need a beer to have this conversation." Nick parked around the corner from the pub. They got out and started down the sidewalk. In the approaching twilight, Finn could see a variety of lit beer signs in the window. "Now that I think about it, I'd like a beer and a new topic. Let's talk football or the BTUs on my new gas grill."

Finn grinned. "Do you want to hear about the new speaker system I installed at my condo?"

"In great detail," Nick said. "With a beer in one hand."

"And a chicken wing in the other?"

"Now you're talking." Nick held open the door of the bar for Finn. Music, laughter and the scent of stale liquor drifted out.

"Is it strange going out in town being the police chief?" Finn asked as they approached the antique bar. Trophy Room had been designed to look like an old English pub with dark paneling and brass fixtures. Rows of shelves and a few glass trophy cases lined the far wall, as it was a town tradition for local teams and star athletes to donate their medals and trophies to the bar for display.

Nick waved to several people and offered friendly greetings to a few more. This was a neighborhood hangout in every sense of the phrase.

"Not anymore," Nick said as they slid into two empty seats at the bar. "I'm not exactly partying like a rock star around here, but I like to keep an eye on things."

"Hey, boys." Finn smiled as Tanya Mehall, who'd babysat him and his sister in their younger years, approached. "Welcome home, Finn," she said, multiple diamond stud earrings glinting in the light. "Always a pleasure, Chief."

"I didn't realize you worked here," Finn told her.

She let out a husky belly laugh, and Finn remembered that she used to sneak cigarettes out on the back porch when he and Ella were supposed to be watching television. "I've been behind the bar about five years now." She leaned in, her familiar bleach-blond hair and high ponytail a throwback to his childhood. "I'd take taming this crowd at their rowdiest over you and your spawn-of-the-devil sister any day."

Finn threw back his head and laughed. Tanya was ten years older than him and the only babysitter who hadn't refused to return to their house after one night with Ella and him. "Did Dad end up paying you double or triple the going rate?"

"Triple," she said without hesitation. "I earned every penny. What's our girl up to these days?"

"She's a travel nurse, focusing on pediatrics,"

Finn reported. "She does a lot of work in Africa and South America."

"Is that so? The wild child has settled down?"

"I'm not sure about that," Finn admitted. Between assignments, Ella had managed to visit every continent on the planet, often backpacking with friends she made during her travels. Finn had done a fine job of ignoring the pain from his childhood. Ella was still on the run from hers. His sister had channeled her energy for good as a nurse, but she still wouldn't make a commitment to stay in one location for more than a few months at a time. "But she's managing in her own way."

"Aren't we all?" Tanya asked with a wink. "What can I get the two of you?"

Finn and Nick each ordered a beer, with Nick adding wings and nachos. The drinks came quickly and Tanya promised the food would follow shortly.

As Finn took a long pull, he turned in his chair to survey the crowd. He recognized a number of people, and even more looked vaguely familiar. But there were also a handful of newbies sprinkled in, whether visitors to the area or new residents he couldn't say. The fact that Starlight was growing made him more confident about the chances of turning things around at the bank for the long term. He didn't want to admit how much Peter Henry's dismal prediction had affected him.

"Some things never change," he said quietly, taking a strange sort of comfort in that. The social scene he was a part of in Seattle consisted of trendy brewpubs and high-end restaurants. He'd thought that was what he wanted from his life, but the more time he spent in Starlight, the less sure he became.

"Aww, hell, no," Nick muttered and Finn felt the immediate change in his friend's demeanor.

"What's wrong?" He followed Nick's gaze to the back of the bar, where a cluster of high-top tables were situated around a couple of pool tables and a shuffleboard game.

He didn't see anything out of the ordinary at first. Then a burly man in dark flannel shifted and he caught sight of a tumble of golden-hued hair. Awareness shot through him. He couldn't get a clear view thanks to the group of twenty-something men surrounding the table, but by the look on Nick's face, Finn already knew who occupied the table where his friend was staring.

"Did you do this on purpose?" Nick's voice was sharp.

Finn shook his head. "I told you they were going to dinner. Why would two women pick the Trophy Room for dinner?"

"Wings," Nick answered simply.

Finn glanced at him.

"Brynn loves wings," Nick clarified. "Everyone in Starlight knows this place serves the best."

"Sorry," Finn said on a sigh. "We can leave if you want to. I'll tell Tanya—"

"Look at the men," Nick said. "They're clustering around them like bees in a flower garden."

"They're two grown women." Finn took a long drink of beer and forced his gaze away from where Kaitlin and Brynn sat. "I'm sure they can handle—"

"One of them just touched Kaitlin's hair."

Finn was out of his seat in an instant, slamming his beer to the top of the bar.

"Here's the food, boys," Tanya said, placing two heaping plates in front of them. "Enjoy."

"I've lost my appetite," Finn muttered when the bartender walked away. He messed with the brim of his ball cap. "What the hell are we supposed to do now?"

Nick plucked a chip from the plate of nachos, melted cheese oozing off the side. "Pretend you don't care."

"I don't care. Not like that."

"Liar."

Finn gave a sharp shake of his head and then picked up the plate of nachos along with his beer. "Grab the wings."

"I'm not going over there."

"It's about time you talked to her anyway."

"I can't talk to her in a crowded bar."

"You have to start somewhere."

"This isn't about Brynn and me."

Finn grinned. "I'm making it about you. Easier for me that way."

Nick grumbled a protest but followed as Finn weaved through groups of people toward Kaitlin's table. Her eyes widened when she noticed him, but she smiled.

"Hello, ladies," Finn said, placing the nachos in the center of the table. "We come bearing food."

Brynn's mouth formed a small O as Nick approached.

"Hey." One of their male admirers held up a hand in protest. "We were here first."

Before Finn could answer, Kaitlin turned to the guy, her shoulders squared. "Excuse me? You say that like you staked a flag on the moon."

"You know what I mean," the man said with a smile that wanted to be charming. "We're all hanging out. No room for anyone else."

"You're done here now," Nick said, moving forward. Finn suddenly had a clear picture of the serious lawman his goof-off friend had become.

Two of the guys took the hint and stepped back but the third edged closer to Brynn, holding out his phone. "Put your number in and I'll text you later."

It was a good thing Nick was off duty because

Finn was pretty sure his friend would have found an excuse to arrest the guy otherwise.

"No, thanks," Brynn said simply. If she detected Nick's brewing temper, she ignored it.

"We can keep things casual," the guy said, not giving up.

Nick made a sound suspiciously close to a growl. This time Brynn did notice and gave him a quelling glance.

She turned back to her would-be suitor with a saccharine-sweet smile. "Let me set you straight, friend. I've been a widow for less than a month and am now the proud single parent of a son who I had when I was still in my teens. As fun as casual sounds, I'm not sure I have it in me at this point. You want to take that on?"

The man swallowed, his Adam's apple bobbing, and slowly pocketed the phone. "Um…well… I should probably go. Have a good night, then."

"You, too," Brynn said with a little wave. She turned back toward the table. "I guess there are benefits and drawbacks to meeting new people." She took a wing from the plate Nick still held and dipped it in the ramekin of ranch dressing. "I come with baggage, and most everyone in Starlight knows it."

"Everyone comes with baggage," Kaitlin said reassuringly.

"Tyler isn't baggage," Nick muttered, shoving over the nachos to make room for the wings.

"Would you date a single mother who just lost her husband?" Brynn asked conversationally.

Finn tried not to cringe as he watched his friend squirm under Brynn's steady gaze.

"N-not you, of course," Nick stammered after a moment.

Although Brynn's expression didn't change, something flashed in her eyes that made Finn want to slap Nick upside the head.

"Of course," Brynn repeated softly.

"Who wants a nacho?" Kaitlin asked, her voice bright.

"You know what I mean," Nick insisted, not taking his eyes off Brynn.

"I do."

"Besides, you don't want to date," he continued, only digging himself a deeper hole as far as Finn was concerned. "It's too soon."

"Thank you for that insight," Brynn told him wryly.

"The nachos look so good," Kaitlin offered into the awkward silence that followed.

"They're the best," Finn agreed.

Brynn stood. "I think I need another beer to go with them."

"Are you driving?" Nick asked, earning an eye roll but no other response from Brynn.

"Anyone else?"

"I'm set," Finn said.

"Me, too," Kaitlin agreed. "Want me to go to the bar with you?"

"I've got it," Brynn answered and turned away.

She started toward the bar, then veered off to where the three men had moved.

"She can't be doing what it looks like she's doing," Nick whispered.

But indeed, Brynn Hale, the sweetest and most accommodating girl Finn had ever met, took the phone of her flannel-clad admirer, tapped something into the screen and handed it back to him with a smile for the ages.

"She did," Kaitlin said with a chuckle.

Nick rounded on her. "That's not funny, and it isn't the Brynn I know."

"How well do you know her at this point?" Kaitlin asked.

Nick's green gaze darkened.

"Kaitlin's right," Finn said, laying a hand on his friend's shoulder. "Even if you don't want to hear it. Brynn's been a married woman for a decade. She's a mother. You can't go right back to how things were in high school just because Daniel died."

"I don't want to go back to high school." Nick's tone was razor sharp. "But she needs…" He ran a hand through his hair. "I don't know what she needs, but it's not a random hookup."

"Give her some credit," Kaitlin said gently. "I don't know her well, but nothing that she's said to me so far has indicated that her husband's death or the circumstances of it is going to send her off the rails. She wants to create a good life for her son."

Nick hitched a thumb toward the trio of hipster lumberjacks. "Then what was that about?"

"I think it was a reaction to your reaction," Kaitlin told him, and Finn appreciated her honesty. "Finn told me how close you and Brynn were in high school. She's not that girl anymore. If you want to be her friend now, figure out how to do that with the woman she's become."

"Good advice," Finn said, gratified when Kaitlin shifted slightly closer to him.

"Yeah," Nick agreed, then drained his beer. He put the empty glass on the table. "But I'm not sure I know how." He nodded at Kaitlin. "I'm glad you and Brynn connected."

"Me, too," Kaitlin agreed.

"You mind giving Finn a ride home?" Nick asked. He drew in an unsteady breath. "I'm not great company right now, and I don't want to irritate Brynn any more than I already have."

Kaitlin nodded. “Sure.”

“I can come with you,” Finn offered.

“Stay,” Nick answered. “I’ll catch up with you later.”

“Nick is like a brother to me, but he was out of line,” Finn said when they were alone.

“Are you sure he was the only one?” Kaitlin gave him a look like he was a recalcitrant schoolboy.

“What did I do?”

She rolled her pretty eyes. “You know I can handle myself in a bar, right?”

“Yes,” he said slowly. “Although I didn’t expect to see you here tonight. When you said the two of you were going out for dinner—”

“Brynn wanted wings.”

“That’s what Nick guessed. Are you mad that we came over?” He shrugged. “Am I cramping your style?”

She flashed a saucy smile that had his blood heating. “I don’t have that kind of style, nor do I want it. I’m glad to see you, Finn.”

He released the breath he hadn’t realized he was holding.

“If we weren’t keeping things between us on the down low, I’d kiss you right now.”

He groaned softly. “Killing me here, Kaitlin.”

"Is Nick interested in Brynn?" she asked suddenly, and all of that glorious heat disappeared.

He glanced over his shoulder to make sure Brynn was still at the bar. "She's newly widowed," he told her as if she didn't know the story.

"That doesn't answer my question. I know they were friends, and then she and Daniel were married when she got pregnant. Did she leave Nick heartbroken back then?"

He shook his head. "It definitely rocked his world along the lines of 'you don't know what you've got until it's gone.' Who knows what their new normal will end up looking like?"

"Where's Nick?"

He turned as Brynn slid back into her seat. "He had to go." Finn smiled. "It's good to see you out, Brynn."

She glanced at her watch. "Actually, you're about to see me disappear. Tyler's car pool will be dropping him off in about twenty minutes."

Finn realized she'd returned empty-handed. "What about that other beer?"

"I didn't want another beer as much as I wanted to avoid Starlight's finest doing his big brother routine with me. Ever since Daniel's death, Nick looks at me like I'm an abandoned puppy. Helpless and pitiful."

"He doesn't think either of those things about you."

She didn't look convinced but only shrugged. "Thank you for a fun night," she said to Kaitlin. "I hope Mara can join us next time."

The two women hugged and Brynn whispered something that had Kaitlin giggling.

"What?" Finn demanded.

"Nothing," Brynn said, then hugged him. "It's nice to have you back in town, even temporarily."

His gut clenched at that reminder, and he purposely didn't look at Kaitlin until Brynn was gone.

"We've got a lot of nachos to get through," he said, his tone light despite the lead balloon currently occupying his insides.

She shook her head. "I don't think so."

Damn. Was this the part where she came to her senses and cut him loose?

Then she leaned closer. "I don't want to ruin my appetite when you promised me dessert. Remember?"

His hulking doubts about the future morphed into a million specks of dust flitting through him. He grabbed her hand and pulled her through the bar like a raging fire licked at their heels. "Where are you parked?" he demanded, surprised he could make his voice work normally when every inch of him was on edge.

She pointed across the street toward her small sedan and he led her forward. Pulling the key fob from her purse, she unlocked the car. They got in without speaking, and Finn wondered if Kaitlin was as blown away by the potent attraction between them as he was.

Then the car lurched forward and she tossed him a sexy grin. "Sorry," she said in a laugh. "You haven't even done anything yet and already my body's reacting."

"That sounds almost like a challenge," he told her, but she playfully swatted away his hand when he would have rested it on her jeans-clad leg.

"I'd like to get home in one piece."

"Good point," he admitted. "I guess for safety reasons you'll just have to imagine all the ways I want to touch you right now."

She sucked in a breath and glanced at him again. "Just so you know, Finn, I have a vivid imagination."

"That's the best thing I've heard all night."

Chapter Fifteen

Kaitlin wasn't sure how she managed the drive from downtown to the Samuelson property with all the wicked thoughts swirling through her mind.

Finn didn't say much, but every few minutes he'd let out a devious little chuckle like he knew exactly how worked up his implied promise made her.

"The main house," he told her as she pulled up the driveway. "I want you in my bed."

She nodded, ignoring the fact that the guest bed in his father's house didn't belong to him. Just as she'd ignored Brynn's comment about Finn being in Starlight temporarily. Kaitlin had learned from a young age to be a master at compartmentalization. She'd had no idea it would serve her so well in her dating life.

Or not *exactly* dating life. If she had to admit the truth, the back-and-forth between Brynn and Nick had gotten to her. Were she and Finn the definition of *casual*? A convenient scratching of an itch neither of them could ignore?

Except nothing about her feelings was convenient. *Complicated* didn't even start to do it justice.

But like a moth drawn to a shining light in the dark, she seemed to have no self-preservation instinct when it came to this man.

She parked the car in front of the house, and he took her hand as they walked to the porch. His thumb traced tiny circles on the inside of her wrist, sending shockwaves of awareness through her body.

Finn was a man on a mission. As soon as they were through the door, he headed for the hallway that led to the bedrooms. "You and me first," he said, his voice low and rumbly. "Actual dessert later." He laced his fingers with hers. "Does that work for you?"

When he glanced at her, she nodded, not trusting her voice to speak. Anticipation built within her, and the moment they crossed the threshold into the guest bedroom, he turned and drew her close.

The kiss was electric, every part of her lighting up like a night sky on the Fourth of July. They tore at each other, need and desire making their movements frenetic. It was difficult to tell where Kaitlin ended and Finn began, which was exactly how she wanted this moment to go.

So when he pulled away, she fought back a whimper of protest.

"I can't go slow," he told her, his gaze at once fierce and tender.

"Then don't." She toed off her shoes and shimmied out of her jeans. "I don't want to wait, Finn."

It was all the invitation he needed. He reached for her again, and they were a tangle of arms and kisses until both of them were undressed and tumbling into the bed together.

Once the condom was in place, he entered her in one long thrust, the shock and pleasure of being filled so completely taking her breath away. They moved together and it was like nothing she'd ever felt. Finn seemed to inherently know exactly how to touch her to drive her wild. It was as if he understood what she wanted before she even realized it.

When her release came, her body turned electric once more and the intensity of the pleasure made her want this moment to last forever. He followed her over the edge a few seconds later. Kaitlin felt like her heart had transferred to the outside of her body, as if she were wearing every bit of her feelings for this man on her skin. Surely he could sense it, that all of her talk about rules and boundaries had disintegrated into a thousand pieces in the wake of what he did to her.

"You're amazing," Finn whispered, rolling onto his back and taking her with him.

I love you.

She rolled her lips inward, pressing them tight to prevent the words from popping out unbidden. If she said those three words to him now, it would ruin everything.

He climbed out of the bed and padded to the bathroom as she tried to control her breathing.

She'd fallen in love with Finn Samuelson. All her talk about being independent and living her own life had just gone straight to hell. Goals and priorities, and she was completely enamored of a man who wasn't going to stay.

How did this make her any different than her mom? Always falling hard for whatever man she took to her bed, brokenhearted when each of them left her behind until she was finally just broken.

Kaitlin had sworn she wouldn't make those same mistakes. Hell, she'd left her old life behind so that she could have a fresh start.

If only Finn felt the same way she did. If only he would stay in Starlight.

She bit down on the inside of her cheek until she tasted blood.

If only she weren't such a softhearted fool.

He'd given her no reason to believe anything had changed between them. In fact, she couldn't shake the conviction that there was more to his boss showing up in Starlight than he was willing to admit. But the way he made love to her—like she was the most precious thing in his world—gave her hope.

Kaitlin hated hope. Hope led to disappointment.

She climbed out of bed and threw on one of his discarded T-shirts.

"You look good in my clothes," he said with a wink as he exited the bathroom. He'd pulled on boxers and a pair of loose basketball shorts. "Are you ready for dessert?"

"Sure," she said, keeping her smile bright. He led the way to the kitchen and pulled out a carton of mint chocolate-chip ice cream from the freezer.

Kaitlin grabbed two spoons from a drawer as Finn took off the lid. "How do you feel about your dad leaving you in charge of the art show?"

He took a spoon from her and sat at the kitchen table, pushing out the chair next to his for her. "I'm suspicious anytime Jack Samuelson voluntarily relinquishes control, but I have no problem making the opening remarks on Saturday. My mom chaired the committee the first year the Starlight Art Festival took place. She'd just taken up watercolor painting and was so excited to make the town some sort of mecca for regional artists. It was the summer before she died, and First Trust has been the event's main sponsor ever since."

"Finn, wow." Kaitlin paused with the spoon halfway to her mouth. "I didn't realize what a personal connection you had to it." She shook her head. "Your dad probably got sick of me trying to convince him to reconsider the amount he'd pledged to fund it. I was worried about the bank's bottom line but had no idea why it meant so much to him."

"I'm sure he appreciated your concern." Finn used one finger to nudge the spoon toward her mouth. "I understand the disconnect, though. It's the same thing I grappled with on Seth's business loan. Things are much simpler when they're just numbers on a page."

"I guess."

He inclined his head. "Or when you establish the rules for something early on?"

Her cheeks heated at the teasing note to his tone. Here was her chance to tell him she wanted to throw her silly guidelines out the window and go all in with him.

But something stopped her.

Doubt. Fear. The possibility that he would break her heart.

"I have another rule for you," she said instead.

His brows furrowed. "I can't wait to hear it."

She pointed her spoon toward him. "No mining for chips."

He glanced down at the container of ice cream, a slow smile curling his lips. He'd dug around, maybe without even realizing it, for the hunks of chocolate embedded in the ice cream. "But the chips are the best part."

She shook her head, trying to keep her expression neutral. "If you dig them all out, the next person will be left with plain ice cream."

"I want the good stuff now," he said unapologetically. He held up his spoon. "I'll share if you say please."

"Please," she whispered, leaning forward. The chocolate was rich and creamy on her tongue. Then Finn kissed her, and after that she forgot all about ice cream.

Finn gulped down another swig of water as he waited to one side of the grandstand on Saturday morning. He'd told Kaitlin he had no problem making the opening remarks for the art festival, but at that point he hadn't considered how his family's history with the event would affect him.

The festival appeared to have quadrupled in size since Finn had last attended. He could still remember that first year. There had been folding tables and makeshift booths with a handful of local artists selling their creations. His mom had been so proud when the last of her watercolors had sold, and she'd insisted on taking the family out to dinner with her profits.

By that Christmas, she'd been gone.

He'd been angry when his dad had stepped in the following year to sponsor the event, offering enough funding to make it worthwhile for the local art community to keep it going. To Finn, the art show had belonged to his mom and he'd avoided downtown annually on the weekend when it took place until the summer he'd left for college.

Now he was back and it was as if his mother's unintended legacy surrounded him.

"We're thrilled to have you with us this year."

He blinked and nodded, forcing himself to focus on Torrey Daniels, the woman who was chairing the event.

"Thanks," he said, clearing his throat when the word came out sounding like a frog's croak.

"Your dad has been so supportive through the

years of the arts community in Starlight. Anytime we have a new idea, he finds a way to make it happen. There aren't too many people like him in the world, willing to put their money toward what they value in life."

Finn sucked in a breath. All the anger he'd felt toward his father through the years felt like so much water under the bridge right now. Maybe Jack had been gruff and unemotional with Finn and Ella, but Finn could clearly see that his dad's love for his late wife permeated everything he did. He guessed that Torrey was in her midforties, with sandy-brown hair cut into a stylish but easy-to-manage bob. She wore a dress of deep purple, a color he imagined his mother would have loved. She would have appreciated everything about the event. The thought made fresh pain engulf his heart, covering the old ache of missing her like an avalanche of emotion.

"Glad to be here," he said, willing the words to sound less lame than they did.

Torrey flashed an awkward smile. "Okay, then. I'm going to start things off, and then I'll ask you to say a few words before I announce the featured artists for this year."

"What does is it mean to be a featured artist?"

"Those are the artists who were given stipends after last year's show," she told him with a frown.

"It's one of the reasons we've gotten so big. Part of the bank's funding goes toward funding artists in each medium. Attendees vote and your father and his committee make the final decision."

"I didn't know that."

"Over the years, several of the artists who've received funding from First Trust have gone on to break out at both the regional and national levels. Many times all a person needs is someone to believe in them."

Finn felt his mouth go dry. "Tell me about it."

"Your father is truly an amazing man."

"I can see why you think that," Finn said quietly, his senses on overload at the influx of new information to process about Jack Samuelson.

Because of Finn's anger, he'd missed out on so much. Not that he'd misjudged his dad exactly. Jack had admittedly been an awful father after his wife died. But that wasn't the whole of him, the way Finn had always believed.

Torrey checked her watch. "Here we go," she told him with an enthusiastic thumbs-up.

Finn clenched and unclenched his fists as he watched her walk toward the podium. She welcomed the artists and the attendees and then thanked the businesses and community of Starlight for their continued support before inviting Finn to join her onstage.

He registered a polite round of applause, but his focus remained on keeping his composure despite the tumult of sentiment his conversation with Torrey had released inside him. "Thank you." He spoke into the microphone, trying not to wince at the low whine of feedback. "I'll be honest," he continued, glancing out at familiar and new-to-him faces. "It's been years since I attended one of these festivals. Before her death, my mom was an aspiring artist and deeply committed to fostering a thriving art scene in Starlight."

He sucked in a breath at what he'd just revealed. Finn didn't talk about his mother's death, and certainly not in this kind of public forum. Another round of applause sounded and his gaze caught and held on Kaitlin. She stood in the center of the crowd and gave him a small smile and nod, like she was proud of him for sharing that bit of himself.

"But I'm happy to be here now," he told the crowd. "I'm impressed by this community and what my father and First Trust have done to support it. In a few minutes, you're going to be introduced to the artists who were funded through a program at First Trust. My dad doesn't just run a bank here in Starlight. He cares about this town and its future. We're all dedicated and hope that when you think about the kind of service you want from a financial institution, you'll remember that commitment."

He took another breath as the understanding of what he wanted from his future dawned on him. He couldn't look at Kaitlin again; otherwise he might rush off the stage and pull her into his arms. She might have rules, but he was about to break every last one of them. He wanted her. For keeps. "We might not be artists at First Trust, but I hope you'll visit our booth and learn more about some of the programs we're offering to help you meet your life goals, no matter what they might be."

As he backed away from the microphone, he couldn't help but notice the applause was more intense than when he'd taken the stage a few minutes earlier.

"You did great," Torrey whispered, gently squeezing his arm as she moved past him.

Finn shook hands with the artists waiting to be introduced, each one thanking him and offering kind words about his father and the way he'd personally supported them over the previous year. Finn wasn't sure whether to be humbled or irritated at how easily his dad seemed to offer encouragement and backing to everyone in his life except Finn.

He couldn't stand to examine the thought too closely or else he'd have to admit his part in that.

Kaitlin was waiting for him behind the line of booths.

"You did great," she said with a huge smile.

His heart hammered in his throat at everything this woman made him feel. Could he say it now? Blurt out that he loved her and hope for the best?

There was no way she couldn't feel something for him. No way his emotions were one-sided. He just had to convince her to take a chance.

"It helped having a friendly face in the audience." He reached for her but she gave small shake of her head, her smile dimming slightly. "We're in public," she whispered.

"I don't care," he answered. "We need to talk, Kaitlin. There's so much…"

"Finn!" He turned as one of the sound guys waved to him from the back of the stage. "Torrey needs you for pictures with the artists."

Finn cursed under his breath.

"Go," Kaitlin said. "I'll be at the First Trust booth all day. We can talk later."

"I don't want to wait."

"Delayed gratification is good for you," she said with a laugh, then stood on tiptoe to brush a quick kiss across his lips. "There's something to tide you over."

"So sweet. I'll find you," he promised before heading back toward the stage.

Chapter Sixteen

It was late in the afternoon before Kaitlin felt like she had a moment to breathe. The bank's booth had been swamped with people all day. Some had been in the crowd that morning and heard Finn's speech, and word of mouth had made talk of First Trust's dedication to the Starlight community spread like wildfire.

Although many longtime locals already did their banking with the institution, Starlight had grown in the past few years. Many of the newer residents were also new to First Trust. Before the recent social media campaign and marketing initiatives, they hadn't done much to attract additional customers.

Jack had always believed that if he engaged in good business practices, he'd have a successful business. Kaitlin wished she'd spoken up earlier about the red flags she'd noticed in the way things had been handled. At this point, they had a good start on making First Trust healthy again, but there was still a lot of work to be done.

She hated to think of doing it without Finn. Why couldn't he see that he belonged in Starlight? His words this morning had caused goose bumps to break out across her arms and legs. He had a history here but also a future.

He'd looked so happy when he'd walked off the stage, and now she wished she'd run into his arms the way she'd wanted to. If he didn't care about being discreet, what did it matter?

She swallowed against the lump rising in the back of her throat. It mattered because her reputation was on the line. As much as she might think he should be in Starlight, until Finn agreed she couldn't put herself out there.

Rolling her shoulders, she glanced down the grassy pathway between the rows of booths. Finn had stopped by several times, but she'd always been talking to people. She'd taken a lunch break but had found him surrounded by a group of Jack's friends, who seemed to be regaling him with embarrassing anecdotes from his youth.

Frustration skittered along the back of her neck. What had he wanted to talk to her about? She hoped with every fiber of her being that it had nothing to do with him leaving town and heading back to his real life in Seattle.

It was too soon. It would be too soon for the rest of her life.

"I'm going to walk around for a few minutes," she told Meg, who'd arrived at the booth minutes earlier for her shift.

"You can even go for the day if you want," the young teller offered. "I think things are slowing down."

Kaitlin nodded. "Thanks, Meg. I'll be here in the morning."

The younger woman flashed a cheeky grin. "No offense, but you might need to get a life."

"You could be right," Kaitlin agreed with a laugh. She wanted a life, here in Starlight with Finn. She'd shut down her emotions when she left Seattle two years ago because they'd caused her nothing but trouble. Being with Finn didn't make her feel weak or powerless. She could be her best self with him, which gave her the courage to believe she could share that she'd fallen in love.

For once, leading with her heart might turn out well.

A jazz quartet played from the grandstand at the center of the park, and she headed there, hoping she'd run into Finn. Her phone was out of battery, so she couldn't call until she charged it. Groups of people still filed along the path and most of the display booths were filled with potential customers. By all accounts, the festival was a huge success, and not for the first time today she wondered why Jack had willingly missed it.

Suddenly she froze as she heard her name called by a familiar voice.

No.

Not here.

She turned, reluctant to face her past and silently praying she'd heard wrong, but there was no mistake. Robbie Marici, her ex-boyfriend and the biggest regret of her life, stood in front of a booth displaying colorful landscape prints.

"You look good, Kaitlin," he said, one side of his mouth curving into a patronizing smirk. "All fresh and clean. It's working for me."

His eyes on her made her feel dirty, and her flight reflex kicked in hard. Panic pricked its way along the back of her neck as she darted a glance around to make sure no one she knew had seen her with this man.

Not that Robbie stood out as anything but a tall, handsome, casually dressed festival attendee. His dark hair was shorter than it had been when they dated, and a few gray strands flecked the sides. He had a naturally lean build and strong features, but there was no misinterpreting the angry glint in his hazel eyes.

"You can't be here," she said, trying to act like this was a normal conversation. "You don't belong."

"Hey, Pot," he said with a dark chuckle. "Meet Kettle. This town isn't where either of us should be, sweetheart."

She gave a small shake of her head and moved out of the way of a couple with a toddler and another baby in a stroller. "I live here. It's my home."

"Right," he agreed, too readily for her liking. "I've been watching you today at your little bank booth. People like you. They *trust* you."

Kaitlin swallowed against the bile rising in her throat. Robbie had been watching her. "So what?"

"So, we can use that to our advantage."

She stepped closer, hitching her head toward the empty area between two booths. Robbie followed, and she ignored the sweat that rolled between her shoulders. It was quieter in the small space, the sound of her pounding heart filling her ears.

"There's no 'we,'" she told him. "There hasn't been for two years."

He shrugged. “I feel like we never really got closure with the way you ran off.”

“Closure,” she said with a sniff. “Give me a break. What do you want, Robbie?”

“There are a lot of old folks in this town. I’m sure they rely on their friendly neighborhood banker.” He leaned in closer. “And if that banker had access to their accounts…”

“Don’t even go there.” She held up a hand. “First, I’m not a banker. I work at the bank but not directly with customers or their accounts. Even if I did, there’s no way I’d get in on one of your stupid schemes. Forget it.”

“Come on,” he urged. “This place has so much potential.”

It did, Kaitlin agreed, but not in the way Robbie believed. Starlight had the potential to be a true home for her, but suddenly her life here felt tainted. She’d been wild in her younger years and knew she might have been convinced to go along with Robbie if she’d stayed with that low-life crowd from her past.

“Just think about it.” He reached out a long finger, trailing it over her jawline and making her want to shudder. “Seriously, Kaitlin, the good-girl thing is hot in a novel kind of way. But it’s not really you. You’re like the rest of us. You got dealt some crappy cards as a kid and life owes you. We all need to take advantage where we can."

"I'm *earning* my place here," she whispered, willing her voice to remain steady.

"I saw your mom a few weeks ago. She was looking kind of rough. I bet some fresh air from a trip out to the valley would help her feel better."

"Don't go there." Kaitlin fisted her hands at her sides as guilt surged through her. She drove into Seattle every month to mail cash to her mother, but they only spoke a few times a year and Cindi Carmody didn't know where Kaitlin lived. She loved her mother but had finally gotten to a breaking point with Cindi's dysfunction and wouldn't invite that into her life again. She also wouldn't let Robbie bring it to her doorstep.

"Give me a call next week when you've had a chance to sit with things." He smiled and she wanted to throw up. "My number hasn't changed."

She didn't move a muscle as he walked past her, brushing against her side in a way that made her think of a slithering snake.

Two years. That was how much freedom she'd had, believing she'd made a clean break from her past. God, she'd been a fool.

She ducked out from behind the row of booths, hurrying toward the street where she'd parked her car this morning. All her thoughts of finding Finn vanished. He'd know immediately that something was wrong. That everything had changed or, more accurately, that it had gone back to the way it used to be.

Fear threatened to swallow her whole, a familiar desolation. How naive to think she'd overcome it. Instead it had been waiting, suppressed by her attempt at achieving happiness but easily set free after a few obscure threats from her ex. But what if they were more than just threats? If he made good on the things he said, the world she'd created would crumble around her in an instant.

It felt as though the life she'd built in Starlight had been little more than a house of cards, blown apart by one gust of menacing wind.

Where did that leave her? Kaitlin didn't know, but she understood nothing in her life could go back to the way it had been when this day began.

Finn stared out the bay window in the breakfast nook of his dad's house the following morning, hoping to see any trace of movement from the guest cottage. Something was definitely not right, and his stomach twisted at the thought that he'd inadvertently messed up simply by acquiescing to his feelings.

Kaitlin had left the art fair yesterday before he'd had a chance to talk to her. He'd called and texted but other than a few irritatingly baffling smiley face emoji, she hadn't responded. Torrey Daniels had asked him to join the festival committee and the featured artists at a reception, so it had been close to eight by the time he returned home.

He'd knocked on the door of the guesthouse, confused and concerned when Kaitlin had opened it only slightly. Her gaze was guarded and he would have sworn she'd been crying, but she told him she was sick and needed a night alone to rest.

As tempted as he'd been to push his way in—and hopefully through whatever walls she was hastening to erect between them—he'd walked away.

Nothing had changed as far as he could tell. Yes, he'd inwardly admitted he loved her and wanted a future together, but *she* didn't know that. Was he that transparent?

And what did it mean that almost as soon as he'd acknowledged his yearning for that type of commitment, she'd shut him out?

He almost couldn't stand to think of it.

"There are binoculars in my office if you really want a close-up look."

Finn turned to see his dad striding into the kitchen, briefcase in his right hand. "How was Seattle?" he asked, eyeing the leather portfolio as his father lifted it onto the counter.

"Productive," Jack answered. "What's going on with the Peeping Tom routine?"

"I'm bird-watching," Finn said dryly. He wasn't about to open himself to his dad's opinion on his love life. "How was a weekend in the city with your girlfriend productive? Don't tell me it's such a whirlwind romance that you went engagement-ring shopping."

His dad scoffed. "Don't be silly. Nanci and I are old friends who enjoy each other's company. She wanted to meet with a potential new coffee bean supplier for her shop and I..." He lifted his gaze to meet Finn's and something about the emotion Finn saw there had his senses kicking into high alert.

"Why did you go to Seattle, Dad?"

"To meet with Peter Henry."

Finn turned from the window, gripping the back of a kitchen chair. "Tell me you were arranging a tee time."

"I'm not golfing with Peter."

"Dad."

Jack opened the briefcase and pulled out a slim folder. "Obviously it will take time, but he worked up an initial offer for First Trust based on the financials you gave to Roger." He slid the manila file folder across the granite countertop. "If you want to take a look."

"What the hell are you talking about?" Finn felt his knuckles start to ache where they ruthlessly tightened on the back of the chair. "He can't come up with an offer in twenty-four hours. It's the damn weekend."

Jack waved away his concern. "Preliminary numbers, but the wheels are in motion."

Finn shook his head. "You're talking nonsense. From the moment I expressed concern about the bank's stability, you've been telling me you wouldn't sell. I've put my life on hold to bail you out, and now that it seems like the plan might succeed, you go to Peter behind my back to—"

"I didn't go to Peter," Jack interrupted, steel lacing his tone. "You're the one who brought him to Starlight."

"He showed up on his own," Finn insisted. "I sent him away with no hope for a deal."

"Do you really expect me to believe that?"

Finn felt his mouth drop open. "Yes. It's the truth."

Jack drew in a deep breath like he was trying to rein in his temper. "I appreciate the work you've put into the bank these past few weeks. It gives us more bargaining power, which I assume was your intent from the start."

"My intent?" Finn muttered. "Are you joking?"

"I've dedicated my life to First Trust," Jack said slowly. "It's our family's legacy."

"I get that," Finn said through clenched teeth.

"But you've also made it clear that it isn't *your* legacy," Jack continued, and the words were like a punch to the gut for Finn. "I don't fault you for it, but I need to think about the future."

The future was all Finn had been thinking about since yesterday. His future in Starlight, and now it was being taken from him before he'd even had a chance to claim it.

"Don't you think you might have mentioned this to me first?"

"I appreciate all you've done," Jack repeated, "but the bank is still mine. I don't need your permission to make decisions about it."

"You never would have given me a real chance," Finn said, bitterness swamping every other emotion he felt. "That's how it's always been. Why do you think I had to leave and not come back for so many years, Dad?"

"We weren't good enough for you," his dad answered immediately.

Finn barked out a harsh laugh. "Try it the other way around. I was never good enough for you. No matter what I did at the bank or in school, it was never enough."

"I'm not going to apologize for pushing you."

"You pushed me right out of your life," Finn whispered.

Jack opened his mouth, shut it again. After a moment he reached forward and plucked the folder off the counter. "You're here now," he said. "But not once have you given me a reason to believe you want to stay."

Fair enough. Finn could admit that to himself, although not out loud.

"Are you going to stay in Starlight?" his father asked, and Finn couldn't help but notice the older man kept any emotion out of his tone. He posed the question as if he were asking Finn what he fancied for dinner.

"Do you want me to?" The question burst from his lips unbidden, and immediately he wanted to take it back. The words revealed too much vulnerability. Finn felt like he had back in high school, trying but never quite feeling like he'd succeeded at garnering his father's approval.

"I want you to be happy."

Finn sucked in a breath, not quite sure how to process his dad's answer.

Then Jack's gaze moved to a place past his shoulder. "What did you do to her?" he demanded.

Finn turned toward the window to see Kaitlin rolling a large suitcase toward her car. As he watched, she popped the trunk and shoved the luggage inside, her movements frantic like she was in a hurry to get away.

"Nothing." He let out a string of curses as she looked over toward the back of his dad's house. Even from this distance he could see the sadness on her delicate features.

"Does she know about your meeting with Peter?" He glanced at his father. Maybe that was the explanation for her strange behavior yesterday.

"No one knows, although she probably understands your time in Starlight is coming to a quick end. I assume you were clear that your arrangement with her was as temporary as your presence at the bank."

Finn didn't bother to offer a retort. He could deal with his father later. Right now, he had to figure out what was going on with Kaitlin.

By the time he'd crossed the lawn, she was hefting out a cardboard box of possessions.

"What's happening right now?" he demanded as he approached her car.

"I'm leaving." She shoved the box into the back seat and straightened. "When your dad gets back, tell him I'll call him."

"He's in the kitchen."

She drew in a breath at that, squeezing her eyes shut for a moment. "I'd hoped to be gone by the time he returned home."

"Gone where?" He reached for her, but she brushed away his hand like she couldn't stand to be touched by him.

"It doesn't matter." She pulled her keys from the front pocket of her jeans. "You're about to return to Seattle anyway. We had rules."

"Forget the rules," he said, frustration making his voice sharper than he meant it to be.

"I can't," she whispered. "When I ignore the rules, I get hurt."

"I'm not going to hurt you, Kaitlin."

She opened her eyes, and he could almost see the sparks flaring in their dark depths. "You're going back to Seattle."

He wanted to deny it. If she'd said the words to him yesterday, he would have. He would have told her he loved her and he wanted to make a life with her here in Starlight. But the folder his dad had placed on the counter minutes earlier had been like a bomb detonating in the middle of Finn's chest. Every doubt he'd had about himself, every moment of feeling unworthy had exploded within him, the shrapnel lodging so deep he wasn't sure he'd ever recover. His father hadn't even bothered to talk to him.

Jack could say what he wanted, but to Finn it felt like an indictment on his own character. Now Kaitlin was ready to take off without a word. He

couldn't help but believe she'd sensed the level of his feelings for her and didn't want that from him.

Rules and leaving. Those felt like flimsy excuses for what she wasn't willing to say out loud. *She didn't want him.*

"Ask me to stay," he whispered, needing to hear the words. Needing some reassurance if he was going to lay himself bare at her feet.

Her eyes filled with tears and she swiped a hand across her cheeks. "I…have to go," she said and climbed into her car before he could argue.

Blood roared in his ears as he watched her drive away, and he was pretty sure the fracturing sound he heard was his heart breaking into pieces.

Chapter Seventeen

Kaitlin sat crossed-legged on the couch in Brynn's cozy family room later that evening. The sweet single mother was next to her, and Mara was perched on the edge of the overstuffed recliner on the other side of the coffee table.

"Why didn't you ask him to stay?" Brynn asked gently.

Kaitlin kept her hands over her face as she shook her head.

"Or tell him you loved him?" Mara added.

"I don't love him," she whispered. "I can't. That would be stupid. I gave up stupid when I moved to Starlight."

When neither of her friends answered, Kaitlin lowered her hands to look at them. She both hated and appreciated the gentle understanding she saw in each of their gazes.

She'd driven away from the Samuelson house with no thought to where she was heading. Certainly not back to Seattle, although she'd have to eventually call Robbie and tell him his little plan wasn't going to work with her gone from the bank.

Then there was Jack. She despised herself for leaving without giving him an explanation. But if she told him about her ex, he'd try to fix it. Maybe that would work, but Kaitlin couldn't stand the possibility of her past tarnishing Jack's opinion of her. Granted, she'd shared a lot with him when he'd first hired her at the bank. She didn't want to ever give him a reason to regret the chance he'd taken on her.

Her rational side understood that most of what Robbie said had been bluster and empty threats. But the part about bringing her mother to Starlight was real and enough to terrify her. Why was it so difficult to start over with a clean slate?

"You're not stupid," Mara said, "but you aren't a liar, either. It's obvious you love him, Kaitlin."

"He's a good man," Brynn added, reaching out to give Kaitlin's leg a gentle pat.

Kaitlin had driven to the edge of town, then pulled over onto the shoulder of the highway and cried for what felt like days. Eventually she'd regained her composure enough to turn the car around and drive to Brynn's.

Her new friend had taken in Kaitlin's tearstained cheeks, then led her into the small midcentury ranch-style house without question. Kaitlin had gone into the guest bedroom, flopped onto the bed and fallen into a deep, dreamless sleep, exhausted from the emotional toll the confrontation with Robbie had taken and devastated by how she'd left things with Finn.

She'd woken to afternoon shadows making their way across the pale yellow walls and walked out to find both Brynn and Mara waiting for her. Brynn had not only called their mutual friend, but also arranged for her boy to sleep over at his grandma's house.

"You seem like you might need a real girls' night," Brynn had told her, and Kaitlin had dissolved into tears once again.

Now she managed a smile for Brynn. "He's a really great guy," she agreed.

"And you love him?" the other woman asked.

Kaitlin managed a shaky nod. "I do."

"Love complicates everything," Mara muttered. "We're better off without it."

"Stop." Brynn held up a hand. "Now you sound like Finn, Nick and our friend Parker. The three of them made some silly pact back in high school to never fall in love."

Kaitlin frowned. "Why?"

"Probably to avoid getting hurt," Mara offered, picking up her wineglass from the coffee table and taking a long drink. "My divorce just about did me in, and think of what happened to Brynn." She tipped her glass toward Kaitlin. "Maybe you've got the right idea."

"I still believe in love," Brynn said. "Finn isn't your dirtbag ex-husband or Daniel. The guys might think they're going to avoid getting hurt, but they'll also miss out on the happiness true love can bring." She smiled at Kaitlin. "You don't want to let that happen."

Kaitlin glanced at Mara, who was staring into the glass of chardonnay like the golden liquid contained the answers to life's greatest mysteries.

"She's right," Mara said after a few moments. "Even though I hate to admit that I was an idiot for choosing the man I did. But you'll be an idiot if you walk away from Finn Samuelson."

"It's too late." Kaitlin sniffed. "I already ruined things by running away. Both Samuelson men probably hate me at this point."

Brynn laughed softly. "I highly doubt that."

"What if I go back and he doesn't want me?"

"You won't know unless you try," Mara said.

"I'll have to tell him about my ex and his threats."

Both women nodded.

"And how bad things really are with my mom." Kaitlin sighed. "I've kept so much of myself and my past hidden."

"Give him a chance," Brynn urged. "It's scary to show someone the ugly parts as well as the pretty, but you won't be able to truly move forward unless you do. And imagine how great it would be to have someone choose to love you no matter what."

"For better or worse," Mara murmured.

"I don't know your ex-husband," Kaitlin told her friend, "but I can guarantee he was the idiot and not you."

Brynn nodded. "You'll just have to pick someone better next time."

"Oh, no." Mara placed her wineglass on the table as she shook her head. "It's all peachy that the two of you still want love, but I'm done with it. The only kind of lovin' I need in my life is battery-operated."

All three women laughed at that, and Kaitlin felt some of the tension ease from her chest. She'd run away out of fear and a bone-deep belief she didn't deserve happiness because her past was less than perfect. But Finn had been the one to tell her that the point of life was to keep working to get better. She'd done that in Starlight, and it was past time she owned the good about herself as well as the rough stuff.

"I need to talk to him," she whispered. "I need him to know I love him and I want a future together if he'll have me."

"He'd be a fool not to," Brynn said. "No one has ever accused Finn Samuelson of being a fool."

"Thank you for everything." Kaitlin shifted on the sofa cushions, leaning over so she could hug Brynn, then smiled at Mara. "I don't know what I would have done today without the two of you. I'm not used to having real friends, and I want you to know how much I appreciate you both."

"Right back at you," Brynn murmured. "It's kind of comforting to know I'm not the only one working to get my life on track. Cry all you want, but don't ask me to make you another convoluted coffee drink."

Kaitlin chuckled at that.

"You know what I like to say?" Mara leaned forward in her chair. "Chicks before di—"

"No!" Brynn and Kaitlin shouted to the other woman at the same time before dissolving into more laughter.

"You're going to meet some kind, gentle man," Kaitlin said, pointing at Mara. "And it's going to change everything."

"Can he be a librarian?" Mara asked dryly. "I bet a librarian would be free of drama."

"Swipe left for no drama," Brynn said. "That's the new dating theme."

Kaitlin uncrossed her legs and stood. "I have to go back to Jack's and find Finn. We need to have this conversation in person." She pressed a hand to her stomach. "Then I'm driving to Seattle to deal with my past instead of running from it."

"That a girl," Mara said, also rising. "I'll walk out with you. Thanks for the wine, Brynn. If we're all going to be messed up, it should be together and with wine."

Kaitlin groaned softly, prompting Mara to reach out and squeeze her hand. "Scratch that," the other woman said. "You're fixing things. Brynn is still hopeful and I'm holding out for a librarian hero."

"With wine," Kaitlin added, returning the gentle squeeze.

"This has been the most fun I've had in ages," Brynn told them as she opened the front door. "Other than the part where you were sad and crying, of course."

"Of course," Kaitlin repeated, giving both of her friends a final hug before walking to her car. Her breath caught at the sight of her possessions crowded in the back seat. Once she saw Finn, she then needed to talk to his dad. Jack had done so much for her since she'd arrived in Starlight, but it was time for her to stand on her own two feet. She wanted her own apartment—maybe she'd even adopt a cat.

Yes, she loved Finn with her whole heart, but she owed it to both of them to move forward, claiming the life she believed she deserved. She'd never thought of herself as particularly strong, but that was who she was going to strive to become. Finn had helped her have confidence in herself and now she had to convince him they were meant to be together.

His car wasn't at Jack's when she pulled up the driveway. She thought about calling him but got out of the sedan instead and walked toward the front door of the rambling rancher.

The door opened as she lifted her hand to knock.

"You took off like a bat out of hell," Jack said, one thick brow arched.

"Can I come in?" she asked.

"Always," he answered immediately, stepping back to allow her to enter. "Did Finn do something to you?"

She followed him into the formal living room, sinking down onto one of the wingback chairs that flanked the upholstered sofa. “My ex-boyfriend came to Starlight yesterday.”

“The lowlife from Seattle?” Jack frowned as he lowered himself onto the couch. “The one who caused so much trouble for you?”

She nodded. “I haven’t talked to him for over two years, but it felt like no time had passed. He was the same jerk I remembered, only this time he wanted me to help him with a scheme to cheat elderly customers at First Trust out of their savings.”

“Bank fraud,” Jack muttered, rubbing a hand across his jaw. “He’s gotten ambitious in your absence.”

“Or more reckless,” she countered. “I told him no, but he made some stupid threats.”

Jack’s shoulders stiffened. He was no longer a strapping young man but could still appear quite formidable when he set his mind to it. “We won’t let him hurt you, Kaitlin.”

She swallowed at the emotion welling in her at his words. “*I* won’t let him hurt me. He also talked about bringing my mom to Starlight, and I don’t want that. She’s toxic but I got caught up in his anger and the power he used to wield in my life. I felt like the only way to deal with it was for me to leave. You’ve been so good to me, Jack. I’d never knowingly bring trouble to your doorstep.”

He chuckled even as he shook his head. "Girl, I've dealt with my wife's death, cancer and almost losing my family's bank. There's no trouble you can throw at me that I can't handle."

"You shouldn't have to—"

"You're part of this community," Jack reminded her. "We take care of our own around here. But nothing is going to be solved by running away."

"I understand," she said, trying to be discreet as she swiped at the corners of her eyes before the tears started to fall. "Do you know when Finn will be back?" She offered a watery smile. "Turns out I've fallen hard for your son, Jack. I need him to know that."

A trickle of unease crawled across the back of her neck at the look Jack gave her. "I guess you weren't the only one who made some hasty decisions without thinking them through."

"What do you mean?"

His shoulders slumped, and she was suddenly reminded of how frail he'd been after his cancer treatments. He'd regained his strength, but now all that vigor seemed to vanish in an instant. "I started the process of selling the bank to AmeriNat."

Kaitlin felt her mouth drop open. "Jack, you can't do that. Why?"

"Having Peter Henry show up here threw me for a loop. I assumed it was Finn's way of giving me the message that it's time to sell. Besides, I want to start thinking about retirement, and I have to ensure the bank is in good hands before I do that. I've made plenty of mistakes but none bigger than letting my grief drive a wedge between me and my son and daughter. Finn has a huge career and he's done it with no help from me. He helped right things at First Trust but I can't expect him to drop everything he's worked for and take over here in Starlight. I didn't think that was what he wanted anyway."

"You didn't talk to him before meeting with Peter?"

Jack shook his head. "I thought I was right, but now he thinks I did this because I don't want him to run First Trust."

Kaitlin thought about Finn's words as he stood next to her car. *Ask me to stay.*

He'd wanted her to throw him an emotional lifeline, and she'd walked away. He wanted to know his dad believed him, and Jack had made a deal without Finn's knowledge.

Her heart clenched at the thought of how hurt and betrayed he must feel right now.

"He's gone back to Seattle?"

"He packed his bags and took off within an hour of you driving away."

"I'm going to make it right with him," she said,

forcing a confidence in her tone that belied the doubts swirling through her mind.

"Maybe for the two of you," Jack said weakly. "But I've pushed him away too many times."

"It's never too late," she insisted. "We have to believe that. I love Finn with all my heart and I know just as strongly that he belongs in Starlight. I can fix this, Jack."

The older man flashed a tender smile. "If anyone can, I know it's you."

Kaitlin swallowed back her uncertainty and returned Jack's smile. This was her chance to prove she had what it took to claim the life of her dreams. And only her entire heart hung in the balance.

"Let's go over the situation one last time so I'm clear about it. You fell in love with an amazing woman, saved the bank and realized how much our hometown meant to you. But no one actually came out and handed you the future wrapped up with a neat little bow so you put on your best pouty face and walked away?"

Finn glared at Parker Johnson over the rim of his beer bottle. They'd been ensconced in a back booth at the Irish pub around the corner from Finn's building for most of the night. It was after eleven, and the events of the day were catching up with Finn. He stifled a yawn and said, "That's not exactly how I'd describe it."

"Which doesn't change the truth of my summation."

"You realize we're not in court at the moment? It's not actually going to help anyone for you to rake me over the coals."

"No worries." Parker patted his shoulder. "This is just a pro bono service I'm providing for a friend."

"With friends like that..." Finn muttered. He'd called Parker on the drive to Seattle, not wanting to spend the evening on his own recounting the one-two punch his dad and Kaitlin had delivered earlier in the day. Parker had been on his way back from a weekend kayaking trip to the San Juan Islands and had finally met up with Finn at O'Malley's after dinner.

No one had more issues with their father than Parker, and as a divorce attorney, he also saw the worst ends of relationships. Finn figured his friend would be up for a venting session to help Finn transform the bulk of his pain to anger. Anger was way easier to deal with than heartbreak.

Instead, Parker had basically told Finn he was acting like a scared, stupid, immature baby-man, which Finn didn't appreciate in the least. But after a couple of beers and a bit of perspective, Finn had to admit his friend had a point.

"Listen," Parker said, aiming a finger toward Finn like a laser pointer. "If there were guarantees in love, then I'd be out of a job. People take chances and most of them get burned in the fallout when things go bad."

Finn blinked. "Is this a pep talk?"

"I'm getting to that part," Parker promised. "Kaitlin is amazing, but she's had her share of hard knocks. She needs you to step up and show her that you're different. Be the man she needs, Finn."

"What if she doesn't actually want me?" Finn forced himself to voice his greatest fear. "If you remember, this is why we swore off love. No risk of getting hurt."

"No chance of really being happy," Parker shot back before draining his glass of whiskey.

"Right." Finn drew in a long breath. He didn't have to ask about Parker's happiness. They were enough alike that Finn already understood. He'd thought his life was fine. He'd had everything under control and that was how he wanted it. Until Kaitlin had spun his world and his heart around in circles, in the process making him see things in a brand-new way.

He could never go back to how it used to be.

Parker placed his palms flat on the scuffed tabletop and leaned forward. "And in case you haven't already realized it, your dad has always wanted you to have the bank." One side of Parker's mouth lifted. "He had a backward way of showing it, but that doesn't mean it isn't true. The question is what you want your life to be. It's all there but you have to stop messing around and claim it."

Finn huffed out a laugh. "Really? You missed your calling as a therapist, Parker."

"Divorce attorney. Therapist." Parker slapped a hand on the table, then stood. "I have many talents."

"I'm going back," Finn said quietly.

"I know." Parker winked. "You can send a bottle of Glenlivet to my office as thanks for the counseling services. Just be sure you never need my courtroom skills."

Finn nodded. "I'll make her happy if she'll have me."

"Good luck."

They went their separate ways on the sidewalk, and anticipation spiraled through Finn as he thought about how to win Kaitlin and make things right with his dad.

He needed some plan…a grand gesture. He glanced at his watch as he entered his building. It was too late to call or text now. In the morning he could…

He stopped in his tracks as the elevator doors swished open and Kaitlin walked into the empty lobby.

She pressed a hand to her chest as her gaze crashed against his, and he wondered if her heart was pounding in the same way as his.

"Hey," she whispered. "I knocked on your door, but obviously you weren't home."

"You're here." *Nice work, Finn. Master of the obvious.* He closed his eyes for a moment and willed himself to regain control of his tumbling emotions.

She looked so beautiful with her blond hair falling around her shoulders and the slight hint of a blush that colored her cheeks. She wore a simple gray sweatshirt and faded jeans, and Finn immediately gained a new appreciation for cotton as sexy.

"I came to the city to see my ex-boyfriend," she told him, her tone measured.

"Oh." Talk about a kick in the—

"He showed up at the art festival yesterday," she continued. "It was bad, Finn. He was nasty and made threats."

Every protective instinct he had went on high alert. "What kind of threats? If he hurt you I'll—"

"He didn't," she assured him. "I won't let him hurt me again, and I made sure he knew that. But he did make me doubt myself." She paused, took a breath. "I was freaking out. That's why I left your dad's the way I did. I'm sorry. It was a cowardly mistake."

"You're one of the bravest people I know," he told her, moving closer. He wanted to reach for her but stopped short. There was too much to say first. "I'm the coward."

He cleared his throat, needing to find the right words. "I wanted to know you were a sure thing before I told you how I felt. That's how afraid I've been of getting hurt." Unable to resist, he took her hand, lacing their fingers together. The feel of her soft skin against his gave him the courage he needed. Now that he had her again, he'd do anything not to lose her.

Even risk his heart.

"I love you, Kaitlin, with my whole heart. I thought I was protecting myself by keeping people at a distance, but there was no way I could resist you. I don't want to because you make me happier than I ever imagined I could be. So happy that it scares the hell out of me." He lifted her hand and brushed a soft kiss across her knuckles. "I know how much it's going to hurt if you don't want me. But if you give me a chance, I promise I'll spend the rest of our lives trying to be the man you deserve."

She extended a finger against his lips. "I have something I need to say."

He waited, not moving or even daring to breathe.

"I love you, Finn Samuelson." A slow smile

spread across her face. "And I'll always be a sure thing with you."

Relief and joy spreading through him, he pulled her closer. She twined her arms around his neck as he kissed her, his heart finally settling into a place that he knew would be his forever home.

"No more rules," he said against her mouth. "It's you and me, Kaitlin. All in."

"Forever," she promised, then pulled back. "What about Starlight?"

"It's home," he said with a quiet certainty that felt like the most natural thing in the world. "I'll make sure my dad doesn't sell the bank, and we're going to be the most boring small-town couple Starlight has ever seen."

"I'll learn to garden," she said with a laugh.

He grinned. "I'll coach Little League."

She kissed him again. "I don't care what we do as long as we're together."

"Forever," he whispered, finally understanding that true love was always worth the risk.

* * * * *

COMING SOON!

We really hope you enjoyed reading this book. If you're looking for more romance, be sure to head to the shops when new books are available on

Thursday 20th March

To see which titles are coming soon, please visit

millsandboon.co.uk/nextmonth

MILLS & BOON

MILLS & BOON

Coming next month

ONE NIGHT WITH HER MILLIONAIRE BOSS
Kandy Shepherd

The rain was coming down so hard it had driven channels into the gravel, forming small gushing streams. The path was well lit, but it was getting more difficult to avoid the streams and save her shoes and she found herself jumping from side to side as if in a game of aquatic hopscotch. She cursed out loud when the umbrella suddenly turned completely inside out. She was left with only a light jacket over her dress for protection against the elements.

Then Ned was there. 'Seems like you could do with some help,' he said. He was sensibly encased in a long oilskin raincoat and held aloft an enormous black umbrella.

'This darn umbrella is useless,' she spluttered and threw it on the ground.

'Don't tell me—you chose it because it was purple.'

'It was the first one I saw,' she fibbed. Of course she'd been attracted to the pattern of purple iris. The possible sturdiness of the umbrella hadn't been a consideration.

'Come here,' he said.

Ned pulled her to him and under the shelter of his umbrella. Suddenly the stinging onslaught of the rain on her face stopped, but she was far too distracted by Ned's closeness to care. She was dry. She was warm. *He was hot.*

'It's great to get rain. We need it. Trouble is when it all comes down like this at once, so much of it runs off.'

'Hopefully it will ease off,' she said.

His chest was a wall of solid muscle. As he led her towards the house, steering her through the channels, she leaned in closer. Just, of course, to make sure she was completely under the shelter of his umbrella.

'We're almost there or I'd pick you up and carry you,' he said.

'*What!*'

'You're a little thing. Nowhere as heavy as a full-grown sheep to sling over my shoulder.'

Before she had a chance to reply, they reached the house. In one fluid movement, Ned ditched his umbrella, put his hands under her armpits, lifted her off the ground and up the steps, depositing her on the veranda. Freya was back on her feet, out of the rain, before she had time to protest.

'Did you just compare me to a sheep?' she said, mock glaring up at him, a smile twitching at the corners of her mouth. His hair was dark with damp and fat drops of water sat on his cheeks. He grinned. Her heart gave that curious lurch of recognition—she didn't know where it came from.

'A ewe, if I'm to be precise,' he said.

'I'm glad you at least amended that to be a lady sheep.' She couldn't resist his grin and responded with one of her own. 'Do you really lift and haul sheep around the place?' If so, no wonder the man was made of muscle.

'If needs be,' he said. 'I grew up learning to do everything that needed to be done with sheep. Rescue them, shear them, sometimes birth them. So yeah, I've had to haul around the odd sheep or two over the years. No special treatment for the boss.'

He sounded so laconic, so laidback, so *manly* she leaned up on tiptoe and kissed him on the cheek. 'Thank you, for rescuing me like a stray sheep caught in the rain.' She froze. *Why did she do that?*

Her lips tingled from the connection to his skin, cool with raindrops. For a crazy moment she'd wanted to taste them, taste *him*. Her gaze connected with his for a long, still moment.

Continue reading
ONE NIGHT WITH HER MILLIONAIRE BOSS
Kandy Shepherd

Available next month
www.millsandboon.co.uk

Copyright © 2020 Kandy Shepherd

MILLS & BOON

THE HEART OF ROMANCE

A ROMANCE FOR EVERY KIND OF READER

MODERN

Prepare to be swept off your feet by sophisticated, sexy and seductive heroes, in some of the world's most glamourous and romantic locations, where power and passion collide.
8 stories per month.

HISTORICAL

Escape with historical heroes from time gone by. Whether your passion is for wicked Regency Rakes, muscled Vikings or rugged Highlanders, awaken the romance of the past.
6 stories per month.

MEDICAL

Set your pulse racing with dedicated, delectable doctors in the high-pressure world of medicine, where emotions run high and passion, comfort and love are the best medicine.
6 stories per month.

True Love

Celebrate true love with tender stories of heartfelt romance, from the rush of falling in love to the joy a new baby can bring, and a focus on the emotional heart of a relationship.
8 stories per month.

Desire

Indulge in secrets and scandal, intense drama and plenty of sizzling hot action with powerful and passionate heroes who have it all: wealth, status, good looks...everything but the right woman.
6 stories per month.

HEROES

Experience all the excitement of a gripping thriller, with an intense romance at its heart. Resourceful, true-to-life women and strong, fearless men face danger and desire - a killer combination!
8 stories per month.

DARE

Sensual love stories featuring smart, sassy heroines you'd want as a best friend, and compelling intense heroes who are worthy of them.
4 stories per month.

To see which titles are coming soon, please visit

millsandboon.co.uk/nextmonth

MILLS & BOON MEDICAL

Pulse-Racing Passion

Set your pulse racing with dedicated, delectable doctors in the high-pressure world of medicine, where emotions run high and passion, comfort and love are the best medicine.

Eight Medical stories published every month, find them all a

millsandboon.co.uk

JOIN US ON SOCIAL MEDIA!

Stay up to date with our latest releases, author news and gossip, special offers and discounts, and all the behind-the-scenes action from Mills & Boon...

millsandboon

millsandboonuk

millsandboon

t might just be true love...

GET YOUR ROMANCE FIX!

MILLS & BOON

— *blog* —

Get the latest romance news, exclusive author interviews, story extracts and much more!

blog.millsandboon.co.uk

LET'S TALK
Romance

For exclusive extracts, competitions and special offers, find us online:

facebook.com/millsandboon
@MillsandBoon
@MillsandBoonUK

Get in touch on 01413 063232

For all the latest titles coming soon, visit
millsandboon.co.uk/nextmonth

WANT EVEN MORE

ROMANCE?

SUBSCRIBE AND SAVE TODAY!

'Mills & Boon books, the perfect way to escape for an hour or so.'

MISS W. DYER

'Excellent service, promptly delivered and very good subscription choices.'

MISS A. PEARSON

'You get fantastic special offers and the chance to get books before they hit the shops.'

MRS V. HALL

Visit millsandboon.co.uk/Subscribe and save on brand new books.

MILLS & BOON
A ROMANCE FOR EVERY READER

FREE delivery direct to your door

EXCLUSIVE offers every month

SAVE up to 25% on pre-paid subscriptions

SUBSCRIBE AND SAVE

millsandboon.co.uk/Subscribe

BEST FRIEND TO PRINCESS BRIDE

KATRINA CUDMORE

SCOTTISH BORDERS LIBRARY SERVICES	
010571905	
Bertrams	11/02/2020
	£6.99

To Edith, thank you for your constant support,
wisdom and friendship.
Love Katrina